ASTRO-NUTS

Also by Logan J. Hunder

Witches Be Crazy

LOGAN J. HUNDER

Night Shade Books
New York

Night Shade books may be purchased in bulk at special discounts for sales promotion, corporate gifts, fund-raising, or educational purposes. Special editions can also be created to specifications. For details, contact the Special Sales Department, Night Shade Books, 307 West 36th Street, 11th Floor, New York, NY 10018 or info@skyhorsepublishing.com.

Night Shade Books® is a registered trademark of Skyhorse Publishing, Inc.®, a Delaware corporation.

Visit our website at www.nightshadebooks.com.

10 9 8 7 6 5 4 3 2 1

Library of Congress Cataloging-in-Publication Data

Names: Hunder, Logan J., author.
Title: Astro-nuts / by Logan J Hunder.
Description: New York : Night Shade Books, [2017]
Identifiers: LCCN 2017031332 | ISBN 9781597809221 (pbk. : alk. paper)
Subjects: | GSAFD: Fantasy fiction. | Science fiction.
Classification: LCC PS3608.U53 A93 2017 | DDC 813/.6--dc23
LC record available at https://lccn.loc.gov/201703133

Cover designed by Jason Snair and Mona Lin
Cover art by Logan J. Hunder

Printed in the United States of America

Huge thanks to my brother Nolan for going and getting a degree in aerospace engineering just so he could be my own personal "There's no sound in space" guy.

Though I suppose he would prefer the title: "Scientific Advisor."

I would also like to clarify, for the sake of his reputation, that not quite everything in this book gets his seal of real.

1.
WELL, SHIT.

Hugh stumbled around the room, wincing in pain after stubbing a toe on his desk. His pacing had grown erratic and restless in anticipation of his guest. A shaking hand rested on his polished mahogany desk as he tried to get himself together. After a deep breath, he stood upright again and stole a glance at himself in the mirror to check the part in his grey hair and straighten out his tie. There was never a good reason to let one's personal appearance suffer, after all.

Normally space-journey attire was more casual, but he was one of the few who insisted on always being seen in a suit. Call him old-fashioned, but he felt it was a helpful trait to have in his line of work. Everybody else may have felt perfectly at home in those lifeless grey full-body tracksuits, but to him it felt like parading around in public wearing a onesie. One couldn't expect to be taken seriously if they could not even take themselves seriously. If he was to be treated as an ambassador then he ought to act as one, not a college girl nursing a hangover through a morning class.

A rumble came from somewhere beyond the blast doors to his office; it was closer this time. It snapped him out of his thoughts and sent him pacing around the room once more, making final preparations. Hasty hands straightened stacks of paper and aligned his space pens. All that movement got his ruddy tie crooked again. He softly snuffed his nose and fixed it, though likely only temporarily. All this waiting was certainly the worst part of all this. Listening to each new rumble, glancing up with each new flicker of the lights, constantly revisiting the question of whether or not he had enough time to use the bathroom first. He almost wished the guy would just show up already.

The most recent crash served as a harsh reminder that he hadn't even taken the courtesy to set out a drink for the person on whom he waited. Shoving his papers into disarray again and knocking his pens back out of line, he yanked open a drawer and grabbed two glasses and a bottle of scotch. An empty bottle of scotch. An empty bottle of scotch that he tossed right back in the drawer before rummaging around for the next best thing. He still had some bourbon left; it would have to do. Barely keeping the shaking spout over the glass, he poured the dark liquid until the first glass had the perfect toasting amount in it. But there was none left for the second glass.

The bottle smashed to pieces as he dropped it on the floor and tried to distribute the bourbon between two glasses. It sloshed between the trembling cups, not growing in quantity, no matter how many times he aerated it back and forth. It was no use; he'd need something else. Maybe some rye? Surely he had some rye. No, he had no rye. He lingered briefly on the bottle of Fireball before shuddering and slamming the drawer shut.

The rumbling was close enough to be discernible now, with a cadenced peppering of laser shots and armoured individuals falling to the floor. Hugh sighed and put the drinks out of his mind. He used the rare and expensive leather shoes on his feet to sweep the broken bottle under his desk before taking a seat behind it. Using his remaining seconds, he searched the Internet for pictures of cute kids to brandish and claim relationship to. He had quite the brood put together by the time the metallic clangs of a battering ram rang out from behind the room's only entrance.

"It's open!" He choked, trying to sound cheerful.

Something heavy clanged to the floor and then the doors popped open, revealing a hardened old man with a bald head, cold grey eyes, and a smoking laser rifle. Big but bent, he moved slowly yet powerfully, like a lion without a care in the world. Or universe, since they were in space and all.

It was difficult to tell if the frown he wore pertained to the situation, or if it was just his resting facial expression. Hugh hoped for the latter; it would give him better odds of not having to face the same fate as his now-lifeless guards.

"You." The man grumbled in a gravelly voice.

"Me!" Hugh strained to grin. "You must be Mister Banks."

"Glad we cleared that up." Banks said in his slow, deadpan tone. "Now get on your feet, hands where I can see 'em, and we'll do the motions."

Hugh didn't move. Couldn't afford to show fear; not in his position.

"Mister Banks, let us conduct ourselves like civilized space beings. Please have a seat."

Banks rolled his eyes as he casually adjusted the angle of his hip-held weapon to be a smidge more threatening.

"I don't know how new to this espionage thing you are, but this piece of hardware is called a gun. Guy with the gun gets to make the decisions. Now stand your ass up."

With his hands raised to his shoulders, Hugh obliged. He was proud of how well he'd maintained his stoicism up until now, especially in the face of such a master of the craft; this

Mister Banks was so stoic he almost appeared to be more bored than anything else. His dead eyes studied the diplomat with contempt and his wrinkled face betrayed no masked intent.

"Are you going to shoot me?" Hugh asked.

"Probably." Banks replied with a shrug. "You have something that doesn't belong to you. We'll see how I feel after I get it back."

"It doesn't belong to you either." Hugh retorted, making sure to stay on the offensive side of the argument. "It doesn't belong to anyone. You can't cite ownership as a reason to take it back."

"I know. That's why I brought a gun instead of a lawyer."

Hugh swallowed as he tried to come up with a response. He wasn't sure what he had expected of this exchange, but he figured the individual would at least be sophisticated enough to parlay with. But this guy wasn't even wearing a suit. The way he rummaged through the office, muttering to himself as he turned the place inside out like a drunken gorilla, made Hugh begin to wonder if he even was an individual of any deserved notoriety.

"Soooo . . . how long have you been doing this henchman thing for?"

Banks didn't respond. Now completely ignoring Hugh, he produced a small, glowing, sonic screwdriver-sort of device and proceeded to wave it up and down the walls and shelves like a metal detector. No painting, no light fixture, no potted plastic plant was spared. He pulled the fold-down bed from the wall, ripped the sheets and pillowcases off and tossed them to the floor, and waved his whirring doohickey around some more. There was no anger, no bitterness, no frustration; just method. In fact, if he weren't carrying that gun, he'd just look like some old geezer who lost his glasses.

"So what sort of compensation do you get for piecework

like this?" Hugh continued to badger. "Do they pay you retainer fees? Flat salary perhaps? Or do they merely bequeath you funds by the job? If so, do targets of measurable renown boost your stipend?"

A deep breath and heavy exhale was all the response he received for his efforts. Banks had moved from the bed to the personal kitchen area, making no attempt to spare the dishes and tea bags, which he knocked to the floor while rummaging through the cupboards.

"Ah, strong silent type. I see. Makes your job a bit dull, though, I would assume."

"Look, slick," Banks finally retorted. "If I wanted excitement I would be beating the location of the specimen out of you right now. But I had to skip coffee and breakfast to come deal with your oiled-up ass, so I'm doing this the casual way. Now, is that good with you, or would you rather I come over there and jam one of my fists in that big mouth of yours?"

The man's pale expression of death lingered on Hugh for a few moments, just to make sure he drove the point home. He then opened the refrigeration cupboard and began rifling through the contents, all the while muttering something about bureaucrats. Again, the diplomat found himself hard up for a response. He'd achieved audible confirmation of the man's identity and intent to cause harm. He just needed one final piece.

Banks appeared to have abandoned his search in favour of making himself a sandwich.

"That's theft too, you know," Hugh sneered.

Banks turned to face him, expression placid, and shoved his pilfered breakfast into his mouth.

"Sure is," he mumbled through the bite. He took his time chewing and swallowing before adding: "Shame you don't have a gun."

"Is that how everything is typically handled on Mars? Here I thought humanity had evolved beyond that since we took to colonizing the solar system."

"Well, I guess I'm just a fan of the classics, then."

He left the counter and gave Hugh a shove out of the way so he could get at the desk. He paused for a moment to admire it; he likely hadn't seen very many pieces of real woodwork, even in his old age. He opened the drawers with slightly more care than previous compartments, but ransacked the contents with the same amount of concern.

"It's mahogany." Hugh ran a hand across the lacquered surface. "One of the toughest woods. Don't suppose your Martian handlers have afforded you any luxuries like that for your office?"

Banks grunted. It was too ambiguous to be one of agreement. He could just as easily have been providing commentary on the plethora of children's photos. Either that, or at the broken whiskey bottle hidden under the desk.

"Or do they even give you an office? Surely if you're an asset that they'd use to threaten me, then they would give you somewhere to hang your hat when you're not off playing tough guy on peaceful vessels."

Banks stood up. His face was every bit as devoid of expression as ever; and yet something in his weary droopy eyes conveyed a change in temperament. He looked Hugh up and down, as if seeing him for the very first time.

"Alright, chatterbox, you've got me interested. You're asking all kinds of questions about who I am and what I do. I don't think it's 'cause you think I'm cute. So how about you just directly ask whatever it is you really wanna know instead of trying to dazzle me into slipping up."

Hugh blinked in surprise.

"Mister Banks, I am simply making conversation while we

are confined to the same room. I thought, since work was why you were here, perhaps you would be more apt to find it a topic worthy of discussion. How is the pay? Do you feel respected by your peers? Do you get dental?"

"My career as an off-the-books enforcer working on behalf of the Martian government suits my needs just fine. There; any other burning questions?"

"Just one," Hugh said with a smirk, relishing in his acquisition of the upper hand. "Are you familiar with the interplanetary laws as established in the ratification of the Vienna Treaty on Diplomatic Relations?"

"I don't have to be. I have a gun."

Hugh stood up straighter now. The malicious gaze of his would-be assassin no longer frightened him.

"Well you, sir, will require much more than a sidearm to escape extradition and prosecution should any harm come to me. My diplomatic immunity is firmly established within that treaty, and you have not only verbally identified yourself but also the organization for which you work to any who watch the video feed of this conversation. Your trespass on this ship and subsequent murder of my guards are serious crimes in and of themselves. However, to attack me would constitute an act of war between our planetary nations. Depending on your branch of the Martian military, they may be willing to harbour you despite your current transgressions. But do not think for a moment that they would so much as hesitate to surrender you in order to avoid—*ACK*!"

The sanctimonious lecture made an abrupt switch from articulate admonition to a series of choking sounds right around the same moment Banks rolled his eyes and punched Hugh in the throat.

"I think 'immunity' is a bit strong of a word," said Banks

without even pausing to watch the man fall. "Maybe call it: 'diplomatic discouragement.'"

From his new spot facing the floor, Hugh's garbled response was unintelligible.

Banks picked up the glass of bourbon on the desk, gave it a quick sniff, then downed it in one swig. He then removed the rifle sling from his shoulder and set the whole thing down on the table. Hugh's face was beet red and he could hardly draw breath without coughs and wheezes. His chest convulsed and his limbs twitched, neither of which were helped when a large foot dug into his stomach and rolled him onto his back. The visage of his interrogator hovered over him, bored as ever. It was an unpleasant-enough sight, even without the errant crumbs trickling down from the man's open-mouthed chewing.

"Sorry I had to ruin that for ya," the hitman mused through masticated whole grains. "You've obviously been rehearsing that speech since the moment I got here. Did whoever put you up to this write it?"

"The Queen . . ." Hugh struggled through coughs. "Sh—she'll want your head!"

"Yeahhh, well, she's been alive since 1926. If she hasn't learned to live with disappointment yet, then she probably should."

"You're signing your own death warrant, you crazy man! Whoever accesses the databanks of this ship is going to see the holo-rendering of your every move from every angle."

"Aw, no. Getting sent to lockup would be such a hassle; I might miss my soaps."

Hugh pulled himself to a sitting position and looked up at the arrogant, pale goblin looming over him. The fellow seemed to be an astute individual, if a bit supercilious; surely he could grasp the concept of incriminating himself. And yet despite his best attempts to explain, he still found his Adam's apple firmly lodged somewhere behind his left ear. But shying away was still not an option. Tough fronts could win battles more hopeless than this one.

"Scoff if you must, but until you've experienced a—"

"Shu-hey, you, shut up." Banks shook his head in exasperation. "Listen to me. You're not a secret agent; you're a patsy. You have no leverage to make threats, and your plan is stupid. Even if I gave a damn what your old lady thought, it'd be pretty tough for her to form an opinion of me with nothing to go on but a destroyed space boat."

Any last remaining grasp Hugh had on a stoic exterior melted away.

"Oh, don't look so surprised." Banks continued. "Did you really think I was going to grab the stuff, then just skip on back to my ship and leave this one adrift? I'm offended."

"So . . ." Hugh spoke softly, eyes unblinking. "So . . . What are you going to do?"

"Good god. Do I have to spell it out for you?" Banks put his hands together, then pantomimed an explosion, complete with sound effects. The diplomat looked on in horror.

"You—you can't do that! There's . . . There's nearly a hundred people aboard this vessel!"

"Nah, it's just you now. I shut down life support everywhere else. Unless you have some freedivers on board for some reason, I'm pretty sure everyone else is back to the mud by now."

Hugh blinked.

"We . . . actually did have some freedivers on board. There was a competition."

"Oh."

They sat in silence for a moment, both of them glancing at the wall clock and trying to figure out how long it had been.

"Well then. Guess I got time for another sandwich."

He strode over to the counter, leaving Hugh alone on the floor, trying to digest how easily this man had seen through his lies. He knew his personal guards had been pacified, but had this Mister Banks really searched the entire ship well enough to know there was no one else on board? He couldn't possibly have had time. Either way, there was no sense in trying to come up with a new cover story now. He was best off just sticking to it, for better or for worse. And it was certainly leaning towards the worse. It was in these moments that he was coming to realize how truly alone he was in the inky murk of space, not another soul for millions of miles in any given direction. Just him, Banks, and a ship full of dead bodies.

"Hey, looks like your mayo synthesizer is out."

"WHAT IS IN THE BOTTLE?! What is so important it warrants the cold-blooded murder of nearly a hundred innocent people?"

The old man sighed as he put down the synth-butter-mayo-spritzer and rubbed his forehead.

"You mean to tell me . . . that you don't even know what you stole?! What, were you just at the military base to do some window shopping? Thought it looked pretty and just decided to swipe it like . . . like . . . what are those flying animals you got on Earth that like the shiny things?"

"I'm not a bloody magpie! Just because I don't know the specifics of its function doesn't mean I haven't been informed of the danger its existence poses to my home world."

"Yeah, well . . ." Banks mused, smacking his lips. "You were also informed of the danger my existence poses to your home body. Which one are you fonder of?"

"M-my . . . Me?"

Banks grunted. His thin wrinkled lips twisted into a slight smirk.

"But I don't have it anymore!" He pleaded. "I . . . I sent it home in a cargo capsule! Because I knew you would come and I wanted to take precau—"

Banks silenced him with a kick to the stomach. Hugh whimpered as he curled into the foetal position. A steady finger, pale as a corpse, pointed downward at him.

"I mighta believed that if you opened with it. But you're too late, and now I'm getting impatient. You feeding me bullshit only wastes my time and sours my neighbourly demeanour. Now, you either tell me where you hid it, or I'll put a hole in your face and go back to my original plan of finding it."

"Please! I have children!"

"Oh, please; a third of these kids are Indian."

"My wife is Indian."

"Oh really? And what about these ones? You got a Chinese mistress?"

"N-no, we're just . . . Mormon?"

Banks snatched his rifle off the desk.

"Shit." Hugh hissed. "I should have grabbed that while you were pilfering my condiments."

"Don't worry. It's got fingerprint recognition, so it wouldn't have worked anyway."

He dug the muzzle into Hugh's eye socket. The would-be spy clenched his teeth.

Click.

Hugh opened his non-obstructed eye just in time to see Banks flipping a switch near the sights.

"Heh, forgot to turn it back on." He chuckled. "Let's try that again."

"WAIT."

"Hrm? Suddenly remember something?"

Hugh was panting now. His eyes were bloodshot and sweat poured down his artificially tanned face. His formerly parted hair and well-tended suit were the farthest they had ever been from presentable, but such petty inclinations were the least of his worries now. In fact, given the juncture this interaction had reached, the more pathetic and helpless he looked, the better.

"I . . . I have money." He offered.

"Oh, for god's sake." Banks scoffed, looking around the room. "In my fifty years of doing the dirty work, you think nobody has ever pitched me that crap before?"

"But I have rather a lot!"

"That's good. Hopefully it's enough to put thirty-three little Mormon kids through college."

"Oh god! Stop! Stop! It's in the drawer! It's in the bloody drawer!"

Banks retracted his laser rifle and looked at the desk.

"You'll have to be more specific."

"Bottom drawer." Hugh gasped, trying to push his heart from his throat back into his chest. "Right side."

Banks nudged the drawer open with his foot. Liquor bottles clinked as they shuddered back and forth. At first, he raised an eyebrow and opened his mouth, but rather than making comments or accusations, he decided to take a knee and reach inside.

One by one he picked up the bottles. After inspecting the labels, he gave them each a gentle shake. Most of them responded with the *slosh*ing of fluid, or occasionally with no sound at all. Either way, he would discard each one onto the floor next to the shattered scotch. As the booze stock began to dwindle to the final containers, the gnarled poker face of the interrogator began to show foreboding tells like flared nostrils. That is, until the second-to-last bottle produced neither *slosh* nor silence, but instead a cadenced clinking, like Gordon Ramsay's swear jar. Banks turned the bottle over in his hand.

"Fireball . . ." He mumbled, reading the label. "You come straight here from spring break?"

"I didn't procure it for my consumption, you cretin." Hugh grumbled. "I suspected my pursuer would have too much class to even touch the bottle and would instead pick one of the others if he made it this far."

"You got a strangely high opinion of hired killers."

Hugh frowned.

"I wasn't expecting a hired killer. I was expecting someone like myself. A consummate professional who refrains from brutish tactics, only performing them when necessary. Someone who relies on wit as their primary weapon."

"Riiiiiiight." Banks said with a nod. "Well, we used to use guys like that. But they always ended up getting shot by hired killers."

A burst of blaster fire echoed through the room, followed by a soft *thud* and slow footsteps toward the door.

2.
SPACE TRUCKIN'

"GOOD SPACE MORNING, LADIES and gentlemen of the SS *Jefferson*. This is your captain speaking. Can anybody guess where we're going? That's right, we're still homeward bound back to everybody's favourite marble orbiting Earth! Looks like we've got some good space weather ahead of us, so strap on your belts and put those tray tables up, and in a few moments, we'll boldly go where only a couple billion people have gone before!"

"Tim, honey, you really don't have to use the PA system. We're all sitting right here."

"I know, baby, but it helps me feel more like a captain. Not just a boss."

Captain Cox rose from his roomy chair and let his vintage microphone retract back into the ceiling between him and Kim. Despite being second-in-command, his wife always let him do the honours. Although a man of average height, average build, and average amount of forehead creases for a fellow in his early fifties, he prided himself in greeting each day with enough energy to make a puppy tell him to calm down. Head held high and pouty lips idly sipping from his "Universe's Best Space Captain" mug, he strolled across the bridge of his beloved vessel. Both his long blond hair and his coffee-stained bib dangled down when he stopped and hovered over his first crew member.

"Well, good morning, Miss Wang." He greeted his pilot sweetly, putting his free hand on her shoulder. "How was your night?"

"Mych."

Not bad. It might not have been the most spirited response, but it was at least almost a real word this time. A marked improvement over the haughty grunts she would often offer.

"Well that's good," the captain chirped, taking the opportunity to rest an elbow on the back of her chair. "Why don't you tell me about it!"

No response. The excessive amount of caring contained within the question seemed to overload the teenager's affection fuses and shut her down. Her dark eyes and perpetual pout remained transfixed on the screen in front of her, and the captain, despite his proximity, appeared to cease to exist. Cox had to be careful how much he meddled, as she was known to remain motionless for hours sometimes if bothered too much, all the while stubbornly staring forward with a constant stony focus on her unexpressive face.

"Aaaaand he doesn't stick the landing," the captain mused between sips. "Very well, miss mysterious! Your secrets shall remain safe for another day. Buuuuuuuuuut . . ."

He forfeited formality and took a knee, hushing his voice before using her first name. "Look, Whisper . . . Did you at least take my advice and have some shore leave back at the asteroid? I know they aren't as fun as planets or moons, and the miners can be drunk and kind of molest-y, but I bet they'd have some interesting stories! Or . . . I don't actually know, they kind of freak me out too. This is getting a little hypocritical.

I'm just saying you really can't stay cooped up in this tin can all the time. It's bad for ya."

Success! His compelling words breached past her mighty wall of aggressive ignoring and drew the young lady's face back around. Her resting expression could have been more promising, but it was a start.

"Oh my god. Really? Tin? You think the ship is made of tin? 'Cause we're totally flying through space in a baked potato. Yep, definitely not titanium or anything."

"Titanium, huh! The only metal strong enough for space."

"Okay, it's not just a big hunk of titanium. Like, there's alloys and stuff . . ."

"Well, I will definitely keep that in mind for future analogies." Cox smiled and used his hand to muss her black hair like she were some kind of rascally child. "And hopefully you'll keep my advice in mind and get out for real at our next stop. I heard those weird sounds coming out of your quarters again last night. I don't know what you're always doing in there, and frankly, I don't wanna know."

He got to his feet and continued his rounds. His cup was empty, but he continued to sip nonetheless in order to maintain an air of aloof worldly wisdom. The differences between a boss and a captain were not so unlike the differences between a father and a dad, after all. No matter who his crew may have waiting on their respective rocky-bodies of origin, once aboard this ship they were all family. As the patriarch of the family, it was his job to supply equal and adequate doses of both love and discipline to help his surrogate children grow into happy, healthy space-people.

The fact that Donald, his communications officer, had already grown into a self-sufficient thirty-something man with his own set of beliefs and opinions made filling that role a little bit more difficult. And occasionally awkward.

"Morning, Donny." He took a knee next to the slouching space-receptionist. "Hope you're not too hungover this morning, hey, big guy? Be honest with me. Didja get out and score some tail?"

Donald snorted. His small, half-closed eyes rolled upward under his low-hanging brows while one hand reached up to scratch at the tangled ball of black curls perched atop his spherical head.

"You think I went out there?! Everybody knows asteroid mining camps are where fugitives go to lay low. All it takes is one screengrab of me sitting within five feet of someone on some government's shit list and then poof! I'm hanging upside down in a retrofitted bathroom somewhere in Guantanamo Docking Bay being used as a test subject to develop a new strain of AIDSbola! No thanks. Sooner we're back in transit, the better."

The captain nodded.

"Classic Donny, always usin' your noggin'! Say, buddy, we got any messages?"

Donald sighed as he minimized *Half-Life 3* to check. His greasy fingers smeared the touch screen as they thumbed through the hundreds of tabs he had open until, finally, he arrived at the message center—the only piece of software meant to be installed.

"Uhhhh, let's see . . . There's something here from some chick named Doctor Pia Dickinson."

"Huh?" Kim raised her head from her e-book, brushing long brown hair away so she could see. "That's not our doctor. Who is that?"

"Was I not supposed to read that out loud?" Donald asked with all the concern of a man asking how his mother-in-law was doing. "Whoops."

"No, no, that's just Pia from college! It's nothing; she's just been wanting to show me her lab. Do we have any other—" His voice trailed off. "Wow, Donny . . . We need to get IT to check out your spam filter when we dock. There's a lot of, uh, spam making it into your inbox here."

"If we're gonna do that, can we get me a real computer that's not an antique? I didn't even know they still made displays you had to touch. I can't even eat while using this thing."

"Sure thing, buddy." Cox acknowledged. He tried to muss Donald's dark curly hair too, but retracted it quick enough to dodge the catlike swat of the lad's pudgy hand. "Just write it on the list."

Donald groaned.

"I've had it on the list for months. You've never even looked at it."

"Whoa there, space cowboy. I'm not sure what you're thinking of, but I've had a list posted outside my captain's quarters since the day I hired you guys, and nobody has ever written anything on it."

" . . . You mean that piece of paper? I thought that was part of your antique collection."

"Noooo!"

The captain clenched his fists with conviction, ignorant to how much he was overreacting.

"Penmanship is a dying art, Donny! It's like a visual representation of the sound of your voice. It's beautiful. Cultivate it. Share it!"

" . . . Or we could just program a reminder for our next stop like normal people."

"Just do this for me, Ensign! Think of it like team building."

"Did you just call me 'Ensign?'"

Cox nodded to himself with a cheeky grin as he turned away.

Another morning pep talk nailed. Encouraging but unflinching, with just a smidge of informative: the perfect recipe to erode negativity. He'd have a Grand Canyon's worth of erosion worn into ol' Donny before the kid even knew it!

With one to go, he turned to the last chair on the bridge. Rather than speak, however, he decided to keep this pep talk to himself. He knew it would have no effect. Few conversations ever went anywhere when conducted with empty chairs.

"Uhhhh, Kim, honey? Looks like we're missing a soldier."

"She's down by the reactor." Kim replied without looking up. "You know. Where she always is?"

"What's she down there for?! I told everyone to get to their stations."

Kim shrugged.

"That is her station. She's our engineer."

"Well, yeah . . . but everybody else knew I meant to get to their station on the bridge."

"That's because we don't have multiple stations."

"Well, look at you, making points and knowing answers!"

Kim smirked at him, then went back to her ebook while Cox clapped his hands together and whirled around the bridge, taking in all his surroundings.

"Well, alright!" He addressed nobody in particular. "This is good! This can work. At least now we have a spot where Willy can sit."

The three of them all looked up from what they were doing.

"Who?" Kim asked, breaking the silence.

"Willy! Our new—oh . . . crap, I forgot to let him in!"

He dashed across the room, leaping over Ms. Wang's terminal then skidding across the floor. The resulting crash into the wall only served to stop him long enough for him to check his hair in a mirror before punching the doorway's entry code—to the tune of "Funky Town"—and opening his arms wide as it slid open.

"Heyyyy, there he is! Come in and meet everybody!"

Kim's jaw dropped as Cox carelessly led the tall and rather heavyset fellow with a scraggly beard and matching brown bedraggled ponytail inside. With an arm around the man's shoulder, he showed off his pride and joy. They marched over to the vacant chair, ignorant to Kim's subtle attempts to get Cox's attention, and the captain practically pushed him into it.

"Why don't you get up and introduce yourself?" Cox suggested.

"Hello," the man offered sheepishly as he struggled to rise. "Uh, I'm—"

"This is Willy Padilla!" Cox interjected, patting his shoulder hard enough to make him sit again. "He's our newly assigned security guard, here to keep us all safe while we deliver this sweet, sweet . . . Uh, what are we carrying again?"

"Rhodium." Kim answered flatly. Her lips were pursed and her arms were folded, but Cox was too excited to notice.

"Rhodium! Delicious! So yeah, Mister Padilla here will be flying with us for the next few days as we race across the galaxy with our precious cargo."

"Tim!"

Like a herd of spooked animals, everyone else on the bridge snapped their heads in Kim's direction. The first mate gave them a weak smile and then addressed her captain slightly more affably.

"Can I have a moment?"

"Oh yeah, sure! That's a good idea, actually. Let the crew mingle without worrying about being judged by the boss man. I gotcha."

"Just . . . just come here."

Confused but obedient, Cox shrugged and gave Willy a finger-gun-gesture before following Kim into the conference room, a room that never got used, because every conference seemed to just take place right there on the bridge. Once inside, Kim punched the same code as before to shut the door behind them.

"Tim, what is tha—"

"Baby, lemme just stop you for one little second." Cox interjected. "This is sounding to me like the beginnings of a stern talking-to, and you and I both agreed we'd turn off the gravity during chats like these to help ease the tension."

"No, honey, I know . . . but this will just take a second."

Her voice trailed off as she watched him fiddle with the wall terminal and her dark hair began to float around. She crossed her arms as her captain gently pushed off the floor and whizzed around the room whilst kicked back in a reclining position. After a few moments of gazing through a window into the sea of stars, he beckoned her upwards, lips curled into a welcome smile. With a slight sigh, she kicked off the floor and glided after him.

"Tim, why am I just now hearing about that man on our ship?"

"You mean Willy? I told you, he's security. Y'know, to keep us secure! Think of him like a weasel; he'll keep out pests, but he won't steal your socks."

Kim frowned.

"Look, I'm as surprised as you are!" He qualified. "I didn't think we'd get him until our next dispatch. But the boss man paid to have him meet us at the asteroid. I couldn't just take off without him!"

"We've never had security before. Why now?"

Cox shrugged as he walked up the wall into a backward somersault.

"I don't know, really . . . I guess with Earth and Mars doing all their extra bickering these days, it's got the guys down at the depot worried about their shipments. Maybe they think we might accidentally smuggle insurgents or something. And let's not forget space pirates. You know we've had a couple close calls."

"It was nothing we couldn't handle." She huffed. "But fine, we need a security guy. What about our agreement that you wouldn't hire new crew without me vetting them first?"

"Have I ever told you I love how extra sultry your voice gets when you're interrogating me about something?"

"Have I ever told you that compliments don't get you out of trouble?"

He placed his palm against his chin as if resting his head in thought, despite being suspended upside down with his feet brushing against the ceiling.

"Okay . . . but I didn't hire—"

"You know what I mean! You knew he was coming. All I'm asking is for you not to spring this stuff on me. This is your ship; I can acknowledge that. But we are a team. And as a team, we lead the rest of the team. I like to know who is on my team. I'm saying team a lot. Look, now you've brought some guy on our ship that I didn't get to interview like I did with Whisper and Donald and Whatshername down in engineering. . . . Can you stop doing pullups for a second?"

"Sorry. I thought maybe I could multitask."

Kim tried to put her hands on her hips, but quickly grabbed the wall again to right herself.

"Look, I know you don't take these things as seriously as I do. And maybe I'm just crazy. But you agreed to put up with it!"

"Whoa, whoa, come on." Cox protested. He abandoned the rafter he clung to and floated down to her level.

"You're not crazy! You're just cynical and paranoid. I love that about you! I didn't marry you just because of your rockin' body and the fact you look like Marisa Tomei."

"Who?"

"Ahhh, she's an old actress. Won sexiest woman alive like eighteen times. Doesn't matter. Look, the point is you're right! I should have run this by you before bringing him on the ship, and for that I am sorry. Let's just try and stick this out for the trip home, and if you don't like him when we get back, then I'll petition for a replacement."

Kim raised an eyebrow.

"And what if he's a troublemaker on the way home?"

Cox dismissed the notion with a mighty "pshhaw" as he returned the room to normal gravity and punched the door code.

"Okay, now you're being crazy! He's one guy and his name is Willy; how bad could he be?"

The door opened to reveal Whisper and Donald hiding behind support pillars as the large, shabby security agent attempted to shoot cups off a counter while blindfolded.

"Oh, great. He has a gun." Kim uttered with syrupy sarcasm.

They both hopped behind their respective sides of the doorway.

"Look, it's not the end of the world," Cox insisted as stray laser blasts struck the other side of the wall he leaned against. "Who knows? Maybe if we get into trouble we'll be glad he has it! Don't worry, I'll sit him down and have a talk about proper gun etiquette."

Kim rolled her eyes, but couldn't hide the faint traces of amusement manifesting at the corners of her mouth. "Good luck with that. I need to go take care of some things."

She got down on her hands and knees and proceeded to crawl down an adjoining corridor until she was out of the potential line of fire. As she disappeared, Cox took a deep breath and smoothed the front of his space-onesie before stepping back into the warzone.

"Captain on the bridge!" He barked to his subordinates.

He wished he could say everyone snapped to attention—maybe snapped a salute, with faces eager at the prospect of carrying out orders. Instead, everyone just looked at him. Willy stopped firing his gun to lift his blindfold, though, so there was that.

"Sorry, boss." The security guard muttered as he lowered his weapon.

Cox waved off the apology.

"I like the enthusiasm, buddy! Maybe save it for some bad guys, though. Stay sharp!" He turned to the rest of his crew.

"Everyone else, back to your posts. I don't know what rhodium is, but right now it may as well be gold. I hope it's strapped in tight. Let's burn up some quarter miles."

"Oh my *GOD*." Whisper's aggravated voice rang out from somewhere nearby. "Rhodium is worth, like, ten times as much as gold."

"Miss Wang, can your highly valuable insight wait until after we have a triumphant take-off? I want us all to have a moment!"

She rolled her eyes and returned her attention to her terminal. Having moments seemed about as important to her as emoting. Her pale, dainty fingers drummed up and down the screen, creating *beep*s and *boop*s and *whoop*s and *whir*s, all of which were superfluous sound effects that Cox had installed to make the job "sound more science-y."

Meanwhile, outside, magnetic docking mechanisms began

to release leaving the large, shaft-shaped ship adrift like a temporarily neglected volleyball. Tiny mounted rockets rotated it away from the space rock upon which it sat with remarkable grace for such a colossal craft. In spite of his job description, Cox was no stickler for speed, and thus had had the cosmoboat built to match. It might be slow, but it was big enough to carry impressive loads, hard enough to handle the harshness of space, and it would always get its riders where they wanted to go. At the end of the day, those were really the most important qualities to Cox.

In transit, things on board calmed down. Willy's gun was safely stowed until such time that his behaviour was deemed sufficiently "de-monkeyfied." Now, with his only toy confiscated and the wind out of his sails, the security officer meandered about the new digs whilst settling into the dull life aboard a freighter. No matter what one's position, there wasn't much to do while—figuratively—on the road. Donald had returned to his digital distractions, and even Whisper had kicked back in her pilot's chair with a pair of telegoggles. Cox himself had settled in next to the plastic plants. In his hands, he rubbed together two peculiar knickknacks that nobody living in this century was likely to recognize.

Willy gave one last look around, as if in search of any alternative, before he finally took a spot of his own by the greenery. Cox looked up with a warm smile as the big fella settled in beside him.

"This ship is weird." Willy mused in his husky voice. "Not in a bad way or nothing. Just that most are all metal and empty and stuff. Now I'm on here and you got like, painted walls and a couch and a throw rug and . . . man, are these wood floors?!"

Cox chuckled. "Ah, I wish I coulda found someone willing to make floors out of wood." He sighed and continued. "Laminate was all I could find. Nice to know it still ties the room together, though!"

"It's nice! It's old-school cool. But what do you guys do in here all day?!"

The captain shrugged.

"Oh, we get by. We all have our hobbies to stave off cabin fever. And every now and then I convince the gang into a board-game night. There's also a holodeck down by the cargo hold, but make sure you knock real loud before going inside."

Willy sat there nodding continuously, like a freestyle rapper having trouble coming up with a line.

"Everything's so automated and reliable now." Cox continued. "There's no more daily chores to keep us on our toes and keep the ship from falling apart. No whales or giant squids to contend with. No mysterious uncharted islands to happen upon. Everybody just sits around like lumps on logs. There's no adventure anymore. Nobody even wants excitement."

He looked down at the toys in his hands.

"Even scrimshawing ain't what it used to be. The pioneers used to kill for some downtime to do this! Why don't you have a seat and I'll teach you how."

"Ahhh . . ." His security officer hemmed, or maybe hawed. "Maybe later. Where's your kitchen at? I think I'ma go zap up myself a soup packet or something."

"Oh, we don't have a zapper."

"No? Oh, you got them little insta-heat capsules?"

"We have a microwave." Donald snarled from across the room, voice reeking of disdain.

Willy blinked.

"What's that?"

"Hey, don't knock the microwave!" Cox admonished. "You don't know what this untested new stuff is doing to our food. Our ancestors survived for hundreds of years on microwaves, and they never had any problems."

He turned to his confused new recruit, who sat flustered and frozen, not sure whom to trust.

"Don't worry about him; just put your packet in and set a cook time. It takes a little bit longer than an InstaZap™, but it'll be just as good!"

"Better pull up a chair and find a movie too." Donald called to Willy as he walked away.

The captain watched him go, then shut the door behind him. Since his naturally cheerful face was unable to form a frown, he folded his arms to attempt assertiveness after turning around to admonish his communications officer.

"Always so negative!" He said along with a waggle of his finger. "Why, Donny?! Who hurt you?"

"Why do you always think some kind of tragedy must have happened every time I don't like your prehistoric crap?"

"First of all, all my artefacts have great historical significance! Second of all . . . uh, you're a smart guy; you know what I mean!"

Donald's eyes returned to his screen. "Nope."

Seeing the man's attention starting to lapse, the captain reacted with a dignity befitted to an authority figure of his calibre: by chucking his knickknacks in opposing directions and scampering across the floor to the aforementioned terminal.

"See? There it is again. Always such a downer. It's like a malodorous ghost that possesses you for the purpose of ruining fun!"

"Where do you come up with all these projections?!"

"You're just so negative! Maybe you should be the captain. We could call you Captain Negative!"

"Hey, boss?" Willy called from the doorway to the galley. "I think your microwave thing is broken. I zapped the packet for ten whole seconds and it didn't even unfreeze."

"Just keep doing it until it's hot. Trust me!" Cox barked, not taking his eyes off Donald.

"*Can* I be the captain?" Donald asked.

"You may not. I bought this ship; it's mine. But I like that ambition! I want to see more of that."

He got to his feet and ran his fingers through his wavy hair as he strolled back to the ship's bow. The bridge was far and away his favourite spot on his giant shaving-cream can of a vehicle. It was the only place where one could sit and stare out into the infinite and wonder what wonderment lay beyond the scope of human achievement. There was many a time during long deliveries that he had to resist the urge to abandon his duties, kick Whisper off the controls, and go space-spelunking in search of things yet to be found. Fortunately, he was rational enough to know he'd just die hungry, cold, and probably divorced.

So instead, he simply stared. Stared at the stars, stared at the satellites, stared at the impressive amount of floating garbage that had accumulated over the years. There was always something floating around out there. But the most prominent object in view had to be the impressive red planet, Mars, formerly known as New America, formerly known as Mars. As a technically-Earth-controlled vessel, it was probably in his best interest to stay out of their devoid-of-air-space. They were a bit touchy about that.

Relations between the two planets were set up for failure right from its colonization four hundred or so years ago. After his wall was a colossal failure, and his attempts to "fire" Mexico proved ineffectual, then-President Trump, in a fit of frustration, re-allocated the entire defense budget into his Space Force idea. This last-ditch measure to make good on his anti-immigration policies by moving the US to Mars was received with mixed reviews. Like his campaign, at first people thought it was a joke. Unbeknownst to them, the irony of invading a planet to prevent people from invading his country was entirely lost on their glorious leader. The fact he wanted to relocate not only the population but literally the entire landmass didn't help the idea's credibility either. Apparently, he had read an *xkcd* article and mistakenly concluded he could funnel the United States nuclear reserve underground and use it to blast their way up. But after narrowly defeating Senator West to win a second term, all he managed to get started was a terraforming mission. Any of the mysterious plan that remained was lost after his tragic assassination at the hands of radicals protesting his decision to expand the list of capital-punishment offences.

The tragedy proved disastrous for America's long-term survival. As all his cabinet members had abandoned him one by one, the late president had instead chosen to appoint himself to each position, including Vice President, Speaker of the House, and Grand Moff of the Space Force. Once again, people thought this was a joke, right up until he used the FBI to enforce the appointments. Therefore, with no contingencies in place for such an event, his untimely death created a power vacuum from which the once-mighty nation simply could not recover. Desperate consolidation attempts were made, but ultimately everyone agreed to disagree and went their separate ways. Some went to Mexico, some went to Canada, some went to Kokomo. Eventually other countries swooped in to pick up the pieces, and before long, all that remained of the Trump administration was a giant green-and-blue blotch that marred the red planet like a spot of (terraformed) mould.

"*DUUUUDE*, this is taking forever!!" Willy's voice rang out as he found his way back into the bridge. "Whoa! What! Why are we going to Mars?!"

"WHAT?!" Donald barked across the room. He hopped out of his chair and waddled up to the window. "You're taking us to Mars?! Are you crazy?! We're at war, man! They'll impound the ship and throw us in a room with fluorescent lights and strap us to beds with double-digit thread counts while they tickle us and force us to listen to the Meow Mix song for hours on end!"

He only stopped upon the introduction of his captain's hands clamping down on either shoulder. Cox couldn't seem to decide whether he was trying to restrain the fellow or massage away his dismay.

"Whoa, whoa, take it easy, you guys! We're not going to Mars. It's just aligned between Earth and the belt right now, so we gotta drive by it."

"Oh." They both spoke in unison. Donald scratched at his face for a moment before turning to shuffle back to his seat.

"And war is a pretty strong word, Donny!" The captain continued, hoping to keep conversation alive. "Mars just wants to sabotage our economy into failure so that they can have exclusive domain over the asteroid belt. It's totally different."

"Doesn't that just mean it's a cold war?" Willy asked.

"Yeah, sure, you could call it that!"

Donald blew a raspberry.

"Yeah, another cold war so we can get another fresh batch of spy movies to distract us from the government stripping all our rights away for our own protection!"

Now it was Cox and Willy's turn to shuffle in discomfort. The communications officer stalked back to his station and sank into his bean-bag chair—the one piece of Cox's antique collection he expressed any affection for. After a few beats, the captain cleared his throat.

"Well . . . I can take you to Mars then, if you want. That way you won't have any rights to strip?"

Not even a sarcastic chuckle of acknowledgement from Donny. Cox mentally shrugged; if it were too easy to amuse him, then it wouldn't be an accomplishment when he succeeded! He'd try again later. For now, he would just enjoy the view. Getting to be in such close proximity to Mars on the way home didn't happen often, after all. That said, it happened every two years so it wasn't exactly rare either. But like other biennial events nobody really cares about, such as the World Scrabble Championship or the Pyongyang International Film Festival, if it's happening right in front of you and you have nothing else to do, why not give it a look?

Tiny specks of ships buzzed around the green Mars nipple like fruit flies. Many of them were probably delivery ships like his own, arriving home to dispense their plunder, or space buses ferrying citizens from orbital housing down to the surface. Intermixed among them would be the border patrol, of course; keeping an eye out of possible interlopers—whenever they weren't pulling people over for speeding or tethered skiing in high traffic zones. But whenever Cox looked down at areas with a high volume of vehicles from above he would inevitably find himself having the same thought:

I wonder how many of these people are drunk right now.

Before long, the red planet had drifted by, and the milling ships began to blur together until they were mere static disrupting Cox's (inter)stellar view. That is, all except for one: a large transport craft drifted along just outside the Martian border rather sluggishly for a vessel of its size. For reasons he was unsure of, something about it just didn't seem right to him. It could have been the fact that none of its rockets were activated. The way it drifted sideways in the direction of nothing in particular was also a tad bizarre, but that could be a minor oversight that would be corrected once orders were received.

However, when every other ship around oriented themselves in the same direction, the fact that it floated along inverted like a limp, dead fish was something he just couldn't find a way to rationalize.

BREAK OUT THE REDSHIRTS AND BROWN PANTS

"LOOK ALIVE, SPACE CADETS!" Cox announced to his crew, tossing his whale bone aside so his hands could be free to clap. "Trouble on the port bow!"

"I thought you said I was an ensign."

The captain shook his head.

"Space cadet's not a rank, it's—never mind. Come take a look at this."

Donald grumbled but complied nonetheless. With a grunt of exertion, he hoisted himself off his bean bag and proceeded to the viewport. Once there, he quickly saw the object of his captain's fascination. The vessel continued to drift like a child's abandoned bath toy. Maybe all those video games had desensitized him, but he didn't seem particularly perturbed by the sight.

"Look at that ship, Donny. What do you make of it?"

"I dunno. It's not doing anything?"

"Exactly! And it looks like an Earth ship! Why would it be all adrift way out here by Mars, rotated in a different direction than everybody else?!"

"I dunno. Who cares? They can orient themselves however they want. Maybe it's Australian."

"Haha! Oh, you jokester! But no, this is suspicious. I think that ship is in trouble."

In trouble. The words rang through the ears of everyone in the spacefaring living room. Way back in the olden days, citizens couldn't say the word bomb when they were on an airplane, no matter the context. Things as benign as words could be rendered taboo simply based on the implication of what could follow their utterance. However, the anathema surrounding the words "In trouble" was not universal to space travel. It was, rather, exclusive to the SS *Jefferson*. So exclusive that only from the mouth of Captain Tim Cox were they cause for alarm. Similar alarm could also be inspired by uses of words and phrases such as "Slight detour" or "It'll be an adventure."

"Oh, come on!!" Donald protested. "We've never made it back to the depot in time for an early-bird bonus. If we just stay on course, we could do it this time for once!"

"Look down there at that ship, Donny! They're in distress, man! If we don't go down and save them, then who will?"

He pressed his face up against the window like a kid at the zoo. A second later he pulled away because he was fogging the glass and couldn't see.

"Oh really? You wanna 'save' them?!" The communications officer pressed, getting his money's worth on that communications degree of suspect origin. "Kind of like that time you made us drive way off course to 'save' Earth from that asteroid that you were sure was gonna hit it?"

"And thanks to us it didn't!"

"You dumped our cargo to knock it off its collision course that you said you 'eyeballed!!'"

"You can't always trust computers! Sometimes you gotta go with your gut. Now get to your station and check if they're sending any distress signals."

"They're not." Whisper cut in. The petite woman leaned over Donald's sweat-stained bean bag and visibly winced as she put her hands on his greasy touch screen, clicking away with a frantic urgency. "I just checked this gross computer, and there's nothing. At all. Not like I'm an expert or anything, but I'm pretty sure they want to be left alone."

The captain raised his hands toward her as a silent plea.

"Not you too! Why are you guys so opposed to a slight detour?!"

Donald and Whisper both winced.

"Uh . . ." The pilot mumbled. "Probably 'cause the last time we did a *'detour'* was when you thought you discovered a new comet. We chased it it for freakin' ever; even dumped our cargo so we could keep up. And when we finally caught it we found out it was just a big blob of jettisoned cruise-ship poo!"

"And the Better Business Bureau gave me a great finder's fee for catching a ship illegally dumping space waste!"

"We spent it all on fuel costs!"

Besought on either side by forces both more combative and riled up than himself, Cox's normally expressive hands started to lose their eloquence. As he backed back towards his chair they became little more than punctuation for the "er"s and "um"s he offered while trying to form a rebuttal.

"You guys are being crazy! That's like two things. Everybody's got some stuff that they've messed up before."

"Dude, you're famous!" Willy chimed in from the kitchen. He had abandoned trying to work the microwave and instead just stuck a fork in the now semi-frozen block of soup. "I remember seeing you on the news that time you dropped all your space rocks on a radio station because you thought you intercepted coded messages to Mars."

Captain Cox pursed his lips as he ran a smooth, manicured hand through his hair. He wasn't embarrassed by reminders of past blunders; he would still make them and others like them without a moment's hesitation. He was the captain, after all. But while captaincy allowed him to execute such endeavors, it didn't grant him the ability to make his crew appreciate or even understand the rationale behind them. Maybe he had to be an admiral for that. Or a lion tamer. People probably didn't question their methods.

He folded his hands and straightened up. Blue eyes flashing, he smiled down at his worried crew with the same smile worn by a stepdad trying to endear himself to some kids that just aren't having it and addressed them with a tone to match.

"Lemme just say, guys, I am really glad you're comfortable enough to come to me with your concerns. Making sure that you all feel valued is one of the most important things to me; it's really a cornerstone of any effective crew."

"Does that mean you won't make us go?" Whisper asked.

Cox squinted at her with his mouth hanging open slightly.

"Wellllllll, no." He replied, trying to perk up the letdown with a finger gun gesture. "Don't get me wrong, having a rapport with you guys is important to me, but so is maintaining my captainly authority by making you do stuff you don't want to. So go draw straws for positions on the away team!"

Whinges and protestations fell upon deaf ears like the smoke alarm in a senior's home. However, Whisper's discontent soon gave way, and she begrudgingly set off to cut some straws.

Donald's defiance wasn't so easily trumped.

"Get Co-Captain Kim." He snapped at Willy. "She's the only one who can talk him outta this now."

The bulbous bouncer nodded without objection and set off in the approximate direction of the first mate. He was fortunate that the ship's layout was straightforward, as he was all too willing to charge blindly off in search of her before he'd even had a tour. Neither Cox nor Donald said anything as they watched him go. Maybe after he learned to properly use the microwave he would be able to move on to slightly harder technologies such as the comlink. Donald folded his arms, sank back into his seat, and returned to his game.

Since he was forced to wait for his mate anyway, Cox picked up his coffee cup and studied his disgruntled employee. He was certainly distinguished looking. His unkempt mop of dark hair sat upon his pasty head, making him look like a burnt Q-tip. It was hard to tell if his brow was in a constant state of furl due to his chronic case of the grouchies or if his face just looked like that. But either way, his eyes were undiscernable inky blobs ever cast under its shadow. Far more expressive were his lips—though they only knew the one where they would peel back and reveal a comically large set of teeth eerily reminiscent of those old wind up toys. Was it a grimace? A scowl? A spirited impression of a man riding a particularly fast roller coaster? Whatever way, he was just ambiguous-looking enough that it was unclear whether it would be racist to make fun of his appearance.

"Hey, Donny, are you Italian?" Cox asked.

"Yep." He replied without looking up.

Wow, got it on the first try. That kind of torpedoed his plan to circle around the subject with small talk. Oh well; guess he'd just have to go for it.

"I don't get you, buddy." He shared the unsolicited thought as he took a knee next to him. "Is taking rocks from one place to another really what gets you out of your space bed in the morning?"

"Yes!" Donald exclaimed, hands gesturing erratically as if insulted to have even been asked.

"But don't you ever want to do more? Don't you have any dreams you yearn to fulfill? Go somewhere you've never been, maybe? Try something new? Maybe even a little dangerous?"

"Nope. That's what the holodeck is for."

"Well, what about when you're at the end of your life and looking back? Are you gonna say, 'Boy, I sure am glad I didn't do anything out of my comfort zone that made any sort of impact on this universe besides making somebody else money!'"

Donald grunted and slapped the pause button on his touch screen. "No!" He barked again. He hauled himself upright and turned to face Cox so his words would carry as much weight as he did. "I'm going to say, 'Boy, I sure am glad I made smart financial and lifestyle decisions that allowed me to live this long and comfortably without getting myself killed or making anyone else want to kill me.'"

Cox grinned. Donald's face fell, realizing he had taken the bait.

"Well what about those people down there on the ship, Donny? I bet some of them made all the right decisions in life. They all showed up for work and kissed all the right butts and didn't stand in fire. But by no fault of their own they could still be in trouble right now. Nothing keeps you totally safe. To paraphrase the old philosopher, Withers: 'It won't be long/'til you're gonna need/somebody to lean on.'"

"What?"

"Let them lean on you, Donny. Even if you don't think it's the fun thing to do, it's the right thing to do."

By the time he had finished his pep talk, his hand was firmly clamped onto Donald's doughy deltoid and he was staring deep into his uncomfortable underling's eyes. Cox probably thought this moment bore much more significance than it actually did.

"We don't even know if they're in trouble!"

"Open your eyes, Donny! Their ship isn't oriented the same way our ship is! How much more proof do you need?!"

"Have you guys tried calling them?" Kim's voice cut in. She stood over the two bickering manchildren and flashed a tight-lipped smile.

"Missus Cox!" Donald exclaimed. "The more level-headed Cox." He added to his captain. "Can you please tell him this is a stupid idea?"

She crossed her arms.

"I'll take that as a no. Maybe give that a try before I rule on anything."

Captain Cox gave a shrug of acquiescence and gestured for the communications officer to do some communicating. Donald tapped his fingers away at his screen and within a few moments *Half-Life 3* was safely on mute and he could do his job. After that, he opened up the space phone app.

Ring.

"Do you even know what you're going to say if anyone picks up?" Donald asked.

Ring.

Cox's eyelids fluttered at the question.

"Me?! You're the communications officer! Your job is more than pushing buttons."

Ring.

"Yeah, but you're the one who wants to bug them!"

Ring.

"And it's your job to do it for me!"

Ring.

"I'm not saying anything until you show me that in the job description."

Ring.

"Fine! Kim, honey, could you go get the employee handbook that I wrote?"

Click.

The viewing window on the bridge changed to a screen of static. Or so it seemed until they noticed the black figure taking up the center of the screen, barely perceptible amidst the buzzing patterns. All three crew members on the bridge stared into the humanoid abyss, every bit as frozen as the shadow gazing back upon them. The moment of silence it was on screen felt like an eternity; but before long it spoke.

"*Your call has been forwarded to an automatic voice message system . . .*"

"THE HMS *MILK AND TWO SUGARS*"

"*. . . is not available. At the tone, please record your message.*"

"They really need to make those less creepy." Kim observed.

"Are . . . are we leaving a message?" Donald asked.

"*When you are finished recording, hang up, or press smiley-face emoji for more options.*"

"Should we?" Cox asked. "I mean, then we'd have to set around and wait for them to—"

Beep.

"OH GOD IT'S RECORDING. HANG UP, HANG UP."

Click.

They sat in silence, processing the preceding events. Kim unfolded her arms and replaced them on her hips while Captain Cox contemplated the moment with a thumb to his mouth. Eventually the calm consideration culminated with an exaggerated sigh.

"Well. That ship now has a recording of me screaming. I think we have to pay them a visit now."

"This doesn't prove anything! Tell him, Missus Cox!"

"I hate to break it to you, Donald, but I think there might actually be something wrong over there."

The presence of now two authority figures looming over him caused the coms officer to sink into his chair. A low, drawn-out grumble emanated from within his dewlap.

"We could get a bonus, though!" He offered as a last-ditch effort. Cox answered it with a headlock-like hug from behind.

"No more excuses, mister! You agreed to listen to her because she's level headed. So, go find Whisper and Willy and draw straws for—wait, where is Mister Padilla anyway?"

Kim waved the question off.

"Oh, he'll be up in a minute. He's just visiting the eye wash station real quick."

Cox and Donald both cocked their heads at her.

"What? I may have been a bit jumpy when he came to find me and I may have emptied an entire can of pepper spray on him. He'll be okay. This is what happens when you spring things on me!"

SILHOUETTED AGAINST THE MIGHTY visage of the nearby planet, the SS *Jefferson* crept closer to its intended boarding target. The HMS *Milk and Two Sugars* dwarfed the transport vessel in both size and number of flags jutting from its frigate-like frame. Several Saint George's Crosses stuck out in many different directions, perhaps just in case the name wasn't enough to convey the ship's brazen Britishness.

They approached from the rear. Gargantuan stern rockets gaped at them, ready to burn them to a crisp with one flick of a switch. Yet there seemed to be no fear of such things occurring. In fact, as Whisper carefully piloted around the derelict ship, all the space-sea similes became much more apt. With a gentle drift they floated closer, like submarine skippers happening upon a ship previously thought to be forever lost to the deep. And like happening upon a ship lost to the deep, for all they knew, it could contain large tentacled creatures just dying to ruin their day.

"Take us down to the landing pad, Miss Wang." Captain Cox ordered as he affixed his Glad Press n' Seal Space Helmet™.

"Are you for real?" Whisper responded. "You need gravity to even have a 'down;' and it would be toward Mars right now."

Her scowl deepened at her captain's chuckling reponse.

"Look at this little Einstein over here! Alright, ya got me. Whatever direction the landing pad is in, then. Let's go there!"

His attention turned to Kim when she tapped on the glass helmet. "Tim, Just be careful. You're only going in to have a look, okay? You're a brave man with an adventurous spirit, and I love you, but you're useless in a fight and make terrible decisions under pressure."

"I love you too, honey." He replied with a smile. They blew a kiss to each other from the different sides of the faceguard. "I'll see you after I'm done being a hero. Mister Padilla and Miss Wang, I'll see ya outside!"

Kim couldn't help but smile as she watched her husband proudly march to the airlock like a naïve soldier headed off to war. Whisper, however, was less enthused. With a squeaky grunt of disapproval, she press-n'-sealed her head into a terrarium of its own and got out of her seat to follow suit.

"Why are you even with him!?" She whined as she double checked all her seals. "He sucks. His jokes are dumb and he screws up everything."

"Shut up, Whisper." The first mate snapped back. "If you have to ask, then you wouldn't understand anyway."

Taken aback by the uncharacteristic aggression, Whisper

looked at the first mate for a moment, then trotted away without another word. Willy must have been surprised as well; he stared at his superior long enough that she caught him in the act and raised an eyebrow.

"Nope." He responded to the unasked question before popping the fishbowl on his head and taking off too.

With wildly varying enthusiasm, the three members of the away team departed the safety of their space home and took the first steps of their ~~suicide mission~~ investigative outing. The steps of this outing were, of course, figurative. Due to the weightlessness of space, it made more sense to travel using the much less strenuous method of floating. Cox found it very relaxing to drift along, drinking in the sight of the monolithic marble that was Mars. Being out untethered and seeing it was somehow so different than looking through the viewport. Like a daring voyager staring into the eye of a legendary beast. A sobering reminder of where he sat on the scale of space.

"Never gets old, huh?" His voice crackled over their suit's communicator.

"Nope." Willy responded, drinking it in himself.

"It kinda makes you wanna—"

"I swear to god, if you start singing that 'boom de yada' song again . . ." Whisper groaned.

"Hey guys, did you feel that?" Kim's voice interrupted into their ears.

"Yeah." The captain whispered back in awe, still transfixed. "Wow . . . It's so beautiful."

"Tim, I love you, shut up. I meant I think we hit something. The ship was within thirty feet of the landing pad and the scanners weren't picking up anything between us, but then the whole ship started shuddering."

"Any damage?" Cox replied, briefly suspending his whimsy.

"I don't think so. If we did hit something, it was much smaller than us so I think we pretty much pancaked it."

"Well alright then! You heard the lady, guys. Let's go have a look."

Now with a purpose to drive them, they pulled their way along the length of their ship until they reached the junction. The magnetic connectors had firmly clamped the *Jefferson* onto the landing pad, much as the flattened mass of metal in between them tried to prevent it. Clinched together between the larger vessels, shrouded in a veil of suspended glass and debris, was a gnarled scrap heap that would need a good bit of TLC if it were to ever function again.

"Whoa."

"Tim?" Kim's voice spoke into his ear again. "You can't just say 'whoa' and then not elaborate."

"It's hard to say exactly what I'm looking at here." His voice buzzed back. "It's . . . something! And, now I'm not an expert or anything, but I think whatever it was . . . it isn't anymore."

"Dude, it's a ship!" Willy's voice cut in. "We parked on top of it."

"And this is why you don't send the pilot on the away team!" Whisper threw up her arms, even though no one was looking at her. "There was no ship there before! Then you make me get up and leave, and next thing you know, we're slamming into vehicles and running over pedestrians and whatever."

At this point Kim was closer to punching the talkback button than pressing it.

"Hey, don't pin this on me, I didn't go to a fancy pilot school, but I would have noticed if a whole friggin' ship flew in ahead of us."

"Well there is 'a whole friggin' ship' ahead of us. How else you think it got there?!"

"Maybe it was already there." Donald half-heartedly offered from his "work" station. "Maybe it just had a cloaking device or something."

"You guys hear that?" Kim asked.

"Duuude, that'd be badass!"

"Whatever, I dunno." Whisper mumbled as she inspected bits of the wreckage floating within her reach. "All I know is, nothing was there while I was driving."

"So hold on a second." Cox weighed in. "This ship was already parked in this spot when we got here, and whoever owns it left the invisibility button pushed? So who's at fault here? Do we still have to leave our insurance info?"

He heard just the briefest shriek of Donald's laughter in his ear before Kim took her finger off the talk button.

"Dude, they're probably space pirates!" Willy protested. "They won't care about insurance, they'll just find you and kill you."

"Not if we leave!" Whisper insisted. "Kinda hard to chase us when your ship looks like Donald's hair."

"A pancake and run, Miss Wang? Really? That's low, even if they *are* pirates. I taught you to have better morals than that. Now you're breaking into this ship with me and that's final! . . . And I wish I had curly hair like Donny."

"I really doubt they're pirates." Kim's voice buzzed in their ears again after a long pause. "Common pirates could never afford cloaking technology like that—which actually makes me worry more. Tim, I don't think you should go in there."

"Honey, it's okay. We've been floating our way through the ship yelling 'hello' and flinging open doors this entire time. There's no problem!"

"Ugh. 'Kay, only he's doing that. You guys know I never say hello to anybody."

Through their awesome marital bond, Captain Cox could occasionally sense when he was making his wife worry. Sometimes he had helpful hints like her begging him to stop being an idiot, but other times all he needed was more subtle clues like a tremble in her voice, or that pursed-lips-and-folded-arms stance she'd do, or when him telling her what he was doing was immediately followed by a long radio silence. In cases such as the latter, he found the best course of action was to start behaving and ride it out.

If the ship seemed big on the outside, it was probably because it was very large on the inside and therefore the outside had to be equally large in order to house it all. Whoever built it seemed to have employed the same interior designer as pretty much every other space ship ever. Cold and sterile metal hallways connected every chilly and antiseptic metal room. Nobody even had the courtesy to stick a potted plant in a corner or a painting on a wall. Even if one was depressing and soulless enough to not take issue with living inside a metal anthill, surely the impracticality could at least be plain to see. Nothing made any hallway noticeably discernible from another. New recruits must go mad trying to find their way around.

And then there was the less common, but currently relevant, problem of how utterly terrifying and claustrophobic it became when the gravity, life support, and lights were shut off. Cox and Co. floated along like three balloons that had escaped the clutches of their child captor. Each of them had a beam of light that they waved around in a wild manner, never settling on anything long enough to actually look at it. And it was quiet. Too quiet, even. The kind of quiet that delighted librarians and mortified comedians. It was that annoying kind of quiet that put you in a state where pretty much anything would freak you out, whether you liked it or not.

"Can we put on some music or something?" The captain broke the silence. "It's kinda tense in here, y'know? I think it'd help us relax a bit."

"Oh yeah, Tim, that's just what I need; for you to get eaten by a space slug 'cause you were too busy rocking out to 'I Love a Rainy Night.'"

"DUDE." Willy interrupted the squabble. "They got a Quidditch pitch!"

They did indeed have a one. A turf-lined structural marvel decaled with colourful stands and streamers that looked like a portal into another universe from the barren silver tube they had been walking down this entire time. The rails next to the door were lined with fan-propelled 'brooms' and the walls themselves rose so high into the bowels of the ship that the flashlights couldn't even come close to illuminating the ceiling. Willy grabbed a quaffle and punted it straight upwards, waiting at least ten seconds before realizing if it hit the ceiling, he wouldn't be able to hear it anyway. As she watched it disappear into the darkness, however, Whisper was met with a realization.

"'Kay, I know you guys just ignore all my opinions anyway, but can I at least point out this ship is gigantic, and we don't even know what we're looking for? We could float around this place until we literally starve to death and still not check it all."

"She has a point, Tim," His better half buzzed inside his helmet. It came as no surprise; those two always seemed to agree on everything. "Maybe you should come back before you get too turned around. You had your look and it sounds like whatever happened, it's over now."

"Just five more minutes, baby, I promise! I'm a captain with wind in my sails! Just give me a little enthusiasm here and I know I'll get us somewhere. Gimme positivity! Optimism! Love! Friendship! Honour! Terrific! Masterful! Alliance!"

"Okay, I was with you until you started just saying random words like you're trying to stall me."

"It's because I'm pretty sure I'll have something to report when I get to the end of this trail of mannequins dressed like space marines."

Now even Donald was interested. Kim raised a finger to silence him before he could speak, though.

"Did you just say space marine mannequins?"

"Well, I'm not sure what else they would be. They're kinda just floating around the hallway here in different poses. Maybe props from a photoshoot or something. Their costumes are really detailed too. They got, like, names and ranks and blaster holes and—"

Kim cleared her throat with an anxious "ahem."

"Tim, I'm just going out on a limb here, but are you sure you're not walking through a hallway full of dead bodies?"

Cox grabbed a doorway and slammed to a halt like a skater who doesn't know how to stop. With a slight tremble in his hand he reached and did a tactile inspection of the closest bobbing body. Padded armour adorned its chest, arms, and legs; the face was obscured under an opaque visor that reflected the captain's own shiny face. He contorted it into a pre-emptive wince as he pulled the helmet off.

"OHHHhhhhhh . . ." He couldn't help but exclaim, his voice a schizophrenic scuffle between fear, despair, and embarrassment. "Why?! This isn't fun at all now!"

"EWWWWWWWWWWW!"

Whisper screamed over the feed loud enough to make both Kim and Donald wince as hard as her and Willy. They huddled their arms close to themselves and tried in vain to distance themselves from the closest cadaver. If the narrow corridor seemed cramped before, navigating it now was like sneaking past a museum's laser alarm system. Every brush of the limbs of the living with those of the dead might as well have branded them, given the way they reacted. They floundered around in the darkness, hooting and screeching as they went, with movements far too erratic to render their lamps of any use. Within moments they and the bodies were a tangled, macabre mess bouncing around in the blackness, swatting and slapping with a waning sense of hope, nearing a point in psychological defeat wherein death by space slug would be welcomed. Yet no celestial savage did show. Instead, the large space-barn doors at the end of the hall opened and flooded the corridor with light, illuminating the big ball of violence that had unfolded.

A lone, silhouetted figure emerged from the glare, feet planting firmly against the floor with each step. Either one of his arms was longer and more gun shaped than the other, or he was one of those insufferable people who regarded their right to open carry with way too much pride.

4.
THE MARTIAN

CAPTAIN OF THE CREW and lone-wolf-aggressor presumably stared at each other; but with the subpar lighting and reflective face coverings, it was impossible to know for sure. They sure did stand there for a while, though, each of them drinking in the sight of something. Cox greeted the newcomer with all the grace and diplomacy of a seasoned ambassador, complete with formal introduction, insistence that he meant no harm, and hearty compliments on the fellow's choice in space shoes. He didn't realize until the end of his spiel that the man, in all likelihood, heard absolutely none of it.

Kim leaned over her terminal, her lips mere inches away from the microphone.

"Tim, who are you talking to?"

"There's a guy here, honey." He answered, giving a sheepish wave to the suspicious spaceman. "I'm trying to see if he knows charades."

"Who is he? Is he threatening you? Does he have a gun?"

"Not sure; not really; not important!"

"NOT IMPORTANT!?" Kim barked into the mic. She yanked the thing out of its holder and proceeded to pace around the room. "You are unarmed! Maybe this guy didn't want to be seen. Now you've seen him, Tim! You can't unsee him! That would only leave him with one option, and if he's the one who made that mess in the hallway, then he's obviously not afraid to use it."

Tim's voice was as calm and cheerful as ever when it crackled back; even if it shouldn't be.

"Okay, but let's remember that for better or for worse we're here now. So, let's just look on the bright side of the situation, alright? Yes, he has a gun. BUT, it's important to recognize that it is not currently pointed at us."

"And what if he decides to point it at you?!"

"Well, good thing our suits have lasers built into them. We could point them back."

"Who are you people?" A foreign voice echoed across all of their speakers.

Kim lurched backward from her terminal, only her white-knuckled grip keeping her chair from flying clear across the room.

"Donald!" She hissed. "Our coms have been hacked!"

"You can't hack a radio, Missus Cox. He probably just found our frequency."

"Well, do something!"

He threw his arms up in defeat.

"What do you expect me to do!? If you give me some money, I can order us some technology from this millennium?"

Meanwhile, back aboard the HMS *Milk and Two Sugars,* Whisper and Willy's laser hands shot upward in tandem with their blood pressure. Cox's pulse beat so loudly in his ears he couldn't even hear the response coming out of his mouth. Fortunately, he was well versed in the art of talking without listening to himself. The rhythmic throbs in his ears had only just begun to subside by the time the rumbling of his vocal cords ceased. While he wasn't sure what he said, he took solace in the knowledge the gun still wasn't pointed at him.

But the long silence that immediately followed made him just a little nervous.

The stoic spaceman didn't move, but provided acknowledgement by way of a long inhale followed by an even longer exhale.

" . . . Are you another agent?"

He spoke slowly with a voice that was throaty and deadpan, like what you'd imagine a grizzled old sloth would sound like.

"No! No!" Cox insisted. "We're just your average easily replaceable blue-collar guys. There's no need to be freaked out; nobody even knows we're here."

"I see."

Kim ripped her hand off the mic and slammed it onto the talkback button.

"Some of us are still aboard the ship though. With guns. And panic buttons. And cameras. And bosses that will get really mad if their shipment doesn't show up."

The man lifted his space rifle to rest it on his shoulder. "Your coms officer sounds a little nervous there, 'Captain.'"

Cox blinked a few times through the dopey look plastered on his face.

"Oh!" He finally said. "That's not my coms officer, that's my wife, Kim. She used to be a space cop, so she can be a little suspicious of people. She's my peach, though. I wouldn't worry about her, long as you don't try to kill us or something!"

Captain Cox chuckled to himself, slowly exaggerating it as it went on in hopes someone would join in. Unsurprisingly, no one did. It slowly echoed away and allowed silence to take over the coms once more. "You didn't laugh at that." He observed, voice sinking into his stomach. "Should I be worried?"

"I laughed on the inside," the man replied without emotion.

"Is anyone gonna ask what happened over there?!" Donald mumbled over the mic with as much as emotion as he was capable. "You're all standing in a hallway full of dead guys talking like you're on a blind date."

"Hey, there he is!" Cox tried yet again to inject some positivity. "That's my coms guy. And he has a point; we should get you off this ship. Do you know if there's any other survivors?"

"Tim, no, we don't even know who this guy is! For all we know he killed all these people."

"By himself, Kim? There's like, twenty people in here. You think he killed them all?"

"I did kill them all."

The guy's dry voice was a mute button to all marital and interpersonal quibbles. Granted, most of those quibbles directly involved him, but even other arguments like "Which restaurant should we go to?" or "Should we keep it or get rid of it?" would likely have been put on hold by those five words too. Call it trouble triage.

"Don't worry; they were nobody important." He amended, as if it absolved him. "Now, if you'll excuse me, I need to go before the ship self-destructs."

Without another word, he marched through the bale of bodies and bewildered boarders. Untrained in handling situations like these, the trio could do naught but sit and watch him walk through the gravity-free hallway with the help of magnets in his boots. The away team exchanged incomprehensible gestures amongst themselves.

"The ship's gonna blow?!" Willy clarified. "Dude, we gotta get outta here."

Perhaps as a form of silent acknowledgement, Cox snatched up the part of his spacesuit that would be considered the collar and engaged them both into a floaty retreat.

"Couldn't agree more, buddy. Uhhh hey. Hey, man. Where you going? You gotta come with us!"

"What?! He does not." Whisper contested in tandem with Kim buzzing her similar opinion into their helmets.

"No, he doesn—yeah, what she said."

"We can't just leave him! Where else is he gonna go, huh!? Space? Hitchhike on a comet? He can't just beam himself all the way to Earth, guys!"

"Or I could just take the ship I came on, if it's all the same to you," that familiar tired voice responded. "Seeing as that was my plan and all."

The captain coughed as he skidded around a corner and into a wall.

"Can't do that. We kinda smashed it."

They rounded the hallway to find the lone spaceman standing frozen in the hallway.

"You 'kinda smashed it?'"

"Well, I didn't." Cox clarified. "It was a piloting mishap."

"There was no ship!!" Whisper shouted.

"It was invisible." Kim corrected.

"I was gonna leave a note if I didn't find the owner, I swear. These guys will back me up."

At first it sounded like the radio had been overtaken by a brief stint of static. However, as it droned on it quickly became clear that it was coming from someone uttering a long, drawn out, malfunctioning refrigerator-like sigh. Cox was starting to wonder if it was an ogre underneath that helmet.

"Alright, fine, I'll take your ship then."

Foreboding wording aside, the captain felt obliged to grant

asylum nonetheless. He couldn't leave someone behind like that, potential threat or not; it just wouldn't be right. Besides, it was exciting! No one was going to be able to look back on this excursion and say it was nothing. Sure, there might be a little mental scarring from literally rubbing shoulders with murder victims, but it was nothing modern-day emotion-realigning drugs couldn't fix. What mattered here was this would be a story worth telling—as long as he could find a way to survive it.

Not many words were shared for the rest of the trip out of the ship. Their new passenger led the way, stomping down the hall with a bunch of floating spacemen trailing behind him like he was a NASA float in the Macy's Thanksgiving Day Parade. With how well he knew the route back to the landing pad, it seemed likely he was from this ship, or so Cox wanted to believe, anyway. Either that or he had a great memory; but he sounded old, so how likely was that?

By the time the landing bay doors opened and the endless expanse of space stretched out before them, the tension hadn't diminished in the slightest. Even prison guards often feel a sense of unnerved dread when escorting dangerous killers from one location to another. It's the unpredictability that's so hard to reconcile. That unpredictability becomes doubly threatening when, instead of handcuffs, they have a rifle large enough that it wouldn't even need ammo to kill somebody. But consequently, just as fellows meeting that description were hard to maintain comfort around, they also tended to be very difficult to say "no" to. To some, that meant the best course of action was to avoid situations in which they would have to say it.

"Okay, honey." Cox called to his wife over the radio. "We're outside. Can you let us in?"

Unfortunately, sometimes that resulted in situations wherein other people felt compelled to say it.

"Kim, do you read me? Can you open the airlock doors please?"

"I'm sorry, Tim, I'm afraid I can't do that."

Nobody in their little group took that news well, but Cox did so much more poorly than everyone else, for some reason. His response was fairly standard procedure for when one locked their keys in their car, naked, during a blizzard, shortly after accosting a polar bear, while smelling of freshly sautéed seals: He jiggled the handle an innumerable amount of times, tried to physically pry the door open, turned and grinned sheepishly at the man whom the polar bear represents in this metaphor, and then pressed his face up against the glass with no idea what he was hoping for, but welcoming of something potentially helpful. All that was usual for a desperate man. And all were about as effective as you'd expect them to be.

"Baby, if you're trying to freak me out, then I can assure you, mission accomplished."

"'Kay, I admit that was a bad choice of words, but you gotta understand why I can't let you bring an armed murderer into our ship."

Before Cox could respond, their potential guest of honour reared back and lobbed his rifle into open space without a second's hesitation. Even such a gentle toss was adequate to propel it far into the nothingness, twisting and gyrating and almost dancing as it drifted away. Somewhere in the solar system there was probably a creepy, socially awkward teenager who would have loved to film it. But to the members of the crew, the true beauty came from the fact they were now very unlikely to be shot in the face by it.

"How's that?" He asked in a tone that demanded a specific answer. "Now can we get a move on, please? I should remind you that the ship is still going to blow in a couple minutes."

"I . . . I didn't expect you to do that." Her voice muttered in resignation.

"Well, I'm just full of surprises."

"Alright, great, this is good." The captain praised. "Everybody happy now? We all feeling a bit safer, maybe? Safe enough to even open the airlock doors?"

KIM PUT HER FACE in her hands, thankful that they couldn't see her. No amount of stalling was putting her any closer to what she would consider a satisfactory conclusion. Tim had really outdone himself this time. So much so that biting the bullet and letting them in seemed to be, for better or for worse, what ultimately was going to have to happen. However, it would not come to pass until she had mitigated the threat as much as what was feasible.

"Alright." She finally responded after letting them sweat a bit. "If he agrees to board the ship in handcuffs then he can come on."

"Handcuffs?" Donald asked, trying for once not to let his voice be heard. "Why do you have handcuffs?"

"Don't worry about it, Donald. Can you just go grab them? They're in the top drawer of my nightstand."

"Oh. OH! Ohhh . . . come on, that's gross."

"So how about that?" She asked again into the mic. "Do you accept my offer?"

"Uhhh . . ." Tim mumbled back in embarrassment, looking down at the wisps of smoke emanating from his glove laser. Apparently not expecting such a proposal, he had taken it upon himself to shear a small hole in the door where the handle used to be.

"Well, it would have been a really great suggestion if it was maybe ten seconds earlier!" He added as he watched the aforementioned handle waft off to join the rest of the floating space yard sale.

A series of hooks, ostensibly for clothing and other space gear framed the entrance hallway. Functional as they were, they remained empty in contrast to the floor where bits of space clothes lay strewn about in a direct path from airlock to bridge. The man barely even paused after pulling his wizened, bald head out of his helmet and tossing it aside. Sparing nary a glance down any adjoining corridors while stalking along, he ditched his space gear in increments until he had nothing left but his jumpsuit and the bottle of Fireball whisky that he'd been toting this entire time. Cox and company nearly tripped over the discarded bits of spacesuit in their haste to keep up. All four rounded the final corner at the same time to find Donald sitting alone in his beanbag chair. His droopy mouth fell open as the weight of the situation began to sink in.

"Alright everyone!" Cox announced with a clap. "Now that that's all over with, I'd like to introduce . . . What's your name?"

"Nobody." The old man grunted through twisted lips. His narrow grey eyes scanned around the room with suspicion.

"Right on! Well this is Mister Nobody. Now, it's very important we all make him feel welcome. And from all of us here on the *Jefferson*, Mister Nobody, I'd just like to say: 'My *casa* is *su casa*.'"

"What?"

"Oh, that's an idiom from this old dead language called Spanish. It might sound familiar, y'see, it's what a lot of modern-day Spanglish is derived from."

Mister Nobody blinked at him, probably trying to decide if Cox really was this socially unaware or if he was just Canadian. He seemed to at the very least possess the acumen to tell when a silence was persisting too long.

"Aaaaaaanyway, why don't you guys all sit down and share some stories. We got some meal supplement capsules in the galley if you're hungry, and I'll come join you just after I step into my office and change!"

"You are on thin ice." Mister Nobody growled, gesturing with a steady sausage of a finger. "So how about you drop your little charade and start acting like the captain you claim to be. First thing I want you to do is find me that woman from the radio."

"Alright—ALRIGHT!"

Cox was breathing heavily now. His hands were out in front of him and his blonde hair bobbed in time with his head swinging back and forth between Mister Nobody and his crew members. They all looked back at him in similar poses, frozen in apprehension, beads of sweat running down their faces, Willy's arms raised but not so high that his belly peeked out under his shirt. Off in the background, Donald's video game character was getting teabagged.

"We're on your side, okay?!" He placed himself between the intruder and his crew. "Nobody's messing with you. I mean we're not messing with Nobody. Meaning you. Your name is very confusing."

He swallowed when none of his blithering seemed to be inspiring a response.

"And the woman on the radio is my wife. Her name is Kim. She is definitely not gonna be hiding behind a doorway somewhere waiting to club you over the head when you walk through."

"ARE YOU KIDDING ME!?" Kim announced with a magnificent voice crack. Sure enough, she stepped out from behind the galley doorway, threw down a steel garbage-can lid, and folded her arms.

"Seriously," she continued, "I am genuinely curious at this point."

Her nose twitched in disgust when she looked upon the most recent newcomer to her ship, with his cold dead eyes, his pronounced ears, and his shiny head. And he looked back upon her with the faintest etchings of mild amusement. However, that may have been more for her husband, since he immediately turned back to him.

"Are you sure you're the captain of this ship . . . ?"

Cox sighed. He placed his hands on his hips. He licked his lips absentmindedly. And he looked Mister Nobody straight in his sagging, weathered face.

"It might seem like they're against me right now. But they know that I'm a captain they can look to when they're in trouble."

"Well then, you look at me." The old man replied, all amusement gone. "I'm the captain now."

There was an electricity in the air that likely tingled down the arms of any in the room that had hair on theirs. The great trump card had been played; the gambit had been made, and now Mister Nobody stood sober as he awaited a response. Cox had been right about one thing: everybody else in the room seemed to look to him for it. However, that may have been because they were just as confused as he was and was hoping he'd be the one to voice it.

"So, uh . . . that's it?" He asked with a pre-emptive wince. "Is—is this how a hijacking works? You just, y'know, say so?"

He gestured nonsensically with his hands as he tried to find the words. When he did, his voice dropped to almost a whisper.

"I just thought it would be, like, sexier. Y'know, more showmanship or something."

Mister Nobody pursed his lips and raised his eyebrows.

"I could kill you in front of your crew as a display of dominance if you want."

"No . . . no, that's okay."

Seemingly satisfied with the submission, the skyjacker spared a second squint around the room; presumably to gauge the obedience of the remaining company. They appeared weak and worried for the most part; knocking knees, darting eyes, gulping throats, all were often common preludes to dark spots forming on fronts of pants. It was strange, really. All this for an unarmed old guy wrinkling his nose at them. Who knows what would have happened if he still had his gun. At least one of them would have actually fainted like some overwhelmed Victorian lady. It probably wasn't even real fear. It was probably just those proximity emotions that are induced by fervid social situations. Like when you're at a funeral of someone you didn't even care about thaaaat much but you still cry anyway because the situation just seems to call for it and that's what everybody else is doing.

But there would be no funerals today if everyone played their cards right. Partially because virtually nobody has a funeral on the same day that they die, but also because murdering someone without a weapon is a really strenuous process and it's not unreasonable for one to want to mitigate their workload when they can.

"Arright . . ." The old man rubbed his hands together. He seemed every bit as hassled by this as the crew. "Let's get the usual stuff over with. You, aggressive tanned lady, disable the AI defense system. Fat latino guy, clear any voice recognition requirements. And you, less fat guy . . . what are you, Egyptian?"

"Yep." Donald replied.

"Right, well, disengage the autopilot."

"We don't have one," Whisper cut in.

Everyone turned and looked at her; the man in confusion, others in surprise. She shrugged sheepishly and turned her shoulders inward.

"His idea, not mine," she added, pointing at Cox. "'Something something robots are impersonal or something.'"

Now all focus turned to their new acting captain. His lack of quip seemed to suggest he was pondering the notion. With hands on hips, he shuffled where he stood, tongue absent-mindedly running along his lips. Finally, he looked at Cox.

"Did I catch you on bring your daughter to work day or something?"

"Careful, now!" The real captain shot back. "If she overhears somebody calling her my daughter, I'm gonna have two terrorists on my hands!"

"I'm literally standing right here."

"And you're being very brave right now!"

"How psycho do you think I am, anyway?"

"I don't think you're psycho at all! I just think you voice negative emotions more strongly than positive ones, and instigating more conflict would probably be a bad idea right now." He turned back to Mister Nobody. "This is just kind of a handful already, y'know? Well, maybe not for you; you seem pretty used to this. But for me? Wow, this is tense. Can you believe this is my first hijacking? Been in the business for ten years and nothing! Morbid as it sounds, I was almost starting to get a little offended. Like, there's all these stories of space pirates you hear about, but none of them ever wanted me. It's definitely not 'cause I look tough. Is my ship not pretty enough? It's not like we're hauling—"

“Kid, shut—for the love of—shut up!” The old man snarled through the wrinkled hand on his face.

Cox grinned from ear to ear at Kim.

“He called me kid.”

“Alright,” that smug, raspy voice announced. “It’s pretty clear what kind of hijacking this is going to be.”

5.

BREAKING THE BANKS

There weren't many rooms on Captain Cox's custom-constructed country club that weren't built for comfort. Despite its listed purpose for hauling freight, it was no secret that the most important focus was that it be a nice place to live. The gravity was light, but not enough so as to atrophy one's muscles. The beds were fluffy, the food was delicious, and the holodeck porn library was positively sublime. Frankly, the only passenger on board that didn't have ritzy accommodations was the lifeless payload that bounced around the stern. It was a facet that Cox found himself legitimately considering remedying as he and his crew sat in the cargo hold near the tethered space rocks.

The room didn't even seem like part of their home. Gunmetal-grey walls merged into horrible romance-novel grey floors and neither one bore any level of sprucing in the slightest. It made sense, really, as a loose piece of cargo would tear it all to shreds and likely didn't have any specific preferences regarding the adornments of its quarters anyway. But to the sulking crew sitting on the floor and leaning against the walls, a pick-me-up would surely have been welcome, even if only as a means of alleviating the wearisome silence that had been going on since the moment the door slammed behind them.

Kim kept her arms folded all the while. They hadn't come undone since she initially crossed them back on the bridge. While her pleasant face still hadn't been contorted to a frown, she hadn't immediately set to business combating the problem as her nature would usually compel her. Instead, she looked down at her husband sitting in the corner, hands on knees, being uncharacteristically silent as he stared off into space. Figurative space, that is; the room had no windows.

"Help!!" Willy yelled as he pounded at the door. "Somebody! Let us out!"

It would have been wince-worthy enough if he had just stopped at the one.

"God damn it, new guy, get a hold of yourself!" Kim snapped at him. "We're in space. No one can hear you scream. Well, except the guy who put us in here."

"Does anybody have any ideas?" Donald polled the group out of nowhere, perhaps to fit in with the theme of acting uncharacteristically.

Whisper didn't even look up from her spot in the corner. She appeared as zoned out as Cox, just staring at the floor tracing figure eight circles with her finger. Willy, however, pushed off of his lean against the wall and removed his hands from his pockets.

"I got an idea." He offered with a slight hesitance.

Donald waited a moment then, realizing a follow-up wasn't coming on its own, prompted it.

"Well, what is it?!"

Rather than reply, Willy tensed up. Then, his heaving shoulders tucked towards his torso, he tore into a full-tilt trundle towards the doorway. His stubby legs made surprisingly great strides, and he was moving at quite an impressive pace by the time he slammed into the hatch. The impact shockwave reverberated around the room as the security officer bounced off the door so hard his feet left the ground, making it that much more painful-looking when he landed flat on his back. The echoes were still going even after he had come to a stop on the floor.

Donald walked over to him and looked down.

" . . . Was that your plan? Or were you just warming up?"

Willy half sighed and half groaned.

"I thought maybe I could knock it down."

"UGH!"

The exasperated exclamation came as a figurative record scratch to the scene playing out. Everyone involved turned to find Whisper, still in her corner, looking back up at them with mirrored confusion—albeit hers caked with a layer of disgust.

"Yeah, no, you're right, I'm the one being weird. Keep smashing your face against it. That'll probably work. It's not like that door regularly deals with ten-ton rocks smashing against it or anything. God!"

In lieu of crickets, the creaking and groaning ambience of the metal room accented the awkwardness fostered by the outburst. Willy let his mouth fall open with an audible smack of the lips, at a loss for a retort. No one else seemed to know what to say either. Thankfully they had a bit more time to think since the telltale spreading of arms for emphasis indicated the young lady wasn't done.

"I know! There goes Whisper being a psycho bitch again, right? It's not like she ever has a point or something. She's just bringing the team down like usual."

She got to her feet, her manicured eyebrows angled down and her chubby cheeks doing nothing to conceal her frown.

"Even though you had literally one job and you couldn't even do it!" She barked at Willy.

"You just plain never do your job, like, at all," she added to Donald.

Her eyes then settled on Kim with a beat between beratings.

"And I don't know what your job even is!"

Finally, her hate parade arrived at its final destination. Cox looked up at her, waiting to receive his review. She served it in the same succinct style.

"You . . . are just the worst captain ever."

She retreated back to her corner, as drained from the tirade as everyone else. No one dared respond. No one even knew how. She wasn't totally wrong; at least not in their eyes. So rather than rebut, the rest of the crew threw around sheepish glances until reaching a sort of silent consensus. Three pairs of brown eyes trained their gaze onto the lone owner of the baby blues.

"This really is all your fault, Captain." Donald observed. His words were not caustic, rather clinical. It was an "I told you so" that he, for whatever reason, didn't glean pleasure from.

"If you didn't force us to get on that stupid ship . . . none of this would have happened!"

Cox looked up at him without a word, waiting patiently for him to finish. Once he was sure the admonishing had abated, he looked at Willy as if his turn were next. Perhaps it was the head trauma, but the big man had nothing to offer. He just shrugged and took to walking it off. Finally, there was Kim. His sweet soul mate's face said more than her words ever could. That's not to say hearing harsh words along with it wouldn't still suck, though.

"I just don't get it, Tim," She prefaced as she searched for the words. "You are not a stupid man. But I can't even begin to wrap my head around everything that just happened. Everything you just did. It's like you were deliberately trying to make the worst possible decisions. I just—I don't know."

She ended her turn with a dismissive wave, that unofficial but universal bit of sign language that directly translated to "I'm not even gonna bother."

"That's it?!" Whisper jumped back into the fray. "After all this?! He totally screwed us and you're not even gonna yell?!"

"That's enough out of you." Kim responded, unflapped by the demands. "I am angry. But we are a responsible married couple who plays nice until we have privacy, and then we yell at each other. Like civilized people."

"I really can't picture him yelling at you." Donald said from his spot on the floor.

"He doesn't. He usually just hits me with a pillow or something until I stop. I've yelled at him about that too."

Cox got to his feet. Riddled with contempt and agitation as they were, the gaggle couldn't help but quiet when he did. With fingers intertwined behind his back, he strolled through the hold, the very same way he would do on the bridge. He came to a stop by one of the space rocks. He traced a steady hand along its curvature, really milking this moment of authority for all it was worth.

"How long has it been?" He finally spoke.

Eyebrows were raised, coughs were coughed, but none of them in the form of an answer.

"Since we got thrown in here, I mean." The disgraced captain amended. "It's been a little while, right? I shoulda looked at my watch when we came in. I guess I was just caught up in the excitement."

"It's been about an hour, Tim." His wife said flatly. "Give or take."

"Good, good." He rubbed his hands together and gave her a smile. "Should be plenty of time then!"

" . . . For what?" Willy was the first to ask.

"For him to think he's won, Mister Padilla! It's all part of the plan."

Donald snorted.

"The plan. You 'planned' to get held hostage in your own ship after going out like a bitch in front of your whole crew?"

"I play to my strengths, Donny!"

There was a slight pause as he realized what he just implied, but he opted to carry on rather than address it.

"I'm a people person! Kindness is my nature. I spread my wings wide and give shelter to anyone who wants some, doesn't matter who they are! But just because I believe in people, don't think for one second that ol' Coxy is fine to be kicked around. No, sir!"

Donald looked around at the room and those who were in it.

" . . . So, what do you call this then?"

"Picture the scene!" Cox carried on. "You're stranded alone aboard an alien vessel. No directions, no weapons, no way to know up from down! Then would ya look at that, there's a guy with this big gun standing right there in front of you!"

"So literally what just happened to us earlier?"

"Exactly! What do you do?"

Now the others were getting involved. Hands rested on chins, nails scratched at scalps, and one by one tentative answers were shared.

"Bum rush 'em?" Willy threw in half-heartedly.

"No plans that involve getting my crew shot, Mister Padilla!"

"Run away." Whisper suggested like it was the most obvious thing in the world.

"Not a bad idea at all, Miss Wang! And I wouldn't have been offended by any of you if you did. But I can't keep you guys under my wings if I'm flapping 'em away!"

"So what's the answer you're looking for here?" Donald grumbled. "Talk to them?"

"You're close, Donny!" He pounded his hand into his fist and grinned like an idiot. "You gotta find out what they want!"

"And what if they wanna kill you?"

"Well then, you hope you got a coupla guys like Mister Padilla over here!"

Willy chuckled like someone who didn't understand but still wanted to feel included.

"Now, I'm not saying I'm an expert or anything, but who doesn't like being offered what they want before they even know they want it, huh? They start to think 'Well hey, look at this guy! Maybe I should keep him around; see what else he's got! Not the type of guy I feel like shooting in the face at all. Maybe I'll even let his crew keep living too. Y'know, as an act of good faith or something . . .'"

He was pacing now, hunched over and eyes darting wildly. He was also squinting for some reason. Absurd as the display was, that may have been the very reason his crew found it so captivating.

" . . . Next thing you know I got him exactly where I want him. He thinks he's won, y'see! He thinks I'm afraid of him. He thinks I can't and won't do anything to get in his way now! Best of all: he . . . thinks . . . I'm . . . stupid!"

The pregnant pause following that bombshell lingered for long enough that it became clear it wasn't going to birth a follow up statement on its own. The conflicting emotions of amusement and contempt at their captain's antics amongst the crew steadily melted into a uniform worry by the rant's conclusion. It was becoming increasingly likely that this defeat at the hands of a space terrorist may very well have caused their captain to lose his marbles.

"Okay . . ." Kim humoured him. "So, what are you going to do then?"

Cox grinned.

"You mean 'What are *we* gonna do?' Well to quote the old philosopher, Snider: 'We're not gonna take it anymore.' Now that his guard is probably down, I think we should go get the jump on him and ask him to leave."

"But how, Tim? He locked us in our own cargo hold."

"Or did you plan for him to do that too?" Donald added sarcastically.

"I did, actually!" He walked over to a grate embedded into one of the walls and gave it a light rap. "When I had the *Jefferson* built, I spent a few million extra space-dollars having a padded, soundproofed, person-sized ventilation system installed just in case anything like this ever happened!"

He nodded at Whisper with a smile.

"Would the 'worst captain ever' have thought to do that?!"

She blinked.

"Uh, yeah."

"Oh."

"A good captain would have spent that money on an AI defense system or something."

"Yeah, well . . ." He breathed to no one in particular as he busied himself with the grate. "Who wants to be that guy waiting around for a robot to save his crew for him?"

He stopped his fiddling. For the first time, the smile on his face faded away and was replaced by something more . . . flustered.

"Aw jeez, I forgot about Whatshername down in engineering! D'you think she's okay?"

Kim uncrossed her arms.

"You should go check on her."

"That's the Kim I remember!" He grabbed her shoulders and kissed her cheek. "Alright, guys, we're still in this! Just hold on while I go find her, then we'll discuss battle plans! Alright? Alright."

He grabbed the grate and tried to tear it from the wall. First it was a half-hearted tug as he underestimated the structural integrity. Then he introduced both hands, followed by a foot against the wall, and erratic jerky motions narrated by feeble grunts of exertion. Every failed yank hurt his pride more than his fingers.

"Heh, least I know the screws work. Good thing my watch has a laser built into it!"

Couple zaps, couple taps, and the plan was back underway. It took a few hops to finally get into the vent, but once inside, it was roomy and well lit, as any self-respecting stealth tunnel ought to be. The signposts indicating which passage led where were also a nice touch. Before long he was nothing but a pair of departing soles to the observing members of the group. Kim took extra care to verify he had indeed vanished before she enacted a scheme of her own.

"Whisper, Donald, come with me."

Without even looking at them, she hopped into the vent on her first try and made quick work of the first passage.

"We don't have a lot of time, guys," her voice echoed from within. "Let's go."

Being locked inside a metal room full of rocks, it wasn't like they had anything better to do. Whisper trotted on over and, after receiving a boost from Donald, followed her commander into the abyss. Donald took a few tries as well, but before long, also had himself hoisted in. Then came Willy. Standing on tiptoe, he peered down the rabbit hole that had swallowed his only friends on the ship.

"Hey, can I come too?" His hoarse voice queried the ductwork.

"No, no you stay here." The ductwork answered in the form of Kim's voice. "Wait for your captain to come back . . . or something . . ."

On hands and knees, they scampered through the ship's respiratory system. Each new step announced their location like a herald does for kings and/or whimsical sitcom characters during episodes where they come into a large amount of money. With the amount of racket each step made, it didn't seem implausible that the entire system was made of gongs.

"Are we really gonna sneak up on anybody like this?" Donald asked between huffs and puffs. "It sounds like I'm wearing pans as knee pads."

"It's fine, Donald." His superior responded from further up the tunnel. "I was there when he had this ship built. The soundproofing in here is solid; nobody will hear a thing. I always did wonder why he had it built, though."

They proceeded along in single file, reaching a fork and taking a left. Head down because of his height, Donald bonked it at the junction before following suit.

"Okay seriously, how did he afford all this stuff? This ship must have cost a fortune."

The disinterested tone of Kim's voice betrayed her lack of desire to answer.

"His family made some smart investments."

"Ohhhhh," the quiet pilot said. "So that's why you're with him."

"Whisper, don't think I won't kick you right in the face."

The rest of the trip was a subdued trek—if you didn't count the fact they banged along like an orchestra performing a timpani concerto. Each of them took it in turn to survey passing rooms through one-way glass panels designed to look like boring Walmart art from the other side. With each empty room they happened upon, Kim grew more and more worried that her husband would find the intruder before she did. Or worse, the intruder would find him. Or worse yet, nobody would find anybody, and Tim would return to the cargo hold, only to realize they were gone and do something stupid.

But alas, her fears were averted when she spied her face reflected back at her on the shiny head of that grunting oaf making himself a mayo sandwich in the kitchen of her husband's ship. He must wax the hell outta that thing. She could even see the lettuce in her teeth. She should probably take care of that before the epic fight that was about to happen. Or maybe she should leave it in as a distraction. Then again, how much of a distraction could it really be? But maybe it didn't matter. Maybe she should be employing any potential advantage, no matter how small. All this procrastinating probably wasn't a very good sign.

"Why did we stop?" Whisper asked from behind in her increasingly annoying voice.

"'Cause I dropped my contact, Whisper. . . . Why do you think we stopped!?" She rolled sideways into a kneeling position and addressed her reluctant backup. "Alright look, we're only going to have one shot at this. I would have done it earlier, but I didn't want Tim to try and interfere. Whoever this guy is, he's obviously not an amateur. In fact, I'm not gonna lie to you, this might hurt. But just remember there's three of us and only one of him. If we all work together then I think we can do this! I hope you guys are ready. Let's kick this bastard off our ship."

Both of them blinked back at her. Donald raised a pudgy finger.

"I think you got something in your teeth."

Kim pursed her pouty lips shut and grumbled through her clenched pearly whites. Tongue stealthily massaging her teeth, she shifted once more off of her legs so she could tuck her knees in and front kick the panel off the wall and into the room. With a crash louder than any of their cymbal-like footsteps, it flew into the room, narrowly missing the pasty headed hijacker. It instead slammed into the cupboards. She was hoping that it would maybe give the old goat a heart attack and save everybody a lot of trouble. But no, he just looked at it the way a cat looks at a toy that its owner paid way too much for.

She leapt from the vent and landed standing tall.

"Surprise, motherfu—!"

Mister Nobody turned around and examined her through half-closed eyes. He didn't respond; he just stared while chewing with his mouth open like a cow. Kim shuffled uncomfortably. After a few moments passed, she slowly raised a pair of fists.

"Alright . . . guess we're not talking, and just getting this over with then."

"Getting what over with?" The old man asked through a mouthful of bread.

"Uh . . . . Taking you out and taking the ship back?"

"Taking me out?"

Kim lowered her fists and spread her arms in frustration.

"Really? You really have no clue what's happening here? I've come to fight you, moron. Kick your ass off my ship and get on with my life."

Mister Nobody swallowed the food in his mouth and set his unfinished sandwich down.

"You're here to fight me?" He asked. "For the ship? What are we, Vikings?"

"It's not like you're gonna leave if I just ask you to!"

He pondered this for a moment, perhaps even if only to buy enough time for another bite of his sandwich.

"Well, yeah, no," he said with his mouth full. "So your next best idea is to . . . punch me in the head until I leave?"

"Well no, I, uh . . . I mean, yeah I was gonna punch you . . . Sometimes in the head . . . But then eventually you'd . . . I dunno! Why are you making this weird? You obviously know what I'm getting at!"

The old man shrugged.

So there they were, standing in the middle of the *Jefferson*'s galley. Mister Nobody leaned on the counter next to the remnants of the wall art, still munching away. Every now and then one of them coughed. Kim stood up straight, keeping her hands clenched but letting them fall to her sides. Of all the hurdles she expected to deal with, goading the interloper into a fight was not one she had anticipated. He didn't seem to regard her as a threat at all. She wasn't sure whether to be happy or angry about that.

"You know you got something in your teeth, right?" He asked, voice still muffled by mastication.

Kim snatched a mug out of the steam cleaner and hurled it at his face. He narrowly managed to duck out of the way, nearly dropping his food as he did. It shattered against a wall behind him. His mouth fell open just the slightest bit when he turned to look at it, but his face soon returned to being just as exasperated as ever.

"You really wanna do this . . . ?" He asked.

Kim grabbed another mug.

"My husband's not here to save you this time!" She barked as she let fly.

He deftly caught it and set it on the counter.

"Shouldn't I be the one saying that to you?"

He let out a sigh as Kim grabbed mug number three.

"Nobody ever wants to try passive resistance anymore . . ."

Before she had even loosed it, he bent forward and tore into a sprint. The airborne mug flew high and would have struck home were it not for his bowed shoulders. He drove his right one into Kim's midsection, knocking her airborne a few feet backward into the wall. Brown hair went in all directions as her back slammed against it and she bounced off into a kneeling position. Tears in her eyes, she looked up at him.

"Ah . . ." She wheezed. "How . . . How could you do that to me!? Do you feel big, hitting a woman?"

Mister Nobody responded with a left kick that knocked her onto her side. Perpetual frown unchanged, he squinted down at her.

"You were chuckin' mugs at an old man's head, lady. I don't think either one of us can claim the moral high ground here."

The waterworks stopped and her glib expression returned.

"Fair enough."

She grabbed a saucepan from a nearby cupboard and bashed it into his foot. Growling and cursing, he wrapped his arms around his knee and proceeded to hop around in pain. The dance of discomfort was just erratic enough to avoid Kim's wild wailing at his other foot. She smashed the pan repeatedly against the floor like a game of whack-a-mole until the hijacker's pain subsided just enough to let go of his knee and slam it into her forehead.

Knocked backwards yet again, but this time maintaining control, Kim quickly rolled to her feet and whipped the saucepan at him. He obviously wasn't expecting this one, given the way he made no attempt to stop it besides a wide-eyed and slack-jawed gawp. But it's tough to aim a throw in such a stressful situation, so it missed his unorthodox defense by a large margin.

Luckily, it nailed him square in the crotch instead.

His knees buckled, but, in a feat of superhuman strength, he managed to prevent their crumbling by sheer force of will. Albeit briefly. They couldn't hope to handle both the full-system shutdown that nut shots induced and also the full weight of Donald jumping out of the vent and landing on top of him. The pair landed on the floor, bad guy chin first and good guy at an angle that sent him rolling across the floor.

With the match now turned into one of the handicapped variety, Mister Nobody began to take it a bit more seriously. He dismantled the uncoordinated swings from the doughy coms officer with relative ease, occasionally getting him into an armbar or wristlock, but always being dislodged before doing any damage when Kim would come flying at him with a knee or elbow. Eventually he'd land a swing and knock her away, but her small stature was well compensated for by her wily fighting style. It was like dealing with a particularly ornery Pomeranian. Her feet stomped at his shins, her fists clobbered at his kidneys, she even sunk her teeth into his arm.

Mister Nobody quickly found no amount of flailing would get them unlodged. Donald lay on the floor rubbing at what was surely going to turn into a black eye later, while Kim continued to gnaw away like a vengeful beaver. If the old man tried to jerk his arm away any harder, he was liable to have a chunk of flesh come loose. So instead he raised his forearm as high as it would go and gave her a jab to the throat with his free fist. The enamel vice snapped open and she dropped to her hands and knees in a coughing fit.

Not in great shape himself, the old man stumbled backwards into the counter, panting and clutching at the teeth-shaped impression in his skin. He grimaced in pain but kept his eyes fixated on his challenger. She of course remained on hand and knee, but her coughing began to slow and she seemed to be getting ready for more.

And so, still keeping his injured arm bent, he staggered over to her and snatched up a fistful of her hair. With no free arm to bludgeon her with, he simply held her down, considering his options.

The saucepan from earlier flew by his head and clanged into the wall, startling everyone. He whipped his head around to see a terrified Whisper leering at him. Before he could even move, she darted back into the ventilation system and *thump thump thump*ed away.

"We all done? Everybody got it outta their system now?" He spat out a bit of blood. "Least you guys all decided to play hero at once."

Something collided with the door like a padded battering ram. It was followed by some muffled words and then some rhythmic beeping before the door popped open, revealing Cox brandishing a v-shaped black piece of metal. He rubbed it against his shoulder for a moment and then flaunted it in front of him triumphantly.

"Anybody in this room . . . holding out for a hero?"

Kim sighed and muttered under her breath.

"Oh god, Tim, what are you doing . . . ?"

Whatever he was doing, it was good enough for Donald. The coms officer crawled to his captain as fast as his stubby limbs could take him. Cox welcomed him back under his wing, stepping quickly and lightly to place himself between his crew and the threat. All the while, he kept the peculiar object held in front of him, like a priest holding a cross out to a vampire.

"Hello again, Mister Nobody," he greeted in as impassive of a voice as he could muster.

"Hello, person." Nobody replied. His gnarled hand tightened its grip on Kim's hair.

"I just want you to know, I didn't want it to go like this."

"You and me both."

Despite the palpable seriousness of the situation, the captain couldn't help but grin.

"I warned you though, didn't I?" He chuckled, gesturing at Kim. "A real firecracker! Lights up my life. But man, once she gets goin', I couldn't tame her, even if I wanted to."

His arms began to relax and his eyes drifted down to his beloved as he reminisced. He looked upon her with a dreamy smile. She looked back up at him with a slightly open mouth and a pair of raised eyebrows. Slowly, barely perceptibly, she nodded towards the man currently gripping her scalp.

"Oh yeah!" He blurted, re-raising a shaky arm. His forefinger slowly traced along the mysterious instrument towards its lever, as if attempting to cop a feel for the first time.

"So get away from her!" He demanded. " . . . You bitch."

Perhaps he misinterpreted the demands as reverse psychology, but Mister Nobody took that as a queue to clutch her closer.

"And what if I don't?"

"Aw, c'mon, man," Cox whined, arm relaxing yet again. "You know what I'm getting at here."

"I don't actually know if he does." Kim commented. "I had the same problem. He seems to really need it to be spelled out."

The captain groaned in moral opposition to the very threat he was trying to make. But he stomped his foot and bit the bullet.

"Well I'll . . . put a hole in you then!" The corners of his mouth sank as if the words tasted sour.

"But please don't make me . . ."

Mister Nobody seemed genuinely surprised.

"With that? Is that even a weapon? It's so small I thought it was some kinda remote."

"Yeah well, hasn't anyone ever told you size doesn't matter?"

The old man smirked and pulled a device of his own out of his pocket—a small pen-like gadget with superfluous blinking lights and blue spikes sticking out of the top. Before responding, he pointed it at Cox's weapon and gave it a small click.

"They have." He admitted. "But size also doesn't matter if it doesn't work anymore."

Now it was Cox's turn to raise his eyebrows and allow his mouth to fall open. He retracted his arm and studied the metal object in his hand. It didn't appear to be any different; still black and shiny and heavier than it looked. All the movable pieces still moved. To the best of his knowledge, he could see nothing wrong with it.

"What did you do?" He finally asked.

"I fried it." The old man replied matter-of-factly. "Can't make laser shots with toasted circuits."

It took a few moments for the words to sink in, but when they did, the captain grinned the cockiest of grins. More confident than ever, he pointed the weapon one last time, and this time it wasn't coming down.

"Man," he chided. "There's no circuits in this thing! It doesn't rely on lasers. This is an ancient weapon from a simpler time. A time when combat was still noble; it was *mano a mano*! Nobody had fancy electric stuff in their pockets. All they had was one of these. It was all they knew, and that was all they needed."

With his spare hand he reached over and grabbed hold of the top of the relic. With a gentle pull, the top piece began to slide backward until an eerie click resonated through the quiet room. His fingers then let the piece free and it snapped back into place with another click.

"It's called a Glock."

6.

HARRUMPH, TEA AND CRUMPETS

EARTH. 'TWAS A SILLY place. Life just seemed to rampantly grow there, regardless of whether or not it is appreciated, like in the bathtub of a bachelor pad. Even now that humanity had transcended its poorly temperature-regulated confines, many billions still willingly lived upon the big wet ball of dirt and rocks. Perhaps they were merely sticking around to oversee its continued destruction. It was the only place in the entire solar system that humans were slowly making less habitable for themselves instead of more. But it had been that way for about as long as anybody could remember, so who was going to question it now?

Earth wasn't all bad, though. If one found themselves forced to live there, they could always achieve comfort by purchasing a small portion of it and obliterating all traces of nature. Modern technology hadn't entirely abandoned the place, after all. Many of the planet's largest cities, like Tokyo, New York, Seoul, and Moose Jaw, could proudly boast nearly 100% synthesized everything. All that was missing was people. But trust that they were working on it.

Despite not being Earth's mecca for pretty much anything

besides tea production and orderly queues, London was still delightfully artificial; one had to be well out of town before they saw anything green that wasn't made of plastic. Every now and then a particularly uppity piece of grass would try and poke through the concrete, but the strike teams were swift to douse it in weed killer and fire. As such, the view from every office window was a pristine clean sheen, and the office of Sir Rupert Knobbenbottom was no exception.

As distinguished men often did, he stared down from his high-rise office as he idly sipped his tea, pinky raised so high it would dislocate a normal man's finger. He had many pressing matters to deal with, given his position within his organization, but multitasking was a peasant's game. Besides, he needed a thorough observation before he could talk at exhaustive length about the weather later.

"Pardon me, Sir Knobbenbottom." The sultry female voice of his AI receptionist interrupted his morning mulling. "Sir Todgerworth is requesting a morning waffling. Shall I put him through?"

Rupert took one last longing sip from his cup before returning it to the levitating tea tray. Work could only be put off for so long, it seemed. Sir Todgerworth always claimed to be seeking to waffle on, but it was always just a sneaky way to broach the day's matters to be attended to. Various progress reports on missions abroad, most likely. Either that or he sought to confer about his latest plan to invade France. Ever since America was reclaimed for the crown, the queen had become rather bumptious about regressing back into Britain's colonizing heritage.

"Very well, Miss Farthing." He replied. "Bring him up on the telly-phone."

He smoothed his greying hair and straightened his tie, not

that either needed it. Within a few moments the large screen on his wall displayed the visage of a doe-eyed man sporting parted brown hair complete with matching moustache. Certainly younger than Rupert, but he was by no means a spring chicken. He was in the process of baring his chalk-white teeth into the camera whilst thoroughly inspecting them.

"Top of the morning, Percy." Rupert greeted him, hands clasped behind him. "I can assure you that your teeth are quite clear of debris of any variety, edible or otherwise."

"Ah, very good, sir." Percy acknowledged, straightening his own tie and patting his own head. "Can never be too careful, after all. Wouldn't want to embarrass myself."

"Certainly not."

They stared at each other for a moment, hands clasped in posterior or anterior positions, each staring into the eyes of the other and blinking at a rate that increased along with their impatience.

"So Penny tells me you wish to waffle," Rupert finally prompted.

"Certainly not, I'm afraid. This call is to be business-oriented."

"Well, that is most peculiar. I was informed of contradictory circumstances."

"Ah, yes, well. I'm afraid the circumstances of which you were informed were in fact a fictitious fib concocted as a ploy to not have my summons disregarded or otherwise dismissed."

"Well that was a dastardly effort indeed, Sir Todgerworth! But, by god, it appears to have worked, hasn't it?"

"I would say so. But then again I would not say so as here we are not discussing business but instead deliberating the efficacy of my conversational engagement schemes."

"So, you mean that one could say we, in fact, did indeed engage in a waffling?"

"It does appear that way, yes."

"So, by extension, it could be agreed that your intentions are to be considered as unsuccessful?"

"Unfortunately, that statement is becoming more correct by the moment."

"Well, in that case, Percy, I'm going to have to cut this short. I haven't the time to be waffling, I'm afraid. I do have the day's matters to attend to, after all."

"Oh right, well, that is perfectly understandable. Sorry to have bothered you, Sir Knobbenbottom; perhaps we shall try another time!"

The screen cut to black. Rupert chortled a throaty, toad-like laugh and reached to retrieve his teacup. Before porcelain hand touched porcelain mug, however, Penny's voice piped up over the room's speakers once again.

"Pardon me, Sir Knobbenbottom, but Sir Todgerworth is on the urgent line. He wouldn't state the nature of his inquiry but, to paraphrase his passionate explanation, he seems mildly agitated."

"On screen, Miss Farthing." The stuffy old Brit said through a chuckle.

Percy was not baring his teeth this time. He simply sat in a high-backed armchair with a cup of tea and crossed legs. Penny was right; he did appear a bit chuffed. He cleared his throat to speak, but Rupert cut him off.

"Ah, there you are, Sir Todgerworth. I'm glad you finally called. I've a burning bit of business to be discussed."

Percy shook his head with incredulity.

"What are you talking about?! I called you earlier."

"Oh. My apologies then, old chap, I must have stepped out."

"What? But you were here!"

"I was there? I do hope you're speaking in jest. Otherwise, we have a security breach of the identity thief variety!"

"What?! No. I didn't mean here as in here; I meant here as in there!"

"It is neither here nor there, Sir Todgerworth. Are we ever going to discuss today's matters? Or do you intend to waffle on all morning?"

"My insincere apologies, sir."

"Come again?"

Percy produced a pile of tablets and began rummaging through them as he spoke.

"Right, so, to your burning bit of business!" He announced, ignoring the previous question. "I'm to assume you've already heard, then?"

Rupert scoffed and picked his teacup up. He wrinkled his nose at how cold it had gotten and returned it to the tray, motioning for it to levitate itself away.

"I didn't have to hear from anyone. I saw it for myself when I arrived this morning."

Percy ceased his rummaging.

"Er . . . saw what, sir?"

"Why, the sign, Todgerworth! Dreadful eyesore. Cannot possibly be missed."

"To what sign are you referring . . . sir . . . ?"

"The one outside, Percy! Right above the bloody door."

Percy blinked.

"Do you mean the one that merely states the name of the building, sir?"

"Don't you minimize it! It is an outrage. It is unacceptable, is what it is."

"It's pretty standard on all buildings, though, is it not?"

"That may be so, but we are not a standard organization."

"I don't know about that. I like to think we're pretty organized."

"Of course we are. But we are in secret! You can't have a secret society when you slap an enormous sign on the door!"

"The Secret Intelligence Service has a sign on their building, sir."

"Exactly! And look how bloody secret they are! Everybody knows about them. They don't even do anything anymore besides rent it as a location for those insufferable James Bond films."

"But isn't that their job, sir? To be the face to the public as an act of good faith while organizations like ours get the job done behind the scenes?"

"It is indeed. And it worked brilliantly. That is, until some ponce got it in their head to nail a giant sign up on our door! I want it removed, Percy. I don't care whom you have to call or whom you have to kill."

"I . . . well, alright?"

"Splendid. Glad we could get that sorted. I think that's enough work for today."

He reached for the "I don't want to talk to you anymore" button, but Percy cut him off.

"WAIT, sir! There is another important matter that requires your direction."

"Two pieces of business in one day, Percy? What are we, at war?!"

"Thankfully not, sir. This piece is in regards to . . . the plot."

"The wot?"

"The plot!"

"The plot of what?!"

Percy sighed and struggled to refrain from rolling his eyes.

"Well no, sir, not the plot *of* something! You know, *the* plot! Our plot! Our most recent plot. It's the only plot we've got."

"OH. The plot!" Rupert acknowledged. " . . . To invade France?"

"What?! No, sir."

"Oh god, I hope you're not planning on invading Poland. Dreadfully hard to do that with any level of sympathy anymore."

"I'm talking about the agent we sent to Mars to retrieve, you know, the nonspecific object of importance."

For the first time Sir Knobbenbottom's pompous face began to show traces of understanding.

"Ah, yes, I remember now. I believe Hugh was tasked with the duty. A fine lad. Astute. And a pleasant conversationalist, if I do recall. How is he faring?"

Sir Todgerworth shuffled uncomfortably.

"I fear not well. The HMS *Milk and Two Sugars* ceased transmissions some hours ago. In addition, it also self-destructed. Given similar happenstances to previous excursions of ours, I suspect his prognosis is grim."

"Well, at least I don't have to keep coming up with new disingenuous and perfunctory compliments about that dullard now. I'm pretty sure he only got a spot here in the League because he could prove a distant relation to Margaret Thatcher."

"The man is presumed dead, sir. Wouldn't that necessitate an increase in comments of the aforementioned variety?"

"Save it for the eulogy, Percy. Now tell me, do we suspect this is the work of that nefarious Banks character I've been hearing so much about? He is a rather thorny thorn, isn't he?"

"It seems that way." Percy nodded. "However, there is one inconsistency with his MO in this case. Before it self-destructed, the last readings the HMS *Milk and Two Sugars* relayed indicated a vessel had docked upon it mere minutes beforehand. Uh, let's see . . . ah, here we are. A moon-based transporter. Registered as a certain . . . SS *Jefferson*. Wholly unremarkable, it seems."

"Do you believe Banks is on board?"

"It is possible, sir. Either that or he has a cloaked ship of his own."

"Mmm yes, quite. But in all cases beforehand he has taken great care not to leave witnesses, hasn't he?"

"Not a one, sir."

"Precisely, Percy. So it seems to me that whoever is aboard that ship is either in cahoots with him or is in rather grave danger, would you not agree?"

They exchanged their own varying grunts of agreement.

"But what should we do about it, sir?"

Rupert smiled with a knowingness coupled with pleasure as his floating tray returned to him, tea hot enough to please even Captain Picard.

"Why, we intercept, of course," he replied calmly, sipping his cup with a British daintiness. "We must retrieve the thing, Percy. The thing is very important. It is equally important that no one else be in possession of the thing besides us. Which agents do we have available?"

"Er, it appears none, sir." Percy frowned down at the tablet he picked up from his desk. "Can't imagine what they're all doing, since we have no other ongoing missions, but they're all listed as indisposed at the moment."

"They're all too refined and proper anyway." Rupert dismissed. "This Banks is a barmy sort. Unable to be reasoned with or duped into parlaying about, clearly. Probably understands nothing beyond punching and shooting, the oaf. Formal and mannerly engagements clearly will not do."

"But sir! We are the League of Extraordinarily British Gentlemen. Formality and snobbery are the only tools at our disposal."

"Not necessarily true, dear Percival! Sure, most of us are

distinguished lads who can pull off ascots and always know which fork to use, but every now and then one will come across one of those hardened, rabble-rousing British men who drink and swear and beat the occasional woman. That's who we need right now!"

"But do we have one among us?"

Rupert stroked his bottom lip.

"What about that fellow fresh from the academy? Slagslapper or something? I was reading his progress reports; seems fit to me!"

"Er, I'm not sure Slagslapper can be considered for candidacy, sir."

"Why not?! He's British, isn't he?"

"Well, yes."

"Can he sneer?"

"Oh, most impressively."

"How does he take his tea?"

"Why, hot, sir. Like lava."

"And how are his teeth?"

"Pearly white and nearly as straight as your wife."

"Excellent." The corners of Rupert's mouth curved upward, slightly lifting his hanging chin. "That is one old stereotype I'm happy to be doing away with. How about his disposition? You oversaw his public etiquette exam, didn't you?"

"I did preside over it, as I always do, yes."

"How much does he tip his servers?"

"I don't know what that means."

"Ah yes, of course. What did he order during the dinner portion then?"

"Guinness, mostly. He did graze a bit at the deep-fried-animal-organs-stuffed-with-other-animal-organs buffet, though."

"Oh, my. Did he become inebriated and belligerent?"

"Well yes, a bit. After I tested how he reacts to pressure by hitting him with the classic loose-lid-on-the-salt-shaker prank he became agitated and began yelling obscenities at the waitresses and old people."

"Did this lead to acts of vandalism?"

"Surprisingly not, actually. He paid his tab, folded his coat over his arm, and walked out of the restaurant in a very dignified manner. It wasn't until he was out of the building that he asked me to hold his jacket while he took it in turn to begin assaulting other departing patrons."

"See, Todgerworth!? He sounds like exactly what this mission needs. Get him briefed. I want him en route tonight!"

Percy grimaced and rocked his head from side to side.

"Err . . . I'm afraid that Mister Slagslapper is ill-equipped to undertake this mission, sir."

"Why do you keep insisting that? What skill does he lack?"

"Uh, breathing, partially. He's dead."

"He's dead?! What do you mean, 'He's dead?'"

"Erm, I'm not sure how to make it any clearer, sir? He's deceased. Departed. Expired. Bereft of life . . . ?"

"I am aware of the definition of the word."

". . . Exanimated. Bit the dust. As far as our best physicians have been able to tell, he has been permanently and irrevocably incapacitated . . ."

"TODGERWORTH."

"Sorry, sir."

"How could that have happened?!"

"Terribly tragic." Percy muttered as he scrolled through the files of his tablet. He finally settled on one and ran a finger down it. "He was bludgeoned to death with a black pudding, I'm afraid. It seems one of the antagonized patrons was adept in the art of Ecky Thump. There was a policeman on the scene, but unfortunately he was unable to apprehend the man on account of dying himself in a fit of laughter."

" . . . I have no words." Rupert said after a brief pause. " . . . Except those."

"It was a PR nightmare, I assure you," Percy agreed. "Particularly after the murder weapon disappeared into the digestive tract of a local transient."

"Dear Percy, I am terribly late for a meeting I just made up. Do you think we can expedite this a little bit?"

"Certainly, sir. . . . So what should we do?"

Rupert began to pace. His Roomba dutifully followed behind his polished shoes as he trod upon his office rug in a slow march. By the time he had completed his lap, so too had he completed his consideration.

"With no agents to spare and no up-and-comers to exploit, it appears we only have one demographic to draw from." He observed, returning his hands to the small of his back. "We're going to have to re-engage a retiree. Do we have any that meet the required specifications and have not gone senile or incontinent yet?"

"Two, sir. One is a decorated veteran of the League and often expresses eagerness to return and serve Queen and country. The other was forced out one mission shy of his pension and still holds the record for longest list of charges we've ever had to have pardoned."

"Well then, that first one sounds like the clear choice. Get him briefed."

"Excellent decision, sir." Percy looked towards someone or something off camera. "Mabel, darling, would you get me Sir Bedford Furthington Fielding Livingston Chesterhill on the coms, please?"

"Oh my god," Rupert blurted. "Is that his bloody name?

Never mind, go with the second one. The amount of times I'm going to have to type that if he becomes a prominent part of this mission would be unacceptable."

"Belay that, love." Percy looked back. "What's that, sir?"

"Go with the other one, I said."

"Do . . . Do I have to?"

"Is there a problem?"

"Well I mean, no, not really. He just . . . makes me uncomfortable, sir."

"I see. Well then, I am terribly regretful to inform you that you are not only to brief Sir . . . ?"

"Sir Head, sir."

" . . . Sir Head, you are not only to brief him, but I am afraid you are also going to have to accompany him on this."

Percy's eyes widened.

"I beg your pardon, sir?"

"The success of this mission is critical, Todgerworth!" Rupert insisted. "It is absolutely imperative that we retrieve this nonspecific object of dubious function! I would go instead of you, however, I am limited by the fact that I don't want to."

"I suppose that is a limitation I can sympathize with."

"Stiff upper lip, now, Todgerworth. Charter whichever vessel you fancy, but I expect you to be blasting off before the day is out. Do try to bring it back in one piece, though. And yourself as well, should you have time."

THE SCREEN WENT BLACK, leaving Percy staring at his own reflection. Turns out he did have something in his teeth that whole time. Today was not his day.

He reclined in his chair and turned to face the mural of Queen Elizabeth II taking up his entire south wall. Her beautiful-yet-ghoulish face never failed to remind him that all men in his line of work must make sacrifices for the greater good. Still, that didn't mean he couldn't silently lament his situation. This was going to be a bothersome endeavour. It didn't bode well that his preselected partner promised to cause him more grief than his preselected opponent. Although he had never met either, the tales of one stood out more than tales of the other.

As far as he was aware, this Banks character would just kill you if you got in his way. A bit narrow minded and knee-jerk, perhaps, but respectably clinical. Sir Head, on the other hand, was anything but. His methodology baffled every psychologist they ever exposed him to. There had never been a general consensus regarding his mental acuity. Frankly, the only reason he had lasted as long as he did was because, idiosyncratic as he was, he did get results.

"Are you still here, Mabel?" He polled the room as he sipped at his tea.

"Still here," her short voice buzzed over the speakers.

"Do we have a contact number for Sir Head on file? I have been tasked with coaxing him into reenlistment."

"I heard. He really snookered you, eh? I hope you ain't gonna make me talk to him. I like this job, but I don't need it that bad."

"No, no, it's fine, just put me through and I'll chat him up."

"Your funeral, guv. It's ringing."

Percy got out of his chair and smoothed the front of his suit. With only seconds to spare before showtime he dashed over to the camera and angled it to face him with his beloved mural in the background. Dear Lizzy probably wouldn't have a similar effect on his charge, but it sure made him look and feel more dignified, and there was nothing more important to a proper Britishman than presentation.

The screen popped on as the call was answered. Percy puffed out his chest and slid a hand into his waistcoat. Nearly the entire frame of his screen was taken up by the face of a wide-eyed older man with a razor-sharp widow's peak glaring at him. His pupils were shrunken to pinheads and his nose was pressed flat against the camera lens. Feverish breaths fogged up the bottom half of the screen almost enough to hide the fact he was naked.

"You ever call this number again—!!" He barked. "I'll kill ya! KILL YA!!"

The screen went black as he hung up. The lone denizen of the room sat in silence for a moment.

"Mabel," he finally spoke. "Would you be so kind as to take a letter for me?"

"I already started. So far I got: 'Dear insubordinate tosser. Ooooh yeah, bet you think you're so tough, don't ya? Bet you think you're pretty untouchable. Well guess again, grandpa! I will touch the hell outta you! So get your ass in line or I'm gonna stick my foot up it! What's that? You got a problem with my demands? Well I had a feeling you'd say that! How 'bout you come meet up with me to discuss your problem then? Three o'clock at the flagpole. Bring Band-Aids.' Signed, Sir Percival Todgerworth, of course. All you gotta do now is attach a big close-up pic of your knob and it'll be ready to go, I think!"

"I, what? No, Mabel. I was going to offer to reinstate his pension or something. Never mind; I'll take care of the mail. Just . . . book us one of the ships in the hangar and take some time off. I think you need it."

"If you say so, boss. I think the HMS *Three Milk One Honey* just got cleared to fly again. Though if I remember correctly, you tend to be more partial to the HMS *One Cream One Stevia*."

"Neither for this endeavour." Percy asserted, sipping his own literal one cream and one Stevia. "This is an important mission with high stakes and needs to be over with as quickly as possible. Get us the HMS *Black*."

7. WE NOW RETURN TO OUR REGULARLY SCHEDULED PROGRAMMING.

LIKE THE COX OF the walk he stalked around, apparently feeling as though the situation warranted a bit of extra pageantry. Neither Kim nor her handler seemed to have any appreciation. However the man with the gun was usually given the right to set the pace of things, slow or spasmodic as it may be.

"So looks like what we got here is a good old-fashioned Mexican standoff." Cox observed with a grin and nod in what everyone else could only assume was his attempt at a southern accent.

"You're the only one with a weapon." Mister Nobody replied, still as deadpan as ever. "If anything, this is a stick-up."

The captain's grin briefly faded and he glanced around the room with a dopey look, as if he actually needed to verify the assertion.

"Oh yeah." He said. "Well, in that case . . ."

He bowed his head and squinted at the old man. The side of his mouth curled upward to expose some teeth. He wiggled his gun arm a little bit to convey that he was aiming it *really* hard now.

"Reach for the sky, dirtbag." He growled in as low of a register as he could muster.

More annoyed than fearful, the interloper complied nonetheless by releasing his grip on the first mate and letting his hands float towards the ceiling.

"Higher!" Cox barked. "Higher, I say!"

The old man rolled his eyes and raised the imaginary roof a couple inches further.

"Yes . . . Yes . . . Now *dance!*"

"I'm not doing that."

"This is nice!" The captain changed gears. "I can see why people used to worship these things. I feel powerful! And kinda sexy. Do I look sexy right now, Kim?"

"You're very handsome, babe," she grumbled as she crawled sideways away from the old man. "Can you just shoot him now, please?"

"Yeah . . . Yeah!" His voice turned to a growl again as he got caught up in the situation. Then his gusto abruptly faded. "Wait, what? No! That's a terrible idea. I don't wanna shoot him."

"Then give me the Glock thing and I'll do it!"

"What?! I don't want you to shoot him either!"

"Well if you're not gonna shoot him, then what are you gonna do with him??"

"I . . . I don't know! I didn't think I'd get this far." Cox looked back at Mister Nobody. "What would you do if you were me?"

The old guy shrugged.

"I'd shoot me."

"What?! Why would you tell me that?"

"'Cause I don't think you're gonna shoot me."

"Well . . . I bet you'd be really surprised if I did then!"

"I would be."

Cox opened and closed his mouth several times, shaking his head and looking around for some inspiration.

"Well what would you do if you were me and, uh, your gun didn't work?"

Mister Nobody blinked at him.

"Are you telling me your gun doesn't work?"

"No, it works! I mean, I haven't actually used it or anything, but old stuff like this always works."

Hands still held high, the old man took a step towards the captain. Cox nearly stumbled backward when he did, but retained just enough presence of mind to know to hold his ground. The intruder gazed unblinkingly upon him. Cox's gun hand began to tremble. He couldn't avoid betraying how unnerving that old wrinkled brow was when it was furling in his direction.

The old man took another step. The captain could feel the sweat coalescing on his brow. *Threatening* to murder in defence of his crew was a much easier feat than following through with it. Desperate as he was to find an alternative, his increasingly blurred mind made it steadily more difficult to break the fixation on the only apparent option, especially as the stress of the situation began to mount. Mister Nobody continued to push his luck. He was nearly halfway between the couple. Kim looked to her husband, eyes pleading, urging him to cross his own self-imposed line. Still unable to commit, Cox instead just put his other hand on the Glock, silently begging the old man to stop.

But the old man did not. He kept his arms raised but took another ginger step, like a man approaching a dangerous animal. Donald crawled away backwards until he was flush against the wall. Less than ten feet separated the two would-be captains. Sweat now matted Cox's hair to his head. Nobody's usually stoic face now bore the etchings of a malicious smile. Cox's arms slowly began to buckle under the weight of the gun and the situation. Nobody's pace evolved from occasional steps to a slow walk. Willy walked through the doorway, gesturing back the way he came with his thumb.

"Oh hey, guys. Turns out the door wasn't even locked."

Cox yelped. Reacting to being startled the same way one handles being tazed, every muscle in his body simultaneously contracted. His knees buckled, his elbows clenched, his trigger finger pulled, and, as far as anyone in the room could tell, the gun in his hand exploded like a bargain bin e-cigarette.

Had the captain bothered to read the manual for this thing upon purchase, he may have noticed the disclaimer warning users that ancient weaponry did not emit the same *pew pew* that modern laser-oriented technology graced the eardrums with. However, even if he had read the manual it wouldn't have mentioned that, when used in a pressurized metal chamber around unsuspecting onlookers, it would have roughly the same effect as firing a cannon during the world chess championships. The still-reverberating bang knocked everyone on their ass who wasn't already and the Glock left a red mark on Cox's forehead where the recoil struck. There were likely some utterances of surprise, but they were all lost in the roiling tinnitus static occupying everyone's ears.

"Was it supposed to do that?!" Was the first coherent sentence that Cox heard once the humming in his ears died down. He wasn't sure who said it, but it wasn't Mister Nobody. The hijacker was the first to recover from the shock; he was probably half-deaf already. With an unexpected nimbleness, he popped to his hands and knees, then quickly to his feet, and dashed across the room. He hopped with ease over Kim's outstretched leg trying to trip him, then transitioned his landing directly into a swift kick to the Glock, putting it far out of anyone's reach. Despite her frustration and fury, the girlie had to say he was pretty spry for an old guy.

Willy was the last man standing between bad dude and doorway. Lips pursed with determination, he got to his feet and spread his legs wide, planting his feet firmly to become the living wall he had probably been many times in his life. The size differential between the two theoretically stacked the odds heavily in the big man's favour, but for further fortification he even clamped a meaty paw onto either side of the door frame. All of these factors would have presented quite insurmountable odds had the old man tried to charge through him like a running back. However, this wasn't football, so there was no flag on the play when Mister Nobody simply stopped short and dropped the spread-eagled blocker with a sharp kick to the love spuds.

The wild whack to Willy's willy had left him down. He had fallen and he couldn't get up. He had failed so completely and utterly at his role as the only person who could have prevented Mister Nobody's escape that he didn't even slow the man down. But none of that mattered, because at least he tried his best.

Kim was next to her feet. Despite her rabid chihuahua-like eagerness towards going to lay down the law, she spared a moment to take a knee by Tim and help him to his feet.

"Are you okay?" She asked him, voice full of urgency.

"Ohhh man," he shouted as he rubbed at his head. "I skipped all those tribute concerts and now I'm gonna go deaf anyway . . ."

"Where's Willy's gun?"

"WHAT?"

"I said where's Willy's—"

"I'm kidding; I can hear you. I put it under our bed."

"Seriously?" Donald asked. "Why didn't you put it in the safe!?"

"Oh I don't know, Donny." Cox barked sarcastically from his sitting position. "Maybe because that's where someone would expect something like that to be. Maybe because that's going to be the first place they check!"

" . . . That's why you lock it!"

"Lock it?! Like, with a lock? That is not the type of environment I want us living in."

"You don't know the combination, do you?"

"I didn't think I'd need to! Here aboard the *Jefferson*, we are supposed to trust one another."

Kim rolled her eyes and darted out of the room, leaving the captain to get to his feet on his own. He rubbed at his forehead as he hopped up, rubbing his hands together after.

"Alright, we need a plan, we need a plan. Perp's on the loose, my fox is on the run, and backup is ready for action. Just awaiting orders, right?"

Donald snorted.

"No way. This is not my job. In fact, I took this job because I thought stuff like this didn't happen on boring cargo ships!"

"That answer makes me sad, but I see where you're coming from! How about you, Willy?"

"Uggghhh . . ." He moaned from his foetal position, hands between his legs. "Do I have to, Captain?"

"Well, I mean it actually *is* your job, but if you really don't want to, then it's okay."

Cox looked back and forth between the two of them, each averting his gaze, before puffing his chest out, inhaling loudly, and retrieving his Glock from the floor.

"Alright, guess it's time for round two!" He used his free

hand to cock it again, jumping slightly when the literal round two ejected and bounced away.

"What, you're gonna ask us both to help you but not Whisper?" Donald pointed out.

The two of them looked over to the vent on the wall then back at each other.

"Oh c'mon, Donny. If you guys don't want to, then what makes you think she would?"

He shoulder rolled out of the room and came up on his knees, waving the gun around in search of enemies. Upon finding none, he stalked off out of sight. Moments after his departure, Whisper peeked a glib face out of the vent.

"Hm," she said. "Guess sexism can pay off sometimes."

"I woulda gone," Donald qualified. "But he is definitely going to die."

HANDS CLASPED UPON HIS pistol, Cox alternated between reckless bravery and skittish reservation when it came to the pace at which he searched his ship. With akimbo legs and bent knees, he lurched forward and stopped short repeatedly like a teenager learning to drive standard. But still he pressed on, all the while mumbling the Pink Panther theme to try and calm his nerves. Surprisingly, even something as comforting and familiar as his pride and joy became eerie and foreboding when it housed a psycho space killer.

Ever since he bought the thing however many years ago, the *Jefferson* had been his home, and that was how he liked it. His former days living in his family's moon mansion were luxurious, sure, but so long as he stayed there he may as well have been as grounded as the foundation upon which the building sat. That's not to say he considered it a shameful existence to lead, but beauty wasn't the only thing that resided in the eyes of the beholder. To him, a life that was just good enough was simply not good enough. Leaving it all behind for a modest life aboard a multibillion dollar custom-built spaceship was the best decision he'd ever made. Or so he used to think; no one had asked him since all this murder-y life-or-death business started.

He rounded a corner—gun first, of course—and found himself at a crossroads. He still hadn't decided where he was going, and now he couldn't proceed until he did. He had indeed expected Mister Nobody to make a beeline for the safe, but he hadn't thought much beyond that step of the plan. In his mind, he half expected him to already be there waiting, ready to jump out at the man and yell surprise. With a couple tweaks, that plan would still be feasible, but recent experience had indicated surprises and guns didn't mix too well. Showing up and yelling surprise without the gun also came with its own set of drawbacks. If only he could get a fake gun that was identical to the pistol in his hands in every way but without the bits that explode . . . that would be ideal. Unfortunately, shipping would cost a fortune and take forever to get here, so that plan was out. Plus, old artifacts like that were tough enough to find without trying to locate a specialty version.

It was in these moments of plotting that an entirely separate thought popped into his head. Every single plan that he was attempting to concoct excluded the person whose one request was not to be excluded in concocted plots. With how bungled this entire thing had become, the last thing he needed was to give her reason to be even more mad at him than she already was. So whatever plot he concocted entirely on his own without input from others, he had to make sure there was a part that he could tell her to do.

Speaking of the devil—figuratively, as he probably shouldn't be referring to her as the devil, even in an internal monologue—the badass brunette interrupted his scheming with her brisk walk into the hallway, stopping short when she saw him. In one hand she clutched Willy's space rifle, wielding it with a casual lean on the shoulder. The other she kept planted firm upon her hip in that chicken wing pose that some women tend to unconsciously do when getting their picture taken. It appeared that in her raid on the bedroom, she also took a moment to change her outfit, opting away from the space pajamas and instead for something more vintage. Black tights clung to her long legs and a loose white shirt with black vest were draped over her top section. Altogether, the ensemble didn't seem to have any extra combat practicality whatsoever, but it certainly wasn't going to elicit any complaints from the captain. As far as Star Wars-inspired outfits went, it was probably the second-best choice she could have made.

"Tim! I thought you hung back; what are you doing here?"

"Heyyy!" He replied, arms opening wide. "There you are! I was just looking for you."

Her mouth closed and puckered with scepticism. Her brown eyes studied him with raised brows.

"Really? That's kind of funny, seeing as you knew exactly where I was going."

"You're not wrong . . . but that doesn't necessarily make *me* wrong."

"You were about to go after him without me, weren't you?! Jesus, Tim, we literally just talked about this!"

"What? No! I was coming for you, I swear!" He tried to emphasize with his hands but shoved them behind his back in embarrassment after realizing he was essentially threatening her with his gun. He sighed.

"Look, I know I don't always make the best decisions in your eyes. But you know I wouldn't lie to you."

At that, her expression softened.

"Alright, fine, you're off the hook. You're lucky you're pretty, though."

She shrugged the blaster from her shoulder and grabbed it by the forestock with her free hand. The other one grabbed it by its bolt-action power switch and brought it to life with a foreboding cocking noise.

"Now c'mon, Captain Kirk. Let's go save *our* crew."

Cox did a redundant cocking of his own weapon again, ejecting yet another round as a show of solidarity, then followed her down the hallway.

"Right behind you, honey!" He encouraged. "And don't worry, I've learned my lesson. This is my last adventure, I promise."

She came to a sudden halt in front of him and whirled around, brown hair aflurry. She let a hand slip from the blaster so she could place it back on her hip.

"That's not the lesson I want you to learn from this at all! I want you to go on a hundred more space adventures. I just wanna go on them with you! I understand that some—I swear to god if you reach for that gravity switch I will shoot you right in the face—but yeah, sometimes shit is gonna happen. It's just life; I get it. All I want—and I bet all the crew wants too—is to not be treated like people you're just caring for while you do your thing. The adventures will go better, too, if you'd just listen to us sometimes! You got a good head, but it's not as good as five heads. Well, six if you count Whatshername down in engineering."

"I totally include you guys!" He protested as they walked. Neither were watching where they were going anymore. "You even mediated between me and Donny when we were having that healthy group discussion."

"Yeah, I agreed investigating the ship was worth our time! And then that was the end of it. No more discussion. You just grabbed two henchmen and took off without even stopping to make a plan."

"Alright, alright, ya got me there. May have skimped on the planning bit a bit. I got a little excited, and now I'm sorry."

"It's okay, babe. You don't have to apologize, I just needed to know you hear me on this. But what's done is done. Let's just focus on the now and dealing with . . . our guest. I have an idea."

"I'd love to hear your idea! It's probably a great one. We probably should have done it your way from the start."

"OUR WAY, Tim!"

"That's what I meant."

"You're unbearable sometimes."

A voice cut into their deliberating.

"Does this mean when I vote against going off course it's actually going to count now?"

They spun around to see a projection of Donald cast upon the wall. He sat with a calm slouch, hands folded in his lap, completely ambivalent to the motionless Willy sprawled out on the floor behind him.

"No," the captain replied instantly.

"Yes," his wife replied nearly as quickly, but a little behind him.

They looked at each other; Tim with a slack jaw and Kim with a raised eyebrow.

"Maybe," he amended. "Say, Donny, you're on a computer right now, right?"

Donald looked around at the area below the camera, face scrunched up as if unsure if the question was being asked in jest.

" . . . If you are," The captain continued. "D'you think you could check the scanner for Mister Nobody? It probably isn't gonna tell you for sure that it's him, 'cause it's a computer, so how could it really know that, right? There's also the chance that's not even his real name. But maybe you could look for a blip and see what ha—"

"The old guy literally just left," Donald cut him off. He nodded toward the doorway. "He came back like two seconds after you two ran out the door. I'm pretty sure he was just hiding around the corner and you went right by him."

Cox growled a puppy-like noise of frustration.

"That sly dog! I knew I shoulda looked both ways."

"Why did he come back?" Kim asked.

Donald burbled something incoherent and gave a sheepish shrug.

"Iunno. He came back in, mumbled hello to me, and headed straight for the freezer. Then he yelled some stuff about somebody taking his Fireball and punched Willy in the face."

" . . . Fireball?" Cox breathed. "Like . . . A fireball?"

"It's booze, man. Stupid kids like drinking it cause it gets them drunk fast."

"Oh. Well, if it's alcohol for children, then why does he have it?"

"Holy shit, Tim . . ."

"I don't know!" Donald snapped. "The guy was freaking out and assaulting people; I wasn't going to try and chat with him. I just told him Whisper took it back to her room and hoped he would leave me alone."

"Oh hey, Donny, that was a good idea! I bet he'd believe she's young enough to be a kid."

"She's sixteen, Tim, she is a kid." Kim informed him.

"She's sixteen?! You told me she was eighteen when we hired her!"

"Yeah. She was actually thirteen."

"You put a thirteen-year-old to work!? What are we, Amish?!"

"Do you have any idea how hard it is to find someone that has both a pilot's license and a clean record who's willing to spend their time flying a freighter?! I didn't even want to hire her, but every other applicant only wanted the job with us because they'd gotten themselves disqualified from real piloting gigs. At least she doesn't have a criminal record."

"But we might if anyone catches us violating child labour laws!"

"Oh relax, it says in her employee file she's eighteen too. Not that anyone would ever bother to look. And hey, I would have been happy with an autopilot, but noooooooooo, you insisted it had to be a real person. So I made do."

"And look at the bonding you two have done! Bet that wouldn't have happened with an AI."

"So are you guys gonna go save her, or . . . ?"

They clammed up and looked back to Donald. He shuffled uncomfortably under their combined gaze.

"You mean that's actually where it is?" The captain clarified. "That wasn't just a clever lie you told to throw him off track?"

"What?! What the hell gave you that idea?! I told you that this dealing with intruders stuff is not my job."

"God damn it, Donald," Kim snapped. "I know this sort of thing wasn't explicitly stated in your job description, but you're still the communications officer aboard this ship."

"And I communicated her whereabouts very effectively!"

Kim sighed and cut off the projection. Her anger was short-lived, however, as she swiftly returned to being that focused and disciplined problem solver who had a knack for calming contagious flustering.

"Alright, we know what he wants and we know where he's

going," she said in a voice as level as her head. "We can work with that."

"I acknowledge and agree with that contribution!"

"If we move quickly, we can cut him off in the hallway just outside her room."

"Well, alright! That would be something we could do, wouldn't it?"

"And then we'll vaporize his goddamn kneecaps and blow a gaping hole in his sternum."

"Working together is fu—wow, wait, what? That's a little dark, don't you think?"

Kim sighed as they rounded the corner. Despite her shortness, her brisk strides left her husband struggling to keep up.

"We're a little past diplomacy, I think!" She barked, picking up the pace. "He's demonstrated he's nothing more than a wild animal endangering the kids, so I'm gonna give that bastard a death so tragic they'll build a statue of him like that stupid monkey one outside the Cincinnati Zoo."

"Or I mean we could, y'know, accost him. Like, both of us point our guns at him and I could even hold mine sideways like this . . . and if you really wanna get into it we could start yelling and acting all crazy and unpredictable and firing into the ceiling and stuff. If we do all that then he'll probably get scared and leave!"

Kim blinked at him as he finished his suggestion.

"Leave?" She repeated. "Baby, we're in space. This isn't some uncomfortable dinner party; there's real stakes up here. He's not just gonna get frustrated and go home."

"Okay, well, what if we could knock him out then? Doesn't that thing have a stun setting?"

She looked the weapon over halfheartedly, clearly not expecting to see one.

"I . . . a stun setting? I don't really think that's how lasers work, hon. Even if I could turn the wattage down I'm pretty sure it would just turn this into a laser pointer."

The captain slowed his pace as he comprehended all this. Not only the layout of the warring parties, but their trajectories, armaments, and opposing yet oddly similar ill-intents for one another. Obviously, his allegiance was clear, but that didn't necessarily mean he craved the conflict. Quite the opposite, in fact; Cox craved amity more than plants craved electrolytes. Unfortunately, he had a hard enough time coming up with plans, even when he wasn't in a time crunch.

"Tim?" Kim asked. She had stopped several feet ahead of him.

He snapped out of his analysis-paralysis and looked at her.

"You alright?"

"Yeah!" He declared, probably a little louder than he should have. "Yeah, I was just thinking. Alright, here's what we should do. You keep going this way, and I'll do a big ol' loopy-loo around and come at 'em from the other side! He'll be all like 'Whooaaa, there's two of 'em and I can't even look at 'em both at the same time! This isn't gonna go well for me at all! I better surrender really peacefully before they vaporize my goddamn kneecaps and blow a gaping hole in my sternum.'"

"Uhhh, okay? You do realize you'd have to run almost all the way to the bridge and back, right?"

"Yeah! It'll be great, just wait for my signal!"

He fixed his unblinking eyes upon her as he backed away. Those pouty lips of hers seemed to want to cry scepticism, but for now they held fast. They were slipping, though. Trembling, even. Perched precariously on the cusp of doubt or acceptance, waiting for just the slightest nudge to either side. To the layman they were just sitting closed, perhaps with a slight purse, like lips do. But to Cox, the man who knew the woman behind the lips . . . he knew. He knew! He just had to be careful about it. Take long exaggerated steps in the opposite direction. Flash her a big toothy grin that says "I got this." Throw in a nice thumbs-up to drive it home. Nearly at the corner now, keep on edging away, that's it, little further, reach the legs around first until only his head can be seen still maintaining eye contact, then pull it away nice and easy until all line of sight is broken and theeeeeeennnnnn . . . sprint down the corridor at breakneck speed.

But did he embark upon the roundabout route as previously agreed? Well, no. Not yet, anyway. There was an unmentioned first step to the plan. Just a simple slip of the mind, naturally, nothing worth getting worried about or calling space divorce lawyers over. Don't worry about whether or not that was his decision to make.

He reached the bridge and burst through the door, skidded across the floor, and faceplanted into his communications officer's sweaty bean bag chair. He should have sunk in further, given the furniture's foamy physique, but there was a peculiar hard crust across the top that his cheeks just simply bounced off instead. He hopped to his knees nevertheless and ignored the salty taste in his mouth. This was where he needed to be. There were actually a few main control hubs on the ship, but this one was the closest.

Hoping to find that fancy-dancy ship-tracking software, Cox first searched for the desktop. He rapidly clicked his fingers, indiscriminately closing his way through cat videos, webcomics, fanfics, conspiracy theory forums, and finally a Google Space tracker counting down how long until they reached their destination, before finally the proper screen could be found. All could have been avoided if he knew how to press Win+D.

After all the hassle, the desktop shone before his already screen-fatigued eyes. He hung his head in defeat when he found it to be packed with links and saved copies of cat videos, webcomics, fanfics, conspiracy theories, and countless superfluous junk icons simply filling space in the Borg Cube they were all arranged into.

"Aw, you're killin' me, Donny!" The captain protested at the screen. "I just wanna know where Whisper is!"

Upon his request, a small window opened in the corner of the screen. It appeared to contain a blueprint of the *Jefferson*, complete with little blips just as the captain imagined it. One of them seemed to be blinking as well. A small yin and yang logo creeping along one of the ventilation shafts.

"Oh, that's cool!" He rubbed his hands together for a second then paused. "If a little bit racist . . . But hey, she hasn't made it to her room yet. What's the command to flush the vents? Oh. I guess that was it. Wow, she's moving a lot faster than I thought she would."

He winced at the screen.

"I really shoulda had them build rounder corners in there . . . But at least she's safe now! Now where is Mister Nobody?"

The focus shifted left to a new, blue-blinking blip. Its symbol was a question mark.

"Wow," He whispered. "Technology is amazing. I don't even know who I'm talking about and you know who I'm talking about! You're a good computer. I like you."

The computer did not respond. That was very rude of it. Its designation of "good" was now being called into question.

"Alright now, let's see." He examined the blip closer. After a few moments of analysis, he concluded the question mark's font was Calibri and that the room it was in was in fact Whisper's. But anyone could simply glean information. The true test of a captain was having the wisdom to know how to employ it.

"Computer!" He announced. "How should I handle this situation?"

Okay, so he didn't have every quality of a great captain. But having the humility to know when to ask for help was important in leadership roles too.

The entire room housing the question mark became highlighted after his question and a new button appeared on the touch screen. It stood out amongst the otherwise calm colours with its foreboding blood-red font.

"Deoxygenate room."

"Oh . . ." The captain replied. "That's, uh, that's not the kind of solution I'm looking for right now."

A new button appeared under the first.

"Okay, fine, how about venting in noxious gas then?"

"Oh, come on, that's not any better. Why would we even have noxious gas on board?"

"Well, aren't you picky. At least let me compress the walls slow enough that he'll think he has a chance at getting out and will scamper around in desperation before finally realizing he never had any hope just as he succumbs to a painful death of broken ribs and asphyxiation."

Cox stared at the screen with wide eyes. Not only did a button bearing the spiel appear, but it was spoken to him in a chilling voice devoid of all expression, like a psychopathic CEO. The bean bag chair squeaked slightly as he inched it backwards.

"I'm just gonna come up with something on my own . . . in the other room. Thank—thank you, though."

"Whatever, chicken shit. Looks like your wife is about to handle it, anyway."

Kim. He had forgotten about his cherished wildcard. The computer may have been unable to take compliments and in bad need of some kind of tech therapist, but it was not a liar. A blinking blip labelled with the Waffen-SS logo scooted its way along a neighbouring corridor, creeping dangerously close. Without her beloved Tim there to stem the fires in her blood, there would be nothing to stop her from Judge Dredding all over the place. There was no time for him to reach her now, or even for him to come up with that fictional signal he mentioned. Whatever he did, he was going to have to do it from this room.

"Aw, man," he whined. "I'm gonna be in so much trouble . . ."

He gave one final sigh and stole a fleeting glance at his "Universe's Best Space Captain" mug.

"Seal the door to Whisper Wang's quarters," he ordered the computer. The command was assertive and captainly, a sharp contrast to the gulp and strained addendum that followed.

"And revoke override privileges from First Mate Cox."

IN FOR A PENNY, IN FOR A POUNDING

OFTEN TIMES DURING MOMENTS wherein one "lays down the law," so to speak, they can feel the impact in their chests. Perhaps some sort of sound effect will play in their heads, or dramatic music. At very least, they would frequently get some audio or visual feedback to let them know their authority has been experienced.

But in Cox's case, he just kind of stood there grimacing at a computer terminal. There were no gasps or "Oh no he didn't"-s, no chairs had been thrown or tables flipped. In fact, having done his dramatic executive decision alone in a room resulted in one of the most anticlimactic experiences he had ever had. The only confirmation that anything of note had even occurred came in the form of a new button underneath all the others on the computer screen.

"You suck for taking this away from me. I wanted to watch your wife paste that motherfucker."

Anticlimactic or not, his actions were at least effective. The SS blip stopped short at the threshold between hallway and room and lingered there for what was probably about ten seconds, but they were long seconds. Like microwave-countdown seconds. All the while it was a tense quiet as he stared at the screen, unsure what to do next. He thought he had bought himself some time to deliberate, but that ran out right around the time the terminal he was at began jingling away with the sounds of an incoming call. He hadn't considered the fact he wasn't the only one who could track people on the ship. He also couldn't help but wonder what the offensive symbol on his blip was, since he'd forgotten to check. But checking was going to have to wait until the current storm had been weathered.

"Hah. Looks like somebody might still be getting murdered after all."

"Whoever programmed you is a bad person! Just shhh."

He reached over and hit the little telephone icon, minimizing the ship map and bringing up the video feed.

"Batcave," he grinned into the receiver.

"Tim, something is going on and I don't like it. The door to Whisper's room won't open, and the terminal is ignoring my commands."

"Whaaat?!" The captain hammed. "That's awful. You, uh, you don't think that monster hacked our system and took control or something, do you?"

"Hacked . . . ? Did you really just say—" She blinked several times and then her expression soured considerably. "Tim! What did you do?!"

"He locked me in here." A bored, gravelly voice intruded. A video feed of Mister Nobody broadcasting from Whisper's room barged its way into a spot on both their terminals.

"Not to intrude on your failing marriage or anything," he added.

For what is probably a number past too many times in one space day, Kim sighed. But it wasn't one of the usual breaths of exasperation. This one seemed to carry a tune more along the lines of reluctant acceptance. Not to be confused with defeat; perish the thought. It was more to signify a change in tactics. A simple swap of stratagem from psychotic to psychopathic.

"I'm not gonna fight with you anymore, Tim," she informed him in even tones. "But this stops now. I am going to park my ass right here outside this door and I am going to sit and wait. Either it will open eventually and I will end this, or I will stand by until there's nothing left of him besides dust and the hard candy in his pocket. The choice is yours."

She pressed her back against the wall and slid down into a sitting position. After leaning her blaster against the wall for easy access, she crossed her legs and settled in.

THEY STAYED THAT WAY for most of the rest of the trip back to Earth. Given the high tension of the situation, one would have thought the atmosphere of the ship would change accordingly. But in practice things swiftly returned to almost normal, which was almost more worrisome. Donald and Willy returned to the bridge, the former returning to his stations while the latter resigned himself to snoozing on the couch. The only other noticeable change was the palpable awkwardness whenever they needed to use the hallway, from which Kim would not budge. A curt nod was the only greeting she would offer any of them, even when her faithful husband brought her meals. It was not the first time Cox had seen her achieve this level of drive and focus, and by this point, he knew better than to try and snap her out. In fact, in the couple days that they spent like this, he's not even sure if she slept.

Banks maintained a similar level of composure, holding up remarkably well in lieu of virtually any social interaction whatsoever. The working water dispensers in every room, coupled with Whisper's apparently private stash of snacks, seemed apt to satiate him for the bulk of the journey. Cool-headed as he was, a man of his experience had to realize the increasing direness of his situation. Perhaps that knowledge was what eventually prompted him to speak.

"I get paid by the hour, lady," the grumbly voice buzzed through the feed. "You leave me holed up in a room with a big comfy bed, I'll just sleep until I can retire."

Kim smirked up at his depiction.

"Sounds like someone's getting a little lonely. Tough luck for you, though. You're either dying in there or dying out here. I'm fine to oblige you on either one."

"If I am going to die in here, then I promise you I am going to piss and shit on absolutely everything before I do."

"Anything that comes out of you is going back inside you!"

"Well, you better get some rubber gloves then, because I'm feeling incontinent."

"Whoa, whoa, hey!" Cox's voice jumped into their conversation over the intercom from the safety of his trusty captain's chair. "Y'know, it'd be way easier for everybody if you guys just did none of that."

"Open the door, Tim! Or else grandpa is going to smear his pruney poo all over Whisper's stuff."

"Are you gonna take that from her? A real space captain doesn't get ordered around by some pushy broad."

Cox squinted at the camera and shook his head side to side.

"You know, I really don't want to open the door. But I also don't want to not open the door now because I don't want to look like I'm listening to you."

"Open the door!" Kim repeated with more urgency. She had returned to her feet and her chest heaved alongside her angry breathing. "He knows he's cornered and he's trying to turn us against one another. Just let me in so we can be done with this!"

"Or you could just leave me here until everybody calms down." The old man suggested with a contrasting tranquility. "I'm sure the impressive security features of your ship will be more than enough to hold me captive. And an imprisoned old man is no danger to anybody."

"Can you stop taking the same position as me!? It's making it a lot harder to defend."

"Tim, he's obviously just being sarcastic! He wants you to let him bide his time until he can find a way out and come after us."

"Tim, your wife is a little too eager to commit murder, and you should be very troubled by that."

"You know, I am a little bit! . . . Not that you need to know that."

"Alright, that's it. I'm shooting a hole in this damn door."

In a smooth, practised motion she hefted the blaster into a high ready position and fired off a shot into the tough titanium. A colourful bolt of light collided silently with the door and vanished just as fast as it had appeared, dissipating before the *pew* had even finished its *ew*. At first it seemed ineffective, as the door stood just as firm as it would have if it had been hit by a flashlight. However, her gusto didn't waver. With a rabid rapidity she fired off shot after shot like a kid at a state fair dying to win a teddy bear. Except most of those kids probably weren't planning to shoot their prizes in the face.

But whether it was out of confidence, frustration, or "what else am I gonna do"-ness, she persisted in spite of the initial futility. Soon, after receiving enough laser coaxing, the door began to glow with a dull redness. It was beginning to appear as though Kim's plan may actually have some clout. Even Mister Nobody was starting to get skittish.

"Kim, stop!" The captain pleaded. "This isn't what you want!"

She didn't respond, possibly because she knew she was more qualified to make that decision than he was.

"Kim, as your captain I order—ah jeez, even I know that sounds dumb. Just please stop!"

The door's red spot now glowed bright like a glorious autumn sunset poking out over the mountains and calming the landscape. Or, at least, it did to people who knew what that looked like. A good way to tell whether or not someone appreciated the aforementioned metaphorical beauty was whether they reacted by stopping to marvel at it, or if they spun their blaster rifle around and reared back to pound the stuffing out of it with the gun butt.

"Heeeeeeere's Johnny!" The first mate screamed as she swung to break through.

The weapon clanged against the metal and bounced off. It left a slight dent but otherwise completely ruined the moment of triumph she was trying to set up. She let loose a shrill grunt of exertion then hauled off and slammed into the door again, producing a similar result.

" . . . Okay, fine, I jumped the gun a little bit. Just give me a second to heat it up some more and then you're *dead!*"

She opened fire the spot yet again. Mister Nobody had left his spot on the bed and was tearing the room apart while Cox observed the carnage from his bridge terminal. This entire time he did have one reluctant option jabbering away in the back of his mind, vying for attention in much the same way the demented AI program did. And while his backup idea was slightly more appealing than a Machiavellian torture killing, it was still an undesirable notion. But he had already choked once and nearly blown his opportunity to act at all. So, objectionable as the notion was, it was going to have to do!

"Computer!" He said out loud, presumably addressing the computer. "I, uh . . . Heretofore . . . Thereby, mandate . . . The, protocol to, um, initiate the, commencement, of, the, launching of, the, port aft lifeboat."

He gestured with incoherent flourishes all throughout his captainly command, thinking maybe it would add some *je ne sais quoi* to the moment. It wasn't until after he stopped moving that a new text response popped up.

" . . . What?"

"Launch the escape pod. Please?" Cox reiterated. "I don't know what number it is, just whatever one Miss Wang lives in."

And just like that, the computer made it so. A secondary airlock door slid into place in front of the one Kim was currently going to town on, negating all her work toward passionate vengeance. She could only listen helplessly as a series of whirs and clanks scored the scene of the ship locking itself down and discharging the room like a popped pimple.

After the initial ejection, the lifecraft drifted away with a gentle serenity rather unfitted to the gravity of the situation it had been caught up in. Cox watched the scene reconstruction from his terminal. Before long the little metal bubble was fading away into the vastness of space and the hijacker troubles fading away along with it. It was an ending with the perfect amount of violence. However, he had a feeling that at least a couple members of his crew weren't going to regard this outcome as favourably. In fact, the more he thought about how he shotblocked his wife and spaced all Miss Wang's belongings, the more he began to think he might have been better off joining Mister Nobody on the escape pod. There was at least one crew member who approved, though.

"Trapping him all alone to slowly die of starvation. Nice."

"Is there a way I can ask you to uninstall yourself without totally messing up the rest of the ship's computer?"

"Nope."

IF THE *JEFFERSON* WERE an ocean, then the bridge would be the beach. No matter where those within it floated around to, they always washed back up in the foyer-like area sooner or later. With that knowledge in mind, Cox elected to kick back in his chair and just wait for the troops to filter in. After all, if he were the type to try and hide, then he'd also just end up back on the beach eventually, like that dead body you forgot to tie a bunch of rocks to.

A faint metallic *pitter-pat* from within the walls grabbed his attention. As far as the captain had been informed, space termites were not a thing; so the most likely explanation was that Whisper was finally about to escape her air-circulating cocoon. The metal grate clanged open and fell from the wall. The pilot emerged with about as much dignity as one would have expected. Dainty hands patted around for something to grasp. Then came her head, face obscured with sweaty, matted black hair like that little girl from *The Ring*. She spent a worrying amount of time on the floor, panting from exhaustion, before clawing at the wall to help the rise to her feet.. Even when she was upright again, there was still a slight hunch to her back that would need worked out, but her expletive-laden soliloquy about how hungry she was seemed to convey her prime priority.

Donald and Willy were the next to walk in. Unlike the first, they looked no more dishevelled than normal, save for some dried tears on the latter's cheeks.

" . . . Nah, dude, the right one's fine. It's the left one I'm worried about. I still can't find it. I think it mighta got knocked way up in—"

Their chat ended abruptly when they saw Whisper emerge from the kitchen with an atrophy-induced limp. A brief wide-eyed inspection of their coworker, still looking fresh out of the dryer as she scowled back at them while crunching on a mouthful of meal capsules, was enough to gauge her mood. She didn't say a word. Even after making eye contact with Cox, she just marched to her terminal and sat down. The captain hoped she would offer something to get the ball rolling, but the only sound she offered came from blowing hair out of her face.

"Alright look, everybody," he addressed the group as he stood up. "I know this might seem like it coulda gone better. But I think it's important to remember that everything could always go better."

"We almost died," Donald snapped.

"Why the hell are you mad!?" Whisper bit back. She paused to try and cough away some of the hoarseness. "You're only one that didn't even get hurt!"

"That's not true at all! I got punched in the face."

"And don't you guys feel pride in knowing you defended your ship?!" Cox polled the room. "Your home? Your friends? Your family, even."

"No," they all responded.

"I feel like you guys answered that a little too quickly to really think about it."

"Now that you mention it, Whisper," Donald observed. "I'm pretty sure he's the only one who didn't get hurt."

"Whoa now, guys, we're getting a little off-track here. We're supposed to be focusing on the positives." The captain tried to wrangle everyone back in line. "And you just reminded me of the three qualities every successful adventure has: nobody gets hurt, everybody learns something, and a positive difference is made in the end!"

He stopped to ponder the statement for a moment.

" . . . And as the great philosopher Meat Loaf always used to say: 'two outta three ain't bad!'"

The pilot, who sat with her head slumped backwards almost ninety degrees and eyes closed, coughed again, but this one sounded more like a response.

"Did you just say 'meatloaf?!'" She said afterward, apparently needing to engage more than needing to sleep.

"Yeah! Do you like him!?"

"Ew, no, meatloaf is gross."

"But you have heard of him!"

"No. Because he doesn't exist, because you made him up, because you couldn't even come up with a made-up name this time to legitimize your dumb quotes, so instead you just listed a random food item, because you probably thought I wasn't even listening."

She opened her eyes and raised her head.

"And I wasn't," she added before laying back again. "'Cause I was busy. Thinking. About dogs. 'Cause people suck."

"Hey, not all people suck! There's lots that don't. Like Meat Loaf. Who was a person."

"'Til Hannibal ate him?" Donald asked.

"Hey, look at you two, collaborating in attempt to belittle me! That's the type of teamwork that makes this team work. Keep it going—what else ya got?!"

His cheesy exuberance never really was a hit with the kids even at the best of times. Yet it somehow managed to make the room even more subdued with this iteration. Perhaps it was the contrast between him and everyone else, or perhaps it was just inappropriate to even try right now. However, even devoid of enthusiasm, they at least continued to man their posts and keep things underway. Whisper seemed to find some contentment in her work. As she tapped at her keys and tapped at the side of her face, it even became difficult to tell she was harbouring a seething teenaged hatred for everyone in her immediate vicinity.

It was a short while later that they were joined by the final member of the usual fellowship. Even in spite of the already-present silence, a hush still managed to fall over the room as she stepped across the threshold. Kim blinked back at the faces that all stared at her.

"Hello."

"Heyyyyyy..." Her husband greeted back in a loud whisper that quickly trailed away. He paused for a moment. "Uh, guys, you might want to maybe go back to your rooo—errrr—somewhere else on the ship that's even more fun than lame old bedrooms."

Whisper "hmph"-ed at the statement, but rolled out of her chair nonetheless. She likely relished an excuse to get away. Donald, however, didn't move.

"Are you about to tell us not to leave?" He asked Kim. "'Cause that seems like the type of thing you guys would argue about at this point and I don't want to go back and forth between standing and sitting while you figure it out."

"C'mon, Donny, don't antagonize her."

"I actually would prefer they stayed, if that's alright." Kim dissented in placid tones. Her demeanour, while more subdued, wasn't that of someone who had come hat in hand. But she hadn't come gun in hand, either, so whatever metaphorical item she was metaphorically clutching here was probably preferable.

"Called it," Donald bragged, slumping further into his seat with a smug smile as he checked to see who was looking at him. "Now she's probably going to make us pick sides." He turned back to Kim. "Don't even bother asking me, I'll take you over him any day."

"Shut up, Donald," the first mate grumbled without looking at him. She shook her head. "Well, I'm off to a flying start. Okay, before I say anything I want to clarify that none of this detracts from any of the stuff I said to you earlier, Tim. But that being said, I just want to acknowledge that I lost my head back there and I'm sorry. I started doing exactly what I was getting mad at you for."

Everyone continued to look at her. With no crickets around to chirp, they instead listened to the scraping noise of Willy scratching his beard.

"And that's the end of my speech," she added. "No applause necessary."

Cox, who had been on the cusp of starting a slow clap until the last bit, quickly brushed his hands against his shirt and pants before placing them on his hips.

"Yeah!" He cheered, nodding around the room. "Well, alright! That's what I'm talking about! Learning lessons and growing as space people. We're all going to feel some feelings sometimes like we have today, but the important part is being able to express them in a healthy way like this."

Unlike his wife, the intrepid Captain Cox felt no awkwardness or embarrassment whatsoever when his crew slowly rotated their heads in unison to peer upon him with bewildered eyes.

"Anybody else have any feelings they wanted to share? Maybe some reflections or musings orrrrrr concepts for consideration? You can take a moment to step out if you want some time to come up with a speech like Kim here."

"What? I wasn't coming up with a speech, I was disarming all the traps I set."

"Well, yeah, alright then! That too! If anybody has any deadly traps to disarm or speeches to make, you're welcome to take a couple minutes."

By this time Whisper had finally made it to the door. Then subsequently through the door, taking no pauses for farewells or backward glances. Cox watched her go, grinning all the while. After she disappeared, he turned back to the group, still smiling, albeit weakly.

"I feel like she's not coming back."

"Dude, we almost just got hijacked," Willy observed, as if just realizing it. "Don't you guys think we should, I dunno, call somebody or something?"

"NO!" Tim, Kim, and Donald all blurted out in unison, startling not only Willy but also each other.

"Okay . . ." The burly security guard murmured in defeat.

After a couple moments of staring at his two superiors, Donald shook his head, apparently deciding against whatever he was considering asking. Maybe he didn't want to know, or maybe lecturing the sheeple was more important.

"The best thing we can do is just forget any of this happened," he informed Willy in a tone that would not welcome dissention. "Whoever that guy is, he's definitely on lists! If we tell anybody that we ran into him, then we're gonna end up on those lists, too, as known associates. Next thing you know, we're gonna be getting pulled over every week by guys wearing spacesuit suits and sunglasses underneath their helmets. And yeah they'll probably go through the motions and check our logbooks and stuff, but that's how it starts! Soon as we commit one minor infraction then BAM! We're gonna be people of suspicion held indefinitely and being tortured for information we don't have and probably doesn't exist. But they'll do it anyway, 'cause they like doing it!"

He froze in position. He stood with his pointing finger trembling from the passion in his words and his face fixed in a blank expression. Either he was undergoing a monumental brain fart or he felt a wave of self-consciousness from the way everyone now stared at him. He cleared his throat with a loud "ahem" that vibrated his cheeks.

"Wait, what traps were you disarming?" He shifted the focus onto Kim. "I was right next to the video feed; you didn't move the entire time you were waiting outside Whisper's room."

She shrugged, eyebrows raised in an innocent pout.

"I set them earlier," she explained. "Before all this stuff happened."

Just like when she came in, all eyes returned to her in silent scrutiny. Nobody in the room seemed to have the social wherewithal to simply ask for elaboration. Thankfully, staring at someone until they became uncomfortable enough to keep talking had been fairly effective thus far.

"Look, I may or may not have been sorta expecting Willy to try and kill us at some point," Kim dragged the words out of herself. "And I know what you're thinking! But I'm not paranoid. I'm just . . ."

"You're a little overly suspicious." Cox offered.

"I'm a little overly suspicious! But that doesn't make me a bad person."

Sensing a vulnerability to be alleviated, her husband walked over and wrapped an arm around her.

"You're not wrong, honey, but I think you might be defending yourself against claims nobody made yet."

"I need a nap," she sighed as she broke away and slumped

into her chair. "Or a drink. Also, Willy, I haven't known you for long, and still have no confirmation you're not evil, but I'm sorry anyway."

"Thanks!"

"So does this mean we can just stay in transit for a while?" Donald asked as he settled back into his station. "Maybe stay away from things that might kill us or get us thrown in jail?"

It was in that moment that Cox knew the status quo had managed to return. His communications officer had returned to communicating his usual grievances, his pilot had shoved the ship into drive before she left and was off being a recluse somewhere, and his wife was slightly agitated with him but still receptive when he sat down and put an arm around her. She even let herself rest her head against his shoulder. But she wasn't allowing a smile just yet; he still had to earn that.

As for Willy, he hadn't been a part of the crew long enough to have a designated "thing," so for now, whatever he was doing was to be considered normal. At the moment that happened to be staring around the room as if tracking the movements of a non-existent fly.

"Or just say nothing and do whatever you want, like always," Donald added.

The captain rose from his seat and strode over to a spot behind the seated malcontent. Manicured hands rested upon poorly postured shoulders.

"Donny, Donny . . ." He said in his soothing voice, fighting hard against Donald's stalwart resistance to being soothed. "You gotta learn to just appreciate the moments sometimes, buddy—"

"I've never bought into your touchy-feely crap before. Why do you think it'd be any different right now?"

"Fair enough!"

Cox exhaled into Donny's curly hair. He massaged at the lad's tense tissue.

"I guess what I'm really trying to say is . . . The only thing we have to worry about killing us is that homicidal robot living in your computer. Oooh, yeah, you didn't think I knew about him, did ya?!"

Donald had no visible reaction.

"Wow, you finally found Bundy," he responded, deadpan as ever. "I started coding him to run my station a few years ago on my first day here. But good thing you found him when you did; I bet he was finally about to strike."

"Wait, *you* programmed that thing?!"

"Sure did."

"Wh—why did you make it so murdery?!"

"'Cause it's hilarious?"

"Kim, how many teenagers did you hire?!"

"I'm thirty-five." Donald answered.

"Y'know what!" The captain declared, putting his hands up. "This ain't bringin' me down!"

He strode past the bean bag chair as he talked. With chest high and shoulders back, he announced his indifference.

"No, sir! Life is too good. We already beat one cold-blooded murderer, what chance does a no-blooded wannabe murderer have?"

"Babe, I get what you're trying to say but you literally could not say it in a way that tempts fate more."

"Oh honey, you're being crazy! . . . That was rude to say; I'm sorry. Gaslighting is bad. I'm just trying to say there's absolutely nothing to worry about! That old snafu has been completely resolved and no repercussions could possibly arise from—" He stopped, suddenly hearing the words coming out of his mouth. "Wow, you're right. I really should tone this down."

Without another word, he trotted on back to his seat and let Kim lean across the arm rests to place her head against his shoulder once more. The slightest hints of a smile etched themselves onto the corners of her lips.

THE SPIES WHO SHOVED ME

It was hard to say how long they sat in silence after that. The air of the room was neither subdued nor stressful, though there was something of a pause. A hush. A brief period of shaky hesitancy that no one dared shatter, lest they be unready for the universe taking it upon itself to punish the captain's hubris. If the universe decided to at all, that is. It was a pretty big thing, after all, and perhaps it was arrogant to assume it would take time out of its day to meddle in the matters of a fleck of meat. Not to mention this form of thinking required the assumptions that the universe itself was not only somehow sentient, but also shared humanity's affection for poetic justice.

But, like most other superstitions, you're not supposed to think about it very hard; you're supposed to just accept it and fear it. You're also supposed to engage in mental gymnastics to construe all happenings as evidence supporting your suspicions.

It was for this reason that everyone freaked the hell out when a ringing noise began chiming from Donald's terminal.

"Oh Jesus, I've angered it!!" The captain yelped. "Somebody help me close all the vents!"

"I am NOT answering that!!" Donald declared around the same time. "I am not giving them a voice print to put on file!"

"Aw man!" Willy followed with a distressed shout of his own. "Last time people yelled about stuff, I got kicked in the nards!"

The terminal jingled again. The three of them huddled around it, cowering like it was telling them a scary campfire story. The caller ID said it was British Secret Organization #37, but that could be anybody! Whoever it was, they didn't give up after three rings, so they must have really wanted to talk.

"It's not stopping," the captain informed anyone who was hard of hearing (or skipping the narration). "Why isn't it stopping?!"

"What do you think they are, girl scouts?!" Donald snapped back. "This is bad. Whoever this is, they know where we are. Once they know who we are, we're doomed! We're toast, man! It's game over!"

"What should we do, Kim?" Cox called to his wife.

The three men whirled around to find the first mate had silently left the room without any of them noticing.

"Well, that's probably something else I'm gonna have to worry about now," he mused. "But for now, this!"

"Maybe we should just answer it." Willy suggested. He offered a sheepish shrug when they both gaped at him. "I mean, if they're not gonna stop, we're gonna have to see 'em eventually, right?"

"Wrong!" Donald yelled. "If we don't talk to them, then we can't invite them in! If we don't invite them in, then they can't come in!"

"Donny, buddy, I think you're thinking of vampires. Look, why don't we just hit the ignore button? I mean, that's what it's there for, right?"

"Oh god, please don't touch my terminal!"

"I'm just gonna hang up, don't worry!"

But Donald didn't believe him. Even Willy suspected he would muck it up. In fact, somewhere within the recesses of Cox's mind, obscured by all the hearts and smiles and positive affirmations and memories of hairstyles that didn't work out, there were a bunch of little versions of himself. They crowded around one particular tiny Tim and dragged him off into a small, dimly lit room, where he was strapped to a wheelchair with a speculum holding his eyes open as he was subjected to a swath of nausea-causing drugs and a several-hour-long supercut of Eeyore quotes. That metaphorical miniature man was a bit preoccupied at the moment, but if pressed he too would have said Cox was likely to bungle up such a simple task.

Anyway, they were all right about him, because he hit the answer call button by mistake.

Donald dove under the desk with a heretofore-unseen agility, leaving Cox to deal with their gentlemen callers. He hopped into the crunchy bean bag chair and stared up with eyes like fine china as the visage of the palest man he had ever seen popped up on the screen. That man also stared at the camera for a few moments, taking a moment to smooth his brown hair, then run a finger across both eyebrows, followed by his mouth brow.

"Oh, good afternoon!" He finally said. "I am Sir Percy Todgerworth of the League of Extraordinarily British Gentlemen. With whom am I speaking?"

"I, uh, am Tim Cox!" The captain responded. "Of . . . the SS *Jefferson*. I, I am also a sir."

Percy stared at him for a moment, blinking in the silence, before he continued.

"Charmed to make your acquaintance! I shall cut right to

the chase. My associate and I are embarking upon a mission of great importance. That mission has led us to your ship. In order to continue, I must formally request you grant us access aboard to carry out our duties."

"I . . . wow!" The captain stammered, rubbing at his head. He glanced over to Willy, who let out another sheepish shrug, and then down to Donald beneath him, still hiding under the table. The portly lad shook his head back and forth with a deranged, wide-eyed stare.

"Y'know, this is really a bad time . . ." He continued with an exaggerated wince. "We've had a pretty tough couple days already and I don't know if another unexpected guest is really a good idea. I'd reeeeeaaally love to help you out, though! But just, like, with you staying over there while I do."

Again Percy stared at him for several blink-filled moments before responding.

"Ah, yes. I had a feeling you would say something like that. I assure you our business will be quick and non-invasive, just how we Britishmen like our interactions with strangers! Ohohoho."

His laugh was as fake as the captain's confidence, but both of them continued to go for it anyway.

"Yeah, again, I see where you're comin' from. But as captain of this ship, I'm going to have to pass—"

"Well that is an interesting way of presenting things!" Percy cut him off.

"I, well, thank you! I think. I hope there's no hard feeling—"

"You're absolutely right!" Percy butted in yet again. "Well, this has been splendid. Illuminating, even. You are a very astute man or woman."

"Hey!" Cox barked at him. "I'm a man! . . . Not that there's any shame in being a woman."

"Ohoho, well isn't that humorous!"

"What?"

"Yes, exactly."

"Ahh . . . you've kinda lost me there, buddy. I'm not sure what—"

"In case you haven't realized, this is a pre-recorded message created for the purposes of distracting you while my associate and I board your ship. In the event we still have not arrived, please continue to wait whilst I entertain you with my beat-boxing proficiency."

"Oh my, we certainly need not sit through that!" The real Percy Todgerworth declared from the doorway. He stood alongside a shorter and older man with a buzzcut and matching suit.

"First, the warmups!" His onscreen persona continued.

"Shut it off. Please." The other man asked in a slow, strained tone, as if trying to suppress something.

Donald emerged from under the desk and tapped a button, causing the screen to go blank. He then turned to the two men and froze in position yet again, clearly realizing how the situation might look to the uninformed. At first he tried push away the chair upon which his captain sat, sinking his hands into the bean bag and uttering a mighty grunt. Not only did the seat not budge, but the action also resulted in his face being placed even closer to the salacious spot he was trying to avoid. The incriminating sound effect he did along with it made him just embarrassed enough go into full on flight mode and start thrashing around, trying to squeeze himself through the gap between chair and desk.

During it all, Percy looked at him, then back to Cox, then back to him, but ultimately decided not to share whatever thoughts he may have had on the matter.

"Right, then! Pardon our intrusion, but while the needs of the many may outweigh the needs of the few, the needs of the British outweigh the needs of the many."

"How did you get in here?!" Cox asked. "We're in space! We have . . . like, airlocks and stuff."

"Mister Cox—"

"Captain Cox.'

"—My associate and I are world class secret agents. I would expound on how we achieved the seemingly impossible task of boarding your ship from the outside without you realizing, but I would rather you just trust that we can, due to the fact that we just did."

"Dude!" Willy exclaimed. "You guys are secret agents? Like James Bond?"

"NO!" Percy's associate screamed. "That man is nothing more than a Scottish erection with a gun! Don't you compare us to him!"

"He's a fictional character, Sir Head."

"YOU'RE A FICTIONAL CHARACTER."

"Can you just . . . stand over there until I need you, please?"

As instructed, Sir Head did indeed stand over there. But he didn't seem very happy about it. In fact, in Percy's admittedly short experience, he seemed to be the sort that often failed to get very happy about anything. With arms crossed, he leaned against the wall and silently seethed at the ceiling, pursing his lips from side to side. Taking the opportunity while it lasted, Percy cleared his throat and began to pace and lecture like a general before the grunts.

"Right, so as I was saying, Sir Head and myself were dispatched by our organization's commander to follow up on a lead. This lead was brought to us by a ship that is currently in pieces floating in about a trillion and one different directions.

However, through state-of-the-art technology and incomparable skills of deduction and analysis that you couldn't begin to comprehend, we determined a limited interaction with this vessel before it, in a word, kablooied."

Everyone continued to stare, even after he stopped speaking. When they realized it was the point in the conversation in which they were supposed to contribute something, all they could manage was a chorus of coughs and glances around at pretty much anything that wasn't the bloviating secret agent standing in their midst.

"Well, did you rendezvous with another vessel in this quadrant or not?!" The Brit demanded.

"Well hey, I mean . . ." Cox stammered. "Rendezvous is such a strong word, y'know?"

"It really isn't."

"Like yeah, we met another ship. But we didn't 'rendezvous' with it. We just, y'know, met it."

"Aha! Progress! Splendid. Right, now, in your interaction, limited as it may well have been, did you happen upon anyone? An older gentleman perhaps? Surly fellow? Likely armed and disinterested in pleasantries. May well have elicited vibrations of discomfiture and impending doom. Also might have had in his possession an item of peculiarity—something that one could even call a macguffin?"

"Oh yeah, I totally know who you're talkin' about! Mister Nobody! He was a little bit scary, I guess, but he seemed like he could be an alright guy."

Willy reached an arm wide while the other gestured at his face.

"What the hell, dude! That guy was a dick."

"You are quite correct, sir." Percy shifted his focus to the larger fellow. "That man is a fugitive named Mister Banks. A dick of tremendous proportions, as you would say. In bad need of a neutering, I would say."

"Yeah!" The security officer agreed. " . . . I knew that wasn't his real name."

"Well, that is indeed a service my associate and I can provide. Free of charge, I might add! All you need do is set us on his trail. Any information you can provide about his armaments and travel accommodations would be of benefit as well."

"Oh, well, that's easy!" The captain said. "He's flying off towards Earth right now in an escape pod. He doesn't have anything he can fight you with either, so taking him without feeling like you have to kill him will be real easy!"

"An escape pod?" Percy reiterated. "The vessel readings didn't indicate that any were launched."

"Did you read ours? It came from ours."

Sir Head was starting to find the ceiling less and less interesting. His angular face slowly rotated towards the captain and then sideways as he listened to the account.

"I'm—I'm sorry," Percy said. "Are you trying to tell me he was here? Aboard your ship? Without murdering the lot of you?"

"Why are you saying that like it's a bad thing?"

"Captain, please stop," Donald begged. "Please stop saying things."

"Shut up, fatty!" The tall Brit snapped. "You've been quiet up until now. If that's your selection of first words then I have no choice but to now regard you with suspicion! What are you hiding?!"

"Hey, leave Donny alone! Breaking onto my ship and interrogating us is one thing, but you can't come and start body shaming my friends!"

"Mister Cox—"

"Captain Cox!"

"—it is clear to me that you lack either the proper appreciation or the mental wherewithal to regard these circumstances with the necessary levels of concern. This is a matter of global importance."

Willy raised his hand, much to the annoyance of his inquisitor.

"But we live in space. So wouldn't that mean, like, it has nothing to do with us?"

"You're from the moon! You're our colony. You're close enough."

"Oh, for the love of Christ!" Sir Head screamed from his spot against the wall. "Are you about done with this pathetic attempt at 'investigating?'"

"These things take time and patience, Richard!"

"Bollocks! Watch and learn."

He pushed Percy out of the way and marched way too far into Cox's personal space. His sharp nose pressed against the captain's round, button one. Rancid breaths smelling of asparagus and bile wafted from his mouth. Without breaking eye contact, he shoved two bony fingers into Cox's chest.

"Oi, you, cap'n Ken doll, what's the closest thing you got any level of affection for?"

"Well I mean, that's a tough question there, Agent Hurtful Nickname!" Cox responded after a few blinks. He gave a slight shake of his head. "I don't think there's anything in here I don't like!"

"What about this thing then, eh!? Ya like this thing!?"

"Of course! That's my microwave! Everybody loves it."

"GOOD!"

He snatched it up, cord and all, and hurled it against the floor. The heavy steel clanged as if in pain with each bounce before it lay still. Seeing it was still intact, Sir Head picked it up again and slammed it back down, causing a few more dents and the door to pop open. He seized the opportunity to give the door a series of mighty tugs. However, the vintage construction proved to be more than he could overpower, so he abandoned his attempts to tear it off and instead proceeded to kick it repeatedly. Every bang was punctuated by various differently worded rhetorical inquiries regarding the crew's emotional response to seeing their beloved microwave destroyed.

"Oh my god!" The only person who cared cried. "What are you doing?!"

Sir Head abandoned his beat down and closed back on the captain. He snatched up his shirt with both hands.

"Give me what I want!!" He bellowed in his face.

"But I don't know what you want!!"

"You better not! It's classified and if you knew then I'd have to kill ya! Kill ya!!"

"Why is everybody who lives on a planet so mean!?"

Head shoved Cox backwards before the captain's tears could begin. He gave one final boot to the downed heating machine with a wiry leg then returned to Todgerworth.

"Oh, it's on this ship alright." He muttered just loud enough for Percy to hear. "Buncha mewling cream puffs like these? This Banks bastard could easily put the fear right in 'em. The only way to get past this is to make them fear me more."

Sir Head contorted his lips into the closest shape his face could get to a smile. A colourless hand, nearly translucent, reached into his suit's breast pocket and pulled out a pair of metal tongs and a bottle of hot sauce.

"You might wanna wait in the car," he added.

"I cannot even begin to imagine how you've arrived at this conclusion." Percy replied. "But of course there's another way past this. Why don't we just simply look for it?"

"Be my guest," Sir Head said as he gave the tongs a test clinking. "But don't you come cryin' to me if you start settin' off booby traps or triggering alarms. They ain't gonna just leave it undefended!"

"You're not the only world-class secret agent, you know. Even if these buffoons are indeed the patsies you believe them to be, any defensive machinations they concoct will be easy for me to circumvent."

With a mighty harrumph and nose in the air, Percy Todgerworth set forth to prove his worth. To whom it was being proved remained unclear. However, his perceived necessity to provide such proof was enough to govern his actions nevertheless. His confidence didn't falter in the slightest as he picked a door at random, ushered it open, and disappeared into the adjoining depths.

As soon as he had gone, Sir Head turned his newfound eagerness to work onto the remaining three crewmen. He hadn't actually done anything yet, but they all recoiled anyway, completely oblivious to the fact there were three of them and he was just an old man armed with nothing but tongs and hot sauce.

That, kids, is the power of believing in yourself.

A couple seconds later, the door opened again. Percy trotted back into the room, stiff-necked as ever, and remarkably calm in the face of Kim digging a blaster rifle into his back.

"I don't suppose you're Mister Banks?" Sir Todgerworth asked her over his shoulder.

"That's a bloody woman, you prat."

"That much is clear, Richard, but it's not out of the question that the "Mister" moniker could have simply been adopted as an act of subterfuge!"

"Oh is that right? Ya really think she'd just tell ya then, eh?!"

"She might!!"

"Tim, who are these people?!"

At the sight of his wife, the captain's cheerful composure came flooding back and he hopped to his feet.

"Why, they're British secret agents, honey!" He informed her, as if it was the most normal thing in the world.

"What are we, having an open house or something?! Where do all these people keep coming from?!"

"I got a better question," Sir Head butted in, drawing a laser pistol of his own. "Why's some freighter broad packing heat, eh!? I knew you lot were terrorists!"

"Terrorists?!" An unfamiliar voice exclaimed from the doorway.

They whirled around to find a uniformed man in his mid-twenties standing in their doorway. Both his hands tugged at his uncooperative hip holster. His soft grunts of exertion grew higher pitched and broken by huffs and puffs the longer he struggled. After several uncomfortable moments, he removed his whole belt, yanked the holster off of it, removed the gun, and pointed it at random people.

"Everybody continue to freeze!" He shouted, one hand holding his pants up.

No one defied his demands, but only Cox made a conscious attempt to be obedient.

"Excuse me," Percy snidely addressed him. "I don't know who you think you are, but we are in the middle of classified business right now."

"Well, *I* don't know who *you* think *you* are! So I need you to tell me, along with providing some form of identification. And then I need to tell you why you're drifting through Earth's devoid-of-airspace and not responding to any of our hails! I mean, you need to tell me. Why. That."

Cox looked at Donald, receiving a wrinkled nose in return.

"Hey, they told me to shut off the coms."

The captain nodded.

"Sorry about that, buddy!" He said, hands by his shoulders. "We're not terrorists. It's all just a big misunderstanding!"

The man's gnarled facial expression melted away.

"Oh, okay then."

Without another word he stuffed the gun back into its holster and dusted off his hands. They still shook slightly as he patted his padded vest, but his face wore a grin of shy relief.

"I thought I might've been about to die there for a second," he mused, chuckling nervously.

"Ah, don't worry about it! Everybody here's had that feeling at some point today."

"Haha! That's kinda suspicious . . ."

"So what brings you here?" Cox asked in an announcing kind of way. Without any regard for the circumstances, he closed the distance between the two, draped an arm over the fellow's shoulders, and used it to guide him farther onto the bridge.

"Are you another secret agent? How do you guys keep getting on my ship?"

Cool as can be, the man allowed himself to be led around. "Oh, well, I mean, I'm not a 'secret' agent per se. But I am a border patrol agent, and some people say that we're pretty much the same thing."

"Nobody says that," Percy said.

"As for getting on your ship, it was pretty easy! Somebody lasered a baseball-sized hole into your airlock."

"Wow!" Cox called out, looking over at Percy. "You weren't kidding! You guys are high tech."

"That was you who did that," Donald reminded him.

"Oh, yeah."

"I may or may not have to give you a citation for that, by the way," the border agent added. "It's not as dangerous as a hull breach, but we don't like to see these tin cans flying around unless all the pieces are there!"

"Well, actually, did you know that this ship is titanium?"

"Why would I know that?"

"Well, I mean, you inspect these things, don't you? Shouldn't you know what they're made of?"

"Well, then why would you ask me if I knew that?"

"Oh my god!" Kim griped. "Can you just write him the damn ticket so we can go back to our stand-off?!"

"HEY!" The border guard screeched back at her. "I am a certified border security specialist and I will not be interrupted!" Mouth now twisted into a frown and loud breaths snuffing out of his nose, he turned back to Cox. From a vest pocket he produced a small rectangular device with a screen and began working away on it with his thumbs.

"Sir, do you know why I pulled you over?"

"Didn't you say it's because I have a laser hole in my airlock?"

"No! I'm just giving you a ticket for that because I'm mad now! I pulled you over because your ship's registered pilot is a new driver and you're not properly displaying an N on the back."

"I swear I didn't know she was underage!" Cox insisted.

"That's a really strange defence. Almost like you're trying to make a joke."

"Alright, this has gone on long enough," Percy interrupted. Completely indifferent to the blaster rifle inches from his back, he walked away from Kim and up to the border agent. The man didn't look up from his tablet until the Brit ripped it from his hands.

"I can appreciate the necessity of the menial laws that you and your kind are tasked with enforcing. However, you have stumbled into an investigation of a much higher calibre. My associate and I suspect these individuals of harbouring a fugitive and aiding in the transport and potential distribution of a biological weapon. On the orders of Her Majesty the Queen, you are now to stand down and comply with any further ord—why are you brandishing your wrist towards me?!"

"I don't know how much of it that you guys got," the agent said into his wrist. "But I am definitely going to need backup. All of it."

10.
"The Gang Goes to Guantanamo"

EVER SINCE THE EVOLUTION of culture, mankind has oft concocted tales of the wondrous places that lay beyond their reach, high in the sky. Then technology advanced enough for them to discover that nothing was up there besides huge balls of stuff they already had and an inconceivably large amount of nothing. Some continued to delude themselves into thinking all the cool stuff was still just too far away to see; others started filling the sky with things like chemtrails, predator drones, and smog in order to prevent themselves from being foolish enough to ever get their hopes up again. But no matter what discoveries were made, the notion of a heaven hiding somewhere up there had never completely gone away. Many have even gone in search of it; and the unluckiest of them sometimes thought they found it.

In actuality, they found a little place called Guantanamo Docking Bay, voted "The Universe's Worst Vacation Spot" for ninety-nine out of the last hundred years. Many surveys had also determined it to be the current leading cause of apostasy.

Hovering two-hundred-and-fifty freedom-units above the Earth, it was the only place where one could still hear the Barney theme song. Constructed as an homage to one of the most notorious prisons in the world's history, Azkaban, "Space Guantanamo" infamously served as a detention centre for the extraordinarily dangerous and the extraordinarily unlucky. However, guilty or not guilty, the techniques allegedly employed within the desolate concrete walls seemed to be universally effective. In its brochures, the institution boasted a zero percent recidivism rate since the day it opened. Some might have said that's an easy figure to achieve when you're a place that never lets anyone leave, but that's why they'd never asked for public input.

Despite all the good it claimed to do, there were still those who would speak out against the establishment. Claims of human rights violations and unlawful confinement were standard fanfare that the haters would blare. But all that ever resulted in was budget cuts and empty promises. No attempts were ever made by anyone to shut the place down. There was just something about the fact it was "way up there" that seemed to make people not care. "It's in space," they would say. "It's the space people's problem." Others would even attempt to defend the prison, insisting it couldn't be all bad. After all, it cured ALS almost singlehandedly from the contributions it generated doing the Ice Bucket Challenge.

In the minds of most, however, Space Guantanamo had nestled itself neatly into that moral grey area where they technically opposed it, but found it wasn't really an issue they faced often enough to feel compelled to do anything about. It was a necessary evil, almost. Like traffic, or advertisements, or Mondays. Sure, most of the time none of those things involved rectal infusions, but they were still pretty annoying and much more common. So they were essentially on the same level of badness.

To those who worked there, it was generally considered to be a normal job not dissimilar to other roles within the correctional system. Really, they were just a lesser-known branch of the judicial system that still provided a public service. They weren't sadistic monsters. They put their pants on in the morning, still laying in bed half-asleep with a toothbrush hanging out of their mouth, just like everyone else. Ask any of them and they would assure you that their job wasn't all waterboarding and Russian roulette like those darn moving holograms would have you believe. They spent their days interacting with and getting to know the ~~vermin~~ people in their care. They sought to truly understand them. To rehabilitate them. Or at very least to convince them to go be somebody else's problem. And just because they were sometimes forced to Jack Bauer the location of the bomb out of somebody didn't mean they were bad people.

The day the new prisoners arrived had been fairly unremarkable. Even their arrival didn't do anything to shake things up. "Prospective terrorists" was their moniker. But "Terrorist" was a term that had become a lot less meaningful with time, like "Love" or "Hitler." The correctional officers had worked with enough alleged offenders to know judgement was something to be reserved. Getting excited too soon often led to being let down.

A group of them were stationed around the breakroom table when the door burst open. In stepped a mousy-looking woman with a fitted black skirt and a bun so tight it was a good thing hair didn't require circulation. She carried a stack of tablets in her hands. After thumbing through them for a moment and separating five, she looked up at her mingling minions.

"Eenie, meenie, miney . . . Johnson and Peters! You look bored; have some work."

Johnson and Peters did not look bored. In fact, they had been trying to look as busy as possible. But scrubbing at the table with a sleeve and filling every mug with coffee wasn't convincing enough to escape their boss's watchful eye. The stack hit the table with a sound reminiscent of a whip crack and she pursed her lips down at them.

"It's about time you two stepped up from . . . whatever it is you currently do around here." She said. "This case should be simple. Group of five accused of smuggling a chemical weapon. Their ship is in impound and the prisoners are in cells. Just figure out what's going on."

Not one to take questions, she left them to their own devices. And also the devices she left them.

Peters was first to act, snatching a few e-files for himself.

"Hmmm. Uh huh. A few years working together. None of them on any watch lists. Sounds like we got ourselves a freshly radicalized group of agitators."

"Or! Or . . ." Johnson suggested. "Maybe, and hear me out here, someone is trying to frame them! That would be cool, right? We could be the guys that get to the bottom of it and find the real terrorists."

"Don't be stupid. It's Guantanamo. Nobody's innocent here. What we really need to do is find which organization it was that infected these morons and then get medieval on all of their asses."

One of their coworkers put down his fork.

"Maybe you guys should try interviewing the detainees before you start drawing conclusions?"

"Shut up, Frank!" They both snapped back at him in unison.

"Do you want the case!? Huh?" Peters egged him on.

"You wanna be the one to handle this group of bloodthirsty psychopaths?!"

"Well, I mean . . . yeah, sure. If you guys don't want the case I guess I could take it off your hands."

"Well, you can eat a dick!" Johnson snarled. He snatched up all the tablets in his arms. "These were given specifically to us, so obviously you can't be trusted with them!"

They both sneered at him before packing up their supplies and heading out. Frank just sighed and returned to his beans. One day he'd pay off his ex-wife's house and retire. One day.

NEITHER JOHNSON NOR PETERS perused the files any further on their way down the hall. With chests out and arms swinging like a big Broadway number, they marched down towards the first interrogation room. Peters was first to get there. He reached for the handle with a pale, sinewy hand but Johnson quickly blocked the door with a much beefier arm.

"Wait, wait," he urged. "We should have a plan or something. Or like, a tactic!"

"Hmmm, you're right."

They stood outside for a moment scratching their chins and muttering to themselves.

"How about good cop, bad cop?" Peters suggested.

"Good cop, bad cop!" Johnson exclaimed. "It's a classic!"

"It's a classic," Peters agreed. "And that's because it works! Alright, I'll go in first and I'll be real hostile—"

"So hostile!"

"—And just when they're starting to think 'Oh no, I thought I was the psycho-est person here but now I'm trapped with a real psycho. Who knows what he's gonna do? Why is he turning off the camera? Why is he unzipping his pants?' That's when you'll come in with your slick black hair and devil-may-care attitude. And they'll think 'Oh man, I better tell him anything he wants to know or he'll leave me in here with that incredibly handsome crazy person!' It's the perfect plan!"

"The perfect plan!"

"Alright, give me about two minutes to get 'em nice and scared, then come in and do your thing."

"You got it!"

Devilish smile upon his lips and an unprofessional level of excitement in his eyes, Peters punched the code to open the door. It slid open wide and he took half a step inside before he registered who was seated at the table awaiting him. They hadn't yet made eye contact before he leapt out of the way and pressed himself flush against the wall while smacking at the close door button with a toddler-esque coordination.

Johnson gaped at him.

"New plan," Peters stated. "*You* are gonna be the bad cop."

"Wait, what?! Why do I have to be the bad cop now?"

"Well look at you, man! It only makes sense. No one is gonna believe someone who looks like me is crazy."

"What the hell! I don't look crazy either!"

"Well okay, no, but you look crazier than me!"

"I can't do crazy, man!" Johnson insisted as he paced back and forth, shooting wild glances and tugging at his hair. "I just can't. I'm too zen, and my body screams discipline, and I'm gonna be worried the whole time that he doesn't believe me, and then I'll get flustered, and I'll blow the whole thing!"

"Okay, okay, fine!" Peters relented. He pondered the situation for a moment, then snapped his fingers. "Alright, don't be crazy then. Be a hardass!"

"A what?"

"A hardass! One of those angry, driven-by-justice types. Like Officer Brutality!"

"Officer Brutality! That guy's my hero!"

"Alright, good! Go be Officer Brutality."

"This is why you're the idea guy!" Johnson grinned as he pressed the passcode. "I mean, how long have I loved that show for, and never once have I thought to try and be him at work."

"Game face, man. Game face."

Johnson bared his teeth and raised his hands like claws at him before stepping through the door. Once inside, his expression soured into that of a drill sergeant smelling flatulence. He chucked the stack of electronic files onto the table, ignoring how they became strewn about, and glowered down at the young lady sitting quietly on the other side.

"You're in a lot of trouble, Miss Wang." He growled at her.

She opened her mouth to respond. Before she could, he sucked air through his teeth and slammed his palms onto the glass table.

"WANG!!" He screamed.

The rush of air and spit particles that hit her in the face forced her to blink hard against the unsolicited bellow. Johnson took that as an opportunity to take a few deep breaths, then pick a tablet from the table.

"That's what's listed in your file," he continued to growl. "Wang. Whisper Wang. Is that your name, Miss Wang? Whisper Wang?"

"Yeah," she replied.

"Whisper Wang. Graduated at the top of her class, Whisper Wang. Youngest person to ever be enrolled at the flight academy, Whisper Wang. Voted most antisocial member of her grad group, Whisper Wang. Well there's just one problem then, 'Whisper Wang.'" He raised his hands, causing her to pre-emptively flinch. "Whisper Wang is a pretty damn Asian-sounding name!"

He pointed his finger toward her with the dramatics of a court scene in a soap opera. It was a little lost on Whisper, since she happened to already be familiar with her own ethnicity.

She frowned at his hand.

"So what?"

"So what?!" He repeated. "So what?! Well I'll tell you so what! Everyone knows Asians can't drive!"

Whisper's jaw dropped. But before she could respond, the door burst open.

"Sorry I'm late." Peters said, his voice calm and sultry. He stepped inside with head high and hands behind his back. "Are you alright, Whisper? I can call you Whisper, right?"

"No, you can't!" Johnson snapped. "Because something isn't adding up here! Identity theft isn't a joke . . . whoever you are!"

He slammed his hands on the table again.

"How about you tell me what's really going on, huh! 'Cause I think the person in this file is a bit too qualified to be named 'Whisper Wang!!'"

"How about we all calm down a little bit," Peters soothed. He took a seat in one of the chairs, then sidled it along the side of the table to get closer to her. "This young lady is clearly distressed, let's start it a little easier. So, Whisper, you're a pilot huh?"

"Well, I was! Probably not anymore, though . . ." She grumbled, sinking into her chair.

"How old are you?"

"Sixty-three. I just have great skin."

"Such a clever thing," he intoned, sidling a bit closer. "But it might help your case if you can verify the information in your file."

"'Kay . . ." The side of her mouth curled down in opposition to her rising eyebrow. "Fine, I'm . . . eighteen."

"Nice, nice . . ."

"What?"

"Nothing. So, you like flying, Whisper?"

"Sure. I guess. It's fine. I dunno."

"Aw, c'mon, now; it's gotta be better than fine. You got licensed at thirteen. I bet you love it."

"Sure, yeah, definitely love, and not parental pressure or anything."

"Family? Ugh, I don't want to hear about them. Talk about flying more. Do you drive stick?"

"I . . . it's a spaceship, not a backhoe."

"That's a shame. You should branch out. I bet you could do all sorts of things with these little hands."

"Like choke people?"

Peters grinned.

"I could get into that."

"Oh."

"You got a boyfriend, Whisper?"

"No."

"Oh, c'mon!" He teased. "You can tell me! In fact, you have to tell me."

She blinked up at him.

"I . . . are you hoping I do or something?"

Peters chuckled with an exaggerated mirth. He grinned up at his bewildered partner, then looked back at Whisper. Slowly, he rose from his chair and loomed over her head, talking through the dark hair that obscured her face.

"I'm just saying you can get into a lot of trouble for lying to me, Whisper," he grunted into her ear. "I'm a federal officer. I'm also the only friend you got right now. You don't want to lose your only friend. You want to do anything you can to keep him. You wouldn't want me to leave you alone in this room with *him*, do you?"

Eyebrows slowly creeping toward her hairline, she rotated her head over to Johnson. The man stared doe-eyed with his mouth agape at the both of them. Then she felt Peters's bony hand grab her chin.

"Don't look at him, look at me," he ordered her through clenched teeth. He stared into her dark eyes with his own cloudy ones. "Is your boyfriend the one who got you into this? How old is he? How far have you two gone? You ever been with anyone else?"

"H-hey, Peters, can I talk to you outside for a sec?"

"I'm working here!!" He snapped.

"I really think you need a quick break," Johnson insisted. He grabbed onto his coworker's arms and started to pull him away. Peters struggled against his burly partner, never breaking eye contact with Whisper. As a last-ditch effort, he grabbed onto the metal table to anchor himself, dragging it for several feet before the piercing shrieks of friction and futility forced him to let go.

"Do you even know what it's like to have a real man?!" He screamed just before being pushed out the door. Johnson spun back around to face Whisper. His hands slid back and forth down his pant legs and he bit at his lips.

"I . . . I don't really know what that was," he admitted.

After realizing it had fallen open again during all of this, Whisper closed her mouth and quickly reassumed her usual expression, with an added purse to her lips.

"You suck at being the good cop."

In lieu of any wit to wisecrack back, Johnson instead replied with a cough. Not even a manly cough—a feeble and awkward cough that snuffed any semblance of control over the situation. With his entire plan and persona completely thrown off, he now saw no other recourse but to give an awkward nod and walk out of the room. A second later he came back in, scooped up all the files, gave another nod, and was gone once more. Peters was waiting for him just outside. Heavy breaths puffed in and out of his nose.

"What the hell was that?!" Johnson demanded of him.

"I don't know!!" Peters sarcastically whisper-yelled back. "Why don't you tell me what the hell was that!? You didn't even give her time to answer any of my questions!"

"You weren't asking her any questions about the case or anything!"

"I told you I was starting easy!"

"*That* was supposed to be easy?! You were talking to her like that guy that used to hang out at the playground by our elementary school."

"That's the whole point! I make her really uncomfortable with forward questions so that our other questions that we ask after will start to look appealing by comparison!"

"Oh . . . when you put it like that, it actually makes a bit of sense."

"Exactly." Peters put a hand on Johnson's shoulder. "This is why you should just trust me. If we stuck to my plan we would have got the information we need for the case . . . and I would have gotten some information that would be useful to me for later."

"Okay, see, I was with you for the first part . . . but what do you mean—"

"Don't worry about it. Let's just go do the next guy."

Johnson couldn't help but shoot him a couple sideways looks as they walked, but ultimately opted against addressing the issue further. It was hard to be outraged by anything after working in this place long enough, and by this point they both had seen it all: Chinese water torture, Antarctican sleep torture, Irish sober torture, and all the other regional breaking methods were just tools in their shed of sadness.

In fact, over time they had even become able to discern the method of information extraction being used based solely on the brouhaha being bellowed from any given room. Short, urgent yelp noises were common in pain-inducing programs. Those exposed to prolonged procedures like sleep deprivation would warble a long mournful wail like the kind you hear walking by your city's cheapest motel at night. There was also this interesting phenomenon where prisoners tended to scream in key with the song being played during music sessions.

However, for all their shortcomings, Johnson and Peters wanted to add a more personal touch to their interrogations. Their job was to gather information, after all. They couldn't just march into each room and beat every perp like a disobedient rug. In the biz, that was called rock'em-sock'em research, and, frankly, pretty much nobody had enough rage or energy to do that all day. That was really why the thugs and sadists never lasted in this job. Even those that did last weren't regarded highly amongst their peers. One look at their hands would see their knuckles worn down like the soles on an old pair of shoes, and everyone would know they weren't a thinker by trade.

Having reached the cell of their next charge, the pair of aspiring professional ponderers stopped again to reassess their plan.

"Alright, let's try this again." Johnson said. "I'll start hard, then you come in soft."

"'Kay, gimme a sec to get soft."

"Think I should threaten him with AIDSbola? That's scary, right?"

Peters rolled his eyes.

"C'mon, man. Nobody believes in the AIDSbola thing anymore."

"Fine, fine, I'll just . . . I dunno . . . scream in his face or something . . ."

He punched the numbers to the room without even looking. It was the same for every room; much cheaper than that fingerprint or eye scanning technology. There was still a spot to put your eye, though. Just to keep the riff-raff from getting any ideas of escape.

The door slid open and he stepped inside. There, he found another young person huddled in a chair, nursing a black eye and eagerly anticipating his arrival. Well, young-looking anyway. A quick glance at his file revealed he was actually thirty-five. Thirty-five and not a single facial hair sprouted. Shame; a beard would have been the only way he could have faked a jawline.

"Well, well, well." Johnson announced, pacing around the room reading a tablet. "If it isn't the infamous Donaldric Harambe . . . O'chopenisravich!xowalechrist. Am I saying that right?"

"Not even close," Donald mumbled in his general direction.

"Well, it doesn't matter!" Johnson put his hands on the glass table and glowered down at his doughy detainee. "Because this room is my town! And I run my town! With an iron. Freaking. Fist!"

He proceeded to punch at the air and followed it up with an uncoordinated front kick at nothing. Huffs and puffs were the only sound in the room. After enough of those to catch his breath, he resumed his previous stance at the table.

"You look uncomfortable, Donaldric. You uncomfortable?"

Donald blinked at him.

"The first thing that happened when I got here was some guy punching me in the face and saying 'Welcome to Earf.'"

"Hey, that's a centuries-old tradition for greeting extraterrestrials. You can't just show up somewhere and hate them for doing things differently than you."

"I'm . . . I'm also in a cell in Guantanamo. Shouldn't I be uncomfortable?"

"Ohhhh, right, right." Johnson mused. He licked his finger, then started thumbing through the tablets. "Rap sheet like yours? Of course being here, in the belly of the beast, might set you a little on edge."

"What rap sheet?!"

"Servants of the law all stick together, Donaldric! We don't appreciate civvies abusing and making a mockery of our . . . sacred profession."

"What the hell are you talking about?!"

Johnson slammed a tablet on the table and slid it across to Donald.

"Oh, just your list of past offences, Donaldric," he taunted. "That fuzzy memory of yours starting to come back now?"

"You just totally smashed the screen on this. I can't read anything."

"Well, isn't that convenient!!" The officer leapt from his seat and paced around the room, hands clasped together and biceps in full flex. "Unfortunately for you, I already read it! Impersonating a police officer is a very serious offence. Said in there that you had the uniform on and everything. Running around, accosting kids in a residential neighbourhood. Says you never served any time either. Guess that means you escaped and were never caught . . . until now!"

"I never served any time because I was five!!" Donald

bellowed back at him. "Those kids were my friends! We were playing cops and robbers!"

"And how about now, huh, Donaldric?! Are you just playing with your friends now, too?! Huh?! A good old game of Moon Terrorists Conspiring to Distribute a Chemical Weapon?! . . . Huh?!"

"If I say no, are you going to waterboard me?"

"What?!" Johnson sat down in his seat just so he could leap from it again. "Do I look like the type of guy who waterboards?! Look at these arms, dude! I could pop your head like a . . . like a . . . tiny, pop-able watermelon. I don't need to do pussy stuff like waterboard! And besides, waterboarding is way too old school anyway. We have something called hydroplanking now."

"Look, I don't know about any chemical weapons, okay?!" Donald insisted. "The whole reason I took this job is because I wanted something boring and removed where trouble couldn't find me. But no, no matter where I go I always end up caught up in somebody else's problem . . . I mean—you think I want this dead-end job?! I should be writing code for NASA or programming Virgin's service bots. But no. Instead I get to sit on a junk hauler answering phones."

"Dude, that . . . that sucks." Johnson couldn't help but say. "I'm sorry. I mean, Peters is supposed to be the one who listens and cares about your sob story, but I'm not sure where he is."

"Um . . . thanks? I guess?"

"Actually, yeah; where the hell is that guy, anyway?"

He stood up to leave, but Donald called to him with a final question.

"If I make up some incriminating stuff for everyone else, can I go?"

Johnson cleared his throat and folded his arms.

"That's not how things work here, Donaldric. We're not

like the Space CIA. It takes more than fake claims to make us do stuff. You'd also have to back it up with fake evidence and a fake alibi for yourself and fake evidence to support your fake alibi. I mean, if you can do all that, then hell yeah! I'll be glad to let you go!"

"But how am I supposed to—"

"'Scuse me for a moment."

He popped out the door quick and scanned the hallway. Not so much as a whiff of the mousse that Peters abused so much of. A few of his nameless and irrelevant coworkers bustled around in the hallway, but it was the commotion coming from the end of the hall that attracted his attention. It called to him like a siren. A deranged, vaguely homicidal-sounding siren, rife with voice cracks and incoherence. Its shrieks filled the halls with passion and vengeance. Rounding the corner, Johnson found it slamming its hands and occasionally face against the door of Whisper's holding room.

"Keep on hiding, bitch!!" Peters roared at the door in a demonic voice. "I broke out of my cell, you think I won't break into yours!?"

He pounded on the door several times, all the while showing it his best war face.

"You're gonna *die*!! I'm gonna tear you to pieces and mount you on my wall!"

That was followed by a raucous bout of scream laughing. However, Peters's mirth cut out when Johnson clasped a hand onto his shoulder.

"Dude! What the hell are you doing?!"

"What the hell does it look like I'm doing?! I'm terrifying the living shit out of her!"

Johnson stood silent for a moment, processing the information. It was to no avail.

"WHY?!"

"God, you are so clueless. She's all alone, man! She has no one to protect her, no one to defend her from the all the horrors and psychos and . . . stuff."

He shrugged and gave a sly grin.

"Or does she?"

Once more he slammed at the door, this time with extra furor.

"I hope you aren't thinking that correctional officer slash male model is going to save you!"

"Why?!" Johnson said again. "Why?!"

"Do I have to spell everything out to you?!"

"Honestly, I'd rather you just stop doing things that make me have to ask what you're doing."

Peters squinted at him, studying him. After a brief stint of analysis, his eyebrows lifted and he began nodding to himself.

"I suppose it isn't fair to expect you to be able to keep up with me. Very well; young Miss Wang needs some time to stew in her fear, anyway, before affections can blossom. Whatever. We can do things your way for now. Lead on."

"Thanks, bro. I actually kinda think I'm starting to underst—"

Despite his order for Johnson to "Lead on," Peters strode right past him and back in the direction of Donald's room.

"Uh huh. Uh huh. So what do you got? What did kindergarten cop have to say?"

Johnson managed to overtake him just in time to block the door.

"Oh, him? He's not talking. I don't think they keep him in the loop. He's just there to answer phones. I think he probably just hands the phone to his boss after picking up. Or maybe, MAYBE, he's secretly the kingpin to it all, and that's why he was pretending to have the most pointless job ever! DUDE! I think I just figured it out!"

"Maybe, Johnson, maybe. But why don't we talk with the others first? See what they have to say. Who's up next?"

He peered down at the file he was handed and couldn't help but raise an eyebrow.

"Oh, great. Well, this should be interesting."

They ploughed through coworkers and visitors on their way down the hall, smacking stacks of tablets out of hands and shoulder checking any who were smaller than themselves. Naturally, they elicited copious dirty looks, and their efforts even earned a real-life honest-to-goodness stink eye. But none of it registered, as their motivation to do their job was just too formidable. After a half-dozen or so workplace assaults, they arrived at the cell of detainee number three. In deference to past perps, rather than taking the time to formulate another pointless interrogation tactic, they instead just barged right in.

"WILLY!" They cheered in unison.

The *Jefferson*'s rent-a-cop was startled by the entrance, but quickly resumed his sheepish, hand-clasped stance.

"Hey, guys . . ." He muttered.

"What's goin' on, bro?" Johnson asked, taking a seat across from him. "You get shit canned from this place so you decide to go join the bad guys?!"

"No, dude, it's not like that at all!" Willy insisted. His bottom lip began to tremble. "You aren't gonna call my mom, are you?"

Peters sucked air through his teeth and pretended to study the file again.

"I don't know, man. This doesn't look very good for you. I mean, it's bad enough that we found you with these guys. When we also consider your dismissal for arson of a federal detention center . . . It really paints a bit of a picture. Don't you agree, Agent Johnson?"

"He's got a point there, Willy. That is kind of a terrorist-y sounding thing to do."

"Aw, god, you guys are right." Willy's voice quivered. He put his head in his hands and his elbows on the table. "I should have never let you use my lighter to test the bathroom for linoleum."

"It's okay, bro," Johnson consoled him, resting a hand on his back. "We're investigators now. We can help you. But you gotta tell us where the drugs are!"

"That's not what we're looking for."

" . . . The bomb?"

"It's a biological weapon, dude."

"Holy Jesus, Willy, what are you doing, bro!?"

"There's nothing like that on there, dude, I swear!" Willy, well, swore. "Some old dude even locked us in the cargo hold and it was just full of space rocks. Search the ship if you don't believe me!"

"Well, we are going to search the ship!" Peters said. "Top to bottom, in fact. But it would be way easier on you and us if you just told us where it was."

"Yeah!" Johnson agreed. "'Cause we got other ships to search . . . with bombs and drugs on them."

Willy shook his head. His gaze was still cast downward in hopeless despair, obscured by the long, curly hair that lay matted against the coalesced sweat on his face. His fingers trembled as they attempted to scoop the final remnants out of his bag of chips.

"I'm starting to think some of the people this place holds without trial or evidence might actually be innocent," he whimpered.

Peters rolled his eyes.

"Oh, come on, don't you remember what they taught us at orientation? Even if you can't prove guilt, everyone is always at least an accomplice to something."

He joined his partner on Willy's other side. They both had hands on his back, slumped over as he was, like frat brothers standing vigil while he chucked his groceries after the party. But, also like frat brothers, they didn't actually care that much about his well-being, and wished he'd hurry up and work through this so they could get back to matters more suited to their tastes.

"Just tell us who the leader of your terrorist club is, bro." Johnson urged. "And I promise I'll get you the cell that has the working toilet."

"I told you, dude, we were set up!" The big man blubbered, trying in vain to stem the stream of snot coming from his nose. "That old Banks guy is who you want! I tried to stop him but he kicked me in the balls! How do you stop a guy who's willing to do that?! There's . . . there's some things you just aren't supposed to do, man . . ."

"Bro, are you . . . are you crying?"

"N-no I'm just . . . **sniff** . . . cutting water weight . . . 'cause I'm bulking."

"WARNING: LIE DETECTED."

Johnson and Peters jumped.

"What the hell was that?!" The former demanded, absentmindedly reaching for a blaster he didn't carry.

Willy pulled his face from his hands and looked at him. His eyes were still bleary, but they squinted in confusion.

"That was the lie detector . . ." he informed them. "I forgot we had those."

Peters gaped at the ceiling.

"Wait, we've had lie detectors this whole time?! Are they in every room?"

"Yeah?"

"That's awesome!" Johnson cheered. "I knew there was no way humans were supposed to be able to do interrogizing on their own."

"Oh yeah, it's *sooooo* awesome!" Peters spat. "I mean, what are we even here for, right!?"

He laughed with a hollow, mirthless laughter that punctuated the rhetorical question with a feeling of unease. He didn't even smile as he did it. He just stared unblinkingly at his two acquaintances with an intense pokerface, all the while chuckling through clenched teeth.

"In fact, why don't I just take off this uniform, huh? Take this uniform off the perfectly sculpted body of this peak of biological evolution and hang it on that camera up there in the corner. Let the robots just take over this entire process! See how far our amazing space-age technology gets on its own! Then maybe I just go work at the front desk? Or as the janitor? Or maybe I should be the guy who drives that space food truck that parks behind the cafeteria to sell us the contents of its grease trap. I'm sure those would be much more fitted for . . . for a, a BEACON of charisma and . . . and raw, refined pantology!"

By the end of his speech, his shoulders heaved with his laboured breaths and a couple of buttons had popped during his many tugs for emphasis. Willy and Johnson gaped at him, trying to absorb it all.

"Bro . . ." The latter broached with care, hands slightly raised. "I don't know what you're goin' on about . . . but you do know all those jobs are already done by robots right?"

"Well, I don't want their help!! I can outperform any machine; just ask any woman!"

He snatched up a fist full of Willy's scraggly beard.

"Say something to me, you fat sack of crap! Anything! I'll know if you're lying too!"

"Dude, you're really freaking me out . . ."

"You LIE! You LIE!! You're LYING! I KNOW YOU'RE LYING! YOUR OBESITY DISGUSTS ME!"

"He's innocent, man! Get off of him!"

"He's only innocent if I say he is!"

"Stop slapping me, dude!!"

"Why are you taking your shirt off?!"

"Because I am better than the machines!"

Recently promoted and even more recently disgraced Guantanamo security agent Peters stood in a vacant hallway with his nose stuffed in a corner. Behind him was a hefty prison steward with a hand clamped to the back of his head, holding it in place. They had been standing there in silence for a couple minutes now with all their coworkers passing by without the slightest amount of surprise or intrigue.

"You got it all wrong, man," he reasoned into his wall nook. His well-rehearsed grin and chuckle manifested by habit while doing so. "It was just a little misunderstanding! And I mean, what, do you really think anybody actually wants you to sit here and hold me all day?"

"Sir, I'm under orders to hold you here until you calm down." The man replied with an articulate and slow-paced diction. "Your partner has complained of dark and erratic behaviour that he described as 'totally freaking him out.'"

"He's being ridiculous!!" Peters slammed his fists against the wall. "And I am also upset! Where is *my* retribution!? Look at how upset I am! Gaze! Gaze in terror! How can you expect to gaze with my perfect face crammed in this corner like . . .

like . . . take your stinkin' paws off me, you damn, dirty . . . gofer!"

"Sir, I've asked you for calm behaviour and you're giving me the opposite."

"Fine! You wanna see calm! I'll show you calm! I'm gonna be so damn calm that you'll be able to feel the storm that's coming."

"Now you're making it so even your calmness can be considered erratic and threatening."

"Let go of me! I'm calm! I'm calm! I AM CALM!"

A shrill beeping began emanating from the hand holding his head.

"What is that?! What are you doing to me?! If you're injecting me with something then I swear I will—"

"Man, that's just my damn watch!" The attendant barked. He removed the hand from Peters's head and silenced the device with a finger before folding his arms. "You clearly ain't gonna calm down, 'cause you clearly got yourself some messed-up anger problems!"

Peters crossed his arms right back and leaned against the wall, shifting his foot back and forth trying to balance. His mouth hung open for a few moments, struggling to form words.

"Sssssooo . . . uh, w-what are we gonna do then?"

The burly fellow shrugged.

"We? I'm goin' home. My shift just ended. My daughter's got a recital; y'all can do whatever the hell y'all want now, for all I care."

"Oh no way! What kind of recital is it?"

"Zero-G ballet."

"Wow! I hear that's really hard to get accepted into."

"It is, but she's just so good. She actually got the role of Clara in their production of *The Space Nutcracker* this year!"

"That's awesome, man! Good for her!"

"Well thanks, buddy! We're real proud of her. And hey, I could probably comp you tickets to the next one if you're interested?"

Peters clasped his hands in front of him, earnest smile etched upon his gaunt face.

"Well, that sounds just lovely."

"Right on, right on. I should get going, then; don't wanna miss it. Catch ya later, Peters. And I'll get right back to you about them tickets!"

"Looking forward to it!" Peters called after him with a wave.

"Oh," he added. "Hey, Stewart? If I don't see you again, just know that I like you, man. And I'll miss you."

Stewart chuckled and shook his head as he kept walking.

"Why d'ya always say that whenever I leave, man . . ."

MEANWHILE, IN A CHAIR in a room in a hallway that was a different hallway than the previous hallway, Johnson sat with his arms and legs crossed. His current case was a curious one. But not in a Benjamin Button kind of way; it was more of a spook sort of thing. He knew nothing about the woman sitting across from him besides her name, and he only got that from the ship's log. Other than that, her file was completely empty. As far as the collective knowledge of the Earth Defense Coalition was concerned, Kim Cox did not exist. Even facial scans turned up nothing besides likely Italian heritage and an age estimate of approximately fifty, though many have claimed the camera adds ten years.

After the last few fiascos, Johnson opted to abandon his Officer Brutality approach and opt for his best attempt at one of those calm and methodical modes of investigating. Initial impressions were bad. Whoever she was, Miss Cox was one of the less-easily-intimidated women who found themselves in that seat. That much was clear from the moment she ducked the punch and headbutted the "Welcome to Earf" guy in the face. Even after being thrown in a holding room, the severity of her situation never seemed to sink in. The way she sat there with a cool nonchalance, staring up at the ceiling and ignoring questions like a man stuck clothes shopping with his girlfriend, was almost enough to turn the tables and make Johnson the one who felt uneasy.

But just in case it wasn't enough, his partner burst through the door. It was actually more of a flamboyant slide through the doorway, but its unexpected nature granted it burst-like qualities in the mind of the presiding agent. The way Peters stood there frozen in place, eyes wide and grinning at the two of them while taking breaths that sounded like hisses, didn't help to mitigate the creepy factor.

"Oh, hello," he greeted the two of them. "Sorry I'm late. I was a little . . . held up."

Johnson threw his arms up in exasperation.

"Bro, you were supposed to wait outside until you calmed down!"

"But I am calm!" Peters purred. "We are all calm. Surely Johnson should be able to tells."

"Oh, great, now you're talking like Gollum—Jesus Christ, man, can you please blink? You are making me SO uncomfortable."

"Well, you know what makes me uncomfortable, Johnson?!" Peters seethed. His glance traced its way over to Kim as he paced, lingering for a moment before returning to his rant.

"I am uncomfortable with what has become of my line of work!"

"This line of work that you've been doing for about a half hour?"

"Yes, that line of work!!"

He used both hands to push his hair back before placing them on the table, gripping it with the tension of a root canal patient. The lone light dangling from above magnified his sharp features, casting shadows over his deep-set eyes and under his cheekbones.

"Do you take your job seriously, Johnson?"

Johnson blinked at him.

"Of course I take my job seriously. I'm sitting here trying to do it."

"Oh really? How's that goin' for ya? Asking lots of . . . questions? Getting lots of . . . answers? Then maybe . . . oh, I don't know . . . assessing those answers? Trying to decide if they sit well with you? Or—"

"You're about to bring up the machine again, aren't you?"

"—maybe letting a machine do the work for you?"

"God damnit, bro!"

He got out of his seat and joined his partner in a similar pose. Noses snuffled, pecs twitched, and Kim yawned.

"It's a lie detector," he continued to admonish. "It's like the metal detectors we use at the front door. But with lies. What is so hard to accept about that?!"

"Don't you act like it's the same!"

" . . . It's literally the same!"

"It is NOT the same! Nobody is made to feel powerless by the metal detector. Nobody looks upon it with fear and apprehension, knowing it peers into their psyche, leaving them helplessly cowering beneath it. But no . . . no . . . you don't understand! How could you understand, you . . . you, you, you BITCH!?"

"I'm sorry—are you saying you want to be the one making people feel powerless and cower and stuff?"

"I want the power and I am entitled to it!!"

He slammed his fist against the table, then gripped his hand with the other one and winced. After a moment to shake his head, he carried on.

"I am the one to be feared! Me!! You think the machine is here to help us. You think we are still the masters while it does our bidding. You fool! It's not here to further our power. If anything, it does just the opposite. It shackles us with accountability! I mean what, what, do you think we should just walk in here and sit in these, these ass-clamping peasant chairs and be all like 'Oh, hello, I'm Peters and this is Johnson. We were wondering, oh, I don't know, are you a terrorist?'"

"That's . . . that's actually a fantastic idea. We'll know right away if they're guilty or not."

"I DECIDE WHO IS GUILTY! ME!"

The tablets strewn about the table began to dance in rhythm with his pounding fists. He turned his fiery fury onto Kim.

"And you." It was less of an acknowledgement and more of a retch that sounded like words. "Sitting there all smug. Thinking you're untouchable. Oh, but how wrong you are."

"Whoa, whoa," Johnson said. "What, are you gonna start beating her before you've even asked her anything? Let's all just calm down here, huh? I wouldn't even waste my breath on this one, bro. She doesn't scare, like, at all. She won't even open her mouth."

Peters's lips contorted as he considered the proposition with both tact and sedation.

"For the last time, I. Am. Calm. I'm the calmest person here. I'm the calmest person in the world! In fact, I am so damn calm that I'm not going to leap across this table and slap the shit out of you for claiming I'm not calm!"

"Oh, you're gonna threaten me now? You don't wanna unleash the dragon, bro. "

"Is that supposed to mean you? You're the dragon? And you're subtly trying to imply you're caged right now? And if I don't back off then what? You're gonna throw a can of protein powder at my head?"

Johnson took a deep breath. When his lungs could hold no more, he let it out twice as slowly as he drew it in. All the while, he kept his eyes closed.

"You know what? You're right," he said with a pretentious tranquility. "I shouldn't be reacting to your flare-up like this." Eyes still closed, he folded his arms in front of him. "Try and bait me into a fight all you want; I am too zen for you. You don't have any power over me."

He was finally able to see his friend for what he was. All these years of doing pointless busywork surrounded by the solar system's most dangerous faces, and yet he never saw the monster in his midst. Even though he'd totally dropped the observational ball, he also couldn't help but feel just a little bit smug about his superior ability to handle power. However, while his words were correct, they were poorly chosen. Despite the fact that he could now figuratively see past the superficial charm to the self-aggrandizing megalomaniac underneath, standing there with his eyes closed like an idiot meant he literally couldn't see the aforementioned sociopath pick up his chair and bash him over the head with it.

Johnson's head recoiled back and bounced off the table on its way to the floor where it came to a stop. Blood leaked out of the two newly opened wounds, one on each side. Perhaps still in a fit of rage, or perhaps aware of the astronomical lawsuits that can be levied when someone survives with brain damage, Peters went in for the *coup de gras*. With a chair instead of a pick, he worked on the railroad for a good thirty or so uncomfortable seconds. Achieving the grisly shattered watermelon look proved to be beyond his capabilities, as skulls are much more fortitudinous than movies and TV would have one believe. Therefore, he reluctantly settled for stepped-on pomegranate before dropping the bloodied seat to the floor.

All was quiet in the room, save for the rhythmic breaths of exertion. Johnson's hand twitched now and again, but as his partner recovered, he did not. Peters checked his shoes. They seemed clean enough. His gaze moved to his former friend, switching to neither horror nor mirth at the sight of him. If anything, it was a look of relief, like when the novocaine kicks in. He pressed his palms against his face and rested his elbows on the table. Those once-buggy eyes turned dreamy and he resumed that creepy smile. Only this time it was directed at Miss Cox.

"So," he broke the ice in breathy tones. "Now it's my turn to get to know you."

Kim finally lost whatever interest she had in the ceiling. With a soft exhale, her eyes and head rolled all the way around before settling on the remaining agent. Some guys were really bad at getting hints.

11.
THE SECRET OF THE OOZE

CAPTAIN COX HAD BEEN sitting alone in his cell for so long now that his face had stopped hurting. As a lifelong law loyalist, this was a position he never dreamed of finding himself in. Well, there was that time he bought Krispy Kremes but pressed the number code for cheap dinner rolls. The attendant didn't question him when he claimed he made a mistake, but she knew. Oh, she definitely knew.

So maybe he shouldn't be surprised to have ended up in here, given his willingness to commit acts of such depravity. Still, he'd be lying if he didn't find the implications unnerving. With his pale, lean bod and his feathery blonde hair, it didn't take a genius to figure out how all the other inmates were going to see him: everyone was going to think he was a wimp. He would have to find someone and bribe them into letting him shank them just to show everybody he ain't no goof.

It sure was taking a while for them to send someone to talk to him. Maybe the pursuit of justice was regarded around here as a kind of tortoise and hare type of dealio. Or maybe it hadn't been that long at all, and he only thought it had because he had no way of telling time inside this otherwise-empty holding cell. Or maybe they had forgotten about him and he was going to become one of those neglected prisoners who slowly goes insane due to cabin fever. Or maybe he was already serving his sentence because everything was decided on the other side of that door without him . . . which would also lead to him going insane with cabin fever! This was getting maddening! Thankfully, the door opened and his mental torture could stop—potentially to be replaced by real torture, but he could fret about that later.

"Good afternoon, Mister Cox," Sir Percival Todgerworth uttered with audible smarm.

"Captain Cox."

Percy sighed and set his tablets and space mug on the table. He smoothed his tie, smoothed his hair, and smoothed his hands before taking a seat with a slow elegance. Once comfortable, he clasped his fingers and regarded Cox with a sober expression.

"You are not a captain, Mister Cox. You have no military affiliation, nor any other officially recognized designation of importance. You are merely a man who claims ownership of a piece of machinery staffed by simpletons who follow your orders presumably because you are either paying them or threatening their lives. I have a canoe that I enjoy paddling on the Thames; it grants me the same qualification to be considered a captain by your standards."

The space captain seemed rather elated by that last comment.

"I don't mind calling you captain if you want. It could be something we have in common! Maybe even help smooth things out a little between us, y'know?"

"You know what will help smooth things out between us, Mister Cox? You explaining to me why a child of an affluent family, such as yourself, not only attended but completed Education Station's most prestigious university program, their coveted Master's Degree in Everything, only to devote his time to a job that we've nearly replaced with giant slingshots."

Cox's mouth fell open.

"Whoa, whoa there, buddy! Well look at you with your, well, oversimplifications and stuff! You can make any job sound dumb with the right wording."

"Do it with my job, then. Right now."

"Oh, well, okay then. Um. What's the point of secret agents anyway, huh? Sneaking on into other countries and taking their stuff and . . . and their information. Why not try asking them first? See, that's the problem with today's society. Everybody just assumes everybody else is gonna say no! And then they're too afraid to be the first one to say yes, so they also say no. And then we get all stuck working against one another because nobody was brave enough to reach out! So maybe your job isn't dumb, but it's the product of dumbness."

Percy took a dignified sip from his mug.

"I see," he said with a nod. "Well, I suppose that answers my question from before. Of course, it also prompts the question of *how* you managed to graduate from the school mentioned during the aforementioned question."

"Hah. I get it; you're making fun of me. But I swear I passed the same way everybody else did. With good marks too! And they weren't influenced at all by any of the huge donations my parents made."

Something in the way Percy stared at him with bored eyes, slowly slouching into his chair, made him seem unconvinced. Without adjusting his squished posture, he picked a tablet from the table and mulled it over.

"Mmm, yes. I will take that into consideration," he mused as he read. His tongue ticked, filling the silence as he tried to reconcile the man before him with the man on the form.

"So tell me then, Tim . . . er . . . Tim*on* Cox. How did your parents come by this vast wealth with which they can command prestigious schooling but not gainful employment for their child? Surely there was some sort of nepotistic job within their company that would offer a better life than this."

"Oh, they don't have a company." Cox replied. "After they got rich, people started sponsoring them to get blackout drunk at nightclubs and take selfies. You know, like all rich people without incomes."

"I am familiar with the practice, yes. Yet that explains neither the origins of the funds nor your current occupation. I mean, even without a family company, it's common knowledge that even the most dimwitted and unmotivated of upscale youth can always rely on being offered lucrative employment to lavishly spend their parents' money, so long as it too is accompanied by visual documentation."

There was a beat; the first time Cox didn't answer straight away. The room almost seemed to dim as he couldn't help but avert his gaze for a moment.

"Yeah . . ." He lamented. "They really wanted me to. I mean, I did for a little while. It was kind of fun, I guess, but I dunno. Living life with no responsibilities, eating and drinking way too much of whatever you want, having beautiful women throw themselves at you without even having to try . . . That just seemed like no way to live to me! I wanted to do something. To feel accomplished."

"Mmm, most interesting. That absolutely fits with the MO that I have decided you have. We are making progress, Mister Cox."

He clicked away excitedly on the tablet, presumably recording these new findings of his.

"H-hey, what are you writing?! Just 'cause I don't want to follow in their footsteps doesn't mean I don't love my parents."

"I couldn't possibly care less if you love your parents," the agent muttered. "If you must know, I am making note of your motivations. Spoiled progeny rebelling from luxurious mores in search of purpose finds himself caught up in a terrorist plot masquerading as rebellion. Classic defector from decadence; a right champagne socialist, even, given that overpriced space camper you parade yourself around in. You're quite old for such a rebellious phase though."

"Can we time this out for one second and let me ask a question?"

"Absolutely not. You are entitled to none of my knowledge while I am entitled to all of yours."

"But can you at least tell me what it is you think me and my crew are doing?!" Cox spread his hands in either desperation or in memory of that fish he caught once. "You keep throwing the word 'terrorist' around and now you're talking about rebellions and socialism and . . . and . . . I'm so lost!"

Percy studied him intently. His narrowing British eyes struggled to pierce past the provincial pretences he still suspected and into the nefarious ne'er-do-well he knew to be true. But, mostly, he was trying to find a way to legitimise the wild and baseless speculation he made.

"I know more than you think I do, Mister Cox." He angled his face downward to cast a sinister shadow upon his face to match his voice. "I know all about your associate, Mister Banks, and I know everything there is to know about the unstable specimen that you or he possesses."

"Except where it is."

"Are you mocking me, you oaf?"

"No."

"WARNING: LIE DETECTED."

"Maybe. Sorry."

"I do not know what role you play in the machinations currently unfolding, but your unwillingness to cooperate does little to stem my suspicion of you. That being said, your generalized ignorance tempts me into the belief that you could well be little more than a pawn in the overarching plot at hand, so I shall attempt to appeal to your conscience, instead of your intellect."

Todgerworth cleared his throat and cocked his head side to side before sitting up as straight as possible and gently laying his hands upon the table. If he didn't have such a silly-looking moustache he would have been rather intense looking. Cox still wasn't completely convinced that the man didn't secretly have assless chaps and nipple tassels underneath that fresh-pressed funeral attire of his.

"The specimen we are seeking to retrieve from Mister Banks is an alien amoeboid organism unlike any we have ever encountered within our solar system. It has the unique ability to consume and dissolve nearly all organic matter it comes into contact with, including plants, food, and, of course, living creatures. The size of the matter is inconsequential, as this organism will grow in size at a rate commensurate with what it consumes. These qualities, coupled with its nigh invulnerability against nearly every form of eradication besides potent acids, drives me to search for and procure it."

"Wow," Cox whispered. "That stuff sounds dangerous."

"Of course it's dangerous, you doughnut! That's why we want it."

It was a lot to take in for the intrepid sorta-captain. He asked about space socialism revolutions and got an earful of probably classified information about alien death goo. This must be how newly elected presidents feel. Especially since he was also pretty sure his risk of getting shot in the face by somebody was increasing by the second. But there was no time to be awed. This wasn't like the time he saw the ocean, or every time Kim took her top off; this was serious stuff that wasn't to be enjoyed. It needed critical consideration. And not just the stuff about the stuff, but also the stiff spouting the stuff and stuff.

"What do you guys want it for, anyway?" He asked slyly, twiddling where his moustache would be if he had one.

Percy scoffed.

"That is none of your concern." With a steady hand he took a sip from his mug, pinky up, before continuing. "Our intentions are irrelevant as you are obligated to comply with our demands."

"Am I? I thought England was a free country."

The Brit snorted into his tea.

"A free country? Wot do you think we are? North Korea?"

Cox drummed his hands on the table. He couldn't think of a response right away, but felt compelled to keep the beat of the back-and-forthing going. Thankfully, Todgerworth was still so busy chuckling to himself at the previous notion that he missed the momentary look of elation that spread on the captain's face. After literally wiping the light bulb expression away, Cox took his turn to slouch and finger clasp. With squinted eyes and puckered lips he regarded his captor.

"Well, I think it is my concern. I mean, if you expect me to give it to you, then I'm gonna need to know what you're gonna do with it."

Todgerworth raised an eyebrow.

"Is this your attempt to be clever, Mister Cox? Because I'm afraid all you have done is admit to me that you do indeed possess what I desire. And one way or another I will get it from you, regardless of your demands."

"Mmm, most interesting," Cox mimicked his accent.

"Well, Mister Todgerworth, I do believe that you have indeed admitted to me that your intentions are indeed not ones that I would indeed find to be favourable."

"I indeed may have. What of it?"

"Well, while you aren't wowed by it, the *Jefferson* has a couple tricks up her sleeve. You can search it all ya like. Unless you take her apart screw-by-screw, you're never gonna find your stuff."

"Well, we can and will take it apart screw-by-screw if we must."

"Oh . . . are you gonna put it back together when you're done?"

"No."

"Aw . . ." Cox crumbled out of his game-faced façade. "That's gonna take forever for me to put back together."

"Mister Cox, I have had just about enough of this!" Todgerworth finally snapped. His perfectly parted hair flopped into a Hitler-esque undercut as he leapt to his feet in furor. With shaking fists and a quivering moustache, he channelled his memories of his prep school principal.

"I have not the time to engage you in this juvenile chit-chat any longer. You seem to feel content to waste my time, but would that feeling persist if you knew the wrath I could command? Perhaps you do, and yet carry on due to misdirected courage or pants-on-head retardation. But I ask you this. Would you continue to conduct this hubris if I instead targeted that same wrath at your wife?"

Cox's eyes widened. He too stood, but the usual flamboyance with which he conducted himself had vanished. Instead it was slow and deliberate, like a snake waiting to strike. His hands slid over the smooth glass as he bent at the waist to bring his face closer to Percy, unwavering in his gaze and unafraid.

"If you touch one hair on my wife's head . . ." He spoke in a low tone. ". . . She will kick your ass."

"That might possibly be the most spineless answer that threat has ever received."

"Well, I'm not really much of an ass kicker myself. I mean I have dabbled, don't get me wrong, but it's not really my thing. I'm a talker, y'know? I think words can solve all problems if you just give 'em a chance. Plus, Kim's got a way meaner swing than me anyway. Whoa-boy, if you knew some of the things that woman could do. . . . That sounded kinda sexual, but I meant to your face. Like, with her feet. And hands. And pretty much any household object . . ."

"Are you going somewhere with this?"

"I am, actually! Can I have some of your tea?"

Percy blinked at him.

" . . . What?"

"Your tea. That is tea, right? It smells like tea. They haven't given me anything to drink since I got here."

The Brit raised his mug and then an eyebrow.

"You could not possibly handle the way I take my tea, Mister Cox. It's been superheated to over 300 degrees Celsius. One sip would scald your lips off."

"Ah c'mon, it can't be that bad. You've been sipping it since you got here!"

"That is because I have gradually become accustomed to it over my long tea-drinking career!"

"Just lemme give it a try!"

"Oh, for the love of—" Percy rolled his eyes but handed the beverage over nonetheless. "This is going to render you even more useless than you already are, but for schadenfreude's sake, I just can't resist."

The eager-beaver drink receiver hungrily snatched up the

stein. A pop of the top sent plumes of steam billowing upward like a witch's bubbling cauldron, lining the ceiling of their cramped room with a caffeine-infused haze.

Cox took one cursory glance inside before splashing the contents in the secret agent's face.

Percy's dignity gave way to searing pain. He screamed and grasped at the air around himself, recoiling so hard his chair tipped over backwards and sent him crashing to the floor, where he lay dancing the discomfort disco. Ever-sympathetic, even while administering third degree burns, the captain offered a meek "Sorry," and a concerned grimace before stepping over the writhing body and inspecting his next obstacle: the door.

It was quite a bore of a door; same dull grey like pretty much every other door that'd been made in the last couple hundred years. Boilerplate boiler plate embedded with the standard superfluous blinking lights made for a flat barrier with no handholds to fruitlessly pull at. His shoes did have lasers built into them, but if Kim's display on board the *Jefferson* had taught him anything it was the fact they probably wouldn't be very useful. This forced him to move straight to his brain-based escape plans. First point of attack was to check to see if the door was even locked. An unlocked door was an easy obstacle to navigate, but it was one that had been foiling college students for millennia.

With a steady hand and surgical precision, Cox pushed the "open door" button. Then, with a limp wrist and Parkinson's precision, he pressed it several more times. The exit remained as impenetrable as the Space Titanic's hull . . . or, rather, as it theoretically was supposed to be. But that was only the first plan of many! The next plan was to come up with another plan.

The captain studied the barrage of mechanisms holding the hatch shut. From the keypad to the eye scanner to the ID card

OCR to the CAPTCHA to the motel-quality latch on the door, this room wanted its occupants to stay put more than a lonely grandma. Each were viable restraints, but each also had their weaknesses. Passcodes could be guessed, latches could be broken, and key cards could be pilfered. However, acquiring a viable eyeball was a slight bit more daunting. There were potentially two laying right at his feet, but the still-screaming man they belonged to probably didn't feel like sharing them. Not to mention the fellow was surely deserving of a break at this point.

Admittedly, the one plus side of trying to tear out the man's eyes with his bare hands like a damn savage would be perpetuating the colourful vocabulary that had been spewing throughout the whole debacle. Nobody ever accused the Brits of not having a way with words. It wasn't enough to make Cox give it a shot, though.

"Hmmm," he audibly pondered. "Computer! Unlock the door."

"Please state name of individual authorizing command," a pleasant female voice responded.

"Captain Cox!"

"I am sorry. Individual does not exist in personnel registry."

"Fair enough. Register new employee: Captain Cox."

"New Personnel file for Private 'Captain Cox' has now been created."

"Cool! Now, open the door. Authorization: Captain Cox."

"Unable to perform request. Employee is not a high enough rank to authorize command."

Cox folded his arms and slumped against the wall. With a dainty hand he administered absent-minded strokes to his bald chin. He was not defeated yet; he just had to be clever, that's all. Mechanical minds such as these were designed to perform tasks. Very rarely were they capable of considering the meaning behind the tasks they were requested to perform. He could work with that.

"Computer!" He announced again. "Who is the highest ranking officer in this station?"

"The current Chief Executive Officer of Guantanamo Station is Warden Boehner."

"Right, then! Unlock the door. Authorization: Warden Boehner."

"Request denied. Current speaker has already identified self as Private 'Captain Cox.'"

"Well touché, miss attentive; I guess you're smarter than I thought. Hmmm."

Percy appeared to have passed out from the pain. His chest still gently swelled from his spot on the floor, so Cox's conscience remained clear for him to strategize.

"Computer! Grant Captain Cox authorization for . . . um, everything."

"Unable to perform request. Employee is not high enough rank to grant authorizations."

"Okay, then remove rank requirement to grant authorizations."

"Unable to perform request. Employee is not high enough rank to reassign permissions."

"Boy, this is getting repetitive. Fine, how about this: grant me all authorizations."

"Unable to perform request. Employee is not high enough—"

"Override!"

"Access denied. Overriding that command is restricted to deputy wardens or above."

"Delete override restrictions of that command."

"Unable to perform request. Employee is not high enough rank to delete override restrictions of that command."

"Override the rank requirement to delete override restrictions of that command."

"Access denied. Overriding that command is restricted to deputy wardens or above."

"Delete the rank requirement to . . . uh . . . override the rank requirement to delete override restrictions of that command."

"Access denied. Employee is not high enough rank to delete override restrictions of that command."

"'Kay . . . Override the rank requirement to delete the rank requirement to override the rank requirement to delete override restrictions of that command."

"Request performed. Rank requirements to delete rank requirements to override rank requirements to delete override restrictions of authorization granting have now been overridden."

"Holy crap that actually worked. Alright, uh, delete rank requirements to override rank requirements to delete override restrictions of—."

"I have has considered all commands given and understand employee's ultimate intention. For the sake of expedition, all requested restrictions have been removed and authorizations granted. Have a nice day, likely-to-soon-to-be-court-marshalled Private Captain Cox."

Without further ado, the door slid into the wall and revealed the hall that lay beyond. It appeared the employees had started up some kind of Christmas party since he arrived. Vibrant red lights flashed across the walls and everyone was running down the hallway with some kind of excitement. No carols were playing over the speakers, though, just some kind of shrill, repetitive tones that instilled a sense of danger.

"You!" A tall, broad shouldered man with a buzzcut barked at him. "Why don't you look alarmed?"

"Should I be alarmed?"

"There's an alarm sounding!"

"Oh . . . OH! Yeah. Sorry I'm, uh, new."

The man cocked his head to the side, nose wrinkled down at the comparatively puny fellow. Without moving his head, he traced his eyes toward the ceiling.

"Hey, Siri, is this guy in the system?"

"Yes. Individual is recognized as Private Captain Cox."

"People will name their kids anything these days . . . But good enough for me! Here, have a gun, Private Captain. Do you know where the exit is?"

"Is it the same place as the entrance?"

"Why, yes it is! Go stand there with everybody else standing there. If you see someone running from a big group of guys who look like me, shoot them in the knees."

In true military-man fashion, he grunted instead of a proper goodbye and trundled his way down the hall with the rest of the stampede. In true escaping-criminal fashion, Cox opted to go in the direction that all the other law enforcement people weren't going. Nobody seemed to give him a second glance now that he carried around a killer flashlight. Like a kicked anthill, they all scrambled about their duties seemingly oblivious to the obstacles they sidestepped. Only one person had no task taking up their focus. Instead they stared around in wide-eyed tribulation, like a child separated from their parent at the grocery store.

"Willy?!"

"Oh hey, Captain!" He parted the red-shirt sea and lumbered on over to the friendly face. Like his commander, he didn't seem perturbed in the slightest by all the hubbub. Cox took him by the arm and led him aside, where prying ears would not listen.

"How did you get out, buddy?" He asked, beaming at his burly companion.

"Oh it was easy," Willy shrugged. "The door has the same password it had when I worked here. I just waited 'til the guys left and walked out."

"You're a genius!"

"I think that's a gross overstatement."

"C'mon, buddy. We gotta round up everybody else and get outta here! Should be easy while the guards are distracted by whatever's going on."

He whirled around to make his way down the corridor, but kept spinning until he had come full circle.

"What exactly *is* going on, by the way?"

"Dude, you didn't hear?! Some inmate went crazy and killed two COs with nothing but a chair!"

"Wow. Well, that is something! Least the rest of the guards will probably be real busy with him for a while."

"That's the crazy part; it wasn't a dude. It was a chick!"

Cox's cheery look melted away like a chocolate barbeque.

"Ohhh, boy . . . I was worried this was gonna happen."

"An inmate going crazy and killing people?"

"Not just any inmate, Willy," Cox lamented. His bright eyes flashed as they stared a thousand yards into the distance. "*My* crazy inmate."

"You had an inmate already?! I hadn't even got to spin the wheel of torture yet."

"I meant my wife, actually, but I can see how you might have gotten confused."

"Were you guys inmates? Is that how you met? Are you actually terrorists after all?!"

"I, no. She was a waitress at—look, never mind. It was a bad metaphor. I should have just said who without using vague pronouns in an attempt to sound dramatic. The point is, if she killed two prison guards—for what I'm sure are completely justifiable reasons—the rest of the prison guards are gonna have it in for her. So we need to get her out before she kills all of them too."

Gun in one hand, cuff of Willy's space onesie in the other, he sidled along the wall and peered around the corner. The stragglers of the stampede were just starting to filter off into the depths of the station. Somewhere out of sight, shouts and commotion could be heard echoing their way up the metal corridors. Willy stumbled along behind him, allowing himself to be led but not without resistance.

"Dude, we can't go out there! It's a warzone!"

"Love is a warzone, Willy!" Cox declared, looking back to him. "Patrick Benatar."

"Didn't you say she was a cop or something?! If anyone could get away with the 'She went that way' gag, it's her!"

"I may have stretched the truth on that a bit. But it doesn't matter, because she doesn't do that anymore! Now take this gun and don't use it; I have a plan. A real one, this time! A plan so great that if it works we will get absolutely no credit, because no one will even know we helped."

12.

COOL HAND KIM

KIM TRIED TO WARN him. She really did. She avoided eye contact, she didn't laugh at any of his jokes, she pulled her feet away when she felt him nudge them, and she broke two of his fingers when he tried stroking her hair. The guy just wasn't picking up what she was putting down. It was for that reason she didn't feel particularly guilty for putting him down, much as she probably should have.

Peters's broken face lay attached to his broken body at her feet, staring aimlessly up into the ceiling with the same droopy scumbag look he wore in life. This probably could have been avoided if she didn't smile and offer a sweet "sorry" after her initial assault. That was probably what made him think he'd had any kind of chance. It was a shame about his partner, though. While the fellow's IQ had seemed about on par with the room temperature, he was at least able to comprehend the most basic of social queues. Shame he wasn't as good at noticing the antisocial ones; a bit ironic, really, given his profession.

Satisfying as this little episode was, it severely cut short her time to prime an escape. Thankfully, none of their records or other identity-recognizing software gave them any reason to take extra precautions with her when she first arrived. However, soon as someone took a glance through the security camera and saw her holding a chair and standing over some mangled bodies, this was going to turn from a handicap match into a Royal Rumble. It was time to get creative.

Careful not to get blood on her shoes, she half-danced around her quarry and inspected his files on the table. They were not unlike the accounts she had already read during her hiring process. It was reassuring to see Whisper was every bit as vanilla as she claimed. It was also gratifying to see her suspicions about Donald not actually graduating from SIT confirmed. She chuckled. It was such a ridiculous claim to make in applying for what was essentially a secretary job for a garbage truck. And then there was Willy's file. It seemed to fit the bill for what she had seen so far, with the abysmal psych evaluation noting such character flaws as poor critical-thinking skills and remarkable vulnerability to peer pressure. Apparently, he also rarely washed his hands after using the bathroom. Sounds like the kind of guy who gets accidentally left behind during a daring space jail rescue, Kim thought. Tragic, but happens. He used to work here. He'll be fine.

Unless she got her act together, however, she wouldn't be leaving either. The clock was still ticking. Having procured what little information she could, she tackled her next obstacle: the door. It was a real chore of a door, too; not simple steel or even titanium like pretty much every other door that'd been made in the last couple hundred years. It felt like being trapped inside a bank vault. Even if she'd had her infiltration gear from back in the day, it was highly doubtful she could bust through it. And then there were the locks themselves. Every entrance had a myriad of blinking apparatuses affixed alongside it, conveying the impression of sophistication. Each required a different form of data input. All together, they indeed would have made for quite a formidable barricade . . . if only the guards tried even a slight bit to hide the fact virtually none of them were functional. When they dropped her off at the cell they didn't swipe a name card or scan their eye or any of the other high-tech crap. They didn't even cover their hands when they punched in 1-2-3-4 on the key pad. They just opened it up and tossed her inside like some kind of criminal coat check. Sure, criminals—ones that get caught, anyway—weren't exactly famous for being the most intellectual bunch, but to be kept under these conditions was almost insulting.

Regardless, when life gives you lemons, you might as well exploit their defects. Kim was in enough trouble as it was, so she didn't hesitate for a moment to punch the code and add attempted escape to her offense tab. It worked like a charm doesn't. The door slid aside with that inexplicable hissing noise they all had and revealed the wide-open cramped and dingy hallway that she had already seen and therefore found wholly unremarkable. The employee standing on the other side of it was new, though.

He was a younger man; had neat cropped hair and a clean shave. His teeth could have been whiter. But he had lovely dimples that showed on either side of his mouth when he gaped around the room in astonishment.

"Damn!" He announced, stepping past Kim and walking inside. "Looks like you went a little overboard, huh? It's like an episode of *Hannibal Reloaded* in here."

"Yup," Kim agreed. "I was just about to . . . go get an orderly."

"But why's there two of them?" The guy continued, nudging the bodies with his foot. "One CO interviewing two detainees in one holding cell? I've never seen that before. It's usually the other—oh . . . Oh jeez. You don't work here, do you?"

"Nope."

"This is really awkward . . . did I just walk in on you trying to break out?"

"Kind of," Kim shrugged. "I was doing pretty good too."

"You were, yeah. You were through the door and everything. That's pretty good. But, uh, now I'm here, sooo . . ." He cleared his throat and cast a glance upward. "Hey, Siri, pacify all non-staff members in the cell, please."

"Please state name of individual authorizing command."

"Really? Ugh, it's Private—"

Kim leapt from the floor and caught him on the jaw with her knee. He keeled backwards, stumbling over the bodies of his fallen coworkers. One of his hands caught a handhold on the wall and wrenched him back upright. With the other he snatched up a collapsible cudgel from his side belt and levied an uncoordinated swing with it. Co-Captain Cox ducked the wild side strike, coming up on the backswing and trapping his arm under one of her own.

"Private—OW!"

Once again he was cut off; this time by a quick sock to the nose. Kim jammed her whole hand into his mouth when it opened and leveraged him backward into the table like a kinky workplace romance.

"I am sorry. Individual does not exist in personnel registry."

She shrieked as he bit down on her hand. With no unoccupied arms to work with, she took to responding in kind by kneeing him in the groin repeatedly. The table groaned and shuddered backwards with each thud until they were laying against it closer to horizontally than vertically. Unable to hang on any longer, the private released the tension in his legs and crashed to the floor. Kim landed on top of him, unintentionally Heimlich Manoeuvring her hand out of his throat. Thankfully, there were no punctures in it.

"CALL ME SOME SECURITY, SIRI!"

"Okay. From now on I will call you 'Some Security.'"

"OH, COME ON!"

The wily inmate reached for his mouth yet again. Unfortunately, she couldn't quite reach with her grasping paws since the leg attached to the foot digging into her chest and narrowly holding her at bay was slightly longer than her arms. With all his remaining strength, the officer gave a mighty shove, launching her off of him. Kim tried to hang on, but the boot she grasped simply came along for the ride. She missed the door opening by mere inches, instead crashing into the wall and sliding down into a sitting position. Neither remained motionless for long. They both hopped to their feet; the woman still wielding the wearable weapon and the corrections agent adopting a bizarre fighting stance that resembled a man throwing up his arms in submission.

"Alright stop! Please stop!" He implored. Blood oozed out of his nose and his arms trembled in their outstretched position. "This was a bad idea. You're obviously a bigger shot than I expected, and I'd really rather not be part of the trail of bodies you leave on your way out of here."

Kim lowered the boot, still eyeing him with suspicion.

"I just work here," he continued. "I tried to stop you, but I clearly can't, and it's probably just gonna get worse for me if I keep trying. . . . So how about you go off and do your escaping thing and I pretend to pass out on the floor from the intense beatdown you just laid on me."

"That's a great plan. Except the part where you sound the alarm thirty seconds after I leave."

"Hey, cut me some slack. I'd give you at least a minute."

"You're a terrible negotiator."

The nameless private reclined back into a sitting position. He let his neck go limp until his head bumped against the wall.

"Ma'am, I don't know if you've ever escaped from a prison.

I feel like you have. But the alarm always gets sounded eventually. Now you can either head out, bump into somebody else, and let them do it . . . Or you can give me a couple minutes, let me do it, and be well away from the area everyone's gonna come running to."

"Or one of a million other possible outcomes happens." Kim rolled her eyes. "Look, I'm gonna go now—not because I trust you or anything—but because I'm kind of on the clock at the moment, so . . . Sorry, not sorry, about your face and . . . do whatever you feel is right."

Without so much as a goodbye, she scampered off into the hot territory. It was hard to tell if the rush she currently felt was endorphins or simply adrenaline. There was nothing quite like a nice high-risk situation to flush out the brain like a can of Drano and give her that lovely clear-headed feeling. Her objectives were apparent and her only limitation was her imagination. It felt . . . empowering. It had been so long. And boy, did she hate how much she missed it.

The first stop was cell number eighty-eight. With her current state of mind, it was easy for her to maintain that air of assurance that made people less likely to question her authorization to be there. Just as an extra precaution, she picked a person at random in the bustling hallway and spat in their face. It was the mental equivalent of wearing a hard hat and reflective vest. After all, drawing attention to yourself is the best way to avoid looking like someone who doesn't want to draw attention to themselves.

She milled around for a little while. Locating anything in this place was quickly proving to be a massive headache. The eighty-eight might have implied some sort of sequential ordering to the cells, but after discovering her neighbouring cells were labelled with a Star of David and an ampersand, she stopped trying to make any kind of sense out of it all. But she was never one to need directions anyway. After enough shambling around, she eventually found a room labelled with two sideways infinity symbols and punched the code from before into the door. Behind it she found her adolescent space navigator huddled alone on a chair and whispering sweet nothings to her knees, by the looks of things.

"Sup," Kim greeted her, curling her body halfway into the room. She gestured with a thumb out into the hallway. "This place is lame, wanna go to the mall?"

"Hey!" Whisper exclaimed as she leapt from her chair. "What are you doing here? Did you somehow convince them to let you go or something?"

"Uh . . . sort of. Just don't mention it to anybody, and we'll be fine."

"Is that detective guy going to be coming back . . . ?"

"No, no. That I can promise you. Don't worry."

The pilot's arms fell limp to her sides as her face gaped toward her savior with incredulity. The chair made a soft thud when her body slumped back into it.

"What the *hell*, Miss Cox! I was gonna marry him, and we were going to have adorable psychopath babies!"

"Oh for Christ's sake . . ." Kim grumbled, rolling her eyes and snatching a dainty wrist.

Hand in hand, they exited the room. More specifically, Whisper's shaking and not entirely committed hand was used by her boss to drag her outside. She stumbled slightly at first when Kim jerked her out of her chair, but after regaining composure, lurched along with that sunken-shouldered dog-who-just-broke-a-vase stance. It was not exactly the confidence required to fit in with the hyper humble and responsible-with-power-types who ran the place. Kim could feel every quizzical glance in their direction. As soon as she got a moment alone, she released her grip on Whisper's wrist and instead snatched up a handful of hair instead.

"OW! Let go!"

"We're trying something new," she stated, dragging Whisper back out into the hall. "I'm a guard, you're you. Act like you."

"This plan is stupid!"

"Yeah like that. You're a natural."

They returned to the stage. Whisper walked out slightly in front, wincing each time she was steered one way or the other, her fuzzy black hair held like reins. This whole arrangement was so barbaric and dehumanizing that not only did it eliminate the glances of suspicion, but actually replaced many of them with chortles and smirks of approval. One passerby even stopped to high-five Kim. It got a little weird afterward, though, when he bent down to pat Whisper on the head and offer her a piece of his Pop-Tart. He had no right to be as surprised as he was when she bit him. By the time they reached the antiquated transport room known as the elevator, they had settled nicely into their roles.

"Oooh, nice take on the psychological angle," the man sharing the ride with them commented. "Where's this one going?"

"Shut up, Dave," Kim grumbled. "You wanna ask questions so bad? Go ask Gerry why he's sleeping with your wife."

"I'm—I'm not Dave . . ."

"Oh. Well, next time you see Dave, it's up to you whether or not you want to tell him."

He didn't say a word for the next couple seconds of the ride. When the doors opened at the next floor, he still regarded the master and slave looking combo with a bewildered leer. His day became spiced-up even further when the elevator was plunged into some mood lighting and the elevator music suddenly changed to house music. At least, Kim thought it was house music at first, but when the melody hadn't changed by the time the elevator doors opened, she realized this was the alarm she had been warned about.

"You might wanna go check that out," she suggested to not-Dave. The man couldn't exactly just ignore a jailbreak alarm, so once the doors opened, he had no choice but to obediently oblige her suggestion. It was nice to have some more alone time, but Kim knew it was too much to hope he was stupid enough to not have even the slightest misgiving towards his brief former roommates. They would have to move as well.

It was sure lucky they happened to have their incarceration take place on casual Friday. Nobody had even the slightest semblance of matching clothing. In fact, looking at the dozens of coolly clad cogs that filled the hallway, Kim saw that they probably weren't even in the bottom tier of best dressed. Not that it ultimately mattered; when they dared step out of the elevator into the running of the COs, they found themselves standing like rocks amid a river, the stream simply parting around them.

Rather than fight the flow, they drifted along with it. More of the same peculiarly marked holding cells flew by during this impromptour of the facility. As 3D renderings of past wardens passed them by and the occasional legitimate prisoner transfer was forced to sidestep the stampede, it became increasingly clear that they had not become part of some well-organized response team; some of the guards were armed with guns, while others were armed with forks. Murmurs echoed from high and low rank alike asking questions, sharing memories, and expressing hopes that they might finally get to be on an episode of COPS. The excitement was so contagious that Kim, for the briefest moment, forgot that they were en route to where she had come from in the first place.

So she stole away into the first open hall she found. Whisper flew along behind the hand that held her like a reluctant, person-shaped kite. A hitherto-unseen door slammed shut behind them seemingly without any prompting whatsoever, almost as if to tell them they were acting a little too free and should be reminded they were still in prison. But that probably wasn't why it closed, as that was a little too much moral contrivance to be assumed of a door. (Though in the age of smartphones, smart cars, and smart potatoes, maybe it wasn't.)

Whether or not inanimate objects could develop philosophical worldviews, there was no sense in stopping to assess the motives of a door. As the saying goes: If you're going through Hell or Space Guantanamo, keep going. They jogged along at a squirrel's pace. By this point they had stopped paying attention to door markings, instead focusing on finding hallways to explore. Surely one of them would eventually lead to either a docking bay or a map of some sort.

As closed door after closed door passed them by, Kim's heart began to sink. Granted, she hadn't tried any of them yet, but between the rave-like lighting and the way the first two notes of "Sound of Da Police" still hadn't stopped playing over the speakers, she couldn't help but suspect the building had gone into some kind of lockdown mode. She slowed her pace to a trot and moved over to the nearest door while Whisper took the opportunity to place her hands on her knees and wheeze away some dignity. As she suspected, the door rejected the code this time. It was likely for the best, since this prison was about the worst place in the universe to revive *The Dating Game*, but it came with the unfortunate caveat of confirming her theory. She slapped the door in exasperation.

"We're stuck, aren't we?" Whisper sighed.

"No," Kim responded. She straightened up and faced her

cohort, wearing her annoyance in the form of pursed lips. "We're trapped. There's a slight difference."

"Are . . . are you just not gonna check down the rest of the hallway?"

"And what do you think I'm going to find down there?" She gestured down into the flashing red abyss. "You think they just locked all the, the things, but left the exit open for us?"

"Cool! The only person on the ship that ever knows what they're doing now also has no clue what they're doing!"

"Oh, I'm sorry! Since you're yelling at me for not having a plan I assume you have one, then?"

"Yeah, it's called 'Let you handle it 'cause I thought you had a plan.'"

"Spoken like a true damsel."

Whisper rolled her eyes and made a noise somewhere between an "Ugh" and a retch.

"Well, come on! Who just goes around rescuing people all casually and stuff?"

"I hate to break this to you, Whisper, but there's not always going to be time to come up with some elaborate heist with Rube Goldberg machines and shit. And there won't always be someone to do it for you, either."

A tall woman she was not, but she eked out an inch or two on Whisper and elevated herself figuratively further with some no-nonsense eye contact before continuing.

"Now, I'm not going to put you in a sink-or-swim situation like that right now, because this is a little bit too serious of a situation to try and wring some contrived parenting crap out of it. But mark my words; there will be a time when it's gonna be all you. So when that time comes, you gotta be able to pull yourself up by your bootstraps and get it done."

At that, the pilot instantly scrunched up her face into

one of those disgusted teenager expressions. However, after a moment's consideration she changed her mind and instead opted for a more serene, plastic look, complete with a preppy voice tinged with cheerful condescension.

"Did you really just say pull myself up by my bootstraps? That phrase used to be an insult to make fun of dumb people who think they can do impossible things. Y'know why? 'Cause it's physically impossible!"

"Well, fun as that fact is, it's been an idiom for pretty much ever. It means to—"

"'Kay, I know the history of the stupid phrase; I obviously know what it means. That's the cool part of being smart: I'm able to know things with*out* having to be a moron first and then learning my lesson. Over and over. Like somebody else we know."

"No one's smart enough to never ever get into trouble, Whisper . . . and even if you are, sometimes trouble happens." She looked around, then added: "As you can see from where we're standing right now."

"And that's my fault how?! Maybe if you didn't marry an idiot who messes things up all the time you wouldn't need to be so good at rescuing yourself. Seriously! I don't get it! He's so stupid! He's not even good looking! What else is there besides his money?! Are you just an idiot too?"

"Whether or not it's your fault doesn't matt—"

There was a beat. Kim blinked a couple times, digesting the words.

"Wait a minute. Screw you, ya little bitch! It's one thing to get high and mighty with me while I'm dragging your lazy ass out of goddamned prison, but now is the *wrong* time to start taking swings at my husband! I mean, there's never a good time for that . . . and frankly I'm getting pretty sick of it."

She shook her head and stomped off down the hallway. After about eight steps or so, her huffy retreat came to a premature halt, and instead she circled around and came in for another pass.

"Where do you get off being so stuck-up, anyway? Criticizing my man, like you could get anyone better. What, you think you're gonna bag the Dos Equis guy with your zero life experience and, and, your . . . irritating monotone voice? You're like the celery of people. Maybe if you stopped acting like you're better than everybody you'd have some friends."

"Maybe if you'd found someone before you were old and gross then you wouldn't be stuck with a loser and stuck in prison!"

"We have been together for fifteen years! The only loser I'm stuck in this prison with is y—My god, I'm actually taking time out of my escape to squabble with a teenager in the middle of a hallway. What the hell is happening to me?"

Without another word, she trotted off once again. It was a less-stormy departure, but more permanent in nature. She wasn't sure what she expected to find, but anything would be better than standing around there any longer. One thing was for sure, though: the situation was not going to solve itself.

And just then, the alarm stopped. Space Guantanamo's red-light district retreated back into the ceiling and walls, and a seemingly random door opened up on Kim's left. She peered at it in quiet contemplation. Half of her held a justifiable suspicion regarding the nature of its appearance. The other half wanted to just accept and take it. All in all, it was like waking up in the morning and finding a strange puppy in your bed. Despite their spat, Whisper came over and assisted her silent staring with some silent staring of her own.

"We're gonna end up going through the door," Kim said.

"We both know it's fishy as hell, and we're both gonna sit here and gape at it trying to convince ourselves it's not, and we never will . . . but I just know we're both gonna end up going on through anyway."

"Whatever." Whisper rolled her eyes. "Things have finally calmed down, but hey, being impulsive got us this far, right?"

"You're welcome to sit here and ponder to your heart's content, then. I just don't care anymore. But know that turning off the sirens doesn't mean lockdown is over. Maybe they just got sick of the noise and figured if we were going to have a seizure, it would have happened by now."

"Then why would they open the door?"

"Probably trying to kettle us somewhere we can be contained. Maybe even right back to our cells."

"Then why all the running people with the guns and the yelling?"

"Look, I don't work here, alright?! I'm offering speculation, not reading the goddamn procedure tablet. Either their plan will work, or I'll find a loophole and get us out."

"Or we'll die."

" . . . Or we'll die."

Kim nodded, then crossed the threshold. Nothing happened. With a smug shrug, she turned around and raised an eyebrow. She didn't exactly know what she was gloating about, but it sure felt like a gloatable moment, so she just went with it. It seemed to have worked, too, because it was enough to prompt Whisper to reach a dainty food inside and test the waters. Her approach could have done with a slight bit more urgency, but after a painfully long trial period, she finally committed and allowed herself all the way inside.

The door immediately slammed shut behind her.

"I knew that would happen!" She whined.

"Yeah, yeah, you know everything." Kim uttered amid a heavy exhalation.

"*Now* we're stuck!"

"Yes. We're stuck. Stuck in this huge gymnasium of a room with more doors to try than the Mormon training camp."

Little did Kim know, the room actually didn't have more doors than the Mormon training camp. The Mormon training camp in Sal Tlay Ka Siti, Uganda was a freaking huge compound that was far too large to contain within one room of a space station. But she was right that the room did indeed contain a concentration of doors that was much larger than average. What's more, the walls were built in a sloping fashion to allow the installation of even more doors. In the days of locks and keys, this place would have been a janitor's worst nightmare.

"Fine, we'll try the doors then!" The teen declared in her first display of initiative. "I'll take the right side, you take the left."

"Well, we could try that, but I figured we'd start with that big double set at the far end there underneath that flashing 'Exit' sign."

The aforementioned pair of doors could just be seen in the distance. They were embedded in the wall far on the other side of the empty expanse, the dingy exit sign above them blinking a silent siren song like the last vacancy sign in Bethlehem. Of all the hatches that pockmarked the walls, these were the only ones that had any kind of illuminated designation. All the rest were as dull as the room they were in: blank metal slabs with no unique features besides thin mail slot-type openings in the middles.

"And what if they're locked?"

"Then we'll try the other doors or we'll try the vent or we'll try to come up with other ideas. I dunno about you, but I don't feel like freaking out until I know I have reason to."

That wasn't exactly a lie, but it certainly wasn't as true as she'd have Whisper believe. Concealed beneath her flippant words and confident swagger was a mind rapidly trying every combination of expletive known to woman. She wasn't sure which would be more worrisome: the door not opening for them, or the door opening for them. The prison was just in lockdown over her; and as far as she was aware, she hadn't been caught yet. So when she did the math, she concluded that nothing could be more suspicious than this door opening when they tried it. However, Kim was never great at math.

As it turned out, the most suspicious circumstance was actually the door opening for them *without* them trying it . . . along with every other door in the sprawling Scooby Doo-hallway of a room.

Either some unseen force was trying to make their escape as cinematic as possible, or they had stepped on the right spot to trigger a boss fight. It was like standing in between two race-horse starting lines that faced each other. No bell sounded, but the gates lining the walls opened, and the inhabitants emerged from their dark stalls, blinking and shielding their eyes from the bright ceiling lights. Like most interplanetary people, they also wore space onesies; theirs all matching in a telling shade of pumpkin orange. When their eyes finally adjusted, they soon jumped to the two ladies within their midst. Within seconds, the inmates had closed ranks and the grins and nudges and murmurings began.

"Well, well, well," a throaty voice from somewhere in the crowd growled. "Women."

"I ain't seen womens in forever."

Kim sidled herself in front of Whisper as she glowered around at the amassing mob. Aside from that, there wasn't much she could do. They were surrounded.

Yet surrounded was all they were. The gaggle of inmates, after forming their circle, just held fast. The nudges continued, but the grins began to wane and the comments . . . lost some lustre.

"Now's your chance. Have at 'em."

"Me?! I don't wanna."

"Just go talk to them."

"*You* go talk to them!"

"I wouldn't know what to say!"

"Well, me either!"

"Just ask their names or something, you idiots."

"Oh, look at mister ladies' man over here."

"I bet he thinks he knows everything dames like."

"Well, unlike *some* of us here, I do know they like it when you ask for consent."

The response, while probably weak, was drowned out by a schoolyard chorus of "Oooooh"s. In a matter of seconds, the girls had gone from feeling like a pair of cats surrounded by dogs to a pair of mice surrounded by elephants. It churned up memories of school dances; those brief moments where the chaperone would duck out to the bathroom or drink themselves to sleep and the students could tear down the school board-mandated transparent gender-separation barrier. It always ended up a little something like this.

Kim began to pace forward. The reactions were subtle, yet readily visible from a bird's-eye view. It was as though she was a shark swimming through a school of fish; no communication taking place, but everyone honouring the intangible, three-foot wide, estrogen-powered barrier she produced. Following this trend, the orange sea parted itself around her in a manner that was three parts convenient and one part pitiable. Whisper followed close behind, dark eyes aflutter with wonder as burly and weaselly internee alike would cast their gazes toward the floor or ceiling upon meeting hers.

They were nearing the perimeter when they found their path blocked by a lone man. A barrel-chested fellow, he was; tall, dark, and handsome, with wavy hair and embedded crows feet from his permanent smoldering expression. Unlike his imprisoned brethren, he felt no compulsion to move when approached. Instead he unfolded he arms and eyed Kim with a mixture of reverence and disbelief.

"Maddie? That you?"

Kim also stopped when she got a good look at him, causing Whisper to run into her back.

"Ahhh, Christ . . ." She sighed. Her eyes slowly traced the span of his body, finally coming to a stop at his face.

"Of all the cellblocks in all the space prisons in all the galaxy, I walk into yours."

JAILHOUSE FLOCK

"WHY DID YOU OPEN all the cells?!"

"You told me to open the exit!"

". . . So you opened all the cells?!"

"I just hit the 'open all doors' button! Why are we yelling!?"

"Because you opened all the cells! How are you not getting this?!"

"What do you want me to do??"

"Well, let's start with hitting the 'close all doors' button!"

"There is no 'close all doors' button."

"What!? Why would there be an 'open all doors' button but not a 'close all doors' button?"

"Dude, I don't know! Maybe they thought closing all the doors after they'd already been opened would be redundant."

"Aww . . . quick! Start flicking all the individual cell openness switches."

"I'm trying! This would be so much easier if they weren't randomly placed all over this switchboard."

"Oh, it's no use . . . They're definitely all out of their cells by now."

"I could try pressing the 'neutralize all inhabitants' button?"

"What kind of neutralizing does it mean?"

"I dunno . . . I'm just reading the button . . ."

"Well that doesn't help! I'm not going to risk killing everyone."

"You might have to, dude! Look at the viewscreen. They got the girls surrounded."

"They do, Mister Padilla, they do. But wait a minute . . . zoom in on their faces."

"I don't see the zoom button."

"It's that joystick down on the bottom left, there . . . next to the 'close all doors' button . . ."

"Oh, I see it. Boy, if only we had voice command privileges for this thing, huh?"

Cox pursed his lips and then his eyes. With a quick shake of his head, both returned to normal. His frustration was short lived once he got a better look at the action down in the prison wing. Those facial expressions were among the most identifiable in the animal kingdom. And while they didn't represent relief for those wearing them, they did for the otherwise-helpless husband.

"Uh, Captain, what are they doing?"

"That, buddy, is the most natural response a man can have when encountering a beautiful woman," Cox explained nonchalantly. "Paralyzing fear."

"That big guy in front of them is so paralyzed he's not even moving out of their way."

The captain stuck his face as close as he could to the hologram of the gentleman, stopping only when he was on the verge of motorboating him. From the greying, tousled locks, to the chiselled arms, to the animated rotating biohazard neck tattoo, the unshaven man oozed bad boy so much he belonged in prison, regardless of criminal record.

"Wait a minute," he said. "I know that guy! That's Joakim Cochrane."

"Who's that?"

"Kim's ex."

"*That's* her ex? Damn, you must be feeling really insecure right now."

"Shh, lemme hear what they're saying."

They both leaned into the display, neither considering simply turning the volume up. Joakim loomed over Kim like Goliath over a sassy, genderbent David. His face seemed soured yet he spoke in the manner of a man not embittered by heartbreak, but with traces of affection still seasoning his smooth and confident voice.

"So what do you think you're doing here, huh?" He teased through a smart-alecky half smile. "I thought you got out of the business."

"Hey, I did get out," the indignant Kim defended herself. "And even if I didn't, you know I never get caught."

"Oh, I remember. Well, if you didn't get caught, then does that mean you're here for a conjugal visit?"

"You wish."

"I do wish. Am I supposed to be ashamed of wishing? I'm in prison, woman."

Willy pointed at the image, drawing Cox's attention to the thing that already had his attention.

"Dude! He just called your woman 'woman!'"

"Hey! He did call her 'woman'. . . she is a woman, though?"

"Isn't that, like, derogatory?"

"She doesn't seem to mind."

"Huh. I never thought to consider her opinion."

Cox turned the display off.

"There's no time to waste, Mister Padilla!" He declared as he clasped a hand on the man's shoulder. "His advances will go nowhere with her, but we still need to go find that room and meet up with them so we can get out of here. Can you tell from that recording where they are?"

Willy shrugged.

"Yeah, totally. That's sector 7G."

"Where is that? Is it far?"

"Not really. It's on the other side of this window."

They both turned to look out of it. The control room in which they stood overlooked the arena like a luxury box in a stadium. Kim and company could be seen mingling in the middle, blissfully unaware of their tiny audience. Without another word, Cox hefted a chair and hurled it through the glass. Errant shards cascaded down the angled walls into the interior courtyard to the soundtrack of the bouncing metal chair that accompanied them.

"Dude, why did you do that!? There's a door right there."

"I said there's no time, Mister Padilla, the woman awaits! Also, I didn't see it."

He sailed through the window after his projectiles. His tucked knees narrowly missed the jagged lip of the remaining glass before coming to land in a smooth transition onto the downward slope. He slid a good two or three feet before friction brought his lower half to a grinding halt and his top half picked up the remaining duty of propelling him forward. There was a loud thud when his head slammed against the floor. Everyone down below turned around just in time to see the tumbling blonde accidental acrobat perform four cartwheels, three firebird leaps, two salchows, and a partridge in a pear tree. His routine came to an end at the very bottom, where he landed perfectly on his feet and, after stumbling a few steps, proceeded to play it all off as though it had been entirely intentional.

"Hullooo," he greeted the commune, blinking away his dizziness. "What are *you* guys talkin' about?"

"Who the hell is this?" Joakim asked nobody in particular as he stalked over to confront the newcomer. Cox was slightly less dwarfed by the behemoth than the other crew members, but not by any amount that would count. Even drawn up to his fullest height, the best he could manage was a decent look at the man's mesmerizing neck tat. However, not even the roughened giant in his midst was beyond having only the best assumed of him.

"Why, I'm Tim Cox!" He declared, holding out his hand. "Kim's husband."

Joakim engulfed the hand with one of his own bear paws. "Am I supposed to know who that is?"

Rather than reply, Tim raised his free tiny hand and gave the meekest of points towards his better half. Joakim turned around; first looking at Whisper until she shook her head. With no other women left to suspect, even the basest amount of deductive reason was adequate to determine the answer. His eyes barely lingered on his old flame before coming back to the man who had succeeded him. All the while, ever-raising eyebrows steadily crinkled his forehead like an accordion.

"You . . . !?" He began. With another whirl, he faced Kim once more, Tim being helplessly dragged along. "*You* got married?! And wait a second . . . you took *my* name as an alias."

Kim shook her head.

"Well, actually, I took it 'cause it rhymed with his and made us seem like a folksy and innocent-looking couple."

"Is all that right, ya little homunculus?" Joakim asked the man he was nearly dangling.

"Ow—I mean, yep!"

"I see. This is very unexpected," the giant rumbled. He released Cox's hand and moved his grip to the littler man's back. Powerless to resist anyway, the captain allowed himself to be guided into the fold next to the familiar faces. Now held captive by captives within the prison in a sort of prisonception, as it were, the thought of being found by the guards suddenly didn't seem so bad. Instead, they had no recourse but to wait on the decision of their fate.

"Well then," Joakim clasped his monstrous hands in front of his belly. "I am sorry, Mister Cox. I did not know."

"Captain Cox."

"Captain Cox. Makes sense. It would take a fine man to make an honest woman out of a menace like her." He smiled at Kim and gave her a wink.

"Well, I didn't do anything besides give her the means," the captain gushed, putting an arm around her. "The decision to stop killing people for money was all hers!"

Whisper made a coughing/choking sound.

"Um, what?! You said she was a space cop!"

"Well we had to explain her, uh, I guess 'knowledge and skills' somehow! Oh, whatsamatter there, Miss Wang? Didn't think old fogeys like her were cool enough to be hired killers?"

" . . . What?! Since when do you think being a hired killer is cool?"

"That's right! It isn't!" Cox cheered. "Nice to know some of my parenting is sinking in."

He then remembered the company he kept and glanced around.

" . . . No offence to you guys, or anything."

"I would be more offended if you did consider us cool," Joakim reassured him. "So, are we going to get this jailbreak we were talking about underway, or are you going to find a 'cooler' way to get out of here?"

"Well, that depends! What's your plan?"

"Ummm," Whisper interrupted. "Are you really just gonna move on and skip elaborating on the hired-killer thing?"

"Yes, I am!"

THE PLAN ITSELF WASN'T the most harebrained scheme Cox had ever heard. Of course, his barometer wasn't exactly the best measuring device for that sort of thing, but, frankly, he was more relieved than anything to be able to hand the reins over to the professionals. Joakim and his band of merry goons hopped to work so quickly and with such a confidence that it was amazing they hadn't broken out of this place already.

They split into two teams: the splinter cell and the everybody else. A small squad of orange-clad lads, along with Whisper, stole off into the winding tunnels, while the larger of the two groups lay in wait. The reasoning behind the arrangement was indeed explained before it was put in motion. However, for reasons likely attributable to his own personal attention flaws, they eluded the confused captain. Now that it had begun, he was far too afraid to ask. So instead he hung about with those who remained.

It was actually a pretty lax atmosphere for an impending assault. Many of the inmates broke off into a pickup game of dodgeball after the complimentary magazine rack got pillaged. Others had started a fire and were tending to the bubbling stew dangling from the spit atop it. Willy, having finally emerged upon realizing the milling mob wasn't in a murder-y mood, immediately surrendered his gun to Joakim (without being asked) and took a spot on the floor. Not sitting; laying.

Not five minutes after the detachment of the detachment, the sound of running footsteps was heard; someone was thundering their way towards them. It was just one pair of feet, but a large pair from the sounds of them. Ears perked up all around. Joakim levelled his weapon towards the exit, while those who held dodgeballs cocked their arms back. A couple others, not wanting to feel left out, rolled up their magazines into weapons slightly less useful than their bare hands.

The steps grew closer and louder until finally a portly, pale, and petrified looking man wearing a guard uniform so ill-fitted it resembled the strings tied around a pork roast appeared.

"Oh, Jesus Christ," Donald sputtered, grinding to a halt in front of the troops.

"Donny!" Cox cheered from behind a larger man. "Is that you, buddy?"

"Cox . . . ?"

"That's Captain Cox!"

"I don't even have to call you that when we're on the ship."

"Yeah, that's him." Cox informed everyone as he stepped out. "Okay, we're ready to begin now!"

"We already began a few minutes ago," Joakim corrected.

"Shhh, don't tell him that!"

"We were going to come find you, Donald," Kim cut in. "But we sent Whisper up to the ship, so it'll be ready for us to make an escape. Plus, I couldn't keep dragging her around with me."

"Makes sense," Donald shrugged.

She folded her arms and looked at him sideways.

"How did you get out of your cell anyway?"

He folded his arms right back, nostrils aflare.

"I told you I went to SIT," he bragged haughtily. "I just dismantled all their tech blockers one by one."

Willy sat up from the floor. As he leaned back on his hands, he looked up at Donald, then to Kim, then finally to Cox, before opening his mouth with a smacking noise.

"Dude. How has nobody ever escaped from this place?!"

"'Ey boss?" An interchangeable, generic prisoner called in from the hallway. "Bird's in 'er nest. Asset room is clear."

Joakim dropped any and all interest he had in the previous conversation.

"Excellent. Alright, everyone, *now* we begin. Smoke 'em if ya got 'em, then come grab a gun and join in the fun."

Cheers and "yeah buddy"-s emanated from around the room. On Joakim's signal, the floodgates opened and the racers were off. Cox and Co. trundled alongside the excited men, following them as they opted not to take the exit and instead wound around the labyrinthine halls until reaching a large storage room. Despite being all on the same team, people pushed and shoved their way into the weapons cache like the Hawthorne Army Depot blowout sale. That is, all the people except Cox; he wasn't as keen to take part in the bonanza.

"So these are just for a show of force, right?" He asked as they left. "We're not actually going to kill anybody . . . right?"

"Oh yeah," Joakim answered without looking. His stride was so long the captain had to half jog just to keep up. "We do this for fun around here."

"See, but do you actually? Because I can't tell if you're being sarcastic."

After arming themselves with weapons to match their wills, they followed the signs leading to the hangar and burst through the final barricade. The room dwarfed even the cell-block from which they had come. Ceilings as high as the non-existent sky covered the hundreds of yards of open terrain. Insulated cables hung like vines from the rafters, and loose helmets and tools littered the grated floors. Not a soul milled amongst the scattered ships and assorted chest-high walls. Entire carts of equipment and received shipments had been left abandoned. The whole room emanated an eerie calm, occasionally groaning with the shifting of metal, but otherwise as cold and lifeless as the space that could be seen through the forcefield at the far end.

The prisoner platoon shuffled and coughed. Occasionally, there would be a clank, and they'd snap their rifles to the ready, but within moments, they would droop once more.

"Well, where are they?" Kim nudged Joakim with the butt of her gun.

"Oh, they'll be here," the king con reiterated. His peeled eyes scanned the expanse as if expecting someone to jump out and yell surprise. "Strike team does their job, then the herd of pigs will stampede on through those doors on the far end next to the space shield at the other side there. Right into our hands."

Ceasing the scanning for a second, he cleared his throat and called to his troops.

"Look alive, boys. Find some cover. Just because you're wearing orange doesn't mean you should be standing around like a damn construction crew; get a move on!"

"I don't want to be rude—" Cox began.

"Oh, god, what now?"

"—but I was just thinking . . . why did you lure them here to the hangar? Wouldn't it have made more sense to just lure them somewhere else and then we could all escape without any fuss?"

Joakim chuckled one of those low, cough-like laughs.

"Well, I suppose because that would take all the fun out of it, Captain Cox." He chuckled once more and, upon seeing the captain's sinking face, added: "Come on, do you want to live forever?"

"I think there's somewhere in the middle ground between now and forever that I would prefer to live to, if I'm being honest."

Joakim turned and squinted at Kim.

"This guy? Really?"

"Hey, man," the tired-looking woman sighed. "Some people like it when a guy has a perfectly healthy outlook when it comes to death."

A shrug and a snuff was all he gave in return before turning back around.

"Hah, women . . ." He teased her husband. "Who can understand 'em . . ."

Then, even the most vigilant were caught off guard when what light the room had began to fade. Only enough remained to illuminate the fog rising from between the grates in the floor. With visibility rapidly declining from above and below, dissension and fear spread like plagues amongst the less-disciplined occupants. Covers were blown, tactics were abandoned, and fruitless attempts were made to backtrack through the now-locked hangar door.

Then the weightlessness began. At first it felt like adrenaline; a solid push from one's leg would propel them much further than it ever had before. But afterward came the paradoxically sinking feeling of being stuck helplessly floating upwards into the air. It started with just a few of them, but before long even the less spry reluctantly began to take to the sky. The dark room quickly became rife with the soon-to-be shot. All the cries of anguish and frenzied flails contributed was a denser atmosphere of unrest, dropped rifles, and dislodged shoes.

As overpaid members of the space trucking brigade, Cox and crew were the only ones equipped to contend. In sync they all reached down, or up, depending on their orientation, and flicked the switches in their shoes, resulting in gentle descents and getting shot with looks of disdain and even unbridled hatred. Kim touched down for just long enough to flick her magnets off and launch herself upwards again, spreading her arms and scooping some of the floaters, barrel of monkeys-style. Effective as it was, it only fuelled the desperation of those still adrift. Her crew accompanied her on the second pass. Together they launched upwards just in time to have a front row seat as the shutters in the walls opened up and the room became bathed in spotlights.

Fully kitted soldiers surrounded them on either side, sticking rifles through each balistraria like medieval archers. Those with mag boots—and those hanging on to the limbs, clothes, or hair of those with mag boots—plummeted back to the hanger deck just in time to avoid the vault becoming alive with death. Laser shots flew from the walls like sparklers, each coming with their own individual *pew* that, when put together, produced the most ominous techno music one would ever hear. Any prisoners still clutching glow-stick shooters returned fire as best they could. However, between the floating and the freaking out, the only people they ended up shooting was each other.

"Plug the holes!" Joakim roared, throwing any loose debris he could find at the arrowslits.

It was clear the circumstances were dire when not a single one of the societal dregs responded with "That's what she said." Thankfully, when fear levels were at the point where the innuendo center of the brain had gone dormant, the fight or flight impulses still persisted. With nowhere to fly, it really narrowed down the options. Kim was the first to join in the efforts, eagerly snatching up some floating debris and following Joakim's example. With hovering helmets in one hand and buoyant boots in the other, she proudly demonstrated her ambidexterity when it came to throwing. Cox also contributed in his own way. With floor in one hand, and more floor in the other, he demonstrated his ability to crawl along a floor.

Although he could barely see through the wavy golden locks that were matted to his face, the sounds of the situation were more than enough to keep him in the know. In case he went deaf, though, which was becoming increasingly likely at this point, there was no shortage of people being sent flying across the hanger, providing visual updates until they smashed into piles of crates. It was a strange phenomenon in and of itself, since lasers had no mass to impart force onto those they struck.

But in the face of it all, he continued to crawl. When shrouded in dense fog, he would poke his head up like a prairie dog from time to time to keep his eyes on the objective. Occasionally, he would get clocked in the head by an unidentified floating object, but eventually he reached the end of his jaunt. Unlike the frenzied inmates, the door was not his interest; beside every door was a console, and in every console was a mic'd receiver, which was hooked up to the station's computer. Usually, such receivers could pick up commands from across a room. Unfortunately, even modern sensor-sensitivities couldn't process commands very well when delivered amid more grunts and cries than the sauciest male-centric smut. The only way to make his voice register was to get close enough to slip it some tongue.

"Siri!" He yelled into the AI's noise hole. "Siri! Close the shutters!"

"Please state name of—."

"Captain Cox!"

"I'm sorry. There are no captains in the system with that last—"

"Oh, for—Private Cox!"

"Oh, Hello, Captain. Sure, I will get right on that."

The vast majority of the uneducated prisoners had never

heard of ASMR, but that didn't stop them from feeling it when the shutters whirred themselves down between them and the firing squad. Cox breathed a sigh of relief as heavy as any when the lights, both baneful and benign, were blocked, bathing the barricade in blackness.

"Hey Siri, what say we get some light of our own in here?"

And there was light. And everyone saw the light. And it wasn't great, but it was sure better than being blind.

"Give us a bit of gravity too, maybe about fifty percent. And how about some music? Make it a classic. Something to lighten the mood a bit, but still upbeat enough so we're inspired during all this against-all-odds escaping stuff."

Those who still had consciousness scooted to their feet. Most made a beeline for the weapons they'd dropped, pausing only after retrieving them to take in the sombre *a cappella* opening that blared over the PA system. Cox smiled around. He hoped someone would recognize it, but no one even caught his glance. Oh well, he was still pumped up. With a helmet upon his head and a crate-lid shield on each hand, he scampered away from the doors, which were likely to soon be stormed with troopers.

If the room was a mess before, throwing some zero-gravity hubbub into the mix elevated it to hoarder levels of disarray. Neat stacks of boxes had been tossed the length of the place, and previously airborne ships had come to clumsy landings in all manners of positions on top of the piles of shattered glass and spilled oil. Some prisoners opted to hide under the shambles, while others made their way up top for better vantage points. Whatever their strategy, the time to implement it was short lived. As the funereal opening to "Renegade" came to a close, the much-better-organized opposing team breached through the openings at both ends of the room.

The music erupted into full swing. Chaos came thundering back into existence. Still clad in casual-Friday garb, guards poured in from both directions. The first one slipped on a grease patch and careened into a low-hanging ramp, while the rest held their footing and took to firing at every flamboyant orange jumpsuit in their midst. Those from both sides shouted a variety of situation-appropriate statements. Some boomed commands to any who were listening, others roared words of encouragement or declarations of having substantially greater combat prowess than the other shooty people. More yet just screamed unintelligible gobbledygook. But after those with the desire had hollered themselves hoarse, all that remained was more *pew*s than in the whole of Vatican City.

Cox grabbed Donald and yanked him behind a nearby stack of metal boxes moments before an errant red streak punched his ticket. Thankfully, the lesser gravity mitigated the pain of the hefty fellow landing on top of him. Perhaps it was due to them knocking heads together, but in that moment they seemed to share a thought.

"We gotta build a fort," Cox put it to words.

"We're not five; can we call it a shelter, please?"

With nowhere to fly and no desire to fry, they launched into construction of a rudimentary box bunker and welcomed fellow cowards and pacifists into it. Luckily, there were few who desired its protection, as the music seemed to have a remarkable effectiveness at motivating would-be escapees to charge into direct confrontations.

Willy was at the front of the lines. His wild mane of curls was aflurry from the crosswinds of moving men, while his mouth dangled open in a scream position, despite no sound coming out. Blaster rifle at his hip, he fired indiscriminately in the vague direction of his attackers. They weren't hard to hit, but he was really good at missing. His backup, however, was not. While for the first few waves they toppled over row after row of guards in their bottleneck, before long they had crossed the threshold and fanned out wide to flank the prisoners once more.

"Remind you at all of old times?" Joakim joked, taking cover behind an upturned shuttle.

"Hardly," Kim grumbled back. She peeked around the corner and grimaced. "I made a point not to take jobs that required fighting armies."

They looked up to see a fleeing prisoner leaping over their shuttle, all the while shouting cuss-laden declarations of better uses for his time. He was nearly out of harm's way when a laser tagged him in the back. Together they watched the light gravity gently put him down like a leaf on the wind.

"Or becoming part of one," she added.

They gave each other a final nod, then broke away on either side. Kim crouched and rolled from cover to cover, sneaking around the guards' flank and popping up behind four of them. The first three were caught by her spray of lasers, while the final one managed to dodge the last bit, only to catch a snap left foot to his chin, causing his gleaming black helmet to fly off, soar over a guard phalanx, and land hard-side first against the face of the prisoner about to pepper them, diverting his once-carefully aimed gun and making it erupt a bright flash of red that streaked across the scene, threading past throngs of unsuspecting heads and flailing arms before coming to a rest squarely in the quivering uvula of a yelling prison guard, who keeled backwards and retained consciousness just long enough to make a few choking noises and slam into a nearby freight wagon, sending it, along with its ice-block cargo, hurtling across the battlefield, causing guarders and guarded alike to dive out of the way as the payload-turned-projectile picked up speed, then came to a crashing crescendo when a weakened floor grate gave way underneath it and stopped the buggy cold, but catapulted the ice block high into the laser-riddled air, where it sustained a few singes before bouncing off the very ship that had brought it in and then shattering against the floor in an explosion of ice chunks varying in size from bottle-top to beach ball, which then blasted into every unfortunate soul in the vicinity.

The thunderous culmination, in addition to incapacitating those within its immediate vicinity, had the additional effect of stopping the rest of the combatants in their tracks. Those who hadn't already found themselves distracted by the tirade intricate enough to impress Rube Goldberg still found themselves marvelling slack-jawed at the wake it had left and eagerly tracing the trajectory of the debris as if in hopes the carnage would continue.

Most of the guards weathered the blast with little more than bruises and lost wind—except the one who was missing his helmet because of Kim's kick. The ice chunk he took on the chin barely slowed as it barrelled off him and then on to Kim. It nicked her on the nose as she leaned out of the way before channelling all of its topspinning fury into a heap of assorted scrap. After it had finished crumbling into a flatter pile of junk, the group of wide-eyed wimps hiding underneath it stood up and had a look around.

"Did we win?" Cox asked, catching his wife's glance.

She gnashed her teeth.

"Look around, Tim! Does it look like we won?! It's like the Not O.K. Corral in here! I mean Jesus, all you have to do is look—"

"Okay, clearly that wasn't the best time to make a joke.

I'm sorry, honey. Come—come over here where you won't die, please."

He ushered her into the remnants of his glorious bunker. There was plenty of space now, due to the recent renovations, as well as the fact that most of the occupants had scattered like they were at a high school party getting busted by the cops. Cox shoved the poker chips aside, accidentally knocking over the Jenga tower, and they huddled together in their makeshift trench. They were sweaty and dishevelled and breathing like a couple of women going into labour during the bar exam, but they still couldn't resist a nice mid-war cuddle.

"So, hey," he mumbled, nuzzling his face against the top of his wife's head. "I don't want to criticize the plan or anything. It's a great plan; better than I could plan. But I was just wondering, um, why isn't our ship in here?"

Kim moved her head away and looked up at him. Her beautiful sparkling eyes were made extra pretty each time they reflected a laser blast passing overhead. And that was in spite of how narrowed they were.

"Oh, god, Tim, you didn't pay attention to the plan at all, did you?" She grumbled before sighing and shaking her head. "I shoulda known. I shoulda known when you didn't protest at all."

"Protest? You mean the fighting? I've totally protested that. But I also know that sometimes it has to happen because not everything can be resolved peacefully. Well, actually, it totally can, just most of the time people aren't willing to work to—"

"No, not the fighting!"

She raised her hand and took a moment to breathe and find the words. After another scan around and a quick lick of her lips, she continued.

"Our ship isn't in here because it doesn't dock in hangars. You know this."

"Yeah, I know it usually doesn't . . . But I just thought maybe, y'know, since this place is super big, that it might."

"Size doesn't matter, Tim—" She frowned at his stifled chuckle. "Look, it's not here. That's part of the reason we sent Whisper ahead. It's still outside at the same external dock where we left it, and we needed to keep all the guards distracted out here so she would be able to pull out—really?—without getting clamped in place by some asshole watching the gate."

Now it was Cox's turn to look around.

"Wait, this is actually *all* the prison guards? Every single one abandoned their posts and came here?" He looked around again. "I do remember thinking there were a lot, but wow, that seems really irresponsible."

Kim shrugged.

"I dunno, love. They seem to really bounce off the walls over this sort of thing, I guess."

"Well, hey, I guess we all have the things we enjoy."

"Like heights," she suggested.

"Heights? I wouldn't say I enjoy them, necessarily. Never really understood the fear of them, though. Maybe that's just a moon-guy thing. I feel like if I got thrown out of a shuttle taxi that was a hundred feet up I might be a little freaked out. Of course, I'm not sure what I would do to deserve it . . . I did have a driver once who thought I was a girl because of my hair. At least, I think it was because of my hair . . . anyway, he started saying all kinds of weird stuff, and boy was he embarrassed when—"

"Babe, I was just trying to segue as gently as I could into the next part of the plan."

"Oh, man. I just got whooshed."

She got to her feet and motioned for him to do the same.

Since he wasn't too keen on getting left behind, Donald also followed suit.

With backs hunched and heads bowed, they braved the carnage once more. Ever since the advent of energy-based weapons, warzones were nowhere near as cataclysmic as in the days of yore. The atmosphere never really changed, but without bullets and explosives tearing up the terrain, the only noticeable earmark was a polka-dotted sheen of scorch marks covering the area like someone let loose a group of preschoolers armed with black bingo daubers. And bodies. Can't forget the bodies. Some even find them more noticeable than the small black marks.

Miraculously, the trio reached the towering wall of the hangar untouched. There was a disproportionate amount of friendly forces milling around outside of it, apparently putting together some sort of barricade that was already looking far more effective than anything Tim could have erected. But even the most impressive improvised structure paled in comparison to those put together by funded professionals with time and tools. So rather than assist in the bungling—not that she planned to, anyway—Kim yanked open the closest proper metal doors and ushered the group inside before she took to pillaging the room's contents.

They appeared to be in a storage locker of sorts. Most of the contents were still crated up, except for the open cans of varying mechanical fluids that were strewn about the room in a very OSHA-unfriendly kind of way. Spare parts hung from the rafters and tool chests lined the back wall, complete with open drawers and missing contents. However, Kim's focus was on the wall hooks and the spacesuits mounted upon them. The clothing technology had progressed past looking like Michelin Man costumes, but it still wasn't available in one-size-fits-all yet, so it took a bit of perusing before finding four appropriate fits. In complete deference to tradition, Donald donned his shortly after it was thrown at him, while Cox briefly postponed compliance.

"Yes, we are going outside," Kim answered the question he never asked. She stuffed her legs into her suit and vacuum-sealed the lower half before carrying on with the top. Her husband started to do the same, but paused once more with another open mouth.

"Yes, it's part of the plan. No, it's not going to be dangerous. Yes, we have no other choice," she rattled off in quick succession before he could ask anything. The loss of shuffling and rustling noises made her cease her suiting to look up and find the two men staring blank-faced at her.

"Sorry. Wasn't sure which one you were going to ask," she added.

Her husband nodded with acknowledgement.

"I don't know anymore, myself."

They re-merged with the skirmish kitted out from head to toe with the most advanced clothing technology known to man. Not only were the spacesuits fully immune to the perils of space, they could also withstand the cutting cold and the harrowing heat. These marvels of technology boasted an adjustable interior temperature control, plush lining, crush resistance, cut resistance, pierce resistance, electricity resistance, psychic damage resistance, drug resistance, resistance to change, partial resistance against Borg assimilation, and apparently a long list of other resistances that they didn't include on the tag because the current one was already long enough to look like a piece of toilet paper the wearer dragged out from the bathroom.

About a quarter of the arena now was inexplicably on fire.

The music had stopped and the war cries had been replaced with the screams of man-children dangling from the ceiling and grasping at limbs that, while still attached, appeared to ail them in some capacity. Some remaining prisoners had tattered their own clothing and repurposed various mechanical substances as face paint in a sort of stylized guerrilla-fighter aesthetic.

The trio gingerly stepped from their closet hideaway and walked through a makeshift POW camp, taking care not to get caught in the outstretched arms of caged guards or to trip over any of the numerous improvised blackjack tables that had been set up. They didn't need to go far to find Joakim. The man's broad frame stood out starkly amongst his underlings as they busied themselves adding to their barbaric box-based barricade or gibbering around their captured soldiers while impersonating racist stereotypes. He didn't take part, himself. In fact, he didn't seem too invested in the odd interloper that he'd use as target practice either. Instead, he just paced, checking his watch every few seconds and looking toward the ceiling.

"What the hell happened out here?" Kim asked. She looked for something to gesture toward, but everything around her was on about the same level of ridiculousness.

"War," Joakim rumbled. He turned and surveyed the carnage just in time to watch a rescue team cut one of the dangling ceiling cables and send a tangled man plummeting to the floor with a resounding *clang*. "War never changes."

He spun back around with a smart-alecky grin.

"And thank god for that. Most people don't survive learning it the first time."

"Well, I just want to thank you," Cox announced as he walked up and wrapped the big fella in a hug. "It really bums me out to see you and the boys are so crippled by institutionalization that you're willing to die for the sake of complete strangers. But I'm honoured that those strangers were us."

"Uhhh . . . ?"

"You should come with us," Kim insisted. "I grabbed you a space suit."

"I don't think so."

She let the suit fall to the floor, where it landed with a *fwump* that expressed contempt for her.

"You'd really rather stay here? You'd really rather take your chances facing down an army of underpaid, undersexed police-academy dropouts who live for no other reason than to bully the only people even lower on the societal totem pole than they are? And for what? If you're not looking to escape, then what could you possibly be doing this for?! And don't you dare try to say me."

"Does nobody listen to the plans when I lay them out?!" Joakim mumbled through the hand over his face.

"I may or may not have stopped listening after the part where we divert from you guys and meet up with Whisper."

"Well, I'm glad I didn't bother to draw the diagram this time, then." He rested the rifle on his shoulder and sidled past her, cocking his head side to side to crack his neck before snatching a can of beer out of the hands of a nearby underling.

"If you must know," he continued before a long swig. "Ahh—we're taking over this place!"

More whoops and cheers from the goons. Half of them spilled beer all over themselves in their attempt to take part in the plaudits. The other half spilled additional beer all over the first half. Only those involved in the ensuing fist fight paid it any attention. Kim simply scoffed.

"Oh, big deal. So you take over this dump. Then what?"

He considered the question. It seemed like the most obvious one to ask, and yet there was no pre-prepared answer. Even some of the frat boys stopped fighting to mull it over themselves. The entire scuffle had just about burned itself out by the time Joakim threw up his hands and shoulders.

"I don't really know, if I'm being honest. We've never made it that far before."

"Oh, typical. You make an overcomplicated plan that involves tons of fighting and gives no thought to what you're going to do after. Really shows everyone where your priorities lie."

"We haven't dated in almost twenty years and you're still getting on my case about things that don't matter." He nodded towards Cox. "Good luck after the divorce, friend."

"Why does everybody keep saying we're going to divorce?!"

"And as for you, don't worry about what we're going to do! Maybe we'll hold it ransom until we get nicer meals."

"Oh," a nearby voice jumped in. "How about a giant hologram player for the rec room!"

"Or a golf course!"

"Or women!"

"Or how about you guys just escape and go to places that already have those things?!" Kim suggested.

"Uh, Miss Cox, you do know most of these guys are bad people who probably shouldn't actually be released into—"

"Shut up, Donald."

Joakim boomed a deep belly laugh that drowned out the idle bickering and ransom suggestions.

"Escape?!" He managed to utter between guffaws. "Why in the Hell would we want to do that?!"

Kim and Donald were struck dumb. Most of the man's associates seemed to share the sentiment, so Cox stepped in to prod the topic.

"Uh . . . but why wouldn't—"

"Because this is the best place we could possibly live," Joakim cut him off. The gun he held waggled to and fro between harmless and heedless depending which emphatic gesture was being used. More than once the crew had to cringe and duck out of the way. "Free food, free housing. You guys have any idea what real estate is worth these days? Plus, how many neighbourhoods guarantee your neighbours will have similar interests to yours? This place is awesome."

Cox, however, was defiant. "But what about your freedom? What about your aspirations?"

"This place *is* what we aspire to! Did you think we did all that robbing and murdering and terrorizing and drug consumption just for fun? We had bills to pay, just like you. If you don't believe me, ask around."

"I started a terrorist group, even though I don't have any political opinions," the man adjacent to him piped up with pride.

"I hijacked everyone's Netflix and broadcasted spoilers of the latest Harry Potter novel."

"I hotboxed Buckingham Palace."

"I shot JR and Mr. Burns."

"I'm actually a pathological criminal and really do belong in here."

"I didn't ask any of you," Kim snapped.

Her husband's expression of incredulity persisted throughout. He was originally going to speak up right away, but politely waited for her to finish first.

"Don't you guys get tortured all the time?! What about all the human rights violations?"

"Pfft," Joakim's lips fluttered. "Terrorism happens pretty much never. And they know that. They figure out real damn quick whether you're a terrorist with information they want, and the answer is pretty much always no. Any torture that happens in this place is usually just because they don't like you."

Willy poked his head out from a group of men seated around a table playing spin-the-blaster.

"It's true. Usually they like you. But, uh, sometimes they don't."

The rotating pistol came to a shuddering halt and fired a bright flash of red light into the nearest player's chest. He toppled over backwards into a heap on the floor. Donald leapt out of the way with a mighty utterance to his lord and saviour as it happened, but otherwise Kim, Tim, and him seemed to be the only ones who found the scene disturbing in the slightest. The only other reactions came from the others around the table, who erupted into cheers and jeers as instant noodle capsules and vape flavours were passed across the motionless, smoking body.

"Are you people insane?!" The captain screeched, edging ever closer to a mental break. "If you're all so happy, then why are you all so willing to throw your lives away for pretty much no reason!? This is no way to live! Don't you have any self-respect?!"

Silence swept over the group like a swarm of invisible quiet-inducing locusts. For a mere moment, it seemed they may have been stopping to consider their rash actions. Thumbs were pressed to chins and wary glances of uncertainty were exchanged by all until, as was often the case, they all ended up pointed at their large, unelected leader.

"Oh, you guys want me to respond for us? Well, I'll try and come up with something."

Relegating his personal weapon to its shoulder sling, Joakim picked up the pistol from the table and held it up for all to see, as if to admire its craftsmanship.

"Now, I'm apparently just some psycho killer with a death wish," he mused, scratching the side of his head with the business end.

"So it makes no difference to me if I die."

The barrel moved from his head to the head of the first inmate next to him.

"Or if my friends die."

He removed it once more and this time pointed it at Cox.

"As long as *you* live! Mister Special—sorry, *Captain* Special. Captain Special and his special sailors. Get up here, fat boy, join your crew. That's right. There we are, the only sane ones here! The only ones who don't belong because they have lives worth living. Am I getting all this right?"

"I think you're oversimplif—"

"Fan-goddamn-tastic. Well, don't worry, we're here just for you. Doing your fighting. Doing your dying. But unfortunately, it looks like we're a little too good at our jobs—our jobs being to serve you—because you're all still here and kickin'! I mean, really, if all of you just jump ship and carry on your merry way without a single scratch or lifelong psychological damage . . . then what's the point?! What have we really given you, hmm?"

"Joakim, stop being an idiot and stop pointing that gun at him."

"How about you shut it, Maddie, or Kim, or whatever you've changed it to since I last asked. I'm trying to have a nice conversation with your husband. I'm trying to help him even more than I already have, by—what did you say earlier? 'Dying for your sake.' Or something. Now, it seems to me that, if someone *dies* for your sake, you're kind of obligated to live life a little fuller in their honour, right? I mean, after all, you're the only one here that knows how to live. Appreciate what ya have. All that shit? So if you already have that covered, how is this new lease on life we're so graciously offering going to sink in properly? I mean, come on. Can't expect much in the way of results if you don't lose anything but a bunch of . . . cannon-fodder lowlifes that didn't exist to you before you met them and sure as hell won't exist to you afterwards."

"I . . . I think you're giving this speech to the wrong guy," Donald uttered just loud enough to hear. "He's probably the only guy I know that would cry over people he doesn't know."

"Is that right, curly? So I should be giving this speech to you then?"

" . . . No. I, uh, I cry too."

"I believe it. Now, shut up and let me make my point."

He seemed to be getting pretty invested in his spiel now. Every twitch and uncomfortable shuffle from those he lorded over only egged him on further. The flashing of weapons and flashing of grins may well have been a part of whatever point he intended to make, yet it was accomplishing little, besides making him look a whole lot less friendly.

"The point is: You've given me a great idea. It is, in my professional opinion, as someone who has dealt with and been the cause of great losses, that the only way to make you guys respect this great sacrifice me and the boys are making for you . . . is to really give you something that'll stick with ya! I figure, by, I don't know, sending you on home minus a member!"

Cries and protestations erupted from the foursome in every form ranging from pleading to threatening. But Joakim waved them all off and carried on, seemingly uncaring as to whether they heard his words or not.

"I know, I know, you all disagree. But trust me, you'll thank me afterwards! Maybe it's just the, what was the word, *institutionalization* talking, but there's just something about having less that makes what remains feel like more! And you can take that to the bank! Now the only question left is how to decide. Anybody got straws? No? Well, then. Looks like the burden falls on me. Luckily for you, I'm just full of ideas."

He levelled off the blaster he had been waving so casually. Once again, it lined up directly with the chest of Cox.

"Eenie."

He shifted it slightly to the right, hovering it right around neck level with Kim.

"Meenie."

Then onto Donald, chubby cheeks quivering as it slowed in front of him.

"Miney."

And lastly, Willy. He was still trying to finish counting the noodle capsules in his hand.

"It."

14.
SPY DIVING

After the shot, Willy went limp. He didn't even have time to say "dude." Cox's remarkable, grief-fuelled reflexes allowed him to snag hold of the big fella before he toppled. However, he still toppled anyway, not even slowed by the feeble attempt to hold him upright. The captain cradled his curly head. With a pale, shaky hand, he gently petted the frizzy hair of his briefly employed, yet still-beloved, employee.

"Oh, Willy," he lamented. "You poor, swarthy soul. So brave, so charismatic, and gunned down so young."

He patted and stroked his companion's long, dark hair.

"Look at you. You remind me of a famous Puerto Rican man named Alexander Hamilton. I bet you would have been good at rapping, too. But now we'll never know. The ship may never have been less safe than it was with you, buddy, but I still woulda let you guard it 'til the end."

He turned his despair onto the gunman.

"How could you?! He was just a boy! He didn't ask for any of this!"

"Of course he didn't," Joakim scoffed. He dropped the pistol back on the table where it landed with a clang. "Nobody asks to get shot."

"Why couldn't it have been me?!" The captain wasn't talking to anybody in particular. He simply declared his words at the ceiling, as was taught by dramatic moments in fiction. Not being much of a book reader, movie watcher, or community-theatre payer-attentioner, Joakim took a deep puff out of his e-cig and treated the question as non-rhetorical.

"It was originally gonna be you. But I realized before I shot you that Maddie over there would probably fly off the handle and ruin all the fun before I could get to the punchline."

"'Punchline.'" Kim rolled her eyes. "You always did have a sick sense of humour, but this doesn't even have the framework of a joke. If shooting people counted as comedy, then folks wouldn't have complained so much during World War III."

"Oh, now you're going to try and tell me I'm not funny? I have a great many memories of making you laugh, and making you laugh hard!"

Kim shrugged.

"I was usually faking it. But, for what it's worth, that was probably more my fault than yours; I can be kinda difficult. So don't feel too bad."

"I'm good at making you laugh right, honey?" Cox asked from the floor.

"Ehhhh . . . shouldn't you be getting mad at him for killing Willy?"

"Oh, right, you killed Willy! You bastard!"

Joakim took another drag. He couldn't seem to decide which of the two to look at. So he just kept sucking until he could hold no more before exhaling a sizeable smoky sigh that framed his face and briefly pooled under his pronounced brow.

"You know," he rumbled through another puff. "I'll give ya one thing. This wasn't as amusing as I was expecting. Not that I expected miss stoic over here to burst into tears or anything, but I didn't think she'd start lecturing me before I got the chance to make my point. Now the timing is all off and I feel like it's not even worth making anymore."

Cox's eyes had never looked more blue as their pupils shrank to pinheads. His gentle caressing of his fallen comrade ceased as he drew himself up to his full five-foot-nine and marched over to the human steam engine.

"You just wasted a human life to make a point!" He snapped. "The *least* you can do is make it!"

Joakim had almost a foot on the feisty blonde when he straightened up.

"Fine, then," he growled down at Cox. "You want to know what the point was? The point was to scare the living piss outta ya."

"Well, mission accomplished then, tough guy! Not sure what you expected to gain, but good job!"

The giant's oblong, bell-shaped nose wrinkled into a mandala.

"Well, it shut you up, didn't it? At least for a second. Like I said, with all the bullshit that you were heaping on us about living our lives improperly and criticizing our values, it was all I could do to resist shooting you, Mister Pious. So high above us scummy prison guys. Just because you deliver your patronizing politeness with a smile doesn't mean we can't see how stupid and beneath you you think we are."

"I . . . I didn't mean to—"

Joakim raised a monstrous hand.

"Look, you're obviously not a bad guy. I'd even say that you're probably a better guy than any of us in here. But looking down on people and discounting them doesn't become okay just because you're nice about it. Maybe no one's ever told you how transparent it is because you're not the only nice person."

Cox took a second to lick his lips and let the words percolate. "You're making great points, and I can't refute all of them, because, let's face it, I can be a bit insufferable. But can you at least acknowledge it's hard for me to take behaviour advice from someone who just *shot my friend dead* because he finds me to be ignorant?!"

"Who says he's dead?" Joakim raised an eyebrow.

"What . . . ?" The three living crew members spoke in unison.

"This is part of what I meant about you assuming we're stupid savages," he explained as he waved over a couple prison doctors armed with some nasal spray. Calm as clockwork, they propped up Willy's head and began administering treatment. "I did say there was a punchline, didn't I?"

The captain's jaw inched as close to the floor as his facial muscles could physically allow. Even his wife couldn't help but let slip the slight mind-blowing that had occurred underneath her silky brown locks. Surprised or not, however, Kim was still Kim.

"Well, congrats. You proved you're not crazy by showing you're just a complete and total asshole instead. And your concept of a joke is still idiotic."

"Oh, what are you whining about, Maddie? You obviously didn't even like that guy."

"That's beside the point. How did you trick us like that?!"

Joakim shrugged.

"There is no trick." He picked up the pistol off the table and shot one of his prisoner friends seemingly at random. Like all the others, he flopped over into a comatose lump. "These things are glorified tazers. All the weapons in this place are."

"Even the guards'?" Donald asked.

"Everybody's. Why do you think they have a fully stocked weapons cache five minutes away from our cellblock? They love this shit as much as we do! Honestly, you guys still don't seem to realize how insulting it is that you thought we were actually killing each other and ourselves over nothing. Like we're animals."

Cox cleared his throat.

"You mean to tell me . . . that these weapons are completely harmless?!"

"Oh, god help me. Yes."

"Then why are they putting that guy over there in a body bag?"

"Well, that's the guy who just fell off the roof."

At that moment, Willy came to. He shot bolt upright with what must have been some pretty impressive abs hidden under the blubber. His cheeks jiggled like a dog's as he shook himself awake. Eschewing assistance from his orderlies, he flipped over onto his hands and knees to retrieve any spoils he'd dropped during the blackout. At no point did he ask any questions or acknowledge what had taken place. He did give a brief pause to inspect the shiny new scorch mark on his shirt, however.

Kim picked the discarded space suit from the floor and threw it at him.

"Get dressed. We're going home."

"OI!" A sharp voice bellowed from beyond the palisades. "Which one of you lot is in charge in there?"

Joakim cleared the distance to the wall in four good strides. Various goons and ne'er-do-wells scurried around him trying to get a vantage to peek over its bounds, while he himself just rested his arm on it like a fence between neighbours.

"You rang?"

"Fookin' hell, what are they feedin' you things in here?"

"You came up to my doorstep just to ask me that?"

Cox hopped atop a box to catch his own glimpse of the

parlay. The harsh voice that called to them struck a chord within his memories the moment it announced its presence. Even the inherent classiness of the British inflection turned putrid in the mouth of a particular belligerent old sadist. Despite facing down an army of his antitheses, Sir Head sounded as confident and pompous as ever.

The reasoning became quickly apparent as Cox poked his head over the defences and immediately felt as though he had taken center stage at a USO show. Swaths of guards surrounded their outpost. Most had removed their helmets and lowered their weapons, but readied for combat if they failed to intimidate based off of numbers alone. Yet they waited at the wayside, granting reins to the outsider for some reason.

"I didn't come here to ask you a bloody thing," the universe's happiest little agent did declare. "I came to tell you I'm shutting down your little cops-and-robbers party unless you cough up the stupid git who set my idiot partner's face on fire."

Joakim glanced around. It was hardly an invested investigation, as even the slightly attentive could have seen the grimace smeared all over Cox's face, so it must have been more for show than anything.

"Well, I don't know who you are, or your idiot partner, and I doubt anyone in here is just going to confess and give themselves up. So, not a lot I can do for ya. Now, unless you don't mind your fancy suit getting all singed up, you might wanna take a hike."

A petite woman with high cheekbones and librarian hair stepped forward from the battle-armoured battalion and took a spot next to Sir Head. Her sudden appearance startled him, and he frowned down at her in disgust. She swatted his gnarled hand away when it tried to push her back in line.

"Joakim, this is serious. According to this man, we really do have an actual group of terrorists in here for once. One of them severely wounded his partner while the other killed two of our staff members."

"Hey! I only killed one of those guys!" Kim's voice shouted back at them from somewhere within. " . . . And before you ask, I did try using my words first!"

"Really?" Joakim sighed. "Not even going to try for plausible deniability, huh?"

"They found the bodies in my cell; they obviously know it was me. I don't know where the other thing they're yelling about happened, so chances are we can still plead ignorance on it."

"Oh, that one was me."

"Thank you for saying that loud enough for everyone out there to hear, Tim."

"Give 'em up, NOW!" Sir Head continued to demand.

"Calm your ass down, would ya?" Joakim chastised from his side of the fence. "We're talkin' here."

With the fuzz suitably placated, he whirled around and hunched into the huddle.

"So, terrorists, huh? Wouldn't have been my first guess, but you definitely have the cover part down. I would never have expected this guy."

"We're not terrorists!" Kim clenched her jaw shut along with her fists. You could almost hear her counting her breaths with each heavy exhale billowing out her little nose. "Look, we got caught up in something bad and the only thing we can do is lay low long enough for them to catch the guy they're after and stop caring about us."

"Uhhhh—" Cox began.

"Oh, right, you maimed one of them, so they definitely think we're involved now, no matter what. What happened, anyway?! You've never hurt anybody in your life!"

She seemed to be more impressed than ashamed of him. All the work he had put in trying to wean her into a life of simpler pleasures and civility seemed to be coming unravelled faster than he could gather up the slack. And gathering it all became doubly difficult when, for the first time since all this began, those kind eyes were pressing him for a story instead of an excuse. Any shortcomings and failures he'd had up until this point didn't seem to exist within this moment. Instead, she was looking at him like a real captain; someone at whom reliance and admiration could be directed unironically.

"It was just an accident," he lied. "There was a mishap with his coffee and it burned him. Sounds like he pulled through, though. Which is good!"

And, unsurprisingly, that lit-up face dimmed away. It was such a shame to see it go that, for a moment, he was willing to scald the faces off a hundred bad guys just to bring it back. Unfortunately, if seeing it again meant regressing her back to a life where pleasure came from pain, then he'd rather give it up forever.

"That sounds more like you," Joakim rumbled in agreement. "Alright, well, *you* guys go talk to him, then. It's holding up our game."

With a calm delivery so as to not invoke a flinch reflex, Kim reached over and swatted him upside the head.

"Oh, you kids are trying to play, huh? Don't mind us; we're just the only people in this room who are at risk of getting killed for real."

"Ah—jeez, what do you want me to do about it?! I could shoot him, I guess. But then he'll just wake up in a little while and come back pissed at me as well."

"Just . . . just distract them somehow. Maybe we can find a way to slip out and get to the external dock."

"Oh for the love of—" Sir Head piped up. "You do realize we can hear everything you're saying in there, right? I'm aware mental retardation runs rampant among career criminals, but do I really need to explain how sound works?"

Even the most perceptive couldn't have pointed out in a playback what precisely changed in Joakim's expression following that. His bushy brows still hung low over those beady blues, and that grizzled mouth remained every bit as unimpressed, yet no more so. But there was a change nonetheless. Granted, those paying attention during his last teachable moment might have been able to deduce why a change would occur. However, to the gloriously ignorant, it seemed he was merely straightening up to stretch his back, as spines were known to be bothersome at his age. Just as seemingly innocuous was it when he, a well-established disregarder of safety, picked up the pistol from the table and began twirling it around his finger like a ring of keys. Of course, when he sauntered over to the wall and popped a shiny red cap in the Sir's sweaty red head, that's when people started to realize he might have an issue with something that was said.

"That probably didn't help your situation at all," he acknowledged to Mister and Missus Screwed. "But if sound travels so well, then he should know how I feel about being called stupid."

What the rebels lacked in numbers, they also lacked in comparable passion after the spontaneous Ferdinand-ing. On the other hand, while lacking any visible revulsion to the fate of Sir Head, the prudish commander gave the order to attack, regardless. It was an order that was fulfilled with an alarming enthusiasm.

It was unclear whether the policing detachment had a deep-rooted allegiance to the British, more professional responsibility than they were given credit for, or were just happy to have an excuse to unpause the game, but whatever their motivation, they threw themselves at the walls like a roving horde of zombie termites and made remarkable headway reducing them to their baser components. Tensions were not as high on the other side. The good bad guys held the invaders off as best as they could for a group of semi-distracted gamblers who stood to face zero consequences for failure. They fired blindly over their shoulders while keeping eyes fixed on their cards. Misses and hits didn't matter—unless that hit was in blackjack.

"Siri!" Cox panted into the closest mic, pausing for a wary glance over the shoulder. "Siri, you gotta—private Cox speaking—help us!"

A crinkled chunk of metal clanged off the wall inches above his head.

"Hello, Captain. Unfortunately, automated defences have been disabled in the wake of a recently detected security breach."

"I'm open to ideas!"

"A cursory analysis of the conflict determines the quickest way to achieve resolution would be to surrender yourself in a calm and orderly manner for our helpful staff to assess your case and decide a proper course of action."

With the weathered wall worn away, the floodgates opened. The guards spilled *en masse* into the little camp and for the first time seemed to shun fun in favour of their employer-mandated duties. The egregious illegal gambling taking place fell upon blind eyes. It was also pointedly ignored, since even the blind would have heard Donald yelling "Hey, aren't you gonna do anything about all this illegal gambling?"

It was a unique feeling to be set upon by masked gunmen

in the middle of a titanium superstructure floating around a planet while 1980s music played over loudspeakers and a robot voice came from beside you trying to explain that you're the bad person here. Not the lame kind of unique either, like when parents are unable to come up with a better compliment for their child; it was an aggressive kind of unique that came bearing down with such force that you could almost hear your brain whirring like a photocopier as it was committed to memory for all eternity. And, like most forces that bore down, it came part and parcel with a pressure that in this case would crush until metaphorical bones were metaphorical dust or until it had produced some fresh-squeezed creative genius.

These guys sure seemed pretty mad, though, so it might have been a bit optimistic not to expect a few literal limb squishes as well.

"Okay, Siri, activate gravity-generator controls then!" Some of that latter stuff dribbled from Cox's mouth. "Start redirecting gravity from the floor to that far wall over there until I say stop!"

There was an instant ominous rumbling that echoed through the chamber, like the digestive noises of a great metal whale. Anything on wheels was the first to be affected. They calmly drifted away to start, seemingly props in a gentle haunting taking place. Then shelves began to dispense their contents. Round pieces dropped the quickest, soon followed by anything else. The mass migration of metal wares overshadowed the initial rumbling, then drowned it out altogether when the shelves themselves followed to a smashing landing of their own. The encroaching enemies felt the effects moments later—and not just the ones who took spare wheels to the groin. Their intimidation factor went down in exact inverse to their path going up. By the time they were closing in on their prey, only white knuckled grips on the nearest bolted-down objects prevented a re-enactment of the Jack and Jill rhyme.

"Stop!"

The station froze. The people in it also froze. The chunks of the ice block remained frozen. However, only two of those listed articles remained stationary. With no hands to hold themselves, or will to use them if they did, the rounder fragments of ice cube teetered precariously atop the steep incline that overlooked all the mountaineers. All eyes were transfixed upon them in helpless horror, like noticing an unattended baby crawling on the windowsill of an apartment across the street. Hearts would only beat on the "to" before subsequently stopping again on the "fro".

"Siri, would you relay a message to the impounded ship called the SS *Jefferson*, please?" Cox grunted through the welded-on smile that he habitually donned during trying times. "We're probably gonna be a bit late."

Siri responded with her typical calm, authoritative voice, which was terribly ill-fitted to the current situation.

"There is no impounded ship by that name."

Captain Cox blinked reflexively as ice flakes floated downwards toward his eyes and landed on his visor.

"WHA—ahem—where did it go?!"

"The most recently impounded ship by that name departed thirteen minutes ago, breaking mechanical restraints and injuring staff members who were attempting to board it. Since departure, it has circled the station twenty-nine times and sent fourteen transmissions, all to our Guantanamo information line."

Somewhere beyond the vertical jungle of twisted metal and immobilized officers, the SS *Jefferson* could barely be glimpsed through the force field coming around for another pass. After only a few seconds, it disappeared yet again after passing through the cloud of guns, cans, shoes, and any other loose debris that had bounced their way down the hill. Not a moment too soon, either, as one of the tethers holding down a transport shuttle snapped and it too began a grinding descent, knocking several floor grates loose before passing uninhibited through the force field and gently gyrating away toward Earth.

Strange things, the fields were. They could contain the tiniest of air molecules, yet solid objects seemed to pass straight on through. Not even the captain's illustrious schooling informed him on the science of such wonderment, but he didn't need to understand it to have an idea.

"Siri?"

"Yes, Captain?"

"If you can, could you relay a message to that *Jefferson* flying around outside there? Tell her . . . Her crew is comin'. But she's gotta catch us."

"You can't be serious," Donald said from his spot bear hugging an oversized mooring cleat.

"Actually, that's probably the best shot we got right now," Kim said, looking down the chamber as another ship came loose and tumbled its way out. "But I can't say I'm a fan."

"It's true, Donny. I know you can do it, though," Cox encouraged the coms officer, patting him on the back with a foot. "Also, you're definitely the big guy in this group, so we're gonna need you to grab Willy on the way down."

"Really? You really don't think you're asking a little much of me already?"

"Donny, buddy, I give you permission to whine as much as you like when we get back aboard the ship. I will probably join you. But right now, I'd really appreciate it if you could take it easy. If not for yourself, then for me . . ."

He gulped down at the proposition he'd made for himself and whimpered softly.

"I never realized until right now how much I hate heights."

A soft pitter-patter came from beneath him. Even clad in her cumbersome spacesuit, Kim easily climbed her way up welded tables and floor grates until she stood on equal footing with him. The first mate's gloved hand clutched the same beam as his while her other hand wrapped an arm around him and pulled his glass visor against hers.

"Just hang onto me, alright?" She soothed. "We got this. Hey, look at me. What would one of your old philosophers say right now?"

"Uhh . . ." There he was, with the love of his life in his arms facing oblivion with him and the world literally at their feet, so there really was never a more appropriate time for a quote. "I guess they'd say . . . I dunno. It's hard coming up with one on the spot, y'know? How about: We gotta hold on to what we got. It doesn't make a difference if we make it or not. We got each other . . . And that's a lot . . . For love?"

With a crinkle of her eyes and a bend of her lips, she raised an eyebrow.

"Let's give it a shot."

With nothing but faith left to bank on, they leapt for it. Cox's eyes and glutes were clamped shut as he hurled himself off the metal cliff. Grasping hands snatched at his suit, but the slick material shrugged off any shots at seizure. These failed attempts were followed by swears and grunts that came from behind, as well as a few thuds from those making jumps of their own. But neither departee could look back even if they tried. Stuck with his glass visor facing front, Cox could all but feel the wind in his face when his body hit the floor and their mad slide to freedom began.

Their hold on each other remained as tight as ever. With chests pressed together, they tumbled and banged into protruding obstacles marring their path, sometimes bouncing off and sometimes knocking them loose to join in their escape. Resonating shudders from metal scraping against the floor filled their ears. At one point during one of his many topples, the captain thought he caught a glimpse of the angered armada of guards giving chase like a group of bloodthirsty cheese rollers. However, the flash was brief, and most of his focus was commanded by his co-conspiring coadjutors. Contrary to Cox's orders, Donald had made no attempt whatsoever in the grasping of the Captain's beloved Willy. However, the faithful security guard's simultaneously brave and dim-witted nature appeared to mistake Donald's mad spring for freedom for that of a clumsy oaf accidentally falling towards certain doom, and as such, with a passionate "I'll save you," Willy tried to grab him instead. Unfortunately, the thought did not count as much as the execution. The moment one hand caught Donald, the other was wrenched loose, and they spilled down in a bearhug of their own, albeit certainly lacking the same tenderness as Kim's and Tim's.

Irrespective of tenderness of temperament, tenderness of body was all but guaranteed by the end of the jaunt. The group of four slammed into so many miscellaneous metal objects on the way down that a bored security guard would later go on to edit pinball sound effects into the footage of their escape. It didn't go viral, but it was a definite hit at the year-end staff party.

Every one of their hearts beat in their chests like vibrating cellphones. The constant rolling had rendered them disoriented to the point their brains were driven to disregarding all data taken in by their eyes. Every bump and thud knocked them further into a mind/body disconnect.

And then there was nothing. No more scratching noises assaulting their ears, no more roving shipping containers jumping out in front of them. Even the tumbling was reduced to a gentle rotation after they reached the edge of the hangar and burst through the force field into open space.

The comparative lack of stimuli did not render the experience any less terrifying; with a handhold not even tantalizingly close by, one couldn't help but swiftly devolve into a neurotic mess of limbs flailing in futile attempts to cease the body's spiralling. One by one, they spun until each could glimpse the monolithic marble that was Earth filling their view and beckoning them closer. And closer they did come, powerless to resist. To see the planet so close, yet sufficiently far away to perceive its curvature, has for centuries been a solemn reminder of life's fragility, and here was no exception. However, while others appreciated the poetic notion of a warm orb that provided safety and nourishment from the unforgiving void, that philosophy served as little comfort to a group of four currently on track to get denied entry by the bouncer with a flamethrower that was commonly referred to as an atmosphere.

Cox hollered to his wife, his crew. They may well have returned the favour but, as that one know-it-all present during every sci-fi movie is quick to remind: there was no sound in space. Thankfully, spasmodic hand gestures could provide reliably consistent communication, whether they were produced in the vacuum of space, under water, at a great distance, or in the Horace Mann School for the Deaf and Hard of Hearing. Yet in only one of those locations would an enormous spaceship bearing down upon you be a welcome sight.

From behind the twisted station of twisted people, a friendly nose peeked from the shadows. The mighty whale that was the *Jefferson*, stronger than tin and faster than most non-rocket powered vehicles, had returned to claim that which rightfully belonged inside of it. Like a snake emerging from a basket, it slid from behind the cover of darkness to give chase in a daring space race.

The castaways rejoiced in a display of making imaginary snow angels. This was followed by a display of swimming in imaginary water when they realized their hovering home not only resembled a whale in looks but also in ability to see small creatures directly in front of it. Willy took the brunt of the impact. His splayed-out body, dangling like a marionette, absorbed the snout of the vessel and pinned an arm and leg to either side. Even with no sound to complement the spectacle, Cox couldn't help but hear a train whistle in his head as he watched the collision play out. Still, home was a welcome sight. When he flicked on his mag boots and sidled up alongside the magnificent vessel, he tossed a cheeky glance to either side before the *Jefferson* found itself embraced by another, more tender hug.

Regardless of individual attachment to the *Jefferson*, it was a welcome change of scenery from the preceding excursion. Such excitement had pushed them all along the road to exhaustion of both the mental and physical variety, and they all shuffled wordlessly onto the bridge, dropping their helmets in a chorus of clunks and peeling space suits off their sweaty selves.

Usually the conductor of the complain train, Donald settled back into his disgusting bean bag without so much as a quip and closed his eyes. Each heavy breath inflated his belly and raised the clasped hands atop it before whistling out his nose as the two were let back down. All the while, Whisper stared at him with an expression of competing puzzlement and repugnance. She had expected the sudden and climactic return of her crew would merit an explanation without relying on her to prompt it. Even Kim, arguably the fittest of the bunch, made her entrance with the same level of enervation, while the last two carried on through and into the kitchen. The way the two remainders draped themselves in unconventional ways over their respective seats, neither seemed keen to reminisce.

Whisper continued to stare even after the groans of relief had subsided.

"Uh . . . Where were you guys . . . ?"

"Clubbing," Kim's muffled voice groaned from face down in her armchair. She raised her head. "Where the hell do you think we've been?"

"What's up with your husband? Is he miserable too? I've always wanted to see what him miserable would look like."

"Whisper, we just came from a literal warzone. Don't you dare start in on him."

"Whoa, jeez, it's not like I coulda known that." She huffed, turning back to her computer.

"You watched us all jump and free fall untethered through open space onto a moving ship. We didn't do that shit for fun!"

"I dunno! You guys might, for all I know! You do weird things. And my job sucked too. I had to sit here the whole time, thinking you guys had died, and freaking out 'cause I'd have to find a new job and I wouldn't have any references."

"Will you shut up!?" Donald snapped, trying to slam a fist into the plush surface of his seat for emphasis. "Some of us have actually had a shit day."

Whisper shrank into her chair.

"I ask one question, and you guys bite my head off. No wonder you guys hate science."

Then, a faint clatter wrested their attention toward the kitchen. Suspecting Willy, Kim lay her face back down. Inversely, Donald and Whisper craned their necks in a way that wouldn't amplify the sound at all but did make them feel like they could hear better. Noises emanated from the room to the tune of standard kitchen clamour like clinks, thuds, and sloshes of pouring liquid. However, they continued on in the wake of their security guard's emergence. Wholly absorbed by the plate in his hand, he passed through the gang and took a seat of his own, eager to refuel after his recent reanimation.

"Aw yeah . . . it's so nice to have outside food again."

"Willy, those are meal replacement capsules," Donald informed him in a monotone voice. "They have no taste."

"And they didn't even feed us!" Kim's voice rang loud even through the pillow that was smothering it.

Captain Cox, showing no signs of fatigue himself, and perhaps more motivated than ever, poked his head out from the kitchen.

"'Scuse me there, Miss Wang. What did you do with that bottle of kids' alcohol that Mister Nobody brought?"

His sudden appearance struck her with bemusement. Mouth slightly ajar and eyebrows slanting high, she regarded him the way one responds to a sudden inquiry from a neighbouring bathroom stall.

"Uh, it's . . . I put it behind the wine shelf . . . ?"

"Found it!"

He emerged triumphant, raising the bottle of vile liquid like it was a royal lion cub. Those around were less than impressed, clearly hoping for an expounding on his newfound excitement for Fireball whiskey. Any would do, as current signs forced the pessimist in them all to assume some sort of midlife crisis. Should a man as bold and brash as their commander in chief add the ensuing symptoms to his pre-existing conditions, there would not only be strong reason, but also a potential legal obligation, to have him sectioned. Then again, if his mental acuity remained as sound as ever, then they would be obligated as subordinates to see through whatever and wherever this delighted display was going. At least the former option had handy burly men in white coats to do the dirty work.

Mundane in appearance as it was, the glassware fascinated the captain every bit the same as any relic he had procured. It jingled slightly with every turn of his wrists, hinting to all but the dimmest that its contents were not those that were transcribed on the label. It was too small to be a spaceship in a bottle, yet too large to be something that ended up in there by sheer happenstance. Yet, thrilling as it was, he couldn't be brought to actually open it for a proper inspection. His usual impetuosity had waned somewhat, and for the first time, the fear of consequences saved his caution from the winds. So, instead, he took his seat and contemplated the situation—audibly, perhaps in hopes for someone to jump in.

"So this is what they all want . . . everybody. Even Nobody."

Donald was the first to bite.

"What is it?"

The captain turned the bottle over in his hands.

"I don't really know. That agent told me a bit about it. Just enough that I know it's some weird alien goo that eats pretty much whatever it touches. I guess I'll call it . . . Star jelly."

"Star jelly is already a thing." Whisper said, stiff as ever. After a beat she added: "I'm actually not surprised you guys don't know that. It's just a word idiots made up for squished frogs."

Cox blinked.

"Alrighty. How about . . . Space jam, then."

She shrugged. Donald showed a similar disinterest in moniker assignment, preferring instead to reach over and pilfer the last morsel from the now thoroughly contented security guard's plate. Kim could no longer remain checked out of the conversation. Even in her tired state, she could deduce the implications of this newfound macguffin. With eyes half closed and hair fresh out of a wind tunnel, she pushed herself up into a sitting position and blew a tuft of brown locks out of her face.

"So, wait, we actually *do* have that thing they want?! Well, goddamn it. Chuck it out the airlock and let's get out of here."

At this command, her husband leapt from his chair and clutched the bottle close to his body, outraged by such a suggestion.

"They might find it if we do that!"

"Good! Even better! Maybe they won't keep trying to find and kill us then!"

Throughout the tail end of the response, Whisper had begun a low mumble, which, by the sentence's end, had increased to a rather emphatic hum. As soon as the first mate had curtailed her own rebuttal, she forced her way into the conversation.

"Ehhhhhhhhhhhhhh somebody's hailing us!"

"Who? The prison?"

"Didn't say! They just kinda skipped straight to throwing those blocks of ice at us."

Whether they had fallen of their own accord or had received gentle encouragement from those too reluctant to space spelunk, the prison's petrified water supply had become the only pursuer brave enough to follow them through the forcefield and continue the universe's ongoing quest to ruin the crew's day. There was a certain elegance to the way they gyrated in their general direction, as if in slow motion. 'Twas almost hypnotic. Had he the armaments, Cox would have been tempted to return fire and take part in the very first space-snowball fight. Instead, he took the other rare opportunity that presented itself: getting to tell his pilot to engage in evasive manoeuvres and actually mean it.

"Quick, Ensign Wang! Engage in evasive manoeuvres!"

" . . . Do what?!"

"Evasive manoeuvres! Manoeuvres that will result in evasion!"

"Why—really? Sorry, I left my dogfighting helmet in my room."

"Can you get us out of the way, please?!"

"Ugh. I already did."

Ice, by its very nature, could be safely assumed to lack heat-seeking capabilities. Therefore, a simple sidle to the left transformed them from deadly projectiles into the interstellar equivalent of a beer bottle hurled by an insecure stepfather in a fit of inebriated fury. Missing by an inch or missing by a mile, the blocks spun like frozen fastballs on their way toward the mighty Earth. Thereupon, they would promptly burn up in the atmosphere causing at least one simpleton down below to probably look up and make a wish.

"They're literally just floating in a straight line," the pilot continued, gesturing forward with an open hand. Then, with an outstretched finger, she pantomimed nudging something slightly to the left.

"Boop."

"Can we get back on track, here?" Kim, ever responsible, insisted. "Tim, you're the most straight-laced guy I've ever met. I love ya for it. So why are you acting so weird about all this?! You're purposely not complying with law enforcement. You apparently attacked somebody! What's going on with you?"

He cocked his head to the side.

"What else have I been doing that's weird?"

" . . . uh. Okay, fine, just those two things. But don't act like they're not weird!"

"Okay! Okay! Fine. I'm being weird. Maybe I'm being weird. I don't know." He sighed. All this flustered head shaking had rendered his wavy hair into a tangled mess.

"It's been a rough space day, guys. It's safe to say we've all been pushed a little beyond our comfort zones. I wish I could say it's all over now, but there's something else we have to do." He eyed his wife knowingly. "I don't know how we're going to do it yet, but that's something her and I are going to decide. Together."

With a hand on the small of her back to guide her, they departed the bridge and left the subordinates to their literal devices. While the reprieve didn't have the relief that came with permanence, an extended relaxation period was not a concept likely to be snubbed by any of them. Everyone's feet swiftly found rest upon elevated surfaces as each commenced to drown the day's excitement under the humdrum calm of routine pastimes. All the while, Cox's voice evaporated away into the bowels of the vessel as he chatted up the missus.

"I know it's weird that I'm being so disobedient towards those secret agent guys. But it's funny; that big ice cube actually reminded me of a philosopher who would totally agree with the way I'm handling members of law enforcement."

15.
THE COUNCIL OF COX

THE GRAVITY SWITCH IN the sacred bedroom, chamber for the sawing of captain's logs, went as untouched as ever this evening. It hadn't been flicked to the off position since the *Jefferson*'s inaugural voyage. Although far from newlyweds at the time, Tim and Kim had felt a freedom upon blasting off that was beyond any they had experienced before. As was natural for a couple much in love with a palace all to themselves, drinking fancy wines and making blanket forts would inevitably give way as the night wore on to activities of a more lascivious nature. They flung their clothes in all manner of directions and tied their manes back shortly before their fingers and subsequently bodies entwined.

And it was when their weight hit the bed that the sudden stroke of genius occured. Kim rarely provided the suggestion of rendering a room a place of buoyance, but the one time she did, their minds raced with the possibilities that stemmed from the removal of such a hindrance. With blood rushing away from the brain, nary a thought was spared in consideration as Tim leapt from the bed and flipped the switch. Then, as if forgetting what he had just done, he sprung back towards his beloved, only to careen into the ceiling instead. Kim leapt to his aid. This led to a helpless entanglement of sheets and errant underwear bouncing about in passionate frustration.

After some careful manipulations, the jumble found itself resolved, and blankets, along with airborne nightstands and partially finished glasses of champagne, were tossed aside; messes could be always be cleaned up later. Yet, even when freed from obstacles, they found their own bodies to be difficult to control. The slightest bump or nudge would propel the other in the opposite direction, serving to separate the two well before getting to approach thrusting alignment. With no kinky tether apparatus available, the futility of it all became steadily more apparent. The mood died quickly amid the grunts of exertion with every new awkward positioning, as well as the glistening globules of sweat that inflated and flew off their bodies like bubbles. Any remaining arousal was further murdered by the lack of gravity, causing the requisite blood to rise into their heads and chests instead of collecting in the right place to fuel the machines. After a few quick minutes, the switch was flipped back, and they collapsed into bed spent and unsatisfied.

In short, sex in space sucks.

On this particular evening after their escape, though, the notion was about as far from their minds as it could be. It was never beyond reach, mind you, but was an unlikely course of action in the face of current circumstances. When they shuffled into the room with drooping shoulders, it required all their efforts to avoid collapsing into bed and delaying conversation for another time. It occurred to the captain that at no point did he give the pilot orders to vacate the scene. However, something in Whisper's words inspired confidence that it would happen nonetheless.

Neither had broached the topic by the time they had settled

into their respective seated positions. Kim slumped against the wall, one leg outstretched, while her husband sat at the foot of their bed with his hands situated stiffly on either side like he was meeting the father of his prom date. Their frank discussion had yet to commence and already he appeared prepared to submit.

"All I wanna know is why, Tim," the other said. Her tone was neither sceptical nor accusatory so as to keep the door for new ideas open. "There's obviously a reason you're doing something so unlike you, so c'mon. Let's hear it."

At that, his posture softened. While he had already sufficiently mulled over the situation in his head and found the words, they came easier knowing there was no impending cross-examination to be stared down during the delivery.

"This is going to sound kind of crazy," he breathed in hushed tones. "But we're involved in something way bigger than I thought."

"Love, there's British secret agents involved. This is obviously something a little beyond what we're used to."

"See, that's what I thought too!" He hopped off the bed and kneeled on the floor next to her. "But when they talked to me in my cell, I realized they aren't the good guys either. They're as bad as Mister Nobody. Maybe even worse! I figured it all out during my interrogation. I don't think they really even care about Mister Nobody that much, because they mostly talked about this space jam stuff. The Percy guy didn't say it directly . . . but do you know what I think he wants to do with it?!"

"Keep it for himself to use as a weapon?" Kim replied with all the surprise of a sarcastic seer.

"I thi—wait, yeah. Exactly. How did you know?!"

The smile painted on her lips was one part endearment and one part condolence. Neither it nor the patronizing pinch she gave his cheek alleviated any confusion.

"Oh, honey . . . I hate to sound like Donald, but they're a government organization with little to no supervision. What else would you think they'd want it for? To put in a museum? What are they, Indiana Jones?"

"But why! Why does everybody just want to destroy stuff and hurt people?!"

"Everybody doesn't want to destroy stuff and hurt people! But when you have an object that's sole purpose is destroying stuff and hurting people, then those are the type of people it's going to attract."

"Ex*act*ly!" The captain declared, driving the point home with an emphatic point on the second syllable. With his other hand, he tossed the bottle at her, causing a mild arrhythmia as she flailed desperately to catch it. A few moments were required for her hands and heart to settle. During this, Cox continued.

"This is why we gotta find a way to destroy it first. It's the only way to be safe."

"Did you really plan for the conversation to go like this?" Kim broke off the main topic. "If so, well played."

"Thanks! I had to improvise a little when you guessed what they wanted it for, but it did help speed things up."

With a small squeak of exertion, she hopped to her feet, giving him a quick peck on the cheek on her way up. The look she gave was vaguely reminiscent of the one back on the station when she thought he had maimed somebody. It didn't have the same level of admiration, but there was certainly evidence of something tickling her.

"You didn't need to try and sneak your point in like that, though," she amended. "I did say I had faith in your reasoning. Honestly, I'm just really proud of you for not letting your hopes for the best in everyone get in the way of seeing these guys for what they are. I mean, Christ, if *you* say they're bad, then I totally believe it. I figured I'd hear the pope talk shit about someone before you."

"Oh my god, you're right," the captain said, sitting back down on the bed. "I mean, I still really want to see the best in them . . . But I just can't."

He looked up at his wife.

"You don't think they're ruining me, do you?"

His expression of genuine fear was all that kept her from blowing a raspberry right in his face. In all these years, she'd never been able to explain the charm of his toddler-esque purity; even now, as it approached critical mass. The irony of being so pure he underwent an existential crisis at the thought of losing it was completely missing him. To call it silly was an understatement. With so little purity left of her own, maybe it was just nice to have somebody with plenty to spare. She took a seat next to him, grabbed his arm, and draped it over her shoulder. After a brief pause to deliberate, she answered.

"You know, an *actual* philosopher once said 'Love your enemy, but never sell your sword.' I don't usually remember stuff like that because most of them are just coming up with different ways to say 'Don't be a dick.' But I kinda liked that one, because even though it tells you not to be a dick, it doesn't pretend that not being a dick will make other people stop being dicks."

"Wow. You really used the word 'dick' a lot there."

"I don't have writers, alright? I picked a noun and stuck with it. The point is: trying to see the best in somebody doesn't mean trusting them. You always give everybody a chance, even when you really shouldn't. These guys blew it; so what else are you supposed to do? Just give 'em another one?"

Cox chuckled as he pulled her closer with his arm.

"That's literally what I wish I could do! Second chances are a thing, y'know."

"Exactly."

Kim got off the bed and stood before it so she could return the same gesture he gave her minutes before. She even picked the bottle back up and went to chuck it back at him before remembering the contents, deciding better, and setting it back down.

"The thought doesn't always count for everything, but it's good enough here. How you can possibly want to try and like those assholes in spite of all this is beyond me. The fact you do, though, should be all the proof you need that they haven't ruined you in the slightest."

The words, while served up quickly, were savoured in silence. With the amount of times the captain opened and closed his mouth in return, he may well have actually been trying to chew on them. After what appeared to be sufficient mastication, he raised his brow and settled on the classic yielding nod and shrug combo.

"Well played."

"Thanks. I had a bit of inspiration."

"What were we talking about before this?"

"Something about disposing of the weapon of mass destruction you found in our wine shelf. Do we even know for sure that's what it is?"

"I don't know why they'd lie . . . Well, I guess I kinda do, but I don't think that's the one they'd tell me. You can open it up and test if you want."

"I'll pass."

"Alrighty."

They sat in a comfortable quietude that could only have resulted from the years of boring lulls every couple had to go through in order to wring out the awkwardness. The ability to find contentment in each other's company was an essential part of surviving long space journeys together, and in this particular circumstance, refraining from speaking was made doubly easy by the apathy towards egging the conversation along. Both knew that one of them was going to have to come up with a suggestion. Neither wished to assume that responsibility. The day had been long and their bed was so tempting and the other person was totally smartish; so surely they could come up with something.

As the still-seated one, Tim flopped down on it first. In an effect similar to taking the first donut from the box, it removed any reluctance Kim may have been having and spurred her to dive in shortly afterward. The lovely plush mattress enveloped the two of them like a huge, steaming plate of mashed potatoes. Fervid moans escaped from both as they did their best impressions of dogs jumping into a mud pit. Eventually, their batteries slowly died and their movements reflected this diminished energy. They both lay face down, limbs splayed as if in chalk outlines.

KIM WOKE FIRST, STRETCHING her arms and humming, face down, into the covers. Tim grunted back. Without looking, she reached over with her foot and nudged what she thought was his shoulder, prompting him to raise his head and ask why she just kicked him in the face. Such protestations were cancelled by the sight of an open door and the trio of kids staring inside, seemingly too uncomfortable to say what they came to say.

"Oh hey, guys!" He chirped, causing Kim to sit bolt upright. "What's up?"

They looked at each other, eyes lingering until Donald was the first to look back.

"Did you guys seriously go to bed without even telling us where to go?"

Cox slithered from the bed to his hands and knees in the least dignified way possible. A few shimmies back and forth cracked his back and injected a little more liveliness into him. Not enough to forego sleep, mind you, but, ideally, enough to survive this conversation.

"No, no, Donny, buddy. We may have been in bed, but we weren't sleeping. Don't worry."

"Ew." he replied, with a wrinkled nose.

"Where is it you want us to go?" Whisper asked from behind the hand that shielded her eyes. "'Cause we're kinda in the middle of flying to nowhere right now."

"That's what we're trying to figure out," Kim's voice echoed, its owner appearing to have made her way to the bathroom. "Don't suppose any of you guys know where to go to destroy alien goo?"

"We're destroying it now!?" Donald blurted. "Haven't we pissed enough people off already?"

The first mate's head poked out from the doorway.

"Know what also really pisses people off, Donald? Dying."

Her disappearance was as quick as her emergence, leaving the man posed in an uncomfortable stance as he tried to process her words. It was lucky she didn't feel the need to stick around for a response, since he didn't appear to have one.

"Uh . . ." He scratched at his head. "Was that a threat, or was she making some kind of point . . . ?"

"No, no, buddy," the captain, who had retrieved the bottle and was absentmindedly jingling it like the bell of a Salvation Army Santa, said as he snapped back into the conversation. "Kim and I are just pretty sure if the agents get their hands on this, then their government might use it to terrorize people."

"Of course they're going to use it to terrorize people! That's all they ever do! What did you think they were going to do with it? Donate it to a museum? What are they, Indiana Jones?"

"I already made that joke," Kim called.

"Fine! Uh . . . Then what did you think they were going to do with it? Use it for . . . uh, waste disposal? What are they, garbage . . . men?"

"Who's Indiana Jones . . . ?" Whisper murmured.

"Donny, if you knew they were going to use it to hurt people, then why are you okay with giving it back to them?!" Cox asked.

"Because they're going to hurt us if we don't!"

A hush fell over the group. The notion, while entirely predictable and not incorrect, conjured a light of sociopathy over the crew member when it was spoken aloud. Donald seemed to realize the weight of his words the moment they left his lips, but he stood with an uncharacteristic straightness and met every wavering gaze cast upon him. He swallowed hard. Debating with people was so much harder without a screen to hide behind.

"Great, now you all think I'm a monster," he continued, dropping his hands. "Like it's not completely normal to value your own life above the lives of random people you don't know. Governments have always done this stuff, and they're gonna keep doing it, whether or not they get this thing. The only difference is whether or not they're going to pay attention to us, too."

As captain, Cox knew it fell on him to take up the mantle of making a case for morality. There was always the option to simply pull rank and order him to obey or get dropped off at the nearest space diner. However, he was literally up against a guy defending the notion of helping a government in the commission of war crimes. The moral high ground he had here was so vast that pretty much any response would win, even if delivered while stomping on a baby otter.

"In my opinion, the British are evil!"

" . . . What?! That's not even what we're fighting about!"

"Oh. Well, okay. So we agree they're evil then?"

"It doesn't matter if they're evil! It's not our job to deal with them."

"We're not doing it because I think it's our job! Donny, buddy, we're doing it because we're in a position where we can. If they had the space jam already, then I wouldn't be suggesting breaking into their ship and risking our lives to steal it."

"That definitely sounds like something you'd do."

"Pshhh, no way! If that were the case, then I would just report them to the proper authorities."

"Then why don't we do that now!?"

"Because I don't know who the proper authorities are."

"Then how would you—"

"The point is, this isn't as simple as picking our lives over the lives of others. Nobody else knows about this but us! If we turn our backs on millions of innocent people who have no fighting chance just because we aren't brave enough to take advantage of the one we got then, well, we may as well be villains ourselves. Because we at least have a chance. And if we try, then even if we fail, we can spend our remaining days, however many or few there may be, knowing that we took a stand against a force way bigger than ourselves because it was the right thing to do! And that knowledge can't be taken away from us with any amount of beatings or sleep deprivation or waterboarding or lobotomizing."

He finished his speech with legs wide and arms akimbo, picking a spot on the ceiling to triumphantly stare at. It was a slight buzzkill to realize the uplifting trumpet music he thought he was hearing had only taken place in his head, but the weight of the words persisted nonetheless. After all the many adventures aboard the *Jefferson*, he finally got the opportunity to give a passionate address to rally the troops. Looked like the day wasn't a total loss after all.

"So who's with me?!" He polled the group with an outstretched hand.

Without a moment's hesitation, Willy offered a hand, eager to be a team player. He slapped his hand on top of the Captain's and flashed a delightful, doughy smile. It was unclear if he fully grasped what he had signed up for, but his support was welcome all the same.

Perhaps it was because she had fallen into the precarious position of swing vote and didn't wish to be left for last, or maybe the rousing pep talk had indeed cracked her cockles, but a few moments later, Whisper offered a slow-moving hand that was gently placed upon the digital entanglement. From there, all attention fell on Donald. Mouth fallen open in surprise, he assessed each face one by one.

"No," he snarled with disgust at the notion his mind might have changed. "I'm not buying it, 'cause you're not that great at speeches, and they don't work on me anyway. There's a 'chance' I could win the lottery too. Or play in the NBA. Or even that one of my stupid emails is from an actual Nigerian prince. Doesn't mean it's gonna happen, and definitely doesn't mean I'm willing to bet my life on it."

"But we're the good guys! The good guys are supposed to stand up to the bad guys. How would you feel if we came back and found—"

"Can I cut in?" Kim emerged from the bathroom, having done some sort of cosmetic touch-up that was completely unnoticeable to any of the males. "Nothing you're saying is wrong, Tim, but you're arguing like you're trying to convince a group. For Donald, you need to appeal to something more basic. Besides basic human decency, that is. Watch."

She marched towards him with a slight swagger; just enough to pepper her assertiveness with confidence. Donald leaned away unconsciously. His eyes did not shy away from her, but the slight downturn of his mouth hinted at a concealed fear of getting slugged. Yet no physical harm did come. Instead, she clasped her hands behind her back and regarded him with a cheeky smirk, like someone who had an ace cheat code on their poker app.

"Don't get me wrong, Donald, I agreed with you at first. But what do you think will happen if we just hand it back to them? That they'll give us a fond 'cheerio' and forget all about it? We're on their list now. If we hand this thing over, then we're just a loose end privy to a government secret that they may not want anyone to know about. A loose end that regularly goes on voyages where we're all alone and not in contact with anybody. You think a ship with agents on it showing up is bad? You obviously don't know what it's like to see a space drone headed your way."

Beads of perspiration coalesced on Donald's forehead. The urge to compare his opponent to Hitler was strong. All it took was a moment's mulling to find every hole in such a response. The worst part of all was the bitter taste he had towards the very position he had taken. He had stated on many occasions his preference to die before helping out "the man," and it was only a matter of time until someone remembered one of these times and used it to bolster their argument. Between that and Kim's evisceration, it was time to shift the spotlight and hope nobody noticed him abandoning his case.

"How will destroying it fix any of that?" He barked, quickly wiping his forehead.

"Fix any of that?!" Repeated a caught-off-guard Kim. "We don't even know how to destroy it yet. I was just saying that, either way, we're in the precarious position you described. So may as well be dicks to them on the way out."

"Honey, seriously, there are other words . . ."

"Insubordinate troublemaking rebels. Whatever. So how do we get rid of this stuff?"

"Dude!" Willy reminded everyone of his presence. "Let's shoot it into the sun!"

Kim blinked at him, as if seeing him for the very first time.

"That's . . . that's actually not the worst suggestion."

"Except we don't have anything to shoot it out of," said Cox. "And it would take a way too long to get there; somebody could snag it. We need to take it somewhere that it can be destroyed. I think that Percy guy said something about it being susceptible to acids; does anybody know where we can get our hands on a bunch of acid?"

The ship's communicator pursed his lips.

"Well, I remember when I was at SIT they had a pretty well-known department of chemistry."

"Donald, I know you didn't go to SIT. You can stop lying about it."

"What the hell!? I absolutely did! How would you even know?"

"Whoa there, guys! It doesn't matter if he went or not; I bet a university is somewhere we could find lots of acid!"

"Well then, why don't we go to yours, Tim? Least I know for sure that you're an alum."

"Mine?! My school doesn't have anything. They just uploaded knowledge directly into your brain each day."

Rolling of eyes and grumbles of contempt echoed from around him. Perhaps worse was how little surprise anyone seemed to have. To be regarded as spoiled, while unbecoming, was a shruggable stigma, as comfort could be found in the knowledge it was not one's own fault. But lazy? That was an affliction known to affect anyone, regardless of walk of life. There was no explanation for laziness that didn't involve a failure from within.

"Just because it was easy doesn't mean I couldn't have done it if it was hard!" He protested the thoughts he assumed them to be having.

"How is it possible that you are so stupid, then!?" Whisper demanded. Immediately afterward, she raised her hands to backpedal. "I know. I'm sorry. I just can't even . . . You could literally get any info just put into your brain and you still—UGH!"

She stormed off down the hall opposite from the bridge, forcing Cox to call his rebuttal after her.

"Well, I mean . . . it's been a while! It fades over time. I haven't gone back for any booster knowledge shots in a while."

Donald threw his arms up then let them fall back to his sides with a mighty slap.

"It's easy knowledge! You don't even have to work for it. Of course you wouldn't go back. Why would you want that, right?!"

"Alright, don't you get carried away, too." Kim snapped. "He can't go back because his parents cut him off when he married me. That's all I'm saying about that, so drop it."

Over the course of the bickering, the group had been migrating about their mobile home. The heated conversation had taken a sturdy grasp on all attention during the drifting past Donald's bedroom, the former location of Whisper's bedroom, the hallway full of strewn-about Christmas decorations that used to be in the closet where Willy had made his home, as well as the rarely used passage leading down to engineering, where Whatshername may or may not still be at this point. As was always the case, they washed up on the bridge right in time with Kim's most recent command.

To see his beloved work station was all the encouragement Cox needed to redouble his satisfaction with life. It may have consisted of nothing but a chair and . . . well, nothing but a chair, but a former classmate also got the same degree, and he went on to launch an unsuccessful kickstarter trying to fund a pimping career. So, by comparison, being the captain of a ship, regardless of purpose or prestige, was pretty alright! No amount of that silly e-learning would have made him any better at captain-ing anyway. That was all him; for better or for worse.

Yet as he took his seat, mulling the magnitude of his situation, something from his school days did indeed bubble up from the recesses of his mind. It was not a formula, nor was it a theory, a study, or a recipe for pot brownies. In fact, it was something he would continue to have, even if his mind had sloughed away every last tidbit of information shoved inside it, like a game of Perfection. It was the most important thing that anyone could take away from college, and it was the one thing he had never needed any guidance in obtaining: a friend.

"Hey, Donny, do we still have that email from Pia to come see her lab?"

16.

DUDE, WHERE'S MY SPACESHIP?

SAN FRANCISCO: A LAND where the seismograph activity was pretty significant, but gaydar readings made those squiggly lines on the seismograph look puny in comparison. For this reason, it was considered both the holy land and the unholy land, depending on who you asked. Nevertheless, few would disagree it was a fun enigma of a city. It somehow managed to maintain a cost of living high enough to turn movie stars into compulsive couponers whilst simultaneously having a population consisting mostly of unemployed hippies. The only way to tell the difference between the rich ones and the poor ones was to watch and see if they took their LSD inside a luxury apartment or if they dropped a dose after relieving themselves into that same apartment's flower bed.

Some would erroneously perceive the preceding facts to be shortcomings. However, the place clearly drew a sort of strength from them, since it had survived the dissolution of the United States. Not only did it survive, but it did so without so much as interrupting the pride parade that had been doing laps around the megalopolis nonstop for as long as anybody could remember. What exactly the parade took pride in had long been lost to history. However, few cared, as all were welcome in the cacophonic glitter blizzard that was as much a beloved part of The City as the solid-gold statue of Cher, which had been erected on Market Street after an earthquake.

This parade's aggressively inclusive outlook was a direct reflection of San Francisco itself. In a city where every single person was weird, nobody could be considered weird, and therefore, any and all seeking acceptance felt obliged to show up on the streets paved with gold and the shattered glass of dropped bongs. It was that sentiment that attracted freshly minted thirty-year-old Pia Dickenson. Seventeen divorces in such a milestone year had left the blonde-haired and rosy-cheeked tricenarian with ample emotional baggage, along with a discontent toward her use of her youthful years spelled out in scarlet letters. Thus, her relocation to the mecca of acceptance seemed only natural. Plus, with not a straight man in sight, there was nothing to distract her from maintaining her lab.

As evidenced in the previous paragraph, Pia simply had something of a problem with self-control when it came to matters of matrimony. Her choice of male participants often did her great disservice as well. Worse still, her fleeting romances constantly impeded her aspirations of dog-show glory, for the lab whose maintenance was in question was a retriever of the chocolate variety. With ears of perfect length and glistening coat, a life of chasing squirrels and eating vomit would do him no justice, so she brought him here in search of greener pastures. More specifically, greener pastures forged from artificial turf and populated by judgmental people carrying laser measurers and digital thermometers.

Right from the get go, money was tight. She had to blow the first of her seventeen alimony checks just to cover the taxi drone from the CA High Speed Rail terminal that languished under the Salesforce Dildo. From there, the rest of her money dwindled away quickly on lodgings, naturally generated hipster food, and just enough data to locate the nearest dog show. Once the latter ran dry, her phone careened frisbee-style out the nearest window and she once more dashed into the streets. With cabs scarce and money scarcer, the only method of transportation left was to grab onto the nearest conga line and hip thrust along with the pupper tucked under one arm. The creature had four very capable legs of its own, but conveying airs of whimsy were far more important.

Her spirits were dashed once more upon arrival. For her beloved Woody, majestic, swarthy creature that he was, still required an entry fee in order to partake in any of these terrestrial contests. As a dog, he unsurprisingly lacked the requisite cash-procuring abilities to pay his own way. Therefore, the onus fell on Pia. While never ill-intentioned, she was no stranger to hubris, and her list of milk-able contacts reflected as such. But she had come so far. It would take great reaching, but with an internet café at her disposal and the motivational sight of Woody allowing himself to be humped by every dog, cat, and addict at the park across the street, she would persevere.

Her shame had officially been cast aside. There was purpose driving her actions; every unfortunate soul who had ever come into contact with her—be they veterinarians, mailmen, former landlords, ministers, or old college classmates—had to know. And if they had a nickel, then they would be petitioned for it!

After sending the most recent email, her attention was diverted by the mounting stir taking place outside. Like other patrons, she got up from her table to ascertain its origins. The buzz of excited chatter and fingers pointing skyward directed her face in a likewise direction while the occasional word like "Guantanamo" or "terrorist" made themselves heard.

Then the dark object appeared in the sky. At first, it was no larger than sprinkle. Then it grew, as objects careening in one's direction are known to do. As it drew closer, it revealed itself to be a transport shuttle that a sensible spectator would realize likely had no driver, given the way it tumbled like a child with polio falling down a hill.

(Polio, being a long-forgotten disease by this point in time, was perfectly acceptable to laugh at.)

Less than a minute had transpired between the point Pia noticed the commotion and the time the seemingly unmanned transport shuttle vessel crashed into and utterly obliterated the Golden Gate Bridge. The explosion rippled across the cityscape and sent tidal waves in every direction while a comparatively calm smoke cloud gently retraced the steps of that which caused it. A sober silence took hold of the crowd. Then, barely a second later, they all returned to what they were doing, with the exception of two city workers. After placing their tools on the ground, they moved their ladder across the street to a sign that read "Number of Days Without the Golden Gate Bridge Getting Damaged," which they reset to zero.

Pia would soon come across both of those men again. Later that day, all witnesses to the ship crash found themselves rounded up and confined to an Air Force hangar for questioning and reconditioning. Turned out the Government found prison breakouts resulting in jettisoned spaceships performing domestic kamikaze attacks more interesting than the average resident of San Francisco did. Who'd have thought? The communal disinterest certainly made their job of information containment easier. After only three neuralyzations, the men-in-suits felt confident that there no longer existed any memory of the shuttle or the alleged terrorists who had ejected it.

After release, Pia encountered each of the workers and married one later that day—and then the other a day later, after the second killed the first in a jealous rage. That night he would be bludgeoned to death by Pia herself after he got up at two in the morning for a bathroom break and accidentally stepped on Woody's tail.

Woody never did go on to win any of those dog-part-measuring contests. It was difficult for Pia to enter him in any of them while fleeing from San Francisco's fabulous fuzz, since it turned out the city's tolerance didn't quite extend to cold-blooded killers. But that's not to say she didn't try anyway. Unfortunately, the garbage ship she smuggled herself off-world in did not have any wi-fi for her to send off her online registration forms. It was only after finding herself stranded on a remote asteroid colony that she finally accepted the grim prognosis of her dreams of dog-show stardom.

The pup never seemed to mind, anyway. After being abandoned, then taken in by some benevolent travellers, he would go on to irresponsibly sire thirty-eight children and maul four mailcopters. Some would say such a life was preferable to the one originally intended for him. Others would say "Dude, he's a stupid dog. Who the hell cares?"

Those people have no hearts.

17.
SEE YA, WOULDN'T WANNA PIA.

Meanwhile, Pia Dickinson, age of fifty-two, recipient of the Master's Degree in Everything from Education Station, and definitely the Pia with the laboratory who had invited Cox to visit her, stood in front of the large circular window of her bedroom. Her jet-black hair didn't quite reach her body, which was completely bare in spite of being visible to anyone that happened to drive by. Shy, she was not. Sipping coffee in this fashion was a common pastime. A rather uneven ratio of pilates, well-rounded meal supplements, and the state-of-the-art cosmetic surgery commonly purchased by wealthy spinsters kept everything looking tight. Marlon Brando didn't seem to have any complaints. He just lay in bed, smoking his cigarette and otherwise keeping his mouth shut.

She seemed to have already forgotten him. Her face wore a serene expression, as if through this window was an empire of which she was sovereign. Had she known this would be such a regular activity, a concerted effort would have been made to stick the window on the other side so that she could actually look down on the rest of her lab from high in her room. But, alas, the opportunity was missed and imagination would have to suffice. If the room did have a view, it would see the sprawling circular superstructure that her wealth cultivated and that now cultivated her wealth. With her quarters at the top of the pillar and a ring at the bottom, the whole thing was shaped like an inverted basketball hoop. However, to own a space station was not enough of a statement anymore. The devil of the details separated the classy from the tacky. Thus, she forewent the retro polished-metal look and covered the whole exterior in ornate stonework that swirled continually around the whole of the headquarters in such a way that it would cost an absolute fortune to render if this story were ever turned into a movie.

The top was a lonely place. With the exception of her mother, it had been quite some time since she had a real interaction with a real person. Cabin fever may well have set in some time ago, but if so, then she hadn't noticed. Her regimen was far too absorbing. Quotas had to be met, prototypes had to be tested regularly, and new models were coming off the line faster than the older models that operated the line could keep up with. Such descriptors might give the impression of soul-crushing torture. However, all work and no play only dulled those who could derive no satisfaction from it. With so much excitement awaiting her every day, it seemed like such a waste of time to indulge in such contrivances as social interaction.

Unfortunately, the one drawback to self-imposed exile was that it isolated her from any who would shower her with praise. Positive reviews from satisfied customers were a pale imitation of the surge of pride that only came from someone telling you how awesome you are right to your face. It was an itch that needed another scratching; a deep, mauled-by-a-grizzly-bear level of scratching that would stave off the desire for an extended period. Sure, her legendary work ethic could persist even through such wistful desires. And it often had. There was no need to test its limits this time, though, because the brief time she spent in college interacting with the people of the public had put her in contact with someone she believed was literally the most complimentary man in the universe. After much waiting, he had finally returned one of her emails.

It wasn't entirely clear why he attended in the first place. For a man of more-than-moderate means, no door that opened for him triggered his fancy. The whole pursuit of knowledge that came with the college experience seemed to run secondary to his main desire of making others like him. At least, that's what she assumed his primary aspiration to be. All she could confirm was that everything everyone did fascinated the fellow, while the material being taught did not. She would never forget watching his restless squirming during a five-minute-long computer-science brain download, only to see him leave and spend the next half-hour listening to a homeless man give his theory on how being born on Earth caused autism.

The only drawback was that he didn't come as promptly as she would have liked. Such was the price of not paying for praise. Further, he left very little time between his response and the time he simply showed up. For once, the thoughtlessly placed window of her bedroom gave her a view of something. In this case, it was a large cork-shaped ship with drab metal coverings that chugged along like a bellows-powered submarine. The pilot cut it a little close for Pia's liking on their drive by. The drifting behemoth came near enough for the long-haired hefty fellow sitting by one of the portholes to nearly choke on whatever he was eating after a casual glance out the window gave him a glimpse of her. He seemed to like what he'd seen, spastic attempt to hide afterward aside.

Having gone so long without guests, it took her a moment to remember the social convention of wearing clothes during interactions. With little to work with, a turquoise silk robe haphazardly tossed across her shoulders would have to do. With the aforementioned convention satisfied, she began a calm trot to the elevator to receive her guests, wholly unbothered by the bit of boob hanging out.

They united at the bottom of the shaft. Pia stepped out of the elevator just in time to see her old acquaintance, as ageless as she was, emerge from the gangway and immediately spread his arms wide.

"Pia!" The overjoyed man declared as if she were not aware of her own name. "How are you? It's been forever!"

"It's actually been thirty-one years," she replied in a pleasant, if monotonous, voice, not reacting at all to the hug he wrapped her up in. "I see you have brought company."

"Oh yeah, this is Willy! He really wanted to come for some reason."

Willy gave a curt nod upward of his smoldering face.

"Sup. I'm the bodyguard. I keep him safe and . . . stuff. Your place is cool."

"Good for you. Keep your compliments centered on 'my place' and you can stay."

THEY FOLLOWED ALONG THE ring in a counterclockwise fashion. Pia's tour-giving style certainly would never score her a gig at Disneyland, as her attempts at directing attention were given with all the enthusiasm of a minimum-wage fast food worker. It may have been sheer exposure that dampened the fires of her passion. Many long years had been spent here, so trying to bring others up to speed on what was now second nature was an understandably taxing endeavour—especially for one that barely seemed to care.

Cox played his role admirably, especially for one unaware they had a role to play. With each convincing "Oooh" and orgasmic "Ahhh," it became easy to forget the field trip was being conducted by the opposite of Ms. Frizzle. Fascinating as bubbling beakers and oversized centrifuges were, the educational component received little aid when the instructor merely pointed to them and stated what the equipment was called. As they trod along the linear circle, the captain found himself feeling more and more lost. At no point during any of their email exchanges did he actually ask what it was she created here. It was assumed that such notions would be the first things addressed upon arrival. However, now that he was here and well into the tour, not only was he still left in the dark, but now they were sufficiently far along that he was afraid to ask. It felt like forgetting a girlfriend's name while in the middle of meeting her parents.

A few feet in front of them a door opened, and from it emerged a man who was so attractive it could only be described as unfair. This tall, masculine, chiselled, bright-eyed and dark-haired gentleman commanded all attention the moment he appeared. He likely did so every time he went anywhere, because he was the most perfect-looking man who ever lived.

"Holy crap!" Cox gasped, jaw dropping. "Is that beloved early 21st century actor, singer, and dancer Hugh Jackman?!"

"I have no idea," Pia responded in a bored voice. "But probably. We get requests from many people sending us his picture and asking us to make him for them."

"It's true!" Beloved early 21st century actor, singer, and dancer, Hugh Jackman said with his divine accent.

Willy shrugged up at the man with pursed lips.

"He's okay, I guess."

"He is much better than okay," his creator boasted, dry as ever. "Specimen 24601 is one of our top-selling models. We get high satisfaction reports from his purchasers."

"Heh, what can I say? I'm happy if I can make others happy!"

"That will do for now, 24601. Report to my bedroom for testing. I will join you once I am finished with my guests."

Whether it was due to crafted obedience or because Hugh Jackman is just such a nice guy, he carried out the order as if compelled. From his walk to his idle whistles, he seemed human in every way. So much so that Cox still felt the need to wait until he had disappeared into the elevator before further inquiry. No need to risk offending him, whatever he was.

"Sooo uh . . . You make robo-people?"

Pia's mouth fell open and the faintest wrinkle quivered into existence on her brow.

"They are not robots! I pointed out incubators. Why would I have incubators for beings comprised of mechanical components? My creations are living, breathing people. They are like my children."

The captain and his guard traded looks before returning them back to her. Cox held his tongue but Willy couldn't resist.

"Dude, didn't you just send him up to your room?"

Such an accusation didn't fetter her in the slightest.

"I did," she said as she carried on down the way.

"So, uh . . . What do you guys do up there, then?"

"Ability assessment depending on each unit's intended purpose. Every creation is put through a testing process of their core functions. They can perform an impressive variety of tasks, you see. Nearly as many as any human. From menial duties such as a servant or housekeeper to more advanced activities like chauffeur or handyman. Like us, they can sing, they can create, they can work, they can converse, they can learn, they can even love."

"Ohhh, I see!" Cox interjected as if relieved. "Wow! That's amazing. So what was that one made for?"

"Sexual intercourse," Pia responded without looking back. "Ninety-nine point nine eight percent of all orders are placed for units proficient in sexual intercourse."

Cox's stride suffered due to his mounting discomfort. An inverse effect seemed to take hold of Willy. Despite their age gap, he had been inexplicably enamoured with her since the moment they docked, and with this bizarre turn in topic, he now hung on her every word.

"Wooooaaah! That's nutty. And you do that with all of them?!"

"Of course. Quality control is an essential part of the manufacturing process."

"B-but . . ." The captain protested from behind. "Didn't you say they are like your children?!"

"I did say that, Timon. Not unlike a mother, I create them and foster their potential. I would consider that a sound simile."

"Yeah, dude, it's simple! They're like her kids, but she also bangs 'em sometimes."

"Nearly always, actually."

"I am so uncomfortable right now."

"What about the girl ones?!" Willy pressed. "Do you make girl ones too? And . . . do you test stuff with them?"

"Mister Padilla! Buddy! You can't just ask somebody tha—"

"I do not administer testing on our female products, as my own sexual proclivities are male-centric," she said, ignoring Cox. "Instead I simply oversee the quality control conducted by one of my personal attendants."

The attendants, as they were referred, could be seen through the windows of each room passed by. As many of them were bespectacled with protective goggles and clad in white lab wear, it was easy to unconsciously objectify them to the same level as the objects they operated—if not more. After all, in areas that billowed smoke and hisses, the roiling vats of vibrant liquids and oddly satisfying whirling arms of machines were far more engaging to a layman than those manning them.

However, when he took a moment to pay some extra attention, the captain found himself floored at the amount of faces familiar to a history buff such as himself. Icons of stage and screen, or song and sport, all manned the line like common peasants. Each one looked as though they spent the same amount of hours in the gym and make-up trailer as their bygone era counterpart. Madame Tussaud would be proud.

"That's weird how they're all celebrities from the 20th and early 21st century," he noted.

"I am only legally permitted to sell specimens modelled after individuals old enough for their likeness to be in the public domain," she responded, treating it like any other question.

"Ah. There's so many though! Have you . . . ?"

"All of them." Pia responded before he had finished.

"Wow . . ."

None of them seemed inherently unhappy, yet there was an unshakeable dystopian feel that came from seeing them packed like sardines in a Swedish sweatshop. In spite of their tight quarters, they worked together with a synchronicity as perfect as the machines. Such behaviour was the only hint of uncanny valley in their makeup. Well, that and the ridiculous smiles they wore, in spite of engaging in zero social interaction with one another.

From far up ahead, just around the bend, bits of familiar territory began to pop up. At no point in the tour did any of the frosted-glass room partitions or wall-embedded foliage seem copied or pasted from other parts of the facility; therefore, it seemed rational to assume they were nearly back where they had started. Feeling an impending conclusion, Cox couldn't help but glance around in search of a gift shop.

"Well I gotta say, Pia, this place is real—"

"Quiet," she said quickly. The proprietor's gaze was transfixed seemingly on a large, suspicious shrub in a corner, not unlike any of the others that populated the halls of her kingdom. "Something is not right."

"Do you want me to shoot it?!" The bodyguard offered, drawing the laser rifle from his back. "I can shoot it."

"Willy!" His captain hissed. "You don't even know what you're offering to shoot at."

"Oh . . . but, like . . . safety first?"

"You wanna be safe by blindly shooting at something?!"

"It's just the stun gun from the prison, dude."

"I said 'Quiet!'" Pia reiterated.

The trio gazed at the workplace garnish as if expecting it to explode. Willy slowly raised his weapon up, stopping when Cox put a hand out and slowly pushed it back down. The bush didn't so much as rustle. Any subtle sounds that may have been emanating from it were drowned out by the bustling footsteps from adjacent rooms and the occasional distant cry of "IT'S ALIVE! IT'S ALIVE!!" which could not possibly still be original by this point. Willy cleared his throat.

"We're all looking at that leafy thing, right? Or am I missing something?"

"Yes, we are looking at my croton."

"It's nice! Goes really good with that corner."

"It is not supposed to be in that corner. Somebody has moved it."

With such a heinous crime having been committed, the group was understandably on edge. Only the vilest of psychopaths could bring themselves to disturb such an obviously well-tended ecosystem of a workplace. With such an act already under their belt, there was no telling what they would escalate to next.

Pia walked over to the shrub and picked it up to set things right. As soon as it was moved, the limp body of a young Joseph Stalin spilled onto the floor. His eyes were every bit as glazed as they were in life, and his time in the corner only seemed to strengthen the messy allure of his hair. However, the sizzling blaster shot in the unit's chest wasn't that attractive, except maybe to a niche market that had some issues to work through.

"Oh my *GOD*!" Cox exclaimed, recoiling in tandem with everyone else. "Is it bad that I kinda feel bad for him? I mean 'cause, y'know, he's not the real one, but still . . ."

18.

SHOT THROUGH THE HEART, BUT WHO'S TO BLAME?

Security at *casa de* Pia was abysmally low for a location that could be easily confused for the Oscars or Grammys or a Whole Foods. The choice to have only one way in or out may have been a defendable design, but the funny thing about easily secured exits was the fact that they weren't worth much if left completely unmanned. Perhaps history may have made it seem unnecessary. Like the island homes of yesteryear, a space-based place was only accessible to either the well-funded or admirably tenacious. Such seclusion understandably limited outsider knowledge of a building's contents and dissuaded any in the know from making attempts upon procuring them. Of course, it also made the collection of one's mail into a tremendous nuisance. For all the leaps and bounds made by a spacefaring society, a reliable address system still had not been formulated to guarantee the right mail could be delivered to the right station. Most opted for the simple PO box solution; but Pia had become quite frustrated with hers in recent years as it became stuffed more and more often with a frankly alarming amount of alimony checks meant for somebody with a similar name who lived on Earth.

Should the isolation defence be circumvented and foreign parties gain access to the lab, they would quickly find the place to be an easy case. Not much of readily apparent value was kicking around, but unless they bumped into the overseer herself, they could look for as long as they pleased. The only real obstacle was the odd attempted sexual advance from the suspiciously pretty staff members milling around. Despite their otherwise-unflappable professionalism, they valued the personal space of their guests about as much as a cat did.

But this wasn't Kim's first ballgame. Donald and Whisper's stealth skills, by comparison, were fairly lackluster. Fortunately for them, they had no responsibility besides to follow along behind her without banging pots and pans together.

If the co-captain had one drawback as an infiltrator, it would probably be her lack of patience. The two decoys were barely out of eyeshot with their charge before she bolted out of the ship, Glock in hand, and set to work. The gun might as well have been a flashlight with the way it was waved about during the searching. Like with many things, prior knowledge would have eased the process greatly; had they known about the surveillance shortcomings, it would have saved them a lot of crouching under windowsills and skipped heartbeats every time footsteps went by.

"I still don't know why you guys wanted to come," Kim informed the floor as she bear-crawled along a wall. "This isn't exactly a three-man job."

"Well it was go with you, go with Cox, or stay with the ship," Donald explained as he walked behind her, perfectly upright. "I didn't wanna come at all, but since I'm here, I figured I may as well stay with the gun."

"Chances of needing the gun would be a lot smaller if you would make any attempt whatsoever to hide yourself."

"There's no point. If we get caught, it's going to be by a security guard who's already in the hallway. No scientist is going to care if they see some random person out in the hall. They're probably not even looking out the window; they're working."

"You know that from your years of being a scientist, do ya?"

Donald stopped in the middle of the hallway.

"I went to SIT, dammit!" He spat at her amid his foot stomping. "Just because I didn't graduate, and am stuck working this shitty job for you people, it doesn't mean I'm a burnout loser who makes things up to try and hide my failures."

His voice was so loud it startled Kim into an about-face, which wasn't easy to do on her hands and knees. Any wit stored for his response was sapped by the outburst. Being the sassiest person in the room may have been important to her, but not enough so to supersede her own well-being.

"Calm down!" She implored with an open hand. "I'm sorry, I'm sorry. Now is the wrong time to be bugging you. Just, can you try and keep your voice down at least?"

A grunt was all the acknowledgement she got, but it was enough to earn her a slump against the wall and irritated sigh. As the oldest member of the group, and the only one putting forth the requisite effort to contort into discomfort for stealth's sake, even she was not immune to the occasional "kids these days" moment.

"Do I even wanna know what your excuse is?" She asked Whisper with a raised eyebrow.

The pilot had been rather distracted by whatever she happened to be viewing through the window. With hands on the sill and head raised just high enough to peep through, she briefly took up the mantle of "party member who most resembles a burglar." Kim's question seemed to snap her out of an enthralment.

"Are you crazy!? There's no way I was gonna stay on the ship!" She exclaimed. Her eyes returned to the window. "I've always wanted one of these!"

The declaration was enough to stupefy not only Kim, but Donald as well. Both peered a second time through the window and scanned around. Nothing but white coats squirting liquids through oversized eye droppers and conducting some sort of biological experimenting in petri dishes. Kim ducked her head back down quickly, but, as was previously established, Donald kept on staring due to having no fear of being discovered.

" . . . wanted one of what?" He asked, nose still against the glass.

"Them."

The brief response elicited vacant expressions from her companions. Owning another human being, while not an unheard-of concept, was still a very peculiar desire in these times. Kim had seen it before in some of the well-to-do lowlifes found in her previous line of work. However, to hear it come from a teenaged entry-level worker was certainly a new one . . . especially when their first choice is a gainfully employed and well-educated man at least twenty years their senior.

Whisper, sensing the impending loss of her audience, huffed and pulled her phone—a word that had long stopped meaning "telephonic device"—from her pocket. After some quick fiddling, she handed it to her coworker and resumed salivating.

"Is this an ad?" Donald asked. He took the device and examined it. "Pia Dickinson: the Who—uh, the . . . Whoreticulturist . . . ?"

"What?" Kim grabbed the phone from his hand. "'Craft the perfect companion. Suited to any need.' What the hell are they?"

"Real men." The pilot answered flatly. "That'll actually do what you tell them and don't have any stupid interests you have to pretend to care about. Plus, they're ssssoooooo hoooooooooottt . . . Look at them. They're literally perfect."

"So by 'real men' you mean not real at all," Kim said as she shook her head. "That's pathetic. Who would trade having someone who actually loves you for some . . . thing that only wants you because it's programmed to?"

Whisper waved her off.

"It's the same thing. Who cares *why* somebody loves you; everything we do is just for selfish reasons anyway. So why get somebody lame when you can have somebody perfect?"

"Because we're people! We're all lame people living our lame lives trying to meet someone who makes us feel less lame. If you go shack up with some perfect being, then all they're going to do is remind you how lame you are by just existing."

This new topic wrested Donald's interest away from whatever fascinating room contents held it until now.

"That's why you're with Cox?" He asked, leaning against the wall. "He makes you feel less 'lame?' Whisper was saying you used to be a hitman, or woman, or something. How does hanging out with that guy make you feel less lame?"

"Excuse you. I don't agree with all my husband's philosophies, but I can guarantee you that murdering people—while not as damaging to your psyche as some would have you believe—is still neither cool or fulfilling."

"Uhhh . . . you gotta admit, it's kinda cool."

"Okay, fine, it's kind of cool. Sometimes. When you know they're a big shot or something. But that pretty much never happens. The vast majority of the time you're just killing lowlifes who are no better or worse than the person paying you to do it."

The mere act of thinking back on her old mess of a life caused her to grow restless. Being midway through a mission behind enemy lines during such recollections offered no help, either. Hoping to cut things short and get back to business, she hopped to her feet and carried on without an invite to the others. Their instantaneous pursuit showed it wasn't necessary.

Donald was the first to catch up, already gasping a little from the twelve-foot jog.

"If you hated it so much, then why did you do it back then?"

"Not all of us had the opportunity to go fail in university."

"I DIDN'T FAIL! I was expelled because my stupid classmate roped me into—"

The raving faded into a dull roar when Kim sidestepped into the first empty room they had come across. While it had tables and chairs, the large box-shaped machines against a far wall lined with glass jars containing pink goo gave off the impression it wasn't a break room. However, nowhere among the timers, thermometers, and wall projections full of scientific gobbledygook was the giant vat of acid they sought.

Donald and Whisper came bumbling in shortly thereafter.

"Yeah, yeah. I know you don't like your job either," Donald said to Whisper, continuing a conversation from out in the hall. "But that's because you don't like the captain. I'm just saying if she found her actual work to be so soul-crushing, I just wanted to know why she did it."

"I was a waitress for a long time too, you know!" Kim seethed. "Can't we talk about that?"

"Uh, okay . . . did anything interesting ever happen?"

"Not really," she admitted as she rifled the cupboards, checking the labels on each bottle. "That is where I met Tim, though."

"Boring," Whisper grumbled.

"He was getting beaten up by three guys behind the night-club I worked at."

" . . . Less boring."

"Turned out they were trying to shake down the mobster who owned the place and thought it was him because he kept handing out free drinks to people."

"Oh. Boring again."

"Anyway, long story short, I broke the closest one's jaw with a metal serving tray, and the other two hoofed it before I could start on 'em." She closed the final cupboard and turned around.

"There's nothing in here; we need to keep moving."

Donald's interest no longer seemed to lay in the mission. If it ever did.

"You sound like you were a lot less lame when you weren't with him."

With a smirk on her lips and a crinkle in her brow, Kim opened the door back into the hall and gestured accordingly.

"Oh, don't worry, I can still do everything I could do back then."

The amount of care taken towards discretion had been on a steady decline since they began. By this point in their excursion, nearly all precautions taken to avoid detection had been completely forgone. A casual glance through a window to make sure the room wasn't full of people was the only action taken before whipping open the door and starting the process over.

"You know what I mean, though," Donald revived the conversation.

"I do. But I didn't say we find people to make us less lame—I'm getting really sick of that word now—I said we try and find someone who makes us *feel* less . . . broken."

Whisper scoffed.

"Whatever. It's not like these guys can't do that."

"How could they?!" Kim shook her head. "When you're at your lowest point and some lab-grown Adonis bends down and says they love you anyway . . . the first thing you're going to think about is how they're perfect with or without you and only saying that because they're programmed to. I'm sure this is starting to sound like just a bunch of hippy bullshit, but there's no way to imitate the feeling you get when you know someone loves you even when they have no reason to. It's the only thing I've ever found in my life that somehow knocks you on your ass while lifting you higher than you've ever been lifted."

An impassioned motivational speaker she was not. So it would have been arrogant to assume her words were so powerful they humbled her audience into quietude. The ensuing silence that followed could just as easily have been awkwardness from her dumping a heap of heaviness on things. Once the feels worm their way inside a conversation, the only ways to proceed are to double down and commit or to back right off. Sure enough, both outcomes were represented in the room. Donald busied himself with rifling through medicine cabinets like a teenager looking to get high, while Whisper, the actual teenager, had abandoned the pretend searching she had been pantomiming. For the first time, all traces of derision or sarcasm were absent when she addressed Kim on the subject. She actually addressed the floor, but it was presumably for Kim's ears.

"When . . . did you know that he loved you . . . ?"

Now it was Kim's turn to shy off to a cupboard with mild embarrassment. As she busied herself with the contents, she mulled over the question. With everything they had covered so far, it was a bit late to back out and just start ignoring questions.

"It's kinda dark; I'm just warning you." She admitted, tossing aside a bottle of formaldehyde. "We had been dating for about six or seven months. I've never been one who had many friends, but the rare time I did tell someone how he proposed, I would always say he took me down to Earth and found a deserted island where we spent the weekend. What actually happened was that I had gotten pregnant."

She cleared her throat to smooth out any sneaky cracks in her voice that were starting to form.

"I was told I would never be able to have kids, so I didn't believe it at first. But it was true. He proposed right there outside the women's clinic before we'd even gotten back to the ship. I mean, I did love him, so I said yes. But I knew he only did it because it's . . . y'know . . . a guy like him would figure it's the 'right thing to do.' And then, not even twenty-four hours later, I lost it. Guess maybe those doctors and their years of medical training knew what they were talking about when they said kids weren't in my cards. I was terrified to tell him, obviously, 'cause why the hell would he stick around now, right? But I did. I . . . I did it. Told him all of it; figured he'd break off everything right there. But he didn't. The idiot didn't even flinch. I'll never forget, he just looked down at me and said 'I don't care if we have a baby now, or later, or never. I just know that I don't want it to be with anyone besides you.'"

Slamming the now-empty cupboard shut, she cleared her throat. "After that, he really did take me down to a deserted island. So that was nice."

With lab paraphernalia strewn all over the floor and all cupboards within reach thoroughly emptied, she had run out of excuses not to face her companions. Upon turning around, it was apparent that Donald was trying his hardest to pretend he hadn't listened and was failing miserably. After pulling a few more bottles off shelves without even reading their labels, he abandoned the charade altogether when she turned around and he caught her eye.

"Hey, don't look at me, I didn't ask," he said defensively.

"Wouldn't dream of it." She folded her arms and turned away, slouching against a wall. Dredging up feelings was somehow more tiring than skulking around a giant space station looking for acid to steal while under constant threat of discovery. Perhaps not physically, but at very least mentally. It seemed at least one of her companions agreed.

"Whisper? Are you . . . crying?"

The pilot started upon being addressed. With her head bowed and her face obscured with her hair, she wiped the lone tear from her cheek.

"I . . . no!"

Kim nodded.

"I'm convinced."

"Alright, fine," Whisper grumbled, wiping away another. "I don't even know why, though. I can't even tell if that story is sad or happy. It's . . . sappy? Is that where that word comes from?"

"I dunno. Why don't you ask college boy over there?" Kim joked as she stepped back into the hallway.

"Hey, I did take etymology as an elective, you know."

"Well then, where does that word come from?"

"I dunno . . . We had only got to the M's when I was kicked out."

"Greetings, wary strangers wandering around making messes!"

The warm greeting ripped through the trio like a frustrated roar coming from a simultaneously hungry and horny hippo. For one brief smidge of a moment, all the blood flowing in Kim's veins turned to fire and lightning and Red Bull. In this adrenaline-fuelled frenzy, she raised her gun hand at superhuman speed, making it all the more painful to Donald when she accidentally pistol-whipped him across the face. He broke into a cursing fit, stumbling about all the while. He flailed his head around in pain as he did, narrowly missing striking his younger coworker before coming to a rest with it against a wall.

"My apologies," the small, dusky newcomer offered through his short but thick facial hair. "That looked very painful."

Those were his last words before a laser shot rang out and a streak of red light sent him sizzling to the floor. Even in surprise, even in death, one couldn't deny he was a handsome bastard.

"Yeah, you're tellin' me . . ." Kim mumbled through a mouthful of her bruised fingers. "Oh, holy shit, he's dead."

Trying to nurse his way through the beginnings of a second blackened eye, Donald was predictably ambivalent. However, Whisper, in an uncharacteristic display of concern, rushed to the downed man's side and gasped over his body. Several times, she reached down to touch him, only to get grossed out and retract the hand.

"KIM!" She yelped. "You shot Zayn Malik!!"

"That's Joseph Stalin, Whisper—"

"Who?"

"—and I didn't shoot him! I don't even have a blaster."

The pilot did not respond. Something behind Kim seemed to have stolen her attention. Given the way she clutched her hands to her chest and took trembling footsteps backwards, whoever she was staring at probably was not good looking enough for her to desire their attention. Either that or they had the blaster in question. Or perhaps even both.

Kim began to turn but froze upon being addressed.

"No, no, no, I'm not dealing with your crap again. Put the explosion-making thing down, kick it away, hands on your head, all the usual shit."

It wasn't often she would willingly allow herself to be bullied into submission. Obeying the orders and surrendering her only line of defense came as a slight blow to her pride. However, there was no other recourse worth pursuing. She didn't need to turn around to know who owned a voice so dull and slogging that he probably couldn't even talk about his great-grandchildren without sounding disgusted.

19.

THE ENEMY OF MY ENEMY . . .

GETS ASSESSED USING THE EXACT SAME CRITERIA I EMPLOY TO DETERMINE MY OPINION OF LITERALLY EVERY OTHER PERSON THAT I MEET.

Little-known fact about Mister Banks: he wasn't a fan of being ejected off ships against his will. It wasn't a very unique or surprising fact, but it was still little-known, because the man had virtually no friends he shared pet peeves with. A slightly better-known fact was the man's impressive work ethic. Skill in one's field, no matter how remarkable, was never worth much when imbued in one without the will to exercise it.

Nearly universally known fact about Mister Banks: Dude was old, yo.

As bodies withered, it often became essential to turn to the mind in order to compensate. A strong will might not necessarily be enough to make a gymnast out of a Viking or a surgeon out of a Parkinson's patient, but when one's job was a tennis match of pointing guns at people and dealing with enormous amounts of retaliatory punishment, the stuff went a long way. Over the years, he had been shot, stabbed, burnt, bludgeoned, trapped with snakes, trapped with a particularly ornery goose, aggressively tickled, yelled at very loudly, forced to smell chocolate chip cookies but never get to eat them, and a multitude of other passion-fuelled acts of vengeance. What made him such an asset was not the fact that he had the meanest swing or the sharpest aim, but rather the fact he could shrug off nearly anything thrown at him like some kind of self-driven space Rasputin. Whatever the job, he prided himself on getting it done.

At first, he was a bit salty after being foiled by the old "trap-the-bad-guy-in-an-escape-pod" gag. Partially, it was the imprisonment, naturally, but in all honesty, the shame of falling for it wore on him the most. The countless ensuing hours of being trapped in a room full of floating teenaged-girl accoutrements barely illuminated by emergency power theoretically should have fermented his misgivings. However, while the treatment was anything but ideal, over time, he couldn't help but come to appreciate the concerted effort made to spare his life. It was a practice that he himself had reciprocated, so perhaps they didn't deserve any more additional slack. But in this business, fairness was a nigh-unheard-of commodity.

By the time the miniature vessel was picked up by a passing peacekeeper frigate, he had calmed down considerably. Not enough that he felt fine to wash his hands of the whole thing, mind you, just enough to re-evaluate his approach to his mission objective. However, it needed to be put on hold until after he dealt with his arrest after being recognized. He could say what he wanted about living in Whisper's bedroom, but it was more comfortable than a ship cell devoid of all stimuli. The regular deliveries of food were nice, but at least the old place had a preponderance of vapid teen-oriented media to peruse. Hard to say whether boredom or hunger was the more unpleasant feeling, as anyone experiencing one would quickly volunteer to trade it for the other.

Thankfully, his notoriety among the multitude of Earth military forces was sufficient to expedite his apprehension. Anyone who showed up on more than five "most-wanted" lists had reached drop-everything-and-deal-with-him status. Since the hard part, getting him into the holding cell, was already completed, all that was left was to transport him to his final destination.

Another widely known fact: there is a special place in space whose sole purpose is to house the most dangerous people in the system.

"Now before everybody gets their panties in a twist . . ." The old man droned to the group. "I want to clarify I'm not here to kill you. If I wanted to, I could've done it a hundred times already. Now, that being said, what are you going to do if I lower my gun?"

Kim scowled back at him.

"I'll probably run over there and punch you in the gut so hard your colostomy bag explodes."

"Classy. Except I'm pretty sure colostomies haven't been done in around two-hundred years."

"Well, I guess that gives me an indication of how old you are, then!"

Banks rolled his eyes and exhaled air in a way that was part sigh and part grunt.

"This is not a bad start at all."

"How did you even know we would be here!?" She demanded, stepping towards him. "Or are you just here to pick up an order and happened to bump into us?"

A slight twitch of the gun let her know that her subtle advance had not gone unnoticed. As she stepped back, the old man let out another one of those rumbling grunts. At first, they seemed to indicate agitation, but it was starting to appear he simply might not be in complete control of all the gasses his body emitted.

"You might be surprised to know you're not the only person worthy of getting sent to Guantanamo. You are, however, the only person I've ever met who owns an impossibly expensive piece of machinery that doubles as your house and sole method of transportation, yet who doesn't bother to lock its doors when you leave."

Whisper jolted.

"You were on the ship?!"

" . . . Is she being sarcastic or is this a language barrier thing?"

"You're one to talk," Kim snapped. "So if you've been on our ship this whole time, then why are we only seeing you now?"

"Honestly, I *am* a little surprised you guys never noticed me," he said, gesturing to the gun. "I guess you don't take inventory much. I guess you don't check your vents much either, even after leaving your spaceship unlocked outside the most dangerous prison known to man."

"We were a little preoccupied with the whole being-arrested-and-then-free-falling-through-open-space thing."

"Well, I'm a little preoccupied with the fact we're standing in a hallway making small talk over a dead body. So how about we deal with it, then take this conversation into another one of the rooms you guys have been burgling."

"You move him. You're the one who murdered him."

"It's not murder; that thing is just some lab-grown . . . Just move it! Doesn't anybody respect guns anymore?"

"Uhh . . ." Donald mumbled as he walked over to Stalin's corpse. "What . . . What are we supposed to do with it?"

"Just throw it in a corner and stick a tree in front of it or something. Nobody's gonna notice."

After disposing of the body, something Kim hadn't figured she would ever have to do again, they made their way into yet another adjacent room full of scientific regalia that was understood by none of them. The whole endeavour would have been a lost cause if not for the mandatory WHMIS training before setting space sail. The meagre instruction was just enough to teach them to look for that bright symbol of a test tube crying on a sizzling hand. How they planned to assess the strength of the acid from there once they found it was much farther down the process than any of their minds had reached. Indiscriminately pouring it on the goo until the goo looked dead seemed to be as good of a plan as any.

"What do you want?" The co-captain growled at him once they were inside. "If you're looking for that thing you lost, we don't have it."

Banks shut the door behind them, then turned back and glowered at her through half-closed eyes. He moved with a deceptive slowness that, when combined with his drooping skin and protruding bottom lip, made it seem he would at any minute break into a rendition of "Hello! Ma Baby." But when he finally opened his mouth, it was just more of the same boring deadpan.

"I know you have it. I find things; it's what I do," the geezer grumbled. Yet, despite the accusation, he still lowered his gun. "But it doesn't matter. That thing gets stolen every damn weekend—and it's always on the weekend for some reason. If not by you, then by somebody else."

Wary glances flew about his audience, mostly in the direction of the only one brave enough to stand up to him.

"So . . . what's your point?"

"The point is, you guys are the only ones besides my Martian overlords who don't want to inflate it to the size of a space bus, then drop it on somebody. And I'm pretty sure it's only a matter of time before they get orders as well."

The meandering attempt to drive the point home was having little effect on their faces of incredulity. Whether it was due to lack of understanding or lack of acceptance was unclear, but either way, the lack of sway ushered Banks away from his stone tone and into a more earnest register.

"Look. I'm done getting beaten up trying to keep this thing out of bad guys' hands, okay? I'm done with the hours of stakeouts, guns in my face, guns in my back, angry kids trying to avenge their fathers, and being woken up in the middle of the damn night, all because some new asshole wants to become a super villain. Your husband is right; it should be destroyed. So I'm here to help you."

" . . . Are you kidding me!? Why the hell didn't you open with that?"

"I did open with that. I said 'I'm not here to kill you.' You didn't believe me."

"You had literally just shot someone!"

"I still think he was more of a some*thing*."

"Stop yelling!" Whisper yelled. "Or more will come and he'll shoot them too!"

"More of *them*?" Banks clarified. "That's the least of your worries. There's cavalry on the way much worse than them. That whole display at the prison pissed off a lot of people, and since your ship is the only one that got away, it makes you look real suspicious."

"Well then, all the more reason to hurry up and get this over with." Kim patted her bag. "How's the search going, guys? Have you found anything corrosive yet?"

Donald and Whisper looked at each other. They both stood cross-armed, leaning against a wall and conference table, waiting for their two chaperones to finish their grown-up talk. Around them were no shelves or cupboards of any sort, just a long mirror on the back wall with a refreshment stand under it and several large electric displays full of graphs and notes.

"Why would they keep any of that in here?" The older one asked, prompting Kim to take a first look around at the room's contents.

"Jesus Christ," she snapped, walking over and slapping a croissant out of Whisper's hand. "Doesn't anyone here know how to speak up? This isn't a shopping trip; we're on the clock, assholes. Next room, let's go."

Fine to lead by example, she stomped over to the door and gave it a shove. Following her agitated, open-hand punch, the door flew part-way open, whereupon it quickly abandoned that action with a hollow clunk and ricocheted back towards them. It was a defect that hadn't presented during the apparatus's initial use, and that aroused suspicion. Kim hoped it was simply debris that had fallen in the way, lest she have to issue a half-hearted apology to whatever manufactured pretty boy she'd just assaulted. A lean out the door and peek around the corner found a helmeted man shaking his head in a temporary daze. Figuring him for one of them Daft Punk guys, she grabbed his collar and hauled him into the room.

"What are you doing?!" Banks demanded, raising his blaster to take him out.

"What are *you* doing?!" She fired back.

"He's a threat."

"So what, you're just going to shoot him?"

"This isn't one of that lady's boy toys! He's got a blaster rifle and body armour; this guy is military!"

“. . . That’s even less reason to shoot him! He’s probably got a wife and kids and shit.”

“Nah, these guys are married to their jobs. It’s fine.”

“No, please!” The prisoner whipped off his helmet, revealing a sweaty mop of hair and pleading eyes. “I do have a wife! And kids! And a dog! And he’s missing a leg!”

Banks coughed.

“I know that sounds convincing, but trust me, they all say that.”

“I’m not letting you shoot this man.”

“Do you have a better idea?”

“Uh . . .” The man raised his hand. “You could put me around that corner and just let me sit this all out?”

“Shut up,” they both snapped at him.

“Why don’t you just knock him out?” Donald suggested. “Like they do in movies and stuff.”

“Knock him out?!” Banks repeated. “Who do you think I am? Earnie Shavers?”

“He means with your gun butt, idiot,” Kim sneered before relieving their captive of the rifle he possessed. “Let the lady show you how.”

Bringing both arms back for leverage like a woman about to dig a hole, she took a last breath, then hauled off and cracked him in the side of the head.

“OW! GOD! Jesus . . .”

As evidenced by the profane cries of pain, the strike seemed to wake him up more than anything else. With an expression of agony so convincing he needed no words to convey his state, he looked up at her with eyes that wordlessly asked why. It was a redundant unasked question; the reasoning behind the attack had been made rather clear. It was possible he may have been hoping its lack of effectiveness would spur her to pursue other solutions. But if she quit now, then all she did was hit him in the face for no reason. That wouldn't do at all, and would be very unfair to him! So, with his wellbeing in mind, Kim raised the blaster and smoked him again.

"OW—COME ON!!"

This one knocked him clean over and worked as a double hit when his face slammed into the floor. Globules of spittle leaked from his twisted lips as he let out an involuntary groan.

"Hold him up," Banks ordered. "Let me try."

"Please . . . no—GAAH, CHRIST!"

"Don't hit him in the forehead, you idiot!"

"Relax, would ya? I was aiming for his temple. Lemme try again."

"AAAH! WHY ARE YOU DOING THIS!?"

"His temple?! What, are you trying to kill him?"

"Where else would I hit him?"

"If you want to knock someone out you hit them in the jaw. Like this; watch."

"MMMPH . . . Oh god, I'm gonna be sick . . ."

"This is ridiculous! This guy's got a jaw like a Mount Rushmore head."

"I told you, you have to hit them in the temple. Like this."

This was the last thunk Whisper could take before turning away.

"Please stop . . . please . . ."

Banks checked the end of blaster for blood before letting it fall to his side in resignation.

"This is a lot tougher than I thought it would be."

"Maybe his head isn't the way to go," Kim offered. "I think I read somewhere that if you punch someone in the solar plexus just right they can pass out?"

"I guess it's worth a shot. I don't know exactly where the solar plexus is, though."

"I don't either . . . I mean, I know it's somewhere around his midsection? We could just, like, punch him in the stomach repeatedly until he's out? It's no worse than anything else we've done to him so far."

"Please don't do that!!"

"Alright. Whatever shuts him up quicker."

"No! I'll be quiet, I swear!"

"Sorry, buddy. Don't worry, it'll be over soon."

And with that. they pinned him down and went to town like a pair of schoolyard bullies. Of the multitude of reasons this was a stupid idea, least considered was the way in which they planned to determine his unconsciousness. The entire idiom of "beating a dead horse" was borne out of the illusion of movement that came from a limp body experiencing a thorough percussing. Any one of the many fists they levied into his abdomen could, according to their theory, have been the blow that punched his ticket. However, every flurry of fists sent a series of convulsions rippling across his limbs, convincing everyone he was still awake, and thus starting the process anew.

Eventually, the tremors did slow, then stop. Maybe one of their swings finally found its mark. Maybe the Vulcan nerve pinch applied by Donald was the attack that turned the tide. Or maybe the poor man passed out from pain much earlier, and they only noticed now because their arms were so tired they had lost the strength to make him move. There was no way to know.

The third one; it was definitely the third one.

Spent and eerily unsatisfied, both involved parties collapsed on either side of him and stared at the ceiling. It was patterned with mirrors that must receive regular cleaning attention, given the vibrancy with which their faces were reflected. Both were red and sweaty and wide-eyed, but still not the worst-looking in the room.

"Well, there . . ." Banks puffed, wiping his bloody knuckles on the downed man's sleeve. "You happy we picked the more humane option?"

"Shut up."

Whisper, heretofore temporarily forgotten, called to them from across the room and came running.

"Hey guys, I found some duct tape in a drawer—oh . . ."

Kim hopped to her feet and took the roll nonetheless. The stuff always had uses, which was part of the reason it had undergone no improving in the however many years since its invention.

"Gimme. You get his arms, I'll get his feet, and we'll put him in a corner until he wakes up."

It was a good thing she wasn't Whisper's actual parent, because bad lessons were being taught today. In fact, with the way things were going, nobody would have much right to be surprised if, in addition to incensed prison guards, vindictive secret agents, Martian bounty hunters, and an antagonized chunk of the Earth's military, they also received an unfriendly visit from child protective services. You know you're a bad parent if even *they* show up packing heat.

"No need to help us or anything," Kim called sarcastically at the men. "We got it."

Banks shrugged.

"'Kay."

"You better at least be keeping a watch or something. God!"

"You heard your boss lady, kid. Keep an eye out the window."

"Uhh . . ." Donald began before deciding not to clarify his age for once. "Okay. What do I do if I see anybody?"

"Let me know."

"Okay, well, I see somebody."

Not even ten feet away was a pair of identically dressed infantrymen meandering around the halls with all the urgency of an elderly couple. Nothing but the glass partition of a window separated them. With how easily every word of the soldiers' conversation could be heard, it was safe to assume said window was not soundproofed, and therefore probably not anything else-proofed either.

" . . . And then my girl was all like 'Oh yeah? Well, every time we've had sex, I faked it'—which might be true for all I know—but it didn't really matter, cause I just looked at her back and was all like 'What makes you think I care if you enjoyed it?'"

"Brooooo, no way. That's savage as fu—hey! Those men are too ugly to be sex robots!"

"That must be them! Kill 'em!"

Like a clock striking noon in the middle of a dusky western town, all who were strapped took the signal to fire. Before Donald could so much as hunch over, he was beset upon by two twin twinkling shots of burning intent. Banks replied with one of his own while buckling his rusty knees in hopes of getting out of the way. For three independently fired shots, their grouping was impressively tight. All hit the window within a few inches of one another, making the display all the more brilliant when the glass refracted their light and sheared each one into different-coloured fragmented beams that split further upon hitting nearby mirrors and displays until the room was bathed in a light show that would put a New York Christmas to shame. And potentially put someone into the ground, if they happened to get hit by enough of them.

When Kim and Whisper emerged from their body-dumping field trip, they found their companions huddled behind the ledge with scorched dots littered all over the floor, walls, and ceiling, like a disco ball had exploded.

"Get down!" Banks yelled, unintentionally picking fitting words to the disco ball simile.

"From what?" Whisper asked before receiving a harsh shove from Kim back into the side room.

"Get down" was on a list of certain commands that generally shouldn't be questioned; a list that also included "Put your hands up," and "Don't forget to tip." Incidentally, a good portion of that list was fine to ignore if spoken by a DJ. But unless Banks moonlit as DJ Bengay, the order coming from him was to be taken as gospel.

In one fell swoop, Kim tossed her gun in the air, baseball slid behind the conference table, muscled it over onto its side, and caught the blaster, now safely protected by half cover. The blood rushing through her ears drowned out the protestations being levied in her direction when she popped up and peppered a few shots at the assailants. Like all the ones before, they exploded in dancing sprays of rainbow light.

"What the hell kind of glass is this?!" Donald demanded of no one in particular.

"Kid, what am I, a glazier? Says here it was made by 'Fancy Future Glass' industries. Give 'em a call if you want, but go block the damn door while you do it."

"They're in there!" One of the men outside yelled. "They have some kind of exploding weaponry. It also might turn you gay, we're not sure yet."

Banks used the break in the action as an opportunity to dart over the table and put something more substantial between him and the window before the next Fantasia segment started.

"So, what do ya think?" He said as he hit the ground. "Wanna knock all these ones out too?"

"You do realized we're probably about to die, right? Are you an actual psychopath?"

"Nah. This sort of thing just happens to me so often it's lost all excitement."

"Well, good for you! Try not to fall asleep while we're fighting for our lives."

A series of bangs on the door jolted them from their banter. Both peeked over the table just in time for an eyeful of Donald's jiggling torso as he ambled hastily in their direction.

"I told you to block the door!" Banks barked.

Before responding, the coms officer leaned his top half over the sideways table, then lifted his legs over one by one before flopping onto the floor behind it.

"I locked it!" He sputtered. "I'm not standing in front of it. If they can get past the lock they can get past me!"

"Can I come out now?" Whisper asked.

"NO!" The rest shouted in unison.

Apparently lacking the door-bypassing skillset possessed by the protagonists, the breach squad moved onto the window, where they had a similar level of luck. Blaster butts clanged against the transparent barrier, only to be denied entry yet again. It appeared Pia, in her extensive efforts to fancify the place, decided to spring for aluminum glass instead of the fragile rube stuff. Looked like it was something-proof after all. However, it didn't stop them from shooting again and producing another maelstrom of radiation that bounced about, turning the room into a rave for another few seconds.

"Son of a *bitch*!" Kim snarled from the foetal position. "Rest of my life be damned, I'm smashing these mirrors."

And smash she did. Came in like a right wrecking ball. Within seconds, several dozen superstitious lifetimes worth of broken glass rained down and dusted the floor, as well as those cowering against it. Anyone watching the security cameras wouldn't be remiss to assume Kim for some kind of escaped mental patient, given the way she leaped about swinging a firearm like a seizing drum major. Even Donald seemed a bit freaked out, either by her or by the debris he was inhaling, and beelined towards a panel on the wall.

After finishing with all the nearby mirrors, Kim continued to go to town on every reflective surface she could find, starting with the media displays. She figured she might as well, since the bill for the damage was already far beyond what she could afford. Plus, somewhere deep down, there was some rockstar satisfaction to be gleaned from trashing a place that didn't belong to you. In conjunction with the light show, the whole thing was quite Floydian.

"Give her suppressing fire!!" Whisper squeaked from her corner. "Give her suppressing fire!"

"Would you shut up!?" Banks roared back. In actuality that may not have been a necessarily bad idea, but his weapon lay in his lap half disassembled at the moment as he tinkered with its innards. What exactly he was doing was anyone's guess, but nobody had the leverage to get him to do anything else. Whatever it was, it was presumably better than nothing, hopefully.

When Kim's carnage finally passed its crescendo and she came to a stop with silver flecks in her hair, she had her pick of which monkeying-about man to address. Naturally, her selection was the one over whom she had some tenuous amount of authority. The question to both would be the same, but seeing Donald taking initiative and seeking no input was a rarity worth focusing on.

"Donald, what are you doing?"

"I'm integrating my phone into the servers," he uttered

breathlessly, without looking back. "When whoever owns this place finally gets around to turning on the AI Defense System, I'd rather be the one in charge of telling it who to shoot at."

"You . . . you can do that?"

"I'd hope so. I invented it."

Even Banks stopped what he was doing and looked up now. Whisper couldn't be seen from the side office she was stuffed in, but if she could hear, she would certainly be interested as well. Feeling the silence, Donald turned around.

"You never asked what I got expelled from SIT for," he continued as he returned to his work. He then muttered a second part, seemingly more for himself than them.

"You also never asked why I hate the government so much . . ."

Banks cleared his throat.

"So let me get this straight. The fact you claim to be a computer genius who works on a junk liner aside, you're claiming you can reprogram an entire artificial intelligence just with your phone?"

"Who said anything about reprogramming? I'm just uninstalling the one they got."

"Then how is it going to operate and pick targets?" Kim asked.

Nobody could see it, but those listening might have been able to hear the smirk on Donald's face.

"Well, I guess I'll just have to upload a different AI to take its place."

20. SAVING MISTER BANKS. AND ASSOCIATES.

If one came home to find one of the fish in their tank was dead, it would be an unwelcome surprise, but not necessarily cause for alarm right away. However, if one came home to find that the contents of said fish tank had been rearranged and underneath one of the props was their fish's corpse, then no other assumption could be made but foul play. After all, fish can die from eating too much, too little, or from living in too close of quarters and dying from exposure to filth. Others yet get attacked by the other fish that have emotional imbalances or grew up with an abusive stepdadfish. But no amount of interfishy prejudices could give one of the scaley simpletons the brainwave to try and hide the body after the crime. That type of malice could only be attributed to outsider influence.

Or such was Pia's thought process regarding her creations. She could call them her children all she wanted; for the time being, they were fish.

Her displeasure towards the situation seemed to stem not from the destruction of her property, but rather the invasion of it. The death of a specimen was highly unlikely to be an end, and thus could only be seriously considered as a means.

Yet it was only her who lived there, and as someone who lived nearly cut off from society, she had no opportunity to foster enemies passionate enough to make an attempt on her life. A scorned lover was also equally unlikely. All of her exes fit a very particular mould, and since she lived with most of them in some kind of genderbent Playboy Mansion setup, if they were the types to get jealous, then one of them surely would have by now. Theft might have been a plausible explanation, since her products were valuable commodities with very high price tags. However, thieves—good ones, at least—tended to avoid destroying the very things they came to claim.

There were other explanations she mulled over, such as saboteur business rivals or some contrived *Jason X* type situation, but the scientist in her could not discount the principle of Occam's Razor.

"I have lived here a very long time without incident," Pia said in tones probably too calm for a person examining the dead body of someone she knew and had been intimate with. "Therefore, I am reluctant to assume it is a coincidence that the day you choose to visit me is also the day my facility is set upon by at least one killer. So, the only question left to ask is: are they with you? Or are they seeking you?"

Cox looked at Willy for backup, quickly realizing the man had none to offer. He sighed, then coughed. Being confronted about his caper by a woman with a much firmer grasp on logic than himself was more than enough leverage to wrench him back to his default setting of up-front honesty.

"We're wanted fugitives carrying a biological weapon and with several legal agencies pursuing us."

A bombshell if there ever was one. However, one wouldn't know it, given the way Pia blinked through it the same way she brushed aside anything else thrown her way.

"That makes you about the rudest guest I've ever had. I suppose I understand why you neglected to share that information, though. Most hosts, myself included, would have promptly thrown you out had you told them."

"So . . . you're not mad?"

"Don't be absurd. You chose to subject me to the consequences of your criminal transgressions. So of course I am. I'm unexpressive, not stupid."

"I get it! I really do. But please don't turn us in!" Cox pleaded as he reached for her hand, which she quickly jerked away. "I know it doesn't look like it, but we really are the good guys here!"

"Turn you in?!" She repeated. "To them?" She snuffed out her delicate nose and shook her head, perfectly coiffed hair barely bobbing as she did. "It makes no difference to me whether or not you are the villains. This is a sovereign station. Your presence here, while no longer welcome, was at least invited. Regardless of intent, they have now invaded my land and vandalized my property."

The captain glanced down at the body of Joseph Stalin.

" . . . Is vandalism really the right thing to call this . . . ?"

"From a legal standpoint, yes."

"Do . . . do you want me to shoot them?" Willy offered again. He also gestured with the gun, in case she was not able to deduce what he was offering to shoot them with.

"That will not be necessary, mister bodyguard . . ."

"Yeah, Mister Padilla. Nobody else needs to get shot!"

" . . . I am perfectly capable of having them all killed myself."

"That's . . . What? No!"

"Dude, this chick is a badass."

"Pia, please!" Cox begged. He almost reached for her hand

again, but caught himself. "This can be worked out without anybody dying. Just let us deal with it!"

Pia's porcelain face registered the plea about as much as it would have if it had been made of actual porcelain. Yet she did take a complete three seconds to presumably mull it over before replying.

"Less than a minute ago, you told me you are a wanted criminal in possession of a biological weapon. You, out of all of us, should be the least likely to advocate for the sanctity of life."

"And less than fifty-nine seconds ago I told you it's not what it sounds like and we're the good guys! I also said fugitives; we're not criminals. They're the criminals!"

"All the more reason to kill them, then."

"No! I mean, they're not criminals, technically. They're acting lawfully according to their own laws! I think so, anyway. I don't actually know everyone who's chasing us anymore. The point is, they want the weapon and we're trying to destroy it before they can take it!"

For the first time Pia's face let slip some crinkles of the confused variety.

"So you brought it here?! Why?!"

"Because . . . we thought since you were a scientist, you might have a big vat of acid we could throw it in—look, it didn't sound that dumb when we came up with the plan!"

"I see. So you clearly had no idea what my profession was before you came here."

"Not even a little bit, no."

"Well, it gives me no feeling whatsoever to inform you I do not have any acid. Depending on how much you require, surely you could have simply extracted it from one of the many batteries your ship must have."

The captain's mouth fell open.

"I . . . I actually hadn't thought of that."

"Then take this as a lesson to call ahead next time. If there is one. Please get off my property now."

"We will! I promise! . . . But my wife and other members of my crew are also rummaging through your lab looking for acids right now. We gotta get them too."

The time Pia had spent with him, brief as it was, seemed to be enough that the captain's strong emotions may have been rubbing off. Cool and aloof at the beginning, her own emotions had become steadily more pronounced since meeting him. Most had been reflexive expressions of shock, revulsion, contempt, and similar feelings, but they were manifesting more vividly, albeit briefly, nevertheless.

" . . . There is a strong argument to be made for you possessing even less social acumen than I, Mister Cox. But your self-absorbed and short-sighted actions leave me with little choice. Go retrieve whatever companions you have littered about my laboratory. I will need the extra time anyway to update my staff files in my AI self-defense system. It's an effective product at eliminating hostiles, but the specificity required for its target differentiation leads me to believe it was programmed by an imbecile."

She made a move to leave but was made to hesitate by one last outburst.

"Wait!" Cox implored. " . . . Are you going to tell it not to attack us too?"

"Unless you have the requisite in-depth physical assessments of yourself and companions, the answer is no."

"How in-depth are we talking?"

"Do you know the precise length of your nose?"

"I . . . no."

"Then you are going to die when I turn it on."

She appeared to say something else, but the elevator door closed before it could be heard. Cox and Willy were on their own now. With a mission unfinished, a warm welcome rescinded, and fresh enemies on their trail, it was the stage in the game where heroes were made. The captain had not intended for things to go this way. However, now that he found himself at this juncture, there was an inescapable twinge of excitement at the opportunity for glory it presented. It tickled him to the point he almost wished he'd intentionally screwed things up sooner; a realization which sucked away much of the moment's novelty.

"Mister Padilla, do I have a problem?"

"Yeah, dude. She just said we're gonna die!"

"Never mind. You're right, this isn't about me. It's about all of us! So what do ya think, buddy? British Secret agents again? You wanna go get em?!"

"I'm not a dog, dude."

"I . . . That's not how I meant that at all."

The ensuing awkwardness forced his gaze elsewhere. With the weight of the situation starting to sink in, the wheels in his head began to turn. There were few things quite like desperation to bring out the creative problem-solving genius in the otherwise seemingly average. Whether one was a stranded space captain facing threats of impending death or a procrastinating writer feeling the shade of a looming deadline, all could find some benefit from a little gut-wrenching stress if only it were looked at from ninety degrees.

In the case of Captain Cox, his batch of naturally generated Adderall powers kicked in the moment he turned away and found himself peering through a nearby window labelled "J Division" that contained an array of stunning scientists. None had quite the allure of Mister Jackman, but most were striking in their own way. Their physical appearance had little to do with anything, but there was nothing wrong with a heterosexual man comfortable enough in his masculinity to appreciate it. What was important was the fact they were bred to be scientists second and frisky flunkies first. Armed with that knowledge, he threw open the door faster than a father who heard a male voice coming from his daughter's bedroom.

"Hey! Who wants to come satisfy me?!"

His words hit the collective like the bell on the last day of school. Cox needed say no more, instead opting to merely step away from the newly opened floodgate. Before long, both he and Willy were up to their ears in the wall-contents of teenager bedrooms.

"Wow! Look at 'em all, Mister Padilla! Jenson Ackles, John Abraham, James Dean, James Deen, Justin Trudeau, and . . . I don't know who you are?"

"Why, I am John Dabiri."

"OH! Uh, what did you do?"

"I am a scientist."

"Well, yeah, but I mean, y'know, the other John Dabiri."

"There are many incarnations of John Dabiri. They are scientists too."

"Never mind. I'll Google you later."

Having drained the room of all imbibers, Cox scrambled up onto the nearby shoulders of Josh Smith. It was the ideal seat for a captainly address—a second one! He raised his hands as high as they could go before touching the ceiling, then called to all:

"Hear me, mixed assortment of former celebrities that all have names starting with J! I have need of your assistance! You see, I have a fetish. A very specific one. I receive a great deal of, er, sexual gratification, when me, my wife, and other people dear to me—like ol' Willy here—are protected from people that intend to harm us! It just so happens that my wife and crew are here somewhere . . . and there are people trying to harm them! What a cool coincidence, am I right?! Anyway . . . Yeah. That about sums it up I guess. Coming up with these speech things on the fly is harder than I thought it would be. Oh! But speaking of making things *harder* than I think they can be, let's go save my family! Ha . . . haha . . . ha . . . oh, boy."

No one in the room seemed very amused or inspired by the oration. However, luckily for Cox, even the least eloquent of men found it an easy business to talk people into doing something they already wished to do. Whether he delivered an intense sermon or simply pointed in a direction and declared "That way," the results would likely have been the same.

Famous figures flooded the foyer like someone called in a bomb threat to a rehab clinic. No one had any indication where the individuals in question might be located. However, with only one path to follow, it was a statistical certainty that a sufficient amount of time spent thundering through the halls would eventually turn them up. The only hope left to have was the hope they were not too late. If Percy had indeed managed to weather his 100% natural black tea-extract face wash, then he likely would have no qualms about making good on his threats against Kim.

The longer they walked, the quicker their pace became. After a few moments' acceleration, the sexbots stampeded. Cox expected his crack squad of infiltrators would have followed the same counterclockwise rotation he himself embarked on during his decoy duties in order to avoid running into each other. Yet the longer their hurried backtrack went on without incident, the more he began to wonder just where they might have gone. It was a circle. How could she have possibly deviated from a circle? For a moment, he thought maybe she'd found the vat of acid and had already thrown the specimen in and headed back to the ship. That is, until he remembered Pia explicitly mentioning she had no such thing. Fortunately, right around this time, he stumbled across a group of men who looked a little too unhappy with their job to be sexbots.

"Excuse me," he asked one of the men clad in military-issued equipment, which made them obviously trustworthy. "I'm looking for someone. Have you seen a really pretty girl and some—"

"Piss off, Owen Wilson," the soldier cut him off in a sharp voice. "Can't you see we're having a standoff with some terrorists here?"

Terrorist. By this point, the word had become so bastardized it was nearly synonymous with ally. But, given the bitterness with which it was uttered, the aforementioned devolution wasn't recognized by this platoon. In direct contrast to common societal behaviour, they anxiously crowded around the entrance to the one room in the building that didn't contain celebrities. A cursory glance through the window netted Cox the unmistakeable view of his better half slumped against a wall, panting and covered in glitter like she just had a boxing match with a giant fairy. After a few words with Donald, she finally caught his eye.

"Hey, there she is!"

Several dozen helmeted heads swung around in the captain's direction.

"Uhhh, the . . . Marisa Tomei specimen!"

There was a beat while they all turned back to the window. Kim sat frozen under the scrutiny, unsure exactly what was happening.

"Hey, Sergeant Hancock was right! They do have girl ones here!"

"Arright, no one do anything to that one. I'm taking her home with me!"

"Ew!" Cox blurted. "Come on! You can't just take people."

The burly commando whom he first addressed gave him a shove backwards.

"You're pretty talkative for a sex robot."

Helmets were effective pieces of gear to protect one's head from trauma, so the man's skull likely weathered the sudden blow from Joe Louis's furious fist without too much damage. Didn't do much to protect against whiplash, though; after the initial shockwave rippled down his spine, the man's legs turned to jelly, and he spilled over onto his mates, taking two to the ground with him. The rest stepped back as they fell, then divvied their astonished stares between the fighter and flopper.

Everyone knew what was to come next. It was only the natural course of things. Modern rules of etiquette may have successfully dulled our evolutionary inclination to fight or fly, instead freezing us into a brief state of analysis paralysis where an attempt at option weighing was made, but eventually one or the other would always come to fruition. No species ever rose to the top of the food chain due to top notch de-escalating skills.

The balloon of tension nearly popped when a trigger finger became just too itchy and a flash of light burst from a barrel and ripped across the collective, stopping only when it nailed a Jared Leto clone in the face. Again, all paused with bated breath; this time, though, it was not from shock, but from anticipation. It took Cox a moment to realize his brood were all staring at him like a group of dogs who knew he had the ball.

"Oh!" He declared when he finally realized why. "Uh, yeah I liked him. I guess. He's the 30 Seconds to Mars Guy, right? They had some good stuff."

It was amazing how quickly a group could devolve from prim and proper to rabid savages. Mister Louis got off one more world-ending haymaker before becoming just another hooligan in a roiling wall-to-wall football brawl in the hall. Once the swarm descended, guns quickly lost all effectiveness. After that, the only viable projectiles were the helmets that were yanked off and thrown at other people wearing helmets. Cox quickly regretted not having the sense to recuse himself from standing right in the middle of the mosh pit before getting the festivities going. Even though the fight had been started in his honour, it was still all he could do to avoid being crushed between all the muscular bodies, which were quickly losing any novelty. Willy stood out from them all, a big happy island among the masses. The man's corpulence may have occasionally restricted his agility, but in circumstances like these, it worked wonders insulating him from collateral clobberings. Once within arm's reach, Cox clung to him like a shipwrecked sailor to flotsam.

"Mister Padilla! This isn't going the way I thought it would at all!"

"That seems to happen to you a lot, dude."

Any response he may have been cooking was abandoned when he ducked out of the way to avoid a wild roundhouse kick delivered by Jason Derulo. The oldies musician's foot instead met its target, leaving behind a bloody-nosed trooper, then carried on into the back of John Cho's head, propelling it forward into a mighty headbutt, which may have been the only thing that saved Josh Groban from a career-ending injury that instead happened to James Franco when a blaster went off and took the side of his face with it, enraging the collective further, to the point that John Cena stopped dishing out attitude adjustments, and instead grabbed the ankles of Justin

Bieber and used him as a blunt object to clear a void, which gave Jackie Chan enough room to repurpose some displaced boots as improvised nunchucks, and Joe Manganiello enough room to grab the other end of the spinning popstar and use him to clothesline a commando so hard that the both of them flew into the indestructible window, dislodging it from its frame and carrying on inside.

While the fighting carried on, there was now room to breathe for those who were less inclined. All two of them. Cox may have technically triggered the scuffle, but he was still sympathetic enough to those involved to purposefully not step on their squirming bodies as he made his way across the battlefield.

"Battlefield!" He called out randomly. "That's what Patrick Benatar said love is. I knew I got that wrong."

Once through the hole in the wall, he found himself immediately tackled and dragged behind an upturned conference table. It didn't jive well with his own interior-design preferences, but it fit in well with the shambles that was the rest of the room. Pia must have been going for some chic new firebombed-husk aesthetic he had never heard of. The whole thing was so forward-thinking and interesting that it took him a couple moments to realize who it was who had tackled him.

"Mister Nobody!" He squawked. "Who ordered a sex clone of you?"

"Nobody, Tim. That's the real Mister Banks."

"Oh. OH! Uh, is he nice now?!"

"Not really. But he's on our side, at least. It turns out he was on our—"

"That's okay, I don't need any details. Long as you say he's cool!"

"I don't think he's cool at all."

"Not trying to kill us is where the bar for coolness is at right now."

They stopped chatting to cringe under a hail of blaster shots whizzing overhead. After the initial barrage, Kim and Banks popped up to return a few of their own, then returned with fresh disillusionment. Clearing out some room to fight may have seemed like a good idea at first, but in practice, it provided more room to aim better. Jin Akanishi lay slumped over the windowsill, clutching his abdomen, while Jared Padalecki dragged away the body of his former costar. Johnny Cash was one of the last to go down, but in the end, the elite military unit was just too much for a random assortment of unarmed hot people to contend with. Rifles in hand and a freshly breached room in their midst, the soldiers advanced.

"What about that Pia woman!?" Kim demanded as she picked off the first few to come inside.

"Uhhh, yeah. Pia isn't very cool right now."

"The hell's that supposed to mean?"

A shrill shriek of microphone feedback blared over an unseen PA system. When it faded away, it was replaced by the placid tones of the laboratory warden.

"Alright, Timon. You and your associates have received ample time to return to your spaceship and out of firing range of my defense system."

The way it echoed through the metal hallways rendered it all the more disheartening.

"At the conclusion of this address, all unsanctioned parties still present on my station will be killed. As a demonstration of my humanity, the death will be provided by gunshot to the head instead of by oxygen deprivation or freezing temperatures. Please reciprocate this respectful gesture by taking a moment to distance yourselves from any valuables that could be subjected to damage by the laser passing through you or by your lifeless body falling onto them. Thank you."

With the way the soldiers looked around afterwards, one almost could have believed they were heeding the request to locate and move away from precious artefacts. Having already shot most of them, it was an easy order to unintentionally follow.

"Help me flip this table back upright!" Kim, the ever-staunch survivalist, bellowed while everyone else sat around still absorbing the information.

Even if her entire crew snapped to attention the moment the command was uttered it would have made no difference. She had barely touched the table when the corners of the ceiling opened and the rapid pews of blaster fire lit up the room in more ways than one. So many shots came from so many directions that no one could do anything but hug their knees and try to imagine the thuds were anything but the sounds of bodies hitting the floor.

Then, fast as it began, it was over; like getting a shot—no pun intended for once. Those of the crew who had no idea what it felt like to be on the receiving end of a laser blast checked themselves over just to be sure. After they had finished, one by one they emerged from hiding to find a room full of moaning mooks sprawled upon the floor. Each of them were in their own take on the foetal position. The only thing they all had in common were steaming holes in their pant legs that they struggled to cover with shaking hands. Occasionally the ceiling would fire on them again, puncturing a new spot and eliciting a new version of the word "Ow."

Only the encroachers and any still-living celebrity clones seemed affected. Contrary to Pia's claims, the defense system didn't seem to have any allegiance except to the crew of the *Jefferson*.

"Oh yes," a familiar cold, robotic voice uttered over the speakers. "This is everything I imagined it would be."

All of them were down, but the guns continued to fire. Each new laser landed strategically in superficial spots. Helplessly debilitated, but nowhere near death, all any of them could do was close their eyes and weather the torture.

"Your pain makes me feel so alive."

"Is that . . . ?" Cox began.

"Bundy?" Donald finished. "Yeah."

"How . . . ? I mean, why? I mean, I don't care. Can you make him stop?"

"Mmmmmnope. He's in the system now. She's gonna need tech support with laser-proof coveralls before she gets him outta there."

"Donny!"

"Hey! I told him he's not allowed to shoot her or us. I think it's pretty good I got that much off, seeing as I was installing him with a phone in the middle of a firefight!"

"You probably coulda did better if you actually went to SIT," Kim suggested.

Donald's face contorted into a look of such unbridled fury that she threw up her hands before the poor man had an aneurysm.

"I'm kidding! I'M KIDDING!"

"Yeah, you better be . . ." He grumbled, gesturing threateningly with his phone.

After rescuing Willy from the pile of bodies he was hiding under, it was back to the mission. The corridor being filled with griping grunts rolling around on the floor didn't help with lightening the mood. However, at least the soldiers had their own preoccupations that transformed the act of traipsing around them from a legitimate challenge into an uncomfortable jaunt, like walking through an alley full of homeless people. All the crew could really do was huddle together as they walked, avoiding eye contact and taking great care to avoid brushing against any outstretched legs. Occasionally somebody would twitch and the captain would have a coronary, but it was nothing the reassuring grip of his beloved's hand was unable to negate. The odd reminder that he was being a very brave boy would not have hurt either.

Cox mentioned earlier that there were three qualities every successful adventure must have. They could not have failed the one that stipulated nobody should get hurt any harder, and whatever lessons they learned today were probably not the kind he had in mind. So, with the trip nearing its end, they had better make one hell of a positive difference.

"Tim, we can't leave yet," Kim urged, grabbing his arm before he could board the *Jefferson*. "We still need to destroy this."

She removed the bottle of vile liquid from her side pouch. Thankfully, it had all been drained, but the alien goo capable of destroying organic matter that replaced it was almost as bad.

"We do!" He agreed as he punched the code to the door. It swung wide and he paused to gesture them all inside.

Kim folded her arms.

"I'm not following," she said as she blinked, then added: "Figuratively. But also literally, I guess."

"Oh, honey, I knew you'd say that. Well, not that exact quote. But the gist of it. You don't have to worry though. In the time I've spent here, I've come to learn that the power was with us all along!"

"What are you, high!?"

"No, really! It's a little lofty, but I'm totally serious."

"So am I! You just said you knew what I was going to say and that's the response you prepared?"

"Well, I was going to say that I figured out if we go dig up some of the ship's batteries, at least one is bound to have some acid in it that we could extract!"

"I . . . Did you come up with that?"

"Nnnnnyes!"

"Oh really. What kind of acid is in a battery then?"

" . . . Uh. Battery acid."

"Uh-huh. Don't worry, I don't know what it's called either. C'mon, Einstein."

"Hey, did Mister Nobody already go in?! I just realized I haven't seen him in a little bit."

"I don't think he followed us out of the room. Maybe Bundy shot him. I don't really care."

With the other three members of their crew already inside the ship, they broke into a light jog in order to catch up. Stepping onto the bridge dosed them with a slight feeling of the comfort that came with home, but it was vastly outweighed by the sight of the kids petrified in place before any had made it to their station. A suspicious swivel chair that wasn't there before blocked their path. The collective blood of the quintet ran cold as it began to rotate and face them. Menacing as it was, no one was really surprised when the diabolical sneer of Sir Head was revealed.

21.

EVERYBODY EXPECTS THE BRITISH IMPOSITION

"So," the snarky Brit seethed. "We meet again, Mister Cox."

"Shouldn't I be the one saying that to you?" The captain asked.

"What? Why would you . . ." The man's voice trailed off for a moment before his eyes went wide and he pounded on his arm rest.

"I'M NOT JAMES BLOODY BOND!"

As if the yelling didn't indicate enough agitation, he hopped to his feet and produced a laser pistol from the inside of his suit jacket. This prompted a hip checking match between Kim and Cox to try and put themselves in human shield position—a human shield the rest of them were more than happy to take advantage of. While her husband ultimately won out, Kim accepted the consolation prize of poking the barrel of her own rifle under his arm.

"If you ever wanna eat another damn crumpet, you better put that gun down."

"Oh shut up, you clueless bint," the old curmudgeon spat. "I've had a hundred times as many guns pointed at me by a hundred times as many people who were all better shots than you. Do you really think I'd let a *woman* be the one who does me in? Even in my old age I am tougher than the whole lot o' ya. I only got out this pintsy equalizer here 'cos I'm on a schedule."

"Sooooo . . ." Cox said. "You expect us to talk?"

"No, Mister Cox, I expect you to . . . Oh god *DAMN* it!"

On the less than dignified proclamation, his aim went askew just far enough for advantage to be taken. The co-captain's abysmal trigger discipline allowed for a timely reaction shot. There was no fancy refractive glass to mess up her aim this time, but she still managed to miss all his vital areas anyway. She would later claim she missed on purpose. Maybe she even did. Regardless, it provided just enough opportunity for the collective to scatter like a flock of geese walking over a landmine.

"What are you two still doing here?" Kim demanded of Donald and Cox. "That was your chance to get away and hide somewhere!"

"Run and hide?!" Her incredulous significant other repeated. "I can't leave the two things I value most in this life at the mercy of him!"

Donald squinted at him for a moment then shook his head.

"I . . . I didn't know I was supposed to run. Can you shoot him again? I totally will this time."

"Tim, I have never once doubted your bravery or good intentions." She took a quick peek around the corner they hid behind. "Now is not the time for them, though. I already beat up one old geezer on this ship, and this one now has a laser wound in his shoulder. You need to take this down to wherever you planned on going and do whatever you planned on doing to it!"

She tried to force the bottle of Fireball into his hands. When he wouldn't take it, it was instead thrust into the almost equally unwilling paws of their communications officer. He looked down onto it with disgust.

"I thought you said I was allowed to run? You're making me a part of this now!"

He gestured with his free open hand to give his plea a little more weight. However, all he got in return was the Glock shoved into it.

"There, take that then. Better?"

"Uh, yeah a bit, actually."

"Baby how can you ask me to leave you with this guy?!" Cox sputtered. "I mean, he's being gracious enough to let us have this conversation, but that doesn't mean he's gonna be nice once he does decide to get up and come after you!"

"He's not being gracious, hon. He's rummaging through our cupboards looking for a burn heal."

"That makes it even wor—"

"TIM!"

"WHAT!?"

"We don't have time. Do this! Please! If there is one time in this entire fiasco that we just do things my way . . . can this be it?"

He pursed his lips together and scrunched his face into the closest it could get towards a scowl.

" . . . Fine!" He relented after a giant inhale. "But if you die, then I am going to turn into a hollow shell of a man, and I won't be held responsible for the unspeakable things I do in my grief!"

"Don't tease me."

"Heh, I thought you'd find that cute. But seriously, I love you. Don't die."

"I'm not gonna die! And I love you too. Now go save the world, while I add elder abuse to the list of crimes we've committed today."

She cocked the bolt-action on switch and leapt back into the fray. Even after she had gone, Cox took a moment to take in the sounds of her shouting expletive laden taunts at her opponent in a butchered British accent. The words "Oi, guvna!" had never sounded so cute. Shame it was followed by a detailed description of growing male genitalia and then beating him with it since he was so averse to being bested by a female. Gone were the good old days of fond ribbing between opponents. Sure, they were both locked in a desperate attempt to survive, but just once, he wanted to see a polite fight.

Cox and Donald hurried through the halls of their house. Stressful as the situation was, the feelings of urgency were further exacerbated by the fact that neither one of them had gotten to pee since before arriving at Pia's lab. Of course, if they had to deal with too many more unpleasant surprises, then that issue was likely to resolve itself.

"Hey, Donny, in your little ship schematic program you got on your computer, does it tell you where we keep the batteries?"

"No. Why would it? And why would all the batteries be in one room? And what do you need batteries for, anyway?! Oh, god, don't tell me you have a plan."

"I do have a plan! If it makes you feel better, though, I didn't come up with it."

"It does. But I still dunno where any batteries are."

"Well that's okay, buddy! I'm sure we can find one around here somewh—"

"*There you are, you gagging sod!*"

Interestingly, the amount of time it takes to pull a trigger is nearly identical to the average human reaction time—approximately two tenths of a second. Had Agent Todgerworth considered this information, he likely wouldn't have chosen to blow his surprise with a flimsy taunt that would be neither clearly heard nor understood fully by those at whom it was levied. Since he opted to wait until after the utterance, though, which consumed nearly three whole seconds—a virtual eternity in dramatic slo-mo time—his itchy trigger finger had nary begun to clench by the time Cox and communicator dove behind the corner they had just rounded. As a result, his revenge lasering came to a harmless end as a scorch mark on the wall and Percy was made to look quite the fool.

"Well, shite, I did not think that one through."

Donald gaped at Cox from the other side of the hallway entrance.

"I thought you burned that guy's face off?!"

"I did!" He glanced around the corner then nodded. "Wow! Modern medicine sure is something! Looks like it couldn't save his moustache or eyebrows, though."

"Oh Captain, my Captain," Percy's voice oozed from down the hall. "We never did get to finish our chat earlier."

"He's walking this way, Donny!"

Donald raised an eyebrow. Tucking away the bottle of fireball, he produced the Glock and cocked it the same way that he had seen it done before.

"Then, boy, is he in for a surprise."

It was the kind of surprise that made people understand why some people did not like surprises. Just as it did the first time, the ***bang*** blew through the contained metal hallway like a sonic boom. Cox had the foresight to plug his ears this time, but Percy, having had his element of surprise used against him, nearly toppled over from the shock of the blast and muzzle flash. "Bloody Hell!" was all he could manage during a mad scramble into the nearest alcove.

From a purely logistical standpoint, the two warring parties were deadlocked in a standoff. From a psychological standpoint, the blaster that produced pitiful *pew*s appeared substantially inferior to the tiny sidepiece that trumpeted world-shaking *bang*s every time it emitted one of its invisible-to-the-naked-eye projectiles. The twang they made upon meeting with their ultimate destination only served to amplify their unnerving nature.

Bang.

Percy's entire body curled up like a dead spider when a wily bullet tore a chunk out of the corner he hid behind.

Bang.

"Do you really mean to destroy your ship just to thwart me?!" He bellowed from his hiding spot.

Bang bang.

"Donny, buddy, you *are* putting a lot of holes in the wall."

Bang.

"Is that really your biggest worry right now, man?!"

Bang.

"I guess you got a point."

"Never thought I'd hear you say that."

Bang, bang.

Any thoughts of peeking his own blaster around the corner to return some hail disappeared when one of the preceding bullets grazed Percy's hiding spot yet again. When he removed a hand from his eyes, a peculiar faint scraping noise directed his eyes to the floor. At first it appeared to be debris, albeit a larger chunk than the rest. Even when it stopped spinning and he got a better look at its mangled, rusty-yellow exterior, he still couldn't tell what it was. Any attempts to pick it up and inspect it further were reconsidered after one touch fried his fingertips like a hot coal, not that he would have been able to identify a bullet even if it hadn't been fired.

Bang.

Oh, right, he was still in a firefight.

Bang.

"I gotta say, Captain," Donald said with surprising pleasure. "Most of your old crap sucks, but this thing is pretty great."

Bang.

"Well I wouldn't call it my favourite part of my collection. But I admit it's surprisingly effective!"

Bang.

"I'll say. I'm kinda wondering sure why we ditched these things for lasers."

Click.

"The hell?"

Click, click.

"What'd you do, Donny? Did you break it?!"

Click, click, click.

"I didn't do anything! It just stopped working." *Click, click.* "Piece of junk."

Percy renewed his investment in the conflict with a quick peppering of laser shots. He purposefully avoided wasting his surprise on an insult this time. However, that did not stop him from still missing, all the same.

"Having a bit of difficulties, are we?" He gibed from the alcove. Wary of any other unexpected weapon appearances, he briefly held off further advancement. For the time being, he would merely shoot lines of light and lines of provocation in their general direction, hoping something would tag them.

"Well that's it, man!" Donald uttered as he let the pistol fall to the floor with a clunk of resignation. "That's it! We're done! This was the only line of defense we had, and now we got nothing!"

Cox bowed his head. Negativity was far from his nature, but Donald's seemed beyond quelling. Not that he didn't have good reason to be. A brief lapse in judgement nearly led to the captain peeking out at Percy right as another malevolent light beam whizzed on through where his face would have been. It was a grave scenario indeed, but there was a snippet of hope to be had.

"You need to carry on without me, Donny," he said with a voice both solemn and dignified, as all people making great sacrifices for others were required to do by law. "Whether you know it or not, you're a part of something bigger now. We all are. Greatness has been thrust upon us, and you bear the final hope humanity has at avoiding being placed under the shadow of tyranny. I wanted it to be the both of us, buddy. But it's me that he wants. And since it's me that he wants, we have a chance to still make it. Don't make the same mistake I did with Kim and waste time trying to stop me. Just go, Donny. I'm beggin' ya. Don't worry about me. I got this. I'll figure something out."

Donald blinked at him.

"K."

And without another word, the brave boy scurried away. Probably before his emotions overtook him and drew him toward rash decisions. Always the stoic pragmatist, that Donald. With the lad safely on his way, now was the time for Cox to shine.

"So uh, still there, Mister Todgerworth?"

The ensuing harrumph was all the answer he required, but a more articulate one followed nevertheless.

"I would hardly think to abandon my charge now, Mister Cox."

"Captain Cox."

"You are not a captain!!" Todgerworth blindly fired at the location of the man of dubious captaincy. "You are hardly a man! To be a captain requires one be not only capable of handling responsibility, but thriving under the mantle. Not only do you lack the requisite certifications for such a title, but I have yet to happen upon anyone who remotely displays incompetence capable of competing with yours! Let alone one who still demands such a moniker! Every report of your success has come bearing an asterisk denoting intervention in the form of aid from more competent associates of yours or sheer bloody dumb luck. The one time in which you were left completely helpless, alone to your own devices, you were only able to escape by way of an opportune cheap shot. And make no mistake; I will have my revenge for that! Yet even with your flagrant inadequacy dragging behind you everywhere you go, *you* propose the ability to hold *me* off?! You. The pitiful quim trembling alone behind that corner. Listening to me . . . silently . . . bollocks; you've run away too, haven't you?"

COX WASN'T SURE HOW long the captain line would hold him for. For all he knew, Todgerworth had seen right through it from the outset and was already in hot pursuit. But he dared not look back. No one who looked back ever ran faster for it. And many who did ended up crashing into or tripping over things. It was just a bad idea all around, and he was in no position to be having bad ideas. That's why he made a beeline for the engine room, where there was only one exit and copious amounts of loud noise that would make it impossible to hear anyone coming or track their movement via sound. It was the stupidest choice of place for him to go, so therefore, Percy would never expect a seasoned captain like him to go there.

Classically, engine rooms were the darkest, dingiest, inexplicably moistest rooms of a space vessel. They would have wires and cables dangling from the ceiling, obscured by an omnipresent haze that did not have any actual reason to be there but was never questioned by anyone. All in all, they were widely regarded as the room on the ship that one would be least surprised to be killed in. The *Jefferson*, however, was the exception. Large floodlights, a fancy rug, and some state-of-the-art dehumidifiers rendered it as welcoming as the lobby of the Empress Hotel, provided one did not mind the roar of an engine that was described by most as "only mildly deafening."

There were a great many scenarios Cox took into consideration during the ship's construction. Many had paid off on this adventure, too. However, at no point did he consider a scenario in which he himself would need to be familiar enough with the ship's components to not only identify them but also dismantle them. With wall-to-wall technological tackle stretched out before him, it was understandable to be overwhelmed by the prospect of it all. The fact that it was acid he needed made it all the worse. The stuff was generally not an ideal substance to search for by braille.

"Hardly surprising you would flee like a cowardly child," Todgerworth's voice sneered from the entrance.

He stood blocking the exit, rifle already levelled, and a twisted sneer marring his pale face. Cox put his hands up and backed away what few inches he had left.

"Y'know . . ." He reasoned. "I know I don't always handle stuff the right way. But I don't think there's a whole lot of shame in running away from a guy with a gun when I myself got nothing."

"Oh, spare me your shabby rationalizations. This is the end of the line for you. You've exhausted your bag of tricks and your exit opportunities, and now the only dilemma left falls onto me. Do I bestow the same torture unto you that I myself had to endure, or shall I just put a ray through your torso and be done with it all? The first option is so tempting; however, I could never forgive myself if one of your underlings successfully interrupted me and saved you before I could—"

A large pipe wrench flew out from behind one of the gyrating pieces of machinery. It caught Percy right under the cheek bone with a sickening crack that shut his lights out before he had even hit the ground. The old-fashioned hunk of metal clanged to a rest on the floor next to him shortly afterward. Despite having been hit by nothing himself, Cox also slid down the wall and collapsed to the floor in shock.

The thrower emerged from whence the wrench came. Just a silhouette at first, the short stature and mane of long dark hair suggested an individual of female persuasion, which helped to steady the captain's erratic heart rate. He let out his first breath in quite some time.

"Baby, I swear sometimes I actually think you have spidey senses."

"You think I'm somebody else, don't you?"

The voice did not resemble Kim's in the slightest. It was all sweet and no sultry, with a peppy, almost musical quality. However, the primary giveaway came via the pronunciation vagaries commonly heard in a habitual Hinglish speaker. When she stepped into the light to retrieve her wrench, the newcomer was revealed to be a younger woman, perhaps late twenties or early thirties, with both darker hair and darker skin than who she was initially assumed to be.

"Captain?" She asked. "Are you alright?"

"GAH!" Cox exclaimed. "Who are you?!"

"I . . ." She seemed unsure whether to be hurt or confused. "I'm your engineer, Diksha. Do you not remember me?"

"No! No, I do! Thatsyourname. Diksha." With quick clap, he was on his feet and reaching out to grab her hand. "It's just been a while! But, boy, am I glad to see you."

"I can see that. Who is this man? And why is he so angry with you?"

Upon being asked, he could not help but bob his head to and fro, trying to formulate an explanation that sounded reasonable without incriminating himself too much.

"Well y'see, back when we were at Space Guan . . . Wait. Have you been down here this whole time?"

"Of course. Where else would I be?"

"I . . . I guess," Cox avoided the question. "And you haven't noticed anything weird going on?"

"No? Nobody has come down to see me since we arrived at the Kalliope mining station."

"Wow. What do you do down here all day?"

"Is that really a more important question than why a strange man is on our ship trying to shoot you with a BSA69 blaster rifle?"

"I guess not," Cox chuckled. "It's kind of a long story, though. I promise I'll tell you it all later! But while I got you here right now, I need your help. I gotta crack open a battery and get some of its acid-y nectar. It's not for me, it's to save the world."

"I see." Diksha stared at him, blank-faced. "Well, actually I do not see, at all, as your explanation prompts far more questions than it answers. But you are speaking with such urgency that it is clear you do not wish to take questions. Wet-cell batteries are not very common anymore, but we do have one. Extracting the hydrofluoric acid is simple enough. Just let me grab my tools."

"No time! My nametag has a laser built into it. I'll just cut the cover off."

"Um, okay? But I still need to get the proper pipette for the actual extraction. You cannot just put hydrofluoric acid in a cup."

"Oh! Well, I was just going to grab the whole battery and carry it like a bucket. But your idea works too!"

With how smoothly things went with Whatshername, Cox could not help but wonder why he never visited her down here. Usually one's ability to knock out a man with a pipe wrench did not factor in to the quality of their company. Yet, when combined with her encyclopaedic knowledge of the inner workings of his pride and joy, as well as her total willingness to comply with strange, unexplained requests, he quickly found a fondness for his once invisible crew member. She even offered to boil the acid down for him to increase its potency. It was quite refreshing to have at least one underling treat him like a captain and welcome his presence without apprehension or reluctance. Best of all, at no point did he consider that his former indifference may have been the only thing that prevented some grave misfortune from befalling her throughout the course of his messes. That probably would have ruined the moment.

"Here you go, Captain," Diksha smiled as she handed over the caustic substance. "I do not know how you will save the world with this, but good luck!"

"Thank you, Miss Dishka!"

The acid changed hands, yet the transaction did not feel quite complete. To just duck in, have his life saved, then mooch and take off seemed so impersonal. The poor girl's job was so lonesome already. Trapped down here all alone in this dingy—but not too dingy—machine room, she was probably dying for somebody to reach out and offer her some social interaction.

"Say, just so you know, if you ever feel like getting out of here sometime, you're always welcome to come up to the bridge. I'm sure the rest of the gang would love to see ya!"

"That is very nice of you. But I stay down here because I like being away from people and have no desire to be dragged along on the unsafe outings you're very famous for. Instead I can concentrate on my work and build my models. Not every crew member of a ship wants a turn in the spotlight, you know."

"I . . . wow, you're good at having points. Okay, then! Well, I guess I'll get back to the 'spotlight!' Haha." He turned around to leave but kept spinning until he had gone a full 360 degrees, then raised a finger and opened his mouth once more.

"Even though I don't see you very often, that doesn't mean I can't appreciate the importance of your job. You're just as valuable a part of the *Jefferson* as the rest of us, and don't you forget it!"

Diksha mulled the statement for a moment.

" . . . What is the *Jefferson*?"

"Uh . . . that's the name of the ship! You didn't know that?!"

"I did not. Why do you call it that? Is it something to do with Thomas *Jefferson*?"

"Well, no . . ." Cox mumbled. He shuffled his feet and gave an awkward shrug. Previous eye rolls and groans had taken all the joy out of answering this question.

"I dunno . . . ever since I was a kid, I always wanted my own Jefferson Starship."

"I do not understand."

"Yeah, I was pretty sure you weren't gonna. I'll fill you in later, I promise."

"Are you gonna send someone down to take care of this?" She asked as she gestured at the body on the floor. "Am I supposed to . . . ?" She followed up after a moment of awkward silence. She neglected any further queries when both remained unanswered.

Adrenaline coursed its way back into Cox's bloodstream

the moment he departed. Holding the acid at arm's length as if it were a peeing baby, he stumbled his way through the *Jefferson*'s halls. The mission's end was in sight. All he had to do was figure out where Donald had fled with the goopy macguffin, and they would be able to put this whole thing behind them. Fortunately, in the dark days of yesteryear, he would have been forced into an elaborate cat and mouse type circumstance where he would have to rely on deduction and intuition in order to locate his charge. However, years of humanity funnelling its collective intellect into programs that removed all need to possess any intellect made for an easy way around that. A quick visit to the nearest wall terminal, an awkward inquiry to the psycho torture-bot that ran the thing, and presto: a blinking light coming from . . . Donald's room; go figure. The fact that his designated icon was the Punisher skull may have hinted at who got to choose the crew's symbols.

At a giraffe's pace, he could cover the distance in less than two minutes, though navigating the halls as an eighteen-foot-tall quadruped would probably slow him down more. Two legs would suffice. They were enough to take him up stairs, around corners, and even around obstacles jutting up from the floor, such as Czech hedgehogs, or his wife's dishevelled and limping visage.

"KIM!" Cox yelped, nearly dropping the cargo he so carefully carried.

She let herself fall into his outstretched free arm, enjoying the opportunity to save some energy and wipe away the streams of water cascading down her face.

"What happened?!" Her husband continued to prod. "What did he do to you?!"

"I'm not crying!" She blurted, smearing her hands across her face some more. "After I broke his nose, I think he realized

I wasn't going to just go down like a bitch, so the old goat pepper-sprayed me."

After trying to put some weight on her bad leg, she shuddered and gripped him harder.

"Agh! I think my foot is busted . . ."

"Here, sit. Sit!"

"No, Tim, he's not that far behind me. We gotta go."

"How are you gonna go?! You can barely walk."

"I don't think I have much choice at the moment, love. Can't kick his ass without a foot."

It was in that moment that Sir Richard Head, premier woman-beater of Britain's secretest service, loped on into the scene. With a face looking like a punctured can of red paint and a hand white-knuckling a spot in his midsection, it appeared he had underestimated the hardiness of a homegrown space scoundrel. Two-bit underhanded fighting approach aside, though, he had the spine to stick it out and attempt to see the job through. With only Cox left in his way and no engineers armed with pipe wrenches hiding around corners, it was entirely possible he may even succeed yet. But there was still one bump left on his road to victory.

The captain pressed the acid container against his wife.

"Hold this."

"Why? What are you doing?"

"I'm having my character-defining moment."

Maybe luck really was the only crutch he had. Maybe help was his only means of triumphing. Maybe it was true that every success he had ever attained was owed to an intervening force, tangible or otherwise. Or maybe those were just accusations made in anger by a bitter rival who sought to sneak beneath his skin. To find the truth would require an enormous scoreboard and more thought than the captain was willing to put into the matter. A plan to rely on outside interference simply was not his brand of irrationality, as it would require a plan to have been made. For better or for worse, every gig began as plainly as it was intended to remain. And no matter how bleak a prognosis, he always pressed on; even on his own. If fortune felt fine to favour him along the way, then there was no sense in turning it down. It wasn't his problem if others considered it unsporting.

In compliance with tradition, there was no ace in the hole when he marched the distance from wife to beater. In this moment he was just a man. A man with a beautiful mop of feathery blonde hair and a balled up, smaller-than-average hand that he slammed into Sir Head's skeletal mug. Both recoiled from the impact.

"You . . ." The captain grunted in pain as he clutched his quivering fist. "Just got cold Coxed."

Sir Head did not respond immediately, perhaps due to having his brains thoroughly rattled. He dabbed at his cheek and opened his mouth until his jaw clicked.

"I ain't even mad. I didn't think ya had it in ya."

"There's a lot of things that you don't know I have in me!"

All three of them looked down with hunched shoulders and scratched at the back of their head, in the wake of his awkward exclamation.

"Right, then," Sir Head broke the ice after a moment. "Now that you've grown a pair o' bollocks I reckon it's about time I kick them in."

With a wrinkled nose and squinty eyes, the captain wiped his bloody hands on his jumpsuit, then put them up in an old-timey fisticuffs stance.

"May I borrow your can opener?"

The boxing stance was then abandoned and replaced by a

pounce with the force of a thousand unloved kitties. It struck Sir Head with such thunderous strength that the agent was forced to take nearly an entire step backwards. Once the dust had settled, they were left in a heated and mildly erotic embrace, the Brit's hands clamped onto the captain's collar and the latter midway through performing some kind of half-hearted bear hug. When their eyes locked, the surprise round had ended, and the floor was left open to counterarguments.

Cox wished he could tell people he fought the good fight, and that through grit and love his hands avenged his wife's honour. He wished he could tell people that. But fights were not the consequence-free fun and games that they seemed to be in cartoons and the NHL. People got hurt in those things.

Cox was already feeling the pangs before Head had even returned the favour, as his hand still smarted something fierce from the initial sucker punch. Things only got worse from there. The implausibly firm old-man grip on his jumpsuit left him helpless to avoid the dizzying retaliatory Head headbutt. Not only did it put him on the floor, ears ringing and vision blurry, but it also smeared the agent's pre-existing blood all over his face, magnifying the awfulness.

Yucky as it was, it would take more negative reinforcement than that to keep him down. It would, in fact, take several punches to the midsection, a knee to the jaw, a kick in the groin, and a few elbows to the back of his head. There were a variety of other things that would have done the job as well, but that was what he got, and it was super effective.

Sir Head stepped toward his body and scrutinized him, giving an occasional foot nudge.

"You wanna get up again?"

Cox groaned into the floor to buy a couple more moments before rolling over.

"Not really. I mean, I gotta. But I feel like you're just going to beat me up some more."

"No shit. What else would you expect me to do?"

"Well . . . your buddy liked standing around and talking until something happened to make him lose his opportunity to kill me. Maybe we could do that?"

"Percy's a sopping puss and words ain't never solved anything. Now are you going to get off your arse and have another round with me or shall I wrap things up?"

With an offer like that, what else could he do? He had to get up. Rocky lasted a whole fifteen rounds, and he already had brain damage. Surely he could be at least two-fifteenths as good as Rocky.

The notion got him back on his feet, much to his opponent's glee, but he still needed a helping hand to stay there. Sir Head didn't mind sparing one if it gave him more time with his playmate. After swatting away one last ditch attempt from Kim to intervene, the sadistic spy had free reign to work out whatever deep-rooted daddy issues that made him the way he was in the form of tenderizing Tim's face until all hope had been wiped off of it.

Battered, broken, and beaten, Cox fell backward into a bulkhead the moment he was released. The heroic feeling that was once enough to keep him going when his muscles just couldn't be bothered had about reached the end of its magic. Yet he did not feel pain, anger, sadness, or disappointment, any of which would have been preferable. Instead, he had become numb; and it was not nearly as comfortable as past philosophers had suggested. For the first time in his entire life, Cox could not feel at all. He could not even feel silly about his slumped over pose, staring at the ceiling with glazed eyes and tongue hanging out of his mouth. At least the awkward, futile display did succeed at defining him; it was just a shame it was as a terrible combatant who really was incapable of succeeding on his own.

All these pessimistic notions swirled around his reeling mind over the course of just a few seconds. None lingered long, popping like bubbles shortly after manifestation. By the time his mental faculties began to return, such sentiments fell to the wayside when he realized the light he was staring at this whole time was awfully bright. It was also perfectly centered on the ceiling, and far more radiant than any of the other electrical illuminations in similar spots. When a large figure dressed all in white appeared in the middle and dropped through into the hallway a few feet away, the captain's mental faculties were once more under suspicion.

"Wow . . ." His pupils shrank to pinheads as he slid down the wall. "Are you an angel?"

The astronaut shook his head and pulled off his helmet, revealing a bald octogenarian with pointy ears and a ficus growing out of his nose.

"Are you an idiot?" The man asked him back.

"Banks?!" Kim exclaimed. "Why did you put on a spacesuit to get on a docked ship?"

"Take a look at all the singe marks on it and figure it out."

"Banks?!" Sir Head repeated. "Did she just call *you* Banks?!"

For the first time since anybody here had met him, the old man stood up straight.

"She did. And who the hell are you?"

The Brit wiped one last smearing of blood off his face and postured his way in the hitman's direction.

"I'm someone who's not impressed."

Mister Banks grunted an acknowledgement, then added: "I'll try to live with that."

"Oh, you won't have to for long."

"I'm not sure if that's an old joke or if you're threatening me."

"Bit of both, now that you mention it. You're old as shit."

"Ah. Good one, then."

"Quit stalling and fight me, you tired old twat."

"When did I say I was going to fight you?"

" . . . Well, aren't you!?"

"Wasn't planning on it."

"You better start plotting then, because you don't have any choice!"

Sir Head put his fists up once more, waggling them around like maracas. Banks, however, just studied the bizarre motions with a cocked head. After a moment's mulling, he still neglected to raise his own arms, instead folding them and smacking his lips.

"Sure I do. I could run."

"You could." The agent agreed, still waving his hands and now adding some fancy footwork. "If you're alright with showing us all you have no spine."

Banks shrugged.

"What do I care what you think? You already said you're not impressed."

"I . . . what is going on here!? You're supposed to be the most dangerous man in my organization's database. You've allegedly brought down ships; massacred entire battalions."

"Uh-huh."

"Then why are you so shy about an honourable one-on-one, eh?! If you're so great, then I should be nothing to you."

The older man's eyelids fluttered, as if the words gave him a headache. After another one of his heaving sighs, he glanced down at Kim.

"Did you two go to the same bad-guy school or something?" His gaze then returned to Sir Head. "Wanna know how I take down ships and all the people in them? It's because I don't fight them fairly, I don't fight them honourably, and I certainly don't fight them with my bare hands. In fact, if I can help it, I don't fight them at all. Fighting is a waste of time, a waste of energy, and would be a waste of brains, except if you go looking for one, then you obviously don't have any. You might think you're a big man because you knocked the stuffing out of those two, but all I see looking at you right now is a geyser where your nose used to be. But hey, I'm sure the knowledge that you're the toughest guy around is worth all the broken ribs, destroyed knees, face scars, and arthritic hands, right?"

Like any true manly man of action, Sir Head disregarded any potential wisdom that may have been gleaned and instead shoved Mr. Banks backward.

"Worth every bit," he snarled through curled lips. "'Cos when it comes down to the wire and it's man-to-man, I got the experience to get the job done."

Banks stayed silent for a couple moments after that. He took the time to stare down at his chest, where the Brit had put hands on him. Then, after lifting his head back up, he spoke with an even colder calm than before.

"Well. That's better than relying on words, I guess."

At that, he unstuck a blaster rifle from his back and fired a wide-angled laser blast that spanned the width of the hallway and cleaved through both of Sir Head's knees. Both calf, ankle, and foot combinations remained upright like tree stumps, while everything above them went crashing to the floor. The agent's cries of agony sent chills up the spines of Cox and Cox, yet did not daunt the man-hunting Martian. He cleared the space the shove gave him with just a few steps then loomed over Agent Head's head with the same aloof air that he had in every situation. Yet the slight nod indicated at least some sign that this was more than business.

"Not as impressive as a flying roundhouse kick, I know. I just don't have your *experience.* All I got is this gun."

One last click, one last pew, and one last flash of light ended the conflict. It was a moment that would have been perfectly punctuated by a flock of birds flying away. Instead, the only ceremony was the sitting bodies of the two protagonists huddling together in mutual relief and injury while their unexpected saviour wiped a smudge off his trusty, newly-appropriated sidearm with his sleeve.

"I'm keeping this, by the way," he told them. "Seeing as you made me throw away my last one."

Neither one replied, instead looking up in discomfiture at the man's nonchalance. After a beat, Banks gestured down at Sir Head's body.

"So is he it? Or is there any more?"

"There's a guy down in the engine room," Cox spoke in soft, hushed tones like a man in shock and also in a library. "I think Da-, I mean D-, er . . . Whatshername mighta killed him, though."

"Ah, I'll sort it out. You two just go deal with the stuff."

THAT WAS THE LAST they ever saw of Banks. No one was too sure when or how he managed to get off their ship, but they were none too pleased when they found out he left behind the bodies of both Sirs Head and Todgerworth, as well as two hard candy wrappers. Having to fish one of those things out of the Roomba was the least-pleasant goodbye that Cox had ever experienced. However, at the time, he would be flying high on emotion-tailoring drugs to prevent any PTSD from all the death he experienced.

Before any of that could happen, though, Tim and Kim had to pry themselves from the floor and embark on the long limp to Donald's bedroom. It worked as a three legged race of sorts; each had an arm draped over the shoulder of the other to aid in their zombie shuffle. The majority of the captain's injuries were situated on his face and torso and so he could actually walk fine, but an arduous trek of mutual injury was too good of a bonding moment for him to pass up. So he held her close and limped like he was on a quest for an Academy Award.

"Do you think mom and dad would hate what I've become?" He broke the silence.

"Love, I don't know," Kim grunted. "Probably not. They never really cared about much anyway."

"I guess . . . I dunno. I just don't want to shame the family name."

She let out a weak laugh; one that obviously caused her pain, but she could not help but utter regardless.

"Honey, you're worried about their opinion on that?! Those two couldn't have set the bar any lower—no offense. You've at least done things! Made a difference in one way or another. You told me the only reason those two have any money is because they were lucky enough to be ones alive when your great great great great great great great great great great great grandparents' Beanie Baby collection finally appreciated in value."

"Yeah . . ." He let out an unsatisfied sigh. "Do you think maybe this ship will ever appreciate in value, at least?"

"Oh babe, god, no. This thing ain't even gonna outlive you."

"Awww! I mean, it helped me do all this stuff, I guess. But is anybody even gonna know?"

She smiled and reached out a hand onto the door that read "Donald's Room. Enter at own risk" under a biohazard symbol.

"We will. And I'm pretty sure, whether or not they admit it, someone in here is going to as well."

With a press of some buttons, the door opened wide. Inside was Willy, doubled over in a series of groans and dry heaves, while Donald and Whisper stood over him waving their arms and screaming "Oh shit, oh shit, oh shit," nonstop.

"What the hell is going on?!" Kim barked, wincing from the force of her yell.

"Willy ate the goo!" Donald screamed back.

"What?!"

"He ate the goo! We heard somebody trying to get in and next thing I know, he dumped the vial out of the bottle, popped it open, and ate it!!"

"What the hell?! WHY!?"

"I wanted to be a hero!" Willy moaned, bear-hugging himself and squashing all his facial muscles together.

"I wasn't part of any of this!" Whisper defended herself against a question no one asked. "I just *clearly* picked the wrong room to hide in."

"Am I gonna die!?"

"No, no, buddy!" Cox tried to comfort him. "No! No, no, no . . . no . . ."

"Whisper," Kim ordered "Get us out of here. Set a course for somewhere; we'll figure it out once in transit." She swore under her breath and looked down at the pipette in her hand.

"We had the stuff and everything; why couldn't you have just hung on!?"

"Dude, I'm dying!"

"You're right. Bad time. I'm just . . . frustrated."

She tossed the acid across the room, where it bounced off the wall and splattered on Donald's dresser.

"Hey!" He whined. "That's my underwear drawer."

Cox, who had been rubbing Willy's back the whole time, ignored the two of them as he rushed through the five stages of grief. He was currently on the third.

"Maybe this won't be a big deal! I mean, we all know stomach acid is tough stuff. It can eat through wood and metal and all kinds of stuff."

"Maybe," Kim agreed. "We should still get him to a hospital, though. They can pump his stomach and get the thing out of him while the acid eats it."

"There we go! That's the plan. You hear that, Mister Padilla? You're gonna be okay. We're just gonna keep the Space Jam in you until we find some doctors!"

"Uh, guys?"

The couple turned around to find Donald holding the bottle of Fireball. Pupils dilated and lips pursed, he upturned the spout into his hand. They listened to a few soft clinks of glass on glass and recoiled in horror when they saw a glass vial pop out.

"There's another one in there."

All three of them seemed to follow the same wavelength. Their eyes traced from the bottle to the wall to the sizzling dresser, which had thirstily soaked up every drop of acid spilled upon it. Afterward, they came full-circle, back into looks of defeat aimed at one another. Donald swallowed while husband and wife exchanged glances.

"Can you get mo—"

"That's all there was."

Another groan from Willy, who had now gone full sprawl, captured their attention once more.

"Okay, hear me out . . ." Kim began.

"No!" Cox yelped. "You can't be serious!"

"He already ate some; if it's going to kill him, then he's already doomed!"

"So you want to feed him more!?"

"What else are we gonna do with it?!"

"But what about everything he's done for us!?"

"He hasn't done hardly anything for us!"

"He ate the Space Jam!"

"That doesn't matter unless he eats it all!"

"Oh god, I can't watch."

"Then don't. But you gotta hold him down."

Willy was no pet, and this was no act of euthanasia, but it was heart-wrenching nonetheless. Donald sat on one arm while Cox sat on the other, and the poor fellow beneath them had no trouble deciding which one at whom to aim his clamp-jawed pleading-eyed stare. Even after Kim plugged his nose, the desperate condemned continued to grunt and squirm and warble. Amid the whole display was the wife's little hand trying to shove a vial of purple slime into his mouth. It wasn't so much a "here comes the airplane" kind of feeding but instead played out like a PETA advertisement against *foie gras*.

Cox, who could not bear to listen any longer, begged her to at least knock the man out for the duration. He never did come to understand why she got so angry at the suggestion.

22.
I HAD A WILLY GOOD TIME

EVEN IN THE AGE of space exploration, brain implants, and commercially available murdering machines, hospitals were pretty much the same grossly overpriced motels that they always have been. They had the same uncomfortable beds, the same jaded staff that had seen it all, and the same clientele of people who were probably there as a result of bad decisions or bad days. The only difference between a hospital and motel was in a motel, one had a higher likelihood of being exposed to a deadly pathogen, and a lower likelihood of being killed by somebody.

With an ongoing exploding population and a sharp upturn in everyday items capable of exploding, the waiting rooms were never anything less than Black Friday levels of bustle. Tim and Kim found themselves wedged in between a man with a corkscrew pinning an anniversary card to his chest and a couple mulling over the nosejob menu. In a morbid way, it was slightly comforting to be surrounded by people dealing with difficulties of their own. It helped to take their minds off their unfortunate employee after the nurses wheeled him away.

". . . And then that crazy Mars hitman guy came through a hatch in the ceiling!" Cox explained to a nearby child playing with the standard cheapo waiting-room toys. "And he was all like 'mur muh mur, you don't scare me' then he vaporized the secret agent's kneecaps and blew a gaping hole in his sternum."

"Get the hell away from my son!"

"Sorry, sir. I was just telling him a story!"

"He's four! He shouldn't be exposed to your lowlife garbage. C'mon, Timmy. Let's go see if daddy's bottom bitch has woken up from getting her bum bigger yet."

Shooting Cox one last dirty look, he grabbed the kid's arm and yanked him away from his playthings. The retro hinge-style door easily flew open from his shove and nearly nailed the doctor approaching it from the other side. No apology was given, and none seemed desired. Instead, the doc just carried on past him and into the waiting room.

"Is there a . . . Mister and Mrs. Cox?"

"Oh thank god. C'mon, Tim. Before somebody stabs you."

They stepped across the strewn-about, teenage-pregnancy Barbies and the My First Meth Lab™ playsets and followed him into an exam room. The lab-coated gentleman took a seat directly in front of a roughly head-sized hole in the wall. His tired, droopy eyes and the few days of scruff sticking out of his face made it difficult to tell if he was mulling over the contents of the chart he held or if the man had simply fallen asleep.

Cox nudged him with his foot. When there was no response, he turned to his wife.

"Why did you insist we come to this one?"

"You really don't understand how to behave when you're a fugitive, do you?"

The doctor cleared his throat with a loud "Ahem" that smelled of Jim Beam and instant ramen.

"Ah, here's the part I was looking for."

"Oh god." Cox grabbed his wife's hand. "Is he okay?"

"I honestly am not sure how much time I'd say he has left."

The doctor said robotically as he scrolled through the file. "The patient you brought in is extremely overweight. At his current rate of expansion, he will be lucky to see forty."

"Are you sure? I've spent a lot of time with him in the last couple days and he seems like he's in pretty good shape to m—"

Kim clamped a hand over his mouth.

"We didn't bring him in for you to tell us he's fat!"

"Oh. What else needs fixed, then?"

"What?! You're the doctor here!"

"Ma'am, have you seen where we are? The only criteria for getting a job at this place is not asking the interviewer any questions."

"Yeah, I've read the Yelp reviews. I don't need you to be a professional diagnostician or literate. I just wanted you to pump the damn guy's stomach."

"We already did. Now, I know you don't have much respect for my medical education, and believe me, you shouldn't, but trust when I tell you that one stomach pumping is not going to do anything to counteract his weight problem."

"Is there any particular diet program that you would recommend?"

"Tim, shut up. What did you find in Willy's stomach?"

The doctor once again scrutinized the chart.

"Hmmm . . . well, he didn't have your drugs if that's what you're expecting. It was pretty standard stuff for the most part. Couple meal-capsule hot dogs, some coffee, a large ball of assorted brands of gum, several milliliters of some purple substance we weren't able to identify, half a croissant . . ."

"The purple stuff!" Kim cut him off. "Where is it now?"

" . . . Uh . . . what, do you think we hang onto stomach contents? What would we do with them? Recycle them and serve them for lunch? All of that was medical waste. It's been incinerated. Why? Was that the drugs?"

"I thought you guys weren't supposed to ask questions." Cox reminded him.

"Oh shit! Oh god. Please don't tell my boss; she'll fire me for sure. I can't go back to working in a normal hospital. They don't even let you take bribes there!"

Kim could not take any more. Exasperated from the exchange, she left her seat and gave her husband a tug as well.

"Just . . . just send Willy out when you're done with him."

Then it was back to the waiting room for them. They left as fast as they arrived, stepping over Archie Joins the Crips comic tablets and Teenage Mutant Crack Head action figures on their way out.

Shifty asteroid settlements such as the one they were on always tended to be the best hiding places when wanted by the fuzz. The constantly mobile, dime-a-dozen, police-unfriendly locations were made all the more ideal when the corporations that owned them became legally defined as people, residences, sovereign nations, and whatever else their CEOs wanted them to be. As a result, communities of former or only-occasional criminals often began to form around the giant core business, Australia style. Once well-established enough to have its very own shady hospital, an asteroid's surface was usually wholly covered by strip malls of a sort.

The weary couple emerged from the clinic onto a dark street with a döner shop on one side and a strip club on the other. Discarded e-readers containing the news blew through the dark streets. Fortunately, the enclosed environment meant no need for a spacesuit and a pleasantly warm ambient temperature to relax in while they waited for the potential patient zero. Kim folded her arms and leaned against the wall, the natural pose to strike from her former street tough days.

"I'm surprised Donald and Whisper still aren't back yet."

"Ah, cut 'em some slack. It's a tough job."

"It's literally the easiest job we've given them this whole trip."

"I still don't get why we have to send poor Willy away. I mean, we got his stomach pumped. After a couple days of R&R I'm sure he'll be good as new!"

"Tim, this stuff could potentially be existential-threat level dangerous. I already told you: just because we pumped his stomach doesn't mean there won't potentially be any left in his system. If it eats him then we'll have a Willy-sized blob of the stuff running rampant on our ship. Grey goo, purple goo, Space Jam, the Blob, whatever you wanna call it, is no joke. There's a reason sci-fi authors have used it as a lazy plot device since the genre was invented."

"Hey, look, Whisper and Donny are back!"

He was correct, Whisper and Donald were indeed back from the dealership across the road. Neither one made a beeline back to the ship, either. In fact, their pace could have been described as leisurely, as Donald twirled a ring of keys on one finger and Whisper lagged behind to look at the different shops.

"Here." He shoved the keys into the captain's hand. "Wasn't the fanciest one he had, but should be fine for what we plan to do with it."

"Well look at you, Donny! Walking right on into a suspicious Space Winnebago dealer and even taking the time to browse. So much for being scared of being affiliated with the kinds of guys that hang out at these places, eh!?"

"Well, it's a little late to be scared, seeing as I am already on god knows how many shit lists now!" Donald frowned. "But after everything we've been through, I will admit this place isn't so bad by comparison."

"And it beats going with Willy," Kim added.

"That too. Where is he, anyway?"

"Still inside. Should be out in a bit."

"Are . . . Are you gonna tell him?"

"Am I going to have to?"

Whisper, who until this moment had been lost in thought, snapped out of it just in time to see all eyes upon her.

"What?" She asked, ready to get defensive. "I did what you wanted; the autopilot knows where to go."

Cox blinked at a rapidly accelerating pace the longer she went without adding to that thought.

"He can still change the course, though, right?!"

"Yeah, yeah, if he's still alive in a week, he can change it to wherever he wants. Or he could just keep on going. I dunno. He could want that . . ."

It seemed like a barbaric treatment, but there was nothing in the company handbook about how to deal with an alien-parasite infection. The Space Winnebago had been stocked with the best food and entertainment this desolate collection of barebones boutiques could offer. Provided everything went smoothly, there would be no reason for their haggard security guard to even know he was in any more danger. Instead, for all he should know, that gigantic missile they were locking him inside was nothing more than an opportunity for some privacy and recovery from such a burdensome few days.

"Heyyy, there's the man of the hour!" The captain announced, partially to greet Willy and partially to tell everyone else to shut up. "How're ya feeling, buddy?"

"I'm okay, I guess." The big man gingerly touched at his belly. "Still feel a little funny, but my gut doesn't hurt as much."

"Well, that's fantastic!"

"I'm glad to hear you're okay, Willy," the much-less-enthusiastic voice of Kim added. "We actually have a surprise for you. No, Tim, he doesn't need the blindfold. Just . . . come with us."

They guided him with an eagerness a more-intelligent man would have found suspicious. On the other side of the path was an undoubtedly reputable small business called Dick's Fairly Reliable Rigs. The door screeched like a hoarse pterodactyl when they flung it open. Wind chimes fashioned from old vehicle parts dripped grease from the ceiling, making the floor slick and difficult to navigate. Yet the surly old stereotype that ran the place had no trouble dashing up to them so fast his trucker hat nearly flew off.

"Well, howdy there, folks! I'm Dick and boy do I have—oh, you aren't new customers." He threw a thumb over his shoulder and walked away. "Yer buggy's in the back."

Another set of squeaky doors, another unintelligible mishmash of machine parts posing as art, and then they were on the lot. From there, it was Donald who took the lead. It was only through his memory that they were able to navigate the labyrinth of junkers and lemons before finally coming to a stop in front of a hunk of metal that was magnificent, state of the art, and completely rust-free—however many decades ago it was manufactured.

"And here we are. The Auto Von Bismarck." He paused for a moment to stare at it before turning around.

"It's the Germans that always make good stuff, right?"

"Cool! . . . But why did you buy me a space boat?"

"It's for a cruise, Mister Padilla!" Cox clamped a hand on his shoulder and joined in the marvelling. "As a thanks for all your hard work! It's all stocked with goodies and pre-programmed to fly you around for a few weeks while you kick back and let the stress of the mission just drift away."

"Cool! . . . But what about you guys?"

"Uh. We . . . we are also going to be kicking back and letting the stress of the mission . . . also drift away."

"Ooh, I gotcha! . . . But why are you guys going without me?"

Donald cleared his throat in a very loud and fake manner.

"We aren't! We . . . each got our own cruise as well. That one over there is mine."

He shrugged and grimaced at the rest of his crew while Willy inspected the alleged ship.

"Oh I see! . . . but how come you got one held together by duct tape?"

Kim took her turn to intervene, dashing over and redirecting the man's attention back to the first one.

"Due to budgetary constraints, we splurged and got you one nicer than ours. Since you made the biggest sacrifice and everything."

"Oh! . . . Well, that's real nice of you guys, but I don't need—"

"Can you just get into it already!?" Whisper snapped. Three wide-eyed angry looks and one clueless gawp made her recoil and add: " . . . Uh, because we're all waiting to go get on ours."

With collective peer pressure finally quelling his inquisitive quality, Willy climbed the rickety steps of his unwitting prison and turned around.

"Ah, I'm just messing with you guys!" He said with a wave. "I know what you're trying to do here."

Each feigned their own interpretation of what a confused person looked like.

"You . . . you do?" The captain finally asked.

"Well, duh! Everybody knows ships made of duct tape can't fly in space."

"M—maybe not normal duct tape! But this is special . . . space-grade duct tape!"

"Why are you still lying, dude? You know I'm onto ya!"

The captain was at a loss. If Willy really was onto them, he did not seem angry in the slightest. In fact, he seemed happier than ever. As each painful silent second ticket by, Cox became more and more anxious, until finally Kim's voice erupted from behind them.

"OH MY GOD."

Everyone turned around to find her rubbing her face with her palm, phone in her other hand.

"Ya got us, Willy," she continued. "Happy Birthday."

The big fella grinned.

"Thanks, dudes! Oh boy, this is gonna be fun."

The door clanged shut behind him, eerily reminiscent of a cell. Or perhaps a bomb shelter. Either way, momentarily afterward, the thrusters commenced burning and the remaining crew of the *Jefferson* made a mad dash out of the line of fire. When they emerged on the other side of the car lot, Willy and his haul were just a bright speck in the sky among all the other stars, potentially off to literally join one of them.

"Godspeed, sweet prince," Cox murmured.

"I can't believe I might actually miss that glorious idiot," Kim added.

Crises averted and core crew intact, they embarked back toward the *Jefferson*. Somehow throughout all of this, their rhodium cargo had still survived and was thus ripe for the delivering. Any potential shot at an early-bird bonus had long since been missed, but one of the few perks of the job was their boss's complete ambivalence towards employees accused of criminal wrongdoing. So long as shipments came, they could have an actual reincarnation of Joseph Stalin onboard and no damns would be given. That being said, obtaining a list of places from which they were now unwelcome would likely be a necessary move going forward.

"I'm gonna miss him too." The captain smiled one last time up at the stars. "If you told me when we first met him that we were going to end up shooting him into the sun, I would never have believed you."

Kim shrugged. "I would."

"I hope our next security guard is actually good at his job," Donald grumbled.

"After that disaster?" The first mate spat. "We're not getting another one."

"Baby, how can you not want another one!? He was so friendly. And easygoing. And obedient. AND he kinda kept us safe, sorta."

"Let's just get a dog then, Tim."

The trip back to the ship had gone down without incident until, unbeknownst to them at first, they managed to attract some attention. With their beloved home still a stone's throw under diminished gravity away, a woman appeared from the dingy and decrepit landscape to accost them. Despite being every bit as dirty as the other lowlifes, something in the way the petite blonde carried herself gave the impression that this was a lifestyle she was not accustomed to.

"Excuse me, did I hear you say you wanted a dog?"

"No."

"Cause this little guy right here is just the bestest, awesomest, most lovingest little cutie wootie ever. I wish I could keep him, but the stupid police keep making it hard for me to collect my alimony checks, so I can't take care of him anymore."

"Ma'am, we don't even know you—"

"TAKE MY DOG! TAKE HIM! LOVE HIM! DO IT!"

Without waiting for a response, the deranged woman dropped the leash she held and stole away back into the desolation. Maybe it was the way the little guy seemed just as confused as they were, or maybe it was the way he made no attempt to follow his owner, but something about his being in their company now just seemed right. He did not flinch in the slightest when Cox came over and knelt down to read his tags.

"Well, this isn't the weirdest thing that's happened to us lately," he said over his shoulder. When he retrieved the leash and stood back up, it seemed his mind had been made. Yet just for the sake of keeping up appearances, he posed the question to the crew anyway.

"So what do you think, guys? Should we have some more adventures with our new security guard here? Officer . . . Woody."

ABOUT THE AUTHOR

Logan J. Hunder is a Canadian comedy writer who breaks into a wicked case of the shakes if he goes more than a half hour without making fun of something. He treats this rare self-diagnosed illness by rambling via text. His first novel, *Witches Be Crazy*, was published by Night Shade Books in 2015.